The Notebook
The Proof
The Third Lie

The Notebook
The Proof
The Third Lie

Three Novels by
Agota Kristof

Grove Press
NEW YORK

The author would like to thank the Pro Helvetia Foundation for its support in the writing of this book. Original French titles in chronological order: *Le grand cahier, La Preuve, Le Troisième Mensonge.*

Printed in the United States of America

Library of Congress Cataloging-in-Publication Data

Kristof, Agota.
    [Novels, English, Selectoins]
    The notebook ; The proof ; The third lie : three novels / by Agota
Kristof.
       p. cm.
    ISBN 978-0-8021-3506-3
    1. Sheridan, Alan. II. Watson, David. III. Romano, Marc. IV. Title.
V. Title: Proof. VI. Title: Third lie.
PQ267.R55A28   1997
843'.914—dc21   97-14269

Design by Laura Hammond Hough

Grove Press
an imprint of Grove Atlantic
154 West 14th Street
New York, NY 10011

Distributed by Publishers Group West

groveatlantic.com

23 24   12 11

Contents

The Notebook

Translated by Alan Sheridan

Arrival at Grandmother's

We arrive from the Big Town. We've been traveling all night. Mother's eyes are red. She's carrying a big cardboard box, and the two of us are each carrying a small suitcase containing our clothes, plus Father's big dictionary, which we pass back and forth when our arms get tired.

We walk for a long time. Grandmother's house is far from the station, at the other end of the Little Town. There are no trams, buses, or cars here. Just a few army trucks driving around.

There aren't many people in the streets. The town is very quiet. Our footsteps echo on the pavement; we walk without speaking, Mother in the middle, between the two of us.

When we get to Grandmother's garden gate, Mother says: "Wait for me here."

We wait for a while, then we go into the garden, walk around the house, and crouch down under a window where we can hear voices. Mother's voice says:

"There's nothing more to eat at home, no bread, no meat, no vegetables, no milk. Nothing. I can't feed them anymore."

Another voice says:

"So you've remembered me. For ten years you didn't give me a thought. You never came. You never wrote."

Mother says:

"You know why. I *loved* my father."

The other voice says:

"Yes, and now you remember that you also have a mother. You come here and ask me to help you."

Mother says:

"I'm not asking anything for myself. I just want my children to survive this war. The Big Town is being bombed night and day, and there's no food left. All the children are being evacuated to the country, with relatives or with strangers, anywhere."

The other voice says:

"Then send them to strangers, anywhere."

Mother says:

"They're your grandsons."

"My grandsons? I don't even know them. How many are there?"

"Two. Two boys. Twins."

The other voice asks:

"What have you done with the others?"

Mother asks:

"What others?"

"Bitches have four or five puppies at a time. You keep one or two and drown the others."

The other voice laughs loudly. Mother says nothing, and the other voice asks:

"They have a father, at least? You aren't married, as far as I know. I wasn't invited to any wedding."

"I am married. Their father is at the front. I haven't had any news of him for six months."

"Then you can put a cross over him."

The other voice laughs again. Mother starts crying. We go back to the garden gate.

Mother comes out of the house with an old woman.

Mother says to us:

"This is your Grandmother. You'll be staying with her for a while, till the end of the war."

Grandmother says:

"It could last a long time. But I'll put them to work, don't you fret. Food isn't free here either."

Mother says:

"I'll send you money. Their clothes are in the suitcases. And there are sheets and blankets in the box. Be good, you two. I'll write you."

She kisses us and goes away crying.

Grandmother laughs very loudly and says to us:

"Sheets and blankets! White shirts and patent leather shoes! *I'll* teach you what life is about!"

We stick our tongues out at Grandmother. She laughs even louder and slaps her thighs.

Grandmother's House

Grandmother's house is five minutes' walk from the last houses in the Little Town. After that, there is nothing but the dusty road, soon blocked off by a barrier. It is forbidden to go any further, a soldier is on guard there. He has a machine gun and binoculars, and when it rains, he takes shelter in a sentry box. We know that beyond the barrier, hidden by the trees, there's a secret military base, and beyond the base, the frontier and another country.

Grandmother's house is surrounded by a garden at the bottom of which is a stream, then the forest.

The garden is planted with all sorts of vegetables and fruit trees. In a corner, there's a hutch, a henhouse, a pigsty, and a shed for the goats. We have tried to ride the biggest of the pigs, but it's impossible to stay on.

The vegetables, the fruit, the rabbits, the ducks, and the chickens are sold at market by Grandmother, as well as the hens' and ducks' eggs and the goat cheese. The pigs are sold to the butcher, who pays for them with money, and with hams and smoked sausage too.

There is also a dog to keep away thieves, and a cat to keep away mice and rats. We mustn't give the cat anything to eat so that he's always hungry.

Grandmother also owns a vineyard on the other side of the road.

You enter the house through the kitchen, which is large and warm. A fire burns all day long in the woodstove. Near the window there's a huge table and a corner seat. We sleep on the seat.

From the kitchen a door leads to Grandmother's bedroom, but it's always locked. Only Grandmother goes there, only at night, to sleep.

There's another room, which can be reached without going through the kitchen, directly from the garden. This room is occupied by a foreign officer. Its door is also locked.

Under the house there's a cellar full of things to eat, and under the roof, an attic where Grandmother doesn't go anymore since we sawed away one of the rungs of the ladder and she fell and hurt herself. The entrance to the attic is just above the officer's door, and we get up there by means of a rope. That's where we hide the notebook, Father's dictionary, and the other things we're obliged to conceal.

In short order we make a key that opens all the doors in the house, and we bore holes in the attic floor. With the key we can move freely about the house when nobody's in, and through the holes we can observe Grandmother and the officer in their rooms, without their suspecting.

Grandmother

Grandmother is Mother's mother. Before coming to live in her house, we didn't even know that Mother still had a mother.

We call her Grandmother.

People call her the Witch. She calls us "sons of a bitch."

Grandmother is small and thin. She has a black shawl on her head. Her clothes are dark gray. She wears old army shoes. When the weather's nice, she goes barefoot. Her face is covered with wrinkles, brown spots, and warts that sprout hairs. She has no teeth left, at least none that can be seen.

Grandmother never washes. She wipes her mouth with the corner of her shawl when she's finished eating or drinking. She doesn't wear underpants. When she wants to urinate, she just stops wherever she happens to be, spreads her legs, and pisses on the ground under her skirt. Of course, she doesn't do it in the house.

Grandmother never undresses. We have watched her in her

8

room at night. She takes off her skirt and there's another skirt underneath. She takes off her blouse and there's another blouse underneath. She goes to bed like that. She doesn't take off her shawl.

Grandmother doesn't say much. Except in the evening. In the evening, she takes a bottle down from a shelf and drinks straight out of it. Soon she starts to talk in a language we don't know. It's not the language the foreign soldiers speak, it's a quite different language.

In that unknown language, Grandmother asks herself questions and answers them. Sometimes she laughs, sometimes she gets angry and shouts. In the end, almost always, she starts crying, she staggers into her room, she drops onto her bed, and we hear her sobbing far into the night.

Our Chores

We have to do certain chores for Grandmother, otherwise she doesn't give us anything to eat and leaves us to spend the night outdoors.

At first we refuse to obey her. We sleep in the garden, we eat fruit and raw vegetables.

In the morning, before daybreak, we see Grandmother leave the house. She says nothing to us. She goes and feeds the animals, milks the goats, then takes them to the bank of the stream, where she ties them to a tree. Then she waters the garden and picks the vegetables and fruit, which she loads into her wheelbarrow. She also puts in a basket full of eggs, a small cage with a rabbit, and a chicken or duck with its legs tied together.

She goes off to market pushing her wheelbarrow, with the strap around her scrawny neck, which forces her head down. She staggers under the weight. The bumps and stones in the road make her lose her balance, but she goes on walking, her feet turned inwards, like a duck. She walks to the town, to the market, without stopping, without putting her wheelbarrow down once.

When she gets back from the market, she makes a soup with the vegetables she hasn't sold, and jams with the fruit. She eats, she goes and has a nap in her vineyard, she sleeps for an hour, then she works in the vineyard, or if there is nothing to do there, she returns to the house, she cuts wood, she feeds the animals again, she brings back the goats, she milks them, she goes out into the forest, comes back with mushrooms and kindling, she makes cheeses, she dries mushrooms and beans, she bottles other vegetables, waters the garden again, puts things away in the cellar, and so on until nightfall.

On the sixth morning, when she leaves the house, we have already watered the garden. We take heavy buckets full of pigfeed from her, we take the goats to the bank of the stream, we help her load the wheelbarrow. When she comes back from the market, we are cutting wood.

At the meal, Grandmother says:

"Now you understand. You have to earn food and shelter."

We say:

"It's not that. The work is hard, but to watch someone working and not do anything is even harder, especially if it's someone old."

Grandmother sniggers:

"Sons of a bitch! You mean you felt sorry for me?"

"No, Grandmother. We just felt ashamed."

In the afternoon, we go and gather wood in the forest. From now on we do all the chores we can.

The Forest and the Stream

The forest is very big, the stream is very small. To get to the forest, we have to cross the stream. When there isn't much water, we can cross it by jumping from one stone to another. But sometimes, when it has rained a lot, the water comes up to our waists, and this water is cold and muddy. We decide to build a bridge with bricks and planks that we find around bombed houses.

Our bridge is strong. We show it to Grandmother. She tries it and says:

"Very good. But don't go too far into the forest. The frontier is nearby, the soldiers will shoot at you. And above all, don't get lost. I won't come looking for you."

When we were building the bridge, we saw fish. They hide under big stones or in the shadow of bushes and trees whose branches meet in places over the stream. We choose the biggest fish, we catch them, and we put them in a sprinkling can filled with water. In the evening, when we take them back to the house, Grandmother says:

"Sons of a bitch! How did you catch them?"

"With our hands. It's easy. You just have to stay still and wait."

"Then catch a lot. As many as you can."

Next day, Grandmother puts the sprinkling can on her wheelbarrow and sells our fish at market.

We often go into the forest, we never get lost, we know where the frontier is. Soon the guards get to know us. They never shoot at us. Grandmother teaches us to tell the difference between edible mushrooms and poisonous ones.

From the forest we bring firewood on our backs, and mushrooms and chestnuts in baskets. We stack the wood neatly against the walls of the house under the porch roof, and we roast chestnuts on the stove if Grandmother isn't there.

Once, deep in the forest, beside a big hole made by a bomb, we find a dead soldier. He is still in one piece, only his eyes missing because of the crows. We take his rifle, his cartridges, and his grenades: we hide the rifle inside a bundle of firewood, the cartridges and grenades in our baskets, under the mushrooms.

When we get back to Grandmother's, we carefully wrap these objects in straw and potato sacks, and bury them under the bench in front of the officer's window.

Dirt

At home, in the Big Town, Mother used to wash us often. In the shower or in the bath. She put clean clothes on us and cut our nails. She went with us to the barber to have our hair cut. We used to brush our teeth after every meal.

At Grandmother's it is impossible to wash. There's no bathroom, there isn't even any running water. We have to go pump water from the well in the yard and carry it back in a bucket. There's no soap in the house, no toothpaste, no washing powder.

Everything in the kitchen is dirty. The red, irregular tiles stick to our feet, the big table sticks to our hands and elbows. The stove is completely black with grease, and the walls all around are black with soot. Although Grandmother washes the dishes, the plates, spoons, and knives are never quite clean and the saucepans are covered with a thick layer of grime. The dishcloths are grayish and have a nasty smell.

At first we didn't even want to eat, especially when we saw

14

how Grandmother cooked the meals, wiping her nose on her
sleeve and never washing her hands. Now we take no notice.

When it's warm, we go and bathe in the stream, we wash
our faces and clean our teeth in the well. When it's cold, it's
impossible to wash properly. There is no receptacle big
enough in the house. Our sheets, our blankets, and our towels
have disappeared. We have never seen the big cardboard box
Mother brought them in again.

Grandmother has sold everything.

We're getting dirtier and dirtier, our clothes too. We take
clean clothes out of our suitcases under the seat, but soon
there are no clean clothes left. The ones we wear keep getting
torn, and our shoes have holes in them. When possible, we go
barefoot and wear only underpants or trousers. The soles of
our feet are getting hard, we no longer feel thorns or stones.
Our skin is getting brown, our legs and arms are covered with
scratches, cuts, scabs, and insect bites. Our nails, which are
never cut, break, and our hair, which is almost white from the
sun, reaches down to our shoulders.

The privy is at the bottom of the garden. There's never any
paper. We wipe ourselves with the biggest leaves from certain
plants.

We smell of a mixture of manure, fish, grass, mushrooms,
smoke, milk, cheese, mud, clay, earth, sweat, urine, and mold.

We smell bad, like Grandmother.

Exercise to Toughen the Body

Grandmother often hits us with her bony hands, a broom, or a damp cloth. She pulls our ears and grabs us by the hair.

Other people also slap and kick us, we don't even know why.

The blows hurt and make us cry.

Falls, scratches, cuts, work, cold, and heat cause pain as well.

We decide to toughen our bodies so we can bear pain without crying.

We start by slapping and then punching one another. Seeing our swollen faces, Grandmother asks:

"Who did that to you?"

"We did, Grandmother."

"You had a fight? Why?"

"For nothing, Grandmother. Don't worry, it's only an exercise."

16

"An exercise? You're crazy! Oh, well, if that's your idea of fun . . ."

We are naked. We hit one another with a belt. At each blow we say:

"It doesn't hurt."

We hit harder, harder and harder.

We put our hands over a flame. We cut our thighs, our arms, our chests with a knife and pour alcohol on our wounds. Each time we say:

"It doesn't hurt."

After a while, we really don't feel anything anymore. It's someone else who gets hurt, someone else who gets burned, who gets cut, who feels pain.

We don't cry anymore.

When Grandmother is angry and shouts at us, we say:

"Stop shouting, Grandmother, hit us instead."

When she hits us, we say:

"More, Grandmother! Look, we are turning the other cheek, as it is written in the Bible. Strike the other cheek too, Grandmother."

She answers:

"May the devil take you with your Bible and your cheeks!"

The Orderly

We are lying on the corner seat in the kitchen. Our heads are touching. We aren't asleep yet, but our eyes are shut. Someone pushes at the door. We open our eyes. We are blinded by the beam of a flashlight. We ask:

"Who's there?"

A man's voice answers:

"No fear. You no fear. Two you are, or I too much drink?"

He laughs, lights the oil lamp on the table, and turns off his flashlight. We can see him properly now. He's a foreign soldier, a private. He says:

"I orderly of captain. You do what there?"

We say:

"We live here. It's Grandmother's house."

"You grandchildren of Witch? I never before see you. You be here since when?"

"For two weeks."

"Ah! I go on leave my home, in my village. Laugh much."

18

We ask:

"How is it you can speak our language?"

He says:

"My mother born here, in your country. Come to work in our country, waitress in café. Meet my father, marry with. When I small, my mother speak me your language. Your country and my country be friends. Fight the enemy together. You two come from where?"

"From the Big Town."

"Big Town, much danger. Bang! Bang!"

"Yes, and nothing left to eat."

"Here good to eat. Apples, pigs, chickens, everything. You stay long time? Or only holidays?"

"We'll stay until the end of the war."

"War soon end. You sleep there? Seat bare, hard, cold. Witch no want take you in room?"

"We don't want to sleep in Grandmother's room. She snores and smells. We had blankets and sheets, but she sold them."

The orderly takes some hot water from the cauldron on the stove and says:

"I must clean room. Captain also return leave tonight or tomorrow morning."

He goes out. A few minutes later, he comes back. He brings us two gray army blankets.

"No sell that, old Witch. If she too mean, you tell me. I bang-bang, I kill."

He laughs again. He covers us up, turns out the lamp, and leaves.

During the day we hide the blankets in the attic.

Exercise to Toughen the Mind

Grandmother says to us:
"Sons of a bitch!"
People say to us:
"Sons of a Witch! Sons of a whore!"
Others say:
"Idiots! Hoodlums! Snot-nosed kids! Asses! Slobs! Pigs! Devils! Bastards! Little shits! Punks! Murderers-to-be!"

When we hear these words, our faces get red, our ears buzz, our eyes sting, our knees tremble.

We don't want to blush or tremble anymore, we want to get used to abuse, to hurtful words.

We sit down at the kitchen table face to face, and looking each other in the eyes, we say more and more terrible words.

One of us says:
"Turd! Asshole!"
The other one says:
"Faggot! Prick!"

20

We go on like that until the words no longer reach our brains, no longer even reach our ears.

We exercise this way for about half an hour a day, then we go out walking in the streets.

We contrive to have people insult us, and we observe that we have now reached the stage where we don't care anymore.

But there are also the old words.

Mother used to say to us:

"My darlings! My loves! My joy! My adorable little babies!"

When we remember these words, our eyes fill with tears.

We must forget these words because nobody says such words to us now and because our memory of them is too heavy a burden to bear.

So we begin our exercise again, in a different way.

We say:

"My darlings! My loves! I love you. . . . I shall never leave you. . . . I shall never love anyone but you. . . . Forever. . . . You are my whole life . . ."

By force of repetition, these words gradually lose their meaning, and the pain they carry in them is assuaged.

School

This happened three years ago.

It's evening. Our parents think we are asleep. They're talking about us in the other room.

Mother says:

"They won't bear being separated."

Father says:

"They'll only be separated during school hours."

Mother says:

"They won't bear it."

"They'll have to. It's necessary for them. Everybody says so. The teachers, the psychologists, everybody. It will be difficult at first, but they'll get used to it."

Mother says:

"No, never. I know it. I know them. They are one and the same person."

Father raises his voice:

"Precisely, it isn't normal. They think together, they act

22

together. They live in a different world. In a world of their own. It isn't very healthy. It's even rather worrying. Yes, they worry me. They're odd. You never know what they might be thinking. They're too advanced for their age. They know too much."

Mother laughs:

"You're not going to reproach them with their intelligence, I hope?"

"It isn't funny. Why are you laughing?"

Mother replies:

"Twins are always a problem. It isn't the end of the world. Everything will sort itself out."

Father says:

"Yes, everything will sort itself out if we separate them. Every individual must have his own life."

A few days later, we start school. We're in different classes. We both sit in the front row.

We are separated from one another by the whole length of the building. This distance between us seems monstrous, the pain is unbearable. It is as if they had taken half our bodies away. We can't keep our balance, we feel dizzy, we fall, we lose consciousness.

We wake up in the ambulance that is taking us to the hospital.

Mother comes to fetch us. She smiles and says:

"You'll be in the same class from tomorrow on."

At home, Father just says to us:

"Fakers!"

Soon he leaves for the front. He's a journalist, a war correspondent.

We go to school for two and a half years. The teachers also

leave for the front; they are replaced by women teachers. Later, the school closes because there are too many air raids.

We have learned reading, writing, and arithmetic.

At Grandmother's we decide to continue our studies without a teacher, by ourselves.

Purchase of Paper, Notebook, and Pencils

At Grandmother's there is no paper, there are no pencils. We go looking for some at a shop called Booksellers and Stationers. We choose a packet of graph paper, two pencils, and a big thick notebook. We place all that on the counter in front of the fat gentleman standing on the other side. We say to him:

"We need these things, but we have no money."

The bookseller says:

"What? But . . . you have to pay."

We repeat:

"We have no money, but we absolutely need these things."

The bookseller says:

"The school is closed. Nobody needs notebooks or pencils."

We say:

"We are having school at home. All alone, by ourselves."

"Ask your parents for money."

"Father is at the front, and Mother has stayed in the Big

25

Town. We live at Grandmother's, she doesn't have any money either."

The bookseller says:

"You can't buy anything without money."

We don't say anything else, we just look at him. He looks at us too. His forehead is damp with sweat. After a while he shouts:

"Don't look at me like that! Get out!"

We say:

"We are quite prepared to effect certain tasks for you in exchange for these things. We could water or weed your garden, for example, carry parcels . . ."

He shouts again:

"I don't have a garden! I don't need you! And in the first place, can't you talk normally?"

"We do talk normally."

"Is it normal, at your age, to say 'quite prepared to effect'?"

"We speak correctly."

"Yes, too correctly. I don't care at all for the way you talk! Nor for your way of looking at me! Get out!"

We ask:

"Do you have any chickens, sir?"

He dabs his white face with a white handkerchief. He asks, without shouting:

"Chickens? Why chickens?"

"Because if you don't have any, we have at our disposal a certain quantity of eggs and can supply you with them in exchange for these things, which are indispensable to us."

The bookseller looks at us and says nothing.

We say:

"The price of eggs increases day by day. On the other hand, the price of paper and pencils . . ."

He throws our paper, our pencils, and our notebook in the direction of the door and yells:

"Get out! I don't need your eggs! Take all that, and don't come back!"

We pick the things up carefully and say:

"We shall be obliged, however, to come back when we have used up all the paper and pencils."

Our Studies

For our studies, we have Father's dictionary and the Bible we found here at Grandmother's, in the attic.

We have lessons in spelling, composition, reading, mental arithmetic, mathematics, and memorization.

We use the dictionary for spelling, to obtain explanations, but also to learn new words, synonyms and antonyms.

We use the Bible for reading aloud, dictation, and memorization. We are thus learning whole pages of the Bible by heart.

This is how a composition lesson proceeds:

We are sitting at the kitchen table with our sheets of graph paper, our pencils, and the notebook. We are alone.

One of us says:

"The title of your composition is: 'Arrival at Grandmother's.' "

The other says:

"The title of your composition is: 'Our Chores.' "

28

We start writing. We have two hours to deal with the subject and two sheets of paper at our disposal.

At the end of two hours we exchange our sheets of paper. Each of us corrects the other's spelling mistakes with the help of the dictionary and writes at the bottom of the page: "Good" or "Not good." If it's "Not good," we throw the composition in the fire and try to deal with the same subject in the next lesson. If it's "Good," we can copy the composition into the notebook.

To decide whether it's "Good" or "Not good," we have a very simple rule: the composition must be true. We must describe what is, what we see, what we hear, what we do.

For example, it is forbidden to write, "Grandmother is like a witch"; but we are allowed to write, "People call Grandmother the Witch."

It is forbidden to write, "The Little Town is beautiful," because the Little Town may be beautiful to us and ugly to someone else.

Similarly, if we write, "The orderly is nice," this isn't a truth, because the orderly may be capable of malicious acts that we know nothing about. So we would simply write, "The orderly has given us some blankets."

We would write, "We eat a lot of walnuts," and not "We love walnuts," because the word "love" is not a reliable word, it lacks precision and objectivity. "To love walnuts" and "to love Mother" don't mean the same thing. The first expression designates a pleasant taste in the mouth, the second a feeling.

Words that define feelings are very vague. It is better to avoid using them and stick to the description of objects, human beings, and oneself, that is to say, to the faithful description of facts.

Our Neighbor and Her Daughter

Our neighbor is not as old as Grandmother. She lives with her daughter in the last house of the Little Town. It is a completely dilapidated shack with several holes in the roof. Around it there is a garden, but it is not cultivated like Grandmother's garden. Nothing grows there but weeds.

The neighbor spends all day sitting on a stool in her garden looking straight in front of her at who knows what. In the evenings or when it rains, her daughter takes her by the arm and leads her indoors. Sometimes her daughter forgets her or isn't there, and then the mother spends the whole night outside, whatever the weather.

People say that our neighbor is mad, that she lost her mind when the man who made her pregnant abandoned her.

Grandmother says that the neighbor is simply lazy and prefers to stay poor rather than get down to work.

The neighbor's daughter is no taller than we are, but she is a bit older. During the day, she begs in the town, outside cafés

30

and at street corners. At the market, she picks up vegetables and rotten fruit that people throw away and takes them home. She also steals anything she can. Several times we have had to chase her out of our garden when she was trying to take fruit and eggs.

Once, we catch her drinking milk by sucking the udder of one of our goats.

When she sees us, she gets up, wipes her mouth on the back of her hand, steps back, and says:

"Don't hurt me!"

She adds:

"I run very fast. You won't catch me."

We look at her. It's the first time we've seen her close up. She has a harelip, she's cross-eyed, she has snot in her nose and yellow dirt in the corners of her red eyes. Her legs and arms are covered with pimples.

She says:

"I'm called Harelip. I like milk."

She smiles. Her teeth are black.

"I like milk, but what I like best is sucking the udder. It's good. It's hard and soft at the same time."

We say nothing. She approaches us.

"I like to suck something else, too."

She stretches out her hand. We step back. She says:

"Don't you want to? Don't you want to play with me? I'd really like to. You're so handsome."

She lowers her head and says:

"I disgust you."

We say:

"No, you don't disgust us."

"I see. You're too young, too shy. But you don't have to be

embarrassed with me. I'll teach you some very amusing games."

We say:

"We never play."

"Then what do you do all day long?"

"We work and study."

"I beg, steal, and play."

"You also look after your mother. You're a good girl."

She comes up to us and says:

"You think I'm a good girl? Really?"

"Yes. And if you need anything for your mother or for yourself, you have only to ask us. We'll give you fruit, vegetables, fish, and milk."

She starts shouting:

"I don't want your fruit, your fish, or your milk! I can steal all that. What I want is for you to love me. Nobody loves me. Not even my mother. But I don't love anybody either. Not my mother and not you! I hate you!"

Exercise in Begging

We put on dirty, torn clothes, we take off our shoes, we soil our faces and hands. We go out into the street. We stop, we wait.

When a foreign officer passes us, we raise our right hands in salute and extend our left hands. Usually the officer walks by without seeing us, without looking at us.

Finally an officer stops. He says something in a language we don't understand. He asks us questions. We don't answer. We stand motionless, one arm raised, the other held out. Then he fumbles in his pockets, places a coin and a bit of chocolate in our dirty hands, and goes off, shaking his head.

We go on waiting.

A woman passes by. We hold out our hands. She says:

"Poor kids. I have nothing to give you."

She strokes our hair.

We say:

"Thank you."

Another woman gives us two apples, another some biscuits.

A woman passes by. We hold out our hands. She stops and says:

"Aren't you ashamed to beg? Come with me, I've got a few easy little jobs for you. Cutting wood, for example, or cleaning up the terrace. You're big enough and strong enough for that. Afterward, if you work well, I'll give you some bread and soup."

We answer:

"We don't want to work for you, madam. We don't want to eat your soup or your bread. We are not hungry."

She asks:

"Then why are you begging?"

"To find out what effect it has and to observe people's reactions."

She walks off, shouting:

"Dirty little hooligans! And impertinent too!"

On our way home, we throw the apples, the biscuits, the chocolate, and the coins in the tall grass by the roadside.

It is impossible to throw away the stroking on our hair.

Harelip

We are fishing in the stream. Harelip runs by. She doesn't see us. She lies down in the grass and lifts her skirt. She isn't wearing underpants. We see her bare buttocks and the hair between her legs. We don't have hair between our legs yet. Harelip has some, but not very much.

Harelip whistles. A dog arrives. It's our dog. She takes him in her arms and rolls with him in the grass. The dog barks, gets loose, shakes himself, and runs off. Harelip calls him gently as she strokes her sex with her fingers.

The dog comes back, sniffs Harelip's sex several times, and starts to lick it.

Harelip spreads her legs and presses the dog's head to her belly with both hands. She breathes very deeply and wriggles.

The dog's sex becomes visible, it gets longer and longer, it is thin and red. The dog raises his head and tries to climb onto Harelip.

Harelip turns over, she is on her knees, she offers her backside to the dog. The dog places his front paws on Harelip's back, his hindquarters trembling. He feels around, gets closer and closer, puts himself between Harelip's legs, and sticks himself against her buttocks. He moves very quickly backward and forward. Harelip gives a cry, and after a moment she falls on her stomach.

The dog walks off slowly.

Harelip lies on the ground for a while, then gets up, sees us, and blushes. She shouts:

"Dirty little spies! What did you see?"

We answer:

"We saw you playing with our dog."

She asks:

"Am I still your friend?"

"Yes. And we'll allow you to play with our dog as much as you like."

"And you won't tell anybody what you saw?"

"We never tell anybody anything. You can depend on us."

She sits down in the grass and cries:

"Only animals love me."

We ask:

"Is it true your mother is mad?"

"No. She's just deaf and blind."

"What happened to her?"

"Nothing. Nothing special. One day she went blind, and later on she went deaf. She says it'll be the same for me. Have you seen my eyes? In the morning, when I wake up, my eyelashes are stuck together and my eyes are full of pus."

We say:

"It's certainly an illness that medicine can cure."

She says:

"Maybe. But how can you go to a doctor without money? Anyway, there aren't any doctors. They're all at the front."

We ask:

"And what about your ears? Do they hurt?"

"No, I don't have any problem with my ears. And I don't think my mother has either. She pretends not to hear anything, that suits her when I ask her questions."

Exercise in Blindness
and Deafness

One of us pretends to be blind, the other deaf. To begin with, by way of training, the blind one ties one of Grandmother's black shawls over his eyes and the deaf one stuffs his ears with grass. The shawl smells bad, like Grandmother.

We hold hands and go out walking during air raids, when people are hiding in their cellars and the streets are deserted.

The deaf one describes what he sees:

"The street is long and straight. It is lined with low single-story houses. They are white, gray, pink, yellow, and blue. At the end of the street, I can see a park with trees and a fountain. The sky is blue, with a few white clouds. I can see planes. Five bombers. They are flying low."

The blind one talks slowly so that the deaf one can read his lips:

"I can hear the planes. They are making a deep sputtering noise. Their engines are laboring. They are full of bombs. Now

38

they've passed over. I can hear the birds again. Otherwise everything is quiet."

The deaf one reads the blind one's lips and answers:

"Yes, the street is empty."

The blind one says:

"Not for long. I can hear footsteps in the side street on the left."

The deaf one says:

"You're right. It's a man."

The blind one asks:

"What is he like?"

The deaf one answers:

"Like all of them. Poor, old."

The blind one says:

"I know. I recognize old men's footsteps. I can also hear that he's barefoot, so he's poor."

The deaf one says:

"He's bald. He's wearing an old army jacket. His trousers are too short. His feet are dirty."

"What about his eyes?"

"I can't see them. He's looking down."

"And his mouth?"

"His lips are too drawn. He must have lost all his teeth."

"And his hands?"

"They're in his pockets. The pockets are huge and filled with something. Potatoes or walnuts, there are bumps showing. He's raising his head, he's looking at us. But I can't make out the color of his eyes."

"Can you see anything else?"

"Lines, deep lines on his face, like scars."

The blind one says:

"I can hear the sirens. The raid is over. Let's go home."

Later, with time, we no longer need a shawl over our eyes or grass in our ears. The one playing the blind man simply turns his gaze inward, and the deaf one shuts his ears to all sounds.

The Deserter

We find a man in the forest. A living man, a young man, without a uniform. He is lying behind a bush. He looks at us without moving.

We ask him:

"Why are you lying there?"

He answers:

"I can't walk anymore. I've come from the other side of the frontier. I've been walking for two weeks. Day and night. Especially night. I'm too weak now. I'm hungry. I haven't eaten for three days."

We ask:

"Why haven't you got a uniform? All young men have a uniform. They are all soldiers."

He says:

"I don't want to be a soldier anymore."

"You don't want to fight the enemy anymore?"

"I don't want to fight anyone. I have no enemies. I want to go home."

"Where is your home?"

"Still a long way off. I'll never get there if I don't find something to eat."

We ask:

"Why don't you go and buy something to eat? Don't you have any money?"

"No, I don't have any money, and I can't be seen. I must hide. No one must see me."

"Why?"

"I left my regiment without leave. I ran away. I'm a deserter. If they found me, I'd be shot or hanged."

We ask:

"Like a murderer?"

"Yes, exactly like a murderer."

"And yet you don't want to kill anyone. You just want to go home."

"Yes, I just want to go home."

We ask:

"What do you want us to bring you to eat?"

"Anything."

"Goat's milk, hard-boiled eggs, bread, fruit?"

"Yes, yes, anything."

We ask:

"And a blanket? The nights are cold, and it often rains."

He says:

"Yes, but you mustn't be seen. And you won't say anything to anybody, will you? Not even to your mother."

We answer:

"No one will see us, we never say anything to anybody, and we have no mother."

When we come back with the food and blanket, he says:

"You're very kind."

We say:

"We weren't trying to be kind. We've brought you these things because you absolutely need them. That's all."

He says again:

"I don't know how to thank you. I'll never forget you."

His eyes fill with tears.

We say:

"Crying is no use, you know. We never cry, even though we aren't men yet, like you."

He smiles and says:

"You're right. Excuse me, I won't do it anymore. It's just because of the exhaustion."

Exercise in Fasting

We announce to Grandmother:

"Today and tomorrow we won't eat. We'll only drink water."

She shrugs her shoulders:

"I couldn't care less. But you'll work as usual."

"Of course, Grandmother."

The first day, she kills a chicken and roasts it in the oven. At midday, she calls us:

"Come and eat!"

We go to the kitchen, it smells very good. We're a bit hungry, but not too much. We watch Grandmother carve up the chicken.

She says:

"It smells good. Can you smell how good it smells? Do you want a leg each?"

"We don't want anything, Grandmother."

"That's a pity, because it's really very good."

She eats with her hands, licking her fingers and wiping them on her apron. She gnaws and sucks the bones.

She says:

"Very tender, this young chicken. I can't imagine anything better."

We say:

"Grandmother, since we've been in your house, you have never cooked a chicken for us."

She says:

"I've cooked one today. Now's your chance."

"You knew we didn't want anything to eat today or tomorrow."

"That's not my fault. This is just more of your damn nonsense."

"It's one of our exercises. To get us used to bearing hunger."

"Then get used to it. Nobody's stopping you."

We leave the kitchen and go out to do our chores in the garden. By the end of the day, we are really very hungry. We drink a lot of water. In the evening, we find it hard to get to sleep. We dream of food.

Next day, at midday, Grandmother finishes the chicken. We watch her eating it in a kind of fog. We're no longer hungry. We feel dizzy.

In the evening, Grandmother makes pancakes with jam and cream cheese. We feel sick and have stomach cramps, but as soon as we go to bed, we fall into a deep sleep. When we get up, Grandmother has already left for the market. We want to have our breakfast, but there is nothing to eat in the kitchen. No bread, no milk, no cheese. Grandmother has locked everything away in the cellar. We could open it, but we decide not to touch anything. We eat raw tomatoes and cucumbers with salt.

Grandmother comes back from the market and says:

"You haven't done your work this morning."

"You should have woken us up, Grandmother."

"You should have woken yourselves up. But just this once, I'll give you something to eat all the same."

She makes us a vegetable soup with what she brings back from the market, as usual. We don't eat much. After the meal, Grandmother says:

"It's a stupid exercise. And bad for the health."

Grandfather's Grave

One day, we see Grandmother leave the house with her sprinkling can and her gardening tools. But instead of going to the vineyard, she sets off in a different direction. We follow her at a distance to find out where she is going.

She goes into the cemetery. She stops in front of a grave and puts down her tools. The cemetery is deserted. There is nobody but Grandmother and us.

Hiding behind bushes and tombstones, we get closer and closer. Grandmother is shortsighted and hard of hearing. We can observe her without her knowing.

She pulls up the weeds on the grave, digs with a spade, rakes the soil, plants flowers, fetches water from the well, and comes back to water the grave.

When she has finished her work, she gathers her tools together, then kneels down in front of the wooden cross, but sitting back on her heels. She joins her hands over her belly as if to say a prayer, but what we hear are mainly oaths:

"Shit . . . bastard . . . pig . . . scum . . . demon . . ."

When Grandmother leaves, we go see the grave: it is very well maintained. We look at the cross: the name written on it is Grandmother's. It is also Mother's maiden name. The Christian name is double, with a hyphen, and those two Christian names are our own Christian names.

On the cross, there are also dates of birth and death. We calculate that Grandfather died at the age of forty-four, twenty-three years ago.

In the evening, we ask Grandmother:

"What was our Grandfather like?"

She says:

"What? You don't have a Grandfather."

"But we used to have."

"No, never. He was already dead when you were born. So you never had a Grandfather."

We ask:

"Why did you poison him?"

She asks:

"What are you talking about?"

"People say you poisoned Grandfather."

"People say . . . people say . . . Let them tell their tales."

"You didn't poison him?"

"Leave me alone, sons of a bitch! Nothing was proved! People will say anything."

We go on:

"We know you didn't like Grandfather. So why do you look after his grave?"

"For that very reason! Because of what people say. To stop them telling their tales! And how do you know I look after his grave, eh? You've been spying on me, sons of a bitch, you've been spying on me again! May the devil take you!"

Exercise in Cruelty

It's Sunday. We catch a chicken and cut its throat as we have seen Grandmother do. We bring the chicken into the kitchen and say:

"You must cook it, Grandmother."

She starts shouting:

"Who gave you permission? You have no right! I give the orders here, you little shits! I won't cook it! I'd rather croak first!"

We say:

"All right. We'll cook it ourselves."

We start to pluck the chicken, but Grandmother snatches it from our hands:

"You don't know how to do it! You filthy little bastards, you'll be the death of me, you're God's punishment on me, that's what you are!"

While the chicken is cooking, Grandmother cries:

"It was the most beautiful one. They took the most beauti-

50

ful one on purpose. It was just ready for the Tuesday market."

As we eat the chicken, we say:

"It's very good, this chicken. We'll eat chicken every Sunday."

"Every Sunday? Are you crazy? Do you want to ruin me?"

"We shall eat a chicken every Sunday, whether you like it or not."

Grandmother starts crying again:

"But what have I done to them? Woe is me! They want to kill me. A poor old defenseless woman. I don't deserve this. And I've been so good to them!"

"Yes, Grandmother, you are good, very good. So it is out of goodness that you will cook a chicken for us every Sunday."

When she calms down a bit, we say to her again:

"When there's something to be killed, you must fetch us. We'll do it."

She says:

"You like that, eh?"

"No, Grandmother, as a matter of fact, we don't like it. It's for that reason that we must get used to it."

She says:

"I see. It's a new exercise. You're right. It's good to know how to kill when you have to."

We begin with fish. We pick them up by the tail and bang their heads against a stone. We soon get used to killing animals intended to be eaten: chickens, rabbits, ducks. Later, we kill animals that it would not have been necessary to kill. We catch frogs, nail them down on a board, and slit their bellies open. We also catch butterflies and pin them to a piece of cardboard. Soon we have a fine collection.

One day we hang our cat, a ginger tom, from the branch

of a tree. As he hangs, he stretches and grows enormous. He has spasms and convulsions. When he isn't moving anymore, we cut him down. He lies sprawled on the grass, motionless, then suddenly gets up and runs off.

Ever since then, we sometimes see him at a distance, but he no longer comes near the house. He doesn't even come to drink the milk we put in front of the door on a little plate.

Grandmother says:

"That cat is getting wilder and wilder."

We say:

"Don't worry, Grandmother, we'll take care of the mice."

We make traps and drown the mice we catch in boiling water.

The Other Children

We meet other children in the Little Town. As the school is closed, they are out all day long. There are big ones and little ones. Some have their homes and mothers here, others are from elsewhere, like us. Especially from the Big Town.

A lot of these children are living with people they didn't know before. They have to work in the fields and vineyards; the people who look after them are not always nice to them.

The big children often attack the smallest ones. They take all they have in their pockets, and sometimes even their clothes. They beat them up too, especially those who come from elsewhere. The young ones from here are protected by their mothers and never go out alone.

We are not protected by anybody, so we learn to defend ourselves against the big ones.

We make weapons: we sharpen stones, we fill socks with sand and gravel. We also have a razor, which we found in the chest in the attic, next to the Bible. We have only to take out our razor and the big boys run away.

One very hot day, we are sitting beside the fountain where people who have no well of their own come to get water. Nearby, some boys who are bigger than us are lying in the grass. It is cool here under the trees near the water, which runs without stopping.

Harelip arrives with a bucket that she places under the spout, which is discharging a thin trickle of water. She waits for her bucket to fill.

When the bucket is full, one of the boys gets up and goes over and spits in it. Harelip empties the bucket, rinses it, and puts it back under the spout.

When the bucket is full again, another boy gets up and spits in it. Harelip puts the rinsed bucket back under the spout. She doesn't wait for the bucket to fill, she fills it only halfway and quickly tries to escape.

One of the boys runs after her, catches her by the arm, and spits in the bucket.

Harelip says:

"Stop it, will you? I have to take clean drinking water back."

The boy says:

"But the water *is* clean. I just spat in it. Are you saying my spit is dirty? My spit is cleaner than anything in your house!"

Harelip empties her bucket and cries.

The boy opens his fly and says:

"Suck it! If you suck me off, we'll let you fill your bucket."

Harelip kneels down. The boy steps back:

"Do you think I'm going to put my cock into your disgusting mouth? Filthy slut!"

He kicks Harelip in the chest and does up his fly.

We go over. We pick Harelip up, take her bucket, rinse it well, and put it under the fountain spout.

One of the boys says to the other two:

"Come on, we have better things to do."

Another says:

"Are you crazy? This is when the fun starts."

The first one says:

"Drop it! I know them. They're dangerous."

"Dangerous? Those little cunts? I'll take care of them, you'll see."

He comes up to us and tries to spit in the bucket, but one of us trips him up, the other hits him on the head with a bag of sand. The boy falls down. He lies on the ground, stunned. The other two look at us. One of them takes a step toward us. The other says:

"Watch out! Those little bastards are capable of anything. Once they split my head open with a stone. They've got a razor too, and they don't hesitate to use it. They'd slit your throat as soon as look at you. They're completely crazy."

The boys leave.

We hand the filled bucket to Harelip. She asks us:

"Why didn't you help me right away?"

"We wanted to see how you defended yourself."

"What would I have been able to do against three big boys?"

"Throw your bucket at their heads, scratch their faces, kick them in the balls, shout and yell. Or run away and come back later."

Winter

It's getting colder and colder. We rummage in our suitcases and put on almost everything we find: several pullovers, several pairs of trousers. But we can't put a second pair of shoes on over the holes in our worn-out town shoes. Anyway, we don't have any others. We don't have gloves or hats either. Our hands and feet are covered with chilblains.

The sky is dark gray, the streets of the town are empty, the stream is frozen, the forest is covered with snow. We can't go there anymore. So we'll soon be out of wood.

We say to Grandmother:

"We need two pairs of rubber boots."

She answers:

"And what else do you need? Where do you expect me to find the money?"

"Grandmother, there's hardly any wood left."

"Then we'll have to go easy on it."

We don't go out anymore. We do all kinds of exercises, we

56

carve various objects out of wood, like spoons and bread-boards, and we study late into the night. Grandmother stays in bed almost all the time. She seldom goes into the kitchen. We are left in peace.

We eat badly, there are no more vegetables and fruit, the hens aren't laying anymore. Every day Grandmother brings some dried beans and a few potatoes up from the cellar—which is full of smoked meats and jars of jam.

The postman comes sometimes. He rings his bicycle bell until Grandmother comes out of the house. He then moistens his pencil, writes something on a bit of paper, and hands the pencil and paper to Grandmother, who puts a cross at the bottom. The postman gives her some money, a package, or a letter and goes off toward town whistling.

Grandmother locks herself in her room with the package or the money. If there's a letter, she throws it into the fire.

We ask:

"Grandmother, why do you throw the letter away without reading it?"

She answers:

"I can't read. I never went to school, I've never done anything but work. I wasn't spoiled like you."

"We could read you the letters you get."

"Nobody must read the letters I get."

We ask:

"Who sends the money? Who sends the packages? Who sends the letters?"

She doesn't answer.

Next day, while she is in the cellar, we scour her room. Under the bed we find an open package. In it there are pullovers, scarves, hats, and gloves. We say nothing to Grandmother, because if we did she would realize that we have a key to her room.

After the evening meal, we wait. Grandmother drinks her brandy, then staggers over to open her bedroom door with the key that hangs from her belt. We follow her and push her from behind. She falls on her bed. We pretend to search and find the package.

We say:

"That's not very nice, Grandmother. We're cold, we have no warm clothes, we can't go out anymore, and you want to sell everything Mother has knitted and sent for us."

Grandmother says nothing, she cries.

We say again:

"It's Mother who sends the money, Mother who writes you letters."

Grandmother says:

"It isn't me she writes. She knows very well I can't read. She never used to write me. Now that you're here, she writes. But I don't need her letters! I don't need anything that comes from her!"

The Postman

From now on we wait for the postman in front of the garden gate. He's an old man with a cap. He has a bicycle with two leather pouches attached to the carrier.

When he arrives, we don't give him time to ring: very quickly we unscrew his bell.

He says:

"Where's your grandmother?"

We say:

"Don't worry about her. Give us what you've brought."

He says:

"There's nothing."

He tries to get away, but we give him a push. He falls in the snow. His bicycle falls on top of him. He swears.

We search his pouches and find a letter and a money order. We take the letter and say:

"Give us the money!"

He says:

"No. It's addressed to your grandmother."

We say:

"But it's intended for us. It's been sent to us by our Mother. If you don't hand it over, we'll keep you from getting up until you freeze to death."

He says:

"All right, all right. Help me get up, one of my legs is crushed under the bike."

We pick up the bicycle and help the postman get up. He is very thin, very light.

He takes the money out of one of his pockets and gives it to us.

We ask:

"Do you want a signature or a cross?"

He says:

"A cross will do. One cross is as good as another."

He adds:

"You're right to stand up for yourselves. Everybody knows what your grandmother's like. There's nobody stingier than her. So it's your mother who sends you all that? She's very nice. I knew her when she was a little girl. She did well to leave. She would never have been able to marry here. With all the gossip . . ."

We ask:

"What gossip?"

"Like how she was supposed to have poisoned her husband. I mean, your grandmother poisoned your grandfather. It's an old story. That's why they call her the Witch."

We say:

"We don't want anyone to speak ill of Grandmother."

The postman turns his bicycle around:

"All right, all right, but you ought to be informed."

We say:

"We were already informed. From now on you will give the mail to us. Otherwise we'll kill you. Understand?"

The postman says:

"You'd be quite capable of it, you've got the makings of murderers. You'll have your mail, it's all the same to me. I couldn't care less about the Witch."

He leaves, pushing his bicycle. He drags his leg to show that we hurt him.

Next day, warmly dressed, we go off to town to buy rubber boots with the money Mother has sent us. We take turns carrying her letter under our shirts.

The Cobbler

The cobbler lives and works in the basement of a house near the station. The room is enormous. In one corner is his bed, in another his kitchen. His workshop faces the window, which is at ground level. The cobbler is sitting on a low stool surrounded by shoes and tools. He looks at us over his spectacles; he looks at our cracked patent-leather shoes.

We say:

"Good morning, sir. We would like warm, waterproof rubber boots. Do you sell them? We have money."

He says:

"Yes, I sell them. But the lined ones, the warm ones, are very expensive."

We say:

"We absolutely need them. Our feet are cold."

We put what money we have on the low table.

The cobbler says:

"It's just enough for one pair. But one pair should do you. You're the same size. You can take turns going out."

"That isn't possible. One of us never goes out without the other. We go everywhere together."

"Ask your parents for more money, then."

"We have no parents. We live with our Grandmother, whom they call the Witch. She won't give us any money."

The cobbler says:

"The Witch is your grandmother? Poor kids! And you've come from her house all the way here in those shoes!"

"Yes, we have. We can't get through the winter without boots. We have to go into the forest to find wood; we have to clear the snow. We absolutely need . . ."

"Two pairs of warm, waterproof boots."

The cobbler laughs and hands us two pairs of boots:

"Try them on."

We try them on; they fit us very well.

We say:

"We'll keep them. We'll pay you for the second pair in the spring when we'll be selling fish and eggs. Or if you prefer, we'll bring you wood."

The cobbler hands us back our money:

"Here, take it. I don't want your money. Buy yourselves some good socks with it. I'll give you the boots because you absolutely need them."

We say:

"We don't like to accept presents."

"And why not?"

"Because we don't like to say thank you."

"Nobody's making you say anything. Be off with you. No.

Wait a moment! Take these slippers and these sandals for the summer and these shoes too. They're very strong. Take whatever you like."

"But why are you giving us all this?"

"I don't need them anymore. I'll be going away soon."

We ask:

"Where are you going?"

"Who knows? They'll take me away and kill me."

We ask:

"Who wants to kill you, and why?"

He says:

"Don't ask questions. Leave now."

We pick up the shoes, the slippers, and the sandals. We have the boots on our feet. We stop at the door and say:

"We hope they won't take you away. Or if they do take you away, we hope they won't kill you. Goodbye, sir, and thank you, thank you very much."

When we get back, Grandmother asks:

"Where did you steal all that, you punks?"

"We didn't steal anything. It's a present. Not everybody is as stingy as you, Grandmother."

The Theft

With our boots and our warm clothes, we can go out again. We slide on the frozen stream, we go look for wood in the forest.

We take an axe and a saw with us. We can no longer collect the dead wood lying on the ground; the layer of snow is too thick. We climb trees, saw off the dead branches, and chop them up with the axe. During this work, we aren't cold. We even sweat. So we can take off our gloves and put them in our pockets so that they won't wear out too quickly.

One day, coming back with our two bundles of firewood, we make a detour to go see Harelip.

The snow in front of the shack has not been cleared, and there are no footprints leading to it. The chimney is not smoking.

We knock on the door, no one answers. We go in. At first we see nothing, it is so dark, but our eyes soon adjust to the gloom.

It's a room that serves as kitchen and bedroom. In the darkest corner, there's a bed. We approach. We call out. Someone moves under the blankets and old clothes; Harelip's head emerges.

We ask:

"Is your mother there?"

She says:

"Yes."

"Is she dead?"

"I don't know."

We put down our wood and light a fire in the stove, because it's as cold in the room as outside. Then we go back to Grandmother's and get some potatoes and dried beans from the cellar. We milk one of the goats and come back to our neighbor's. We heat the milk. We melt some snow in a saucepan and cook the beans in it. We bake the potatoes in the oven.

Harelip gets up and totters over to a chair by the fire.

Our neighbor isn't dead. We pour some goat's milk into her mouth. We say to Harelip:

"When all this is ready, eat and give some to your mother. We'll be back."

With the money the cobbler gave back to us, we have bought a few pairs of socks, but we haven't spent it all. We go into a grocer's to buy some flour, and take some salt and sugar without paying for them. We also go to the butchers's; we buy a small slab of bacon and take a big sausage without paying for it. We return to Harelip's. She and her mother have already eaten everything. The mother is still in bed, Harelip is washing up.

We say to her:

"We'll bring you a bundle of firewood every day. Some

beans and potatoes too. But for the rest, you need money. We don't have any more. Without money, you can't go into a shop. You have to buy something if you're going to steal something else."

She says:

"You really are smart. You're right. They don't even let me into the shops. I'd never have thought you were capable of stealing."

We say:

"Why not? It will be our exercise in cunning. But we need a little money. Absolutely."

She thinks about it and says:

"Go ask the parish priest. He used to give me money sometimes when I let him see my slit."

"He asked you to do that?"

"Yes. And sometimes he put his finger in. And afterward he gave me money not to tell anybody. Tell him Harelip and her mother need money."

Blackmail

We go see the parish priest. He lives next to the church in a big house.

We pull on the bellpull. An old woman opens the door:

"What do you want?"

"We want to see the parish priest."

"Why?"

"It's for someone who is going to die."

The old woman takes us into a waiting room. She knocks on a door:

"Father," she shouts, "it's for an extreme unction."

A voice answers from behind the door:

"I'm coming. Tell them to wait."

We wait a few minutes. A tall, thin man with a severe face comes out of the room. He is wearing a sort of white and gold cloak over his dark clothes. He asks us:

"Where is it? Who sent you?"

"Harelip and her mother."

68

He says:

"What is the precise name of these people?"

"We don't know their precise name. The mother is blind and deaf. She lives in the last house in town. They are dying of hunger and cold."

The priest says:

"Although I know absolutely nothing about these people, I am willing to give them extreme unction. Let's go. Lead the way."

We say:

"They don't need extreme unction yet. They need a little money. We've brought them wood, a few potatoes, and some dried beans, but we can't do any more. Harelip has sent us here. You used to give her a little money sometimes."

The priest says:

"It's quite possible. I give money to a lot of poor people. I can't remember all of them. Here!"

He fumbles in his pockets under his cloak and gives us a few coins. We take them and say:

"That's not very much. It's too little. It isn't even enough to buy a loaf of bread."

He says:

"I'm sorry. There are a lot of poor people. And the faithful have almost stopped giving offerings. Everybody is in difficulties at the moment. Off with you now, and God bless you!"

We say:

"We can accept this sum for today, but we will have to come back tomorrow."

"What? What is that supposed to mean? Tomorrow? I shan't let you in. Get out of here immediately."

"Tomorrow we will ring the bell until you let us in. We will knock at the windows, we will kick at your door and tell everybody what you did to Harelip."

"I never did anything to Harelip. I don't even know who she is. She must be making these things up. The stories of a mentally deficient child will not be taken seriously. No one will believe you. Everything she says is untrue!"

We say:

"It hardly matters whether it's true or false. The point is the slander. People love scandal."

The priest sits down on a chair and mops his face with a handkerchief.

"It's monstrous. Have you any idea what you're doing?"

"Yes, sir. Blackmail."

"At your age . . . It's deplorable."

"Yes, it's deplorable that we've been forced to this. But Harelip and her mother absolutely need money."

The priest gets up, takes off his cloak, and says:

"It is a trial sent from God. How much do you want? I'm not rich, you know."

"Ten times what you have already given us. Once a week. We aren't asking you for the impossible."

He takes the money out of his pocket and gives it to us:

"Come every Saturday. But don't imagine for a moment that I'm doing this because I'm giving in to your blackmail. I'm doing it out of charity."

We say:

"That's exactly what we expected of you, Father."

Accusations

One afternoon the orderly comes into the kitchen. We haven't seen him for a long time. He says:

"You come help unload jeep?"

We put on our boots and follow him out to the jeep, which is parked on the road in front of the garden gate. The orderly hands us crates and cardboard boxes, which we carry into the officer's room.

We ask:

"Is the officer coming this evening? We still haven't ever seen him."

The orderly says:

"Officer no come winter here. Perhaps come never. He unhappy in love. Perhaps find another later. Forget. Stories like that not for you. You bring wood to heat room."

We bring wood and make a fire in the small metal stove. The orderly opens the crates and boxes and puts on the table bottles of wine, brandy, beer, and lots of things to eat: sausages, cans of meat and vegetables, rice, biscuits, chocolate, sugar, and coffee.

The orderly opens a bottle, starts to drink, and says:

"I heat food in mess kit on camp stove. Tonight eat, drink, sing with friends. Celebrate victory against the enemy. We soon win war with new wonder weapon."

We ask:

"So the war will be over soon?"

He says:

"Yes, very soon. Why you look like that at food on the table? If you hungry, eat chocolate, biscuits, sausage."

We say:

"There are people dying of hunger."

"So what? No think of that. Many people die of hunger or other things. We no think. We eat and not die."

He laughs. We say:

"We know a blind, deaf woman who lives near here with her daughter. They won't survive this winter."

"Is not my fault."

"Yes, it is your fault. Yours and your country's. You brought us the war."

"Before the war, how they do to eat, the blind woman and daughter?"

"Before the war, they lived on charity. People gave them old clothes and shoes. They brought them food. Now nobody gives anything anymore. People are all poor or are afraid of becoming so. The war has made them stingy and selfish."

The orderly shouts:

"I no care all that! Enough! Silence!"

"Yes, you don't care, and you eat our food."

"Not your food. I take that in barracks stores."

"Everything on that table comes from our country: the drinks, the canned food, the biscuits, the sugar. Our country feeds your army."

The orderly goes red in the face. He sits down on the bed and holds his head in his hands:

"You think I want war and come to your filthy country? I much better at home, quiet, make chairs and tables. Drink wine of my country, have fun with nice girls at home. Here everybody unkind, you too, little children. You say all my fault. What I can do? If I say I no go to war, no come in your country, I shot. You take all, go take all on table. Celebration finished. I sad, you too mean with me."

We say:

"We don't want to take everything, just a few cans and a little chocolate. But from time to time, at least during the winter, you could bring us some powdered milk, flour, or anything else to eat."

He says:

"Good. That I can. You come with me tomorrow to blind woman's house. But you nice with me after. Yes?"

We say:

"Yes."

The orderly laughs. His friends arrive. We leave. We hear them singing all night.

The Priest's Housekeeper

One morning, towards the end of winter, we are sitting in the kitchen with Grandmother. There is a knock on the door; a young woman comes in. She says:

"Good morning. I've come for some potatoes for . . ."

She stops speaking and looks at us:

"Why, they're adorable!"

She takes a stool and sits down:

"Come here, you."

We don't move.

"Or you."

We don't move. She laughs:

"Come on, come here. Are you afraid of me?"

We say:

"We're afraid of nobody."

We go over to her; she says:

"Heavens! How beautiful you are! But how dirty you are!"

Grandmother asks:

"What do you want?"

"Potatoes for the priest. Why are you so dirty? Don't you ever wash?"

Grandmother says angrily:

"It's none of your business. Why didn't the old woman come?"

The young woman laughs again:

"The old woman? She was younger than you. But she died yesterday. She was my aunt. I'm replacing her at the priest's house."

Grandmother says:

"She was five years older than me. She died, just like that . . . How many potatoes do you want?"

"Ten kilos, or more, if you have them. And some apples. And also . . . what else have you got? The priest is as thin as a rake, and there's nothing in his larder."

Grandmother says:

"You should have thought of that in the autumn."

"I wasn't there in the autumn. I've only been there since yesterday evening."

Grandmother says:

"I'm warning you, at this time of year, food of any sort costs plenty."

The young woman laughs again:

"Name your price. We don't have any choice. There's almost nothing left in the shops."

"Soon there'll be nothing left anywhere."

Grandmother sniggers and goes out. We are left alone with the priest's housekeeper. She asks us:

"Why don't you ever wash?"

"There's no bathroom, no soap. It isn't possible to wash."

"And your clothes! What a mess! Don't you have any other clothes!"

"We have some in the suitcases under the seat, but they're all dirty and torn. Grandmother never washes them."

"The Witch is your grandmother? Wonders never cease!"

Grandmother comes back with two sacks:

"That'll be ten silver coins or one gold coin. I don't take bills. They'll soon be worth nothing at all, they're just paper."

The housekeeper asks:

"What's in the sacks?"

Grandmother answers:

"Food. Take it or leave it."

"I'll take it. I'll bring you the money tomorrow. Can the boys help me carry the sacks?"

"They can if they want to. They don't always want to. They don't obey anybody."

The housekeeper asks us:

"You will do that for me, won't you? You'll each carry a sack, and I'll carry your suitcases."

Grandmother asks:

"What's all this about suitcases?"

"I'm going to wash their dirty clothes. I'll bring them back tomorrow with the money."

Grandmother sniggers:

"Wash their clothes? Well, if you've got nothing better to do . . ."

We go off with the housekeeper. We follow her to the priest's house. We see her two blond braids dancing over her black shawl, two long, thick braids. They reach down to her waist. Her hips dance under her red skirt. We can just see a bit of her legs between the skirt and her boots. Her stockings are black, and the one on the right has a run.

The Bath

We arrive at the priest's house with the housekeeper. She lets us in by the back door. We put the sacks down in the larder and go to the washhouse. There are lots of ropes stretched across the room to hold the washing. There are receptacles of every kind, including a zinc bathtub of odd shape, like a deep armchair.

The housekeeper opens our suitcases, puts our clothes in cold water to soak, then starts a fire to heat water in two big cauldrons. She says:

"I'll wash what you need for now right away. While you're bathing, it will dry. I'll bring you the other clothes tomorrow or the day after. They also need mending."

She pours hot water into the bathtub; she adds cold water to it:

"Well, who's first?"

We don't move. She says:

"Who's it going to be, you or you? Come on, get undressed!"

We ask:

"Are you going to stay here while we bathe?"

She laughs very loudly:

"What! Of course I'm going to stay here! I'll even rub your backs and wash your hair. You're not going to be embarrassed in front of me, are you? I'm almost old enough to be your mother."

We still don't move. So she starts to undress:

"Oh, well. Then I'll go first. You see, I'm not embarrassed to undress in front of you. You're only little boys."

She hums to herself, but her face goes red when she realizes we're staring at her. She has taut, pointed breasts like overinflated balloons. Her skin is very white, and she has a lot of blond hair everywhere. Not only between her legs and under her arms, but also on her belly and thighs. She goes on singing in the water, rubbing herself with a washcloth. When she gets out of the bath, she quickly slips into a robe. She changes the water in the tub and starts to do the washing with her back turned to us. Then we get undressed and get into the tub together. There's plenty of room for both of us.

After a while, the housekeeper hands us two large white towels:

"I hope you scrubbed yourselves well all over."

We sit down on a bench, wrapped up in our towels, waiting for our clothes to dry. The washhouse is full of steam and very warm. The housekeeper comes over with a pair of scissors:

"Now I'm going to cut your nails. And stop making a fuss; I won't eat you."

She cuts our fingernails and our toenails. She also cuts our hair. She kisses us on the face and on the neck; and she never stops talking:

"Oh! What pretty little feet, how sweet they are, all clean now! Oh! What adorable ears, what a soft, soft neck! Oh! How I'd love to have two pretty, handsome little boys like you all to myself! I'd tickle them all over, all over, all over."

She strokes and kisses our whole bodies. She tickles us with her tongue on our necks, under our arms, between our buttocks. She kneels down in front of the bench and sucks our penises, which swell and harden in her mouth.

She is now sitting between us; she presses us to her:

"If I had two beautiful little babies like you, I'd give them lovely sweet milk to drink, here, like this."

She draws our heads to her breasts, which are sticking out of her robe, and we suck the pink ends, which have become very hard. She puts her hands under her robe and rubs herself between the legs:

"What a pity you aren't older! Oh! How nice it is, how nice it is to play with you!"

She sighs, pants, then stiffens suddenly.

As we are leaving, she says to us:

"You'll come back every Saturday to bathe. You'll bring your dirty clothes with you. I want you to be always clean."

We say:

"We'll bring you wood in exchange for your work. And fish and mushrooms when there are any."

The Priest

The following Saturday, we go back to have our bath. Afterward, the housekeeper says to us:

"Come to the kitchen. I'll make some tea and we'll have some bread and butter."

We are eating the bread and butter when the priest comes into the kitchen.

We say:

"Good morning, sir."

The housekeeper says:

"Father, these are my protégés. They're the grandsons of the old woman people call the Witch."

The priest says:

"Yes, I know them. Come with me."

We follow him. We go through a room in which there is nothing but a big round table surrounded by chairs, and a crucifix on the wall. Then we go into a dark room whose walls are lined with books from floor to ceiling. Opposite the door,

a prie-dieu with a crucifix; near the window, a desk; a narrow
bed in a corner, three chairs in a row against the wall: that's
all the furniture in the room.

The priest says:

"You've changed a lot. You're clean. You look like two
angels. Sit down."

He pulls two chairs up opposite his desk; we sit down. He
sits down behind his desk. He hands us an envelope:

"Here's the money."

As we take the envelope, we say:

"Soon you'll be able to stop giving these. In the summer,
Harelip manages by herself."

The priest says:

"No. I shall go on helping these two women. I'm ashamed
that I did not do so earlier. And now, let's talk about something else, shall we?"

He looks at us; we say nothing. He says:

"I never see you in church."

"We don't go there."

"Do you pray sometimes?"

"No, we don't pray."

"Poor lost lambs. I shall pray for you. Can you read, at
least?"

"Yes, sir. We can read."

The priest hands us a book:

"Here, read this. You will find in it beautiful stories about
Jesus Christ and the lives of the saints."

"We know these stories already. We have a Bible. We have
read the Old Testament and the New."

The priest raises his dark eyebrows:

"What? You have read all of the Holy Bible?"

"Yes, sir. We even know several passages by heart."

"Which ones, for example?"

"Passages from Genesis, Exodus, Ecclesiastes, Revelation, and others."

The priest is silent for a while, then he says:

"So you know the Ten Commandments. Do you obey them?"

"No, sir, we do not obey them. Nobody obeys them. It is written, 'Thou shalt not kill,' and everybody kills."

The priest says:

"Alas . . . it's the war."

We say:

"We would like to read other books besides the Bible, but we don't have any. You have a lot of books. You could lend us some."

"These books are too difficult for you."

"Are they more difficult than the Bible?"

The priest looks at us. He asks:

"What kind of books would you like to read?"

"History books and geography books. Books that tell true things, not invented things."

The priest says:

"By next Saturday, I shall find some books that will be suitable for you. Leave me now. Go back to the kitchen and finish your tea."

The Housekeeper and the Orderly

We are picking cherries in the garden with the housekeeper. The orderly and the foreign officer arrive in the jeep. The officer walks straight past us and goes into his room. The orderly stops near us and says:

"Good morning, little friends. Good morning, pretty maiden. Cherries already ripe? I love much cherries, I love much pretty young lady."

The officer calls from the window. The orderly has to go into the house. The housekeeper says to us:

"Why didn't you tell me there were men in your house?"

"They're foreigners."

"So what? What a handsome man he is, the officer!"

We ask:

"Don't you like the orderly?"

"He's short and fat."

"But he's nice and amusing. And he speaks our language well."

She says:

"I don't care. It's the officer I like."

The officer comes and sits on the bench in front of his window. The housekeeper's basket is already full of cherries, she could go back to the priest's house, but she stays. She looks at the officer and laughs very loudly. She hangs from the branch of a tree, she swings, she jumps, she lies in the grass, and finally she throws a daisy at the officer's feet. The officer gets up and goes back to his room. Soon afterward, he comes out and goes off in his jeep.

The orderly leans out the window and shouts:

"Who come help poor man clean very dirty room?"

We say:

"We'll be glad to help you."

He says:

"Need a woman to help. Need pretty young lady."

We say to the housekeeper:

"Come on. Let's help him a bit."

All three of us go into the officer's room. The housekeeper picks up a broom and starts to sweep. The orderly sits down on the bed and says:

"I dream. A princess, I see in dream. Princess must pinch me to wake up."

The housekeeper laughs and pinches the orderly's cheek very hard.

The orderly shouts:

"I awake now. I also want pinch wicked princess."

He takes the housekeeper in his arms and pinches her bottom. The housekeeper struggles, but the orderly holds her very tight. He says to us:

"You, outside! And shut the door."

We ask the housekeeper:

"Do you want us to stay?"

She laughs:

"What for? I can take care of myself."

So we leave the room and shut the door behind us. The housekeeper comes to the window, smiles at us, draws the shutters, and closes the window. We go up to the attic and watch what is happening in the officer's room through the holes.

The orderly and the housekeeper are lying on the bed. The housekeeper is completely naked; the orderly has just his shirt and socks on. He's lying on the housekeeper, and they're both moving back and forth, right and left. The orderly grunts like Grandmother's pig, and the housekeeper screams as if in pain, but she also laughs at the same time and cries:

"Yes, yes, yes, oh, oh, oh!"

From that day on, the housekeeper comes back often and shuts herself up with the orderly. We sometimes look at them, but not always.

The orderly prefers the housekeeper to bend over or squat on all fours, and he takes her from behind.

The housekeeper prefers the orderly to lie on his back. Then she sits on the orderly's belly and moves up and down, as if she were riding a horse.

The orderly sometimes gives the housekeeper silk stockings or eau de cologne.

The Foreign Officer

We are doing our immobility exercise in the garden. It's hot. We are lying on our backs in the shade of the walnut tree. Through the leaves, we see the sky and the clouds. The leaves of the tree are motionless; the clouds also seem to be, but if we look at them for a long time, very attentively, we notice that they change shape and stretch out.

Grandmother comes out of the house. As she walks past us, she kicks sand and gravel into our faces and over our bodies. She mutters something and goes into the vineyard for her nap.

The officer is sitting, stripped to the waist, his eyes shut, on the bench in front of his room, his head leaning against the white wall, in full sunlight. Suddenly he comes toward us; he speaks to us, but we don't answer, we don't look at him. He goes back to his bench.

Later, the orderly says to us:

"The officer want you come speak to him."

We don't answer. He says again:

"You get up and come. Officer angry if you not obey."

We don't move.

The officer says something, and the orderly goes into the room. We hear him singing as he cleans up.

When the sun touches the roof of the house beside the chimney, we get up. We go over to the officer. We stop in front of him. He calls the orderly. We ask:

"What does he want?"

The officer asks some questions; the orderly translates:

"The officer ask why you not move, why not speak."

We answer:

"We were doing our immobility exercise."

The orderly translates again:

"The officer say you do many exercises. Also other kinds. He have seen you hit each other with belt."

"That was our toughening exercise."

"The officer ask why you do all that."

"To get used to pain."

"He ask you have pleasure in pain."

"No. We only want to overcome pain, heat, cold, hunger, whatever causes pain."

"The officer admiration for you. He think you extraordinary."

The officer adds a few words. The orderly says:

"Good, finished. I must go now. You too, scram, go fishing."

But the officer holds us by the arm, smiling, and makes a sign for the orderly to go. The orderly takes a few steps, then turns back:

"You leave! Quick! Go for walk in town."

The officer looks at him, and the orderly walks on to the garden gate, where he shouts to us again:

"Beat it, you two! No stay! Not understand, fools?"

He goes off. The officer smiles at us and takes us into his room. He sits down on a chair, draws us to him, picks us up, and sits us on his knees. We put our arms around his neck, we press ourselves against his hairy chest. He rocks us to and fro.

Beneath us, between the officer's legs, we feel a warm movement. We look at one another, then we look the officer in the eyes. He gently pushes us away, he ruffles our hair, he stands up. He hands us two whips and lies face down on his belly. He says only one word, which, without knowing his language, we understand.

We hit. First one, then the other.

The officer's back is scored with red lines. We hit harder and harder. The officer moans and, without changing position, pulls his trousers and shorts down to his ankles. We hit his white buttocks, his thighs, his legs, his back, his neck, his shoulders, as hard as we can, and everything gets red.

The officer's body, hair, clothes, the sheets, the rug, our hands, our arms are red. The blood even spurts into our eyes, mingles with our sweat, and we go on hitting until the man utters a final, inhuman cry and we drop, exhausted, at the foot of his bed.

The Foreign Language

The officer brings us a dictionary in which we can learn his language. We learn the words; the orderly corrects our pronunciation. A few weeks later, we speak this new language fluently. We continue to make progress. The orderly no longer has to translate. The officer is very pleased with us. He gives us a harmonica. He also gives us a key to his room so we can get in when we want to (as we were already doing with our key, but secretly). Now we no longer need to hide, and we can do whatever we like there: eat biscuits and chocolate, smoke cigarettes.

We often go into that room, because everything is clean there and it's more peaceful than the kitchen. That's where we usually do our studying.

The officer has a gramophone and records. Lying on the bed, we listen to music. Once, to please the officer, we play his country's national anthem. But he gets angry and smashes the record with his fist.

Sometimes we sleep on the bed, which is very wide. One morning, the orderly finds us there; he isn't happy:

"You very foolish! You no more do silly thing like that. What happen one time if the officer come back at night?"

"What could happen? There's enough room for him too."

The orderly says:

"You very stupid. One time you pay for stupidity. If the officer hurt you, I kill him."

"He won't hurt us. Don't worry about us."

One night, the officer comes home and finds us asleep on his bed. The light from the oil lamp wakes us. We ask:

"Do you want us to go to the kitchen?"

The officer strokes our heads and says:

"Stay there. Do stay."

He undresses and lies down between us. He puts his arms around us, he whispers in our ears:

"Sleep. I love you. Sleep in peace."

We go back to sleep. Later, near morning, we want to get up, but the officer holds us back:

"Don't move. Keep sleeping."

"We want to urinate. We have to go."

"Don't go. Do it here."

We ask:

"Where?"

He says:

"On me. Yes. Don't be afraid. Piss! On my face."

We do it, then we go out into the garden, because the bed is all wet. The sun is already rising; we start our morning chores.

The Officer's Friend

Sometimes the officer comes back with a friend, another, younger officer. They spend the evening together, and the friend stays over. We have observed them several times through the hole in the ceiling.

It's a summer's evening. The orderly is making something on the camp stove. He puts a cloth on the table, and we arrange flowers on it. The officer and his friend are sitting at the table; they are drinking. Later, they eat. The orderly eats near the door, sitting on a stool. Then they drink again. Meanwhile, we take care of the music. We change the records and wind up the gramophone.

The officer's friend says:

"These kids annoy me. Send them out."

The officer asks:

"Jealous?"

The friend answers:

"Of them? Don't be absurd! Two little savages."

"They're handsome, don't you think?"

"Perhaps. I haven't looked at them."

"Really, you haven't looked at them. Then look at them."

The friend blushes:

"What do you mean? They annoy me with their sneaky ways. As if they were listening to us, spying on us."

"But they are listening to us. They speak our language perfectly. They understand everything."

The friend goes pale and gets up:

"This is too much! I'm leaving!"

The officer says:

"Don't be a fool. Off you go, kids."

We leave the room and go up to the attic. We look and listen.

The officer's friend says:

"You made me look ridiculous in front of those stupid kids."

The officer says:

"Those are the two most intelligent children I have ever met."

The friend says:

"You're just saying that to hurt me, to make me suffer. You'll do anything to torment and humiliate me. One day I'll kill you!"

The officer throws his revolver on the table:

"If only you would! Take it. Kill me! Go on!"

The friend picks up the revolver and points it at the officer:

"I will. You'll see, I will. The next time you mention him, the other one, I'll kill you."

The officer closes his eyes, smiles:

"He was handsome . . . young . . . strong . . . graceful

. . . delicate . . . cultivated . . . tender . . . dreamy . . . brave
. . . arrogant. . . . I loved him. He died on the Eastern front.
He was nineteen. I can't live without him."

The friend throws the revolver on the table and says:

"Swine!"

The officer opens his eyes, looks at his friend:

"What lack of courage! What lack of character!"

The friend says:

"Then do it yourself if you have so much courage, and so
much grief. If you can't live without him, follow him into
death. Or do you need me to help you? I'm not crazy! Die! Die
alone!"

The officer picks up the revolver and puts it to his temple.
We come down from the attic. The orderly is sitting in front
of the open door of the room. We ask him:

"Do you think he's going to kill himself?"

The orderly laughs:

"You not fear. They always do that when drink too much.
I unload two revolvers before."

We go into the room and say to the officer:

"We'll kill you if you really want us to. Give us your
revolver."

The friend says:

"Little bastards!"

The officer smiles and says:

"Thank you. That's very kind of you, but we were only
playing. Go to bed now."

He gets up to shut the door behind us and sees the orderly:

"Are you still there?"

The orderly says:

"I haven't been given permission to go."

"Be off with you! I want to be left in peace! Understand?"
Through the door we can still hear him saying to his friend:
"What a lesson for you, you weakling!"

We also hear the noise of a fight, blows, the crash of chairs
being knocked over, a fall, shouts, panting. Then there is
silence.

Our First Show

The housekeeper often sings. Old popular songs and the latest songs about the war. We listen to these songs and practice them on our harmonica. We also ask the orderly to teach us songs of his country.

Late one evening, when Grandmother is already in bed, we go into town. Near the castle, in an old street, we stop in front of a low house. Noise, voices, and smoke are coming from the door, which opens on a staircase. We go down the stone steps and find ourselves in a cellar converted into a café. Men are standing or sitting on wooden benches and barrels, drinking wine. Most of them are old, but there are also a few young ones and three women. No one takes any notice of us.

One of us starts to play the harmonica, and the other sings a well-known song about a woman waiting for her husband, who has gone to war and will come home soon, victorious.

Gradually everybody turns toward us; the voices die down. We sing and play louder and louder, we hear our melody resound and echo from the vaulted ceiling of the cellar, as if it were someone else playing and singing.

Our song finished, we look up at the tired, hollow faces. A woman laughs and applauds. A young one-armed man says in a husky voice:

"More. Play something else!"

We change roles. The one who had the harmonica hands it to the other, and we begin a new song.

A very thin man staggers up to us and shouts in our faces:

"Silence, dogs!"

He pushes us roughly aside, one to the right, one to the left; we lose our balance; the harmonica falls. The man goes up the stairs holding on to the wall. We can still hear him shouting in the street:

"Why can't they all shut up!"

We pick the harmonica up and clean it off. Someone says:

"He's deaf."

Someone else says:

"He's not only deaf. He's completely mad."

An old man strokes our hair. Tears are flowing from his sunken, black-ringed eyes.

"What misery! What a miserable world! Poor kids! Poor world!"

A woman says:

"Deaf or mad, at least he came back. You too, you came back."

She sits on the one-armed man's lap. The man says:

"You're right, my beauty, I came back. But what am I going to work with? How am I going to hold a board I want to saw? With my empty coat sleeve?"

Another young man, sitting on a bench, laughs and says:

"I too came back. But I'm paralyzed from the waist down. The legs and all the rest. I'll never get it up again. I'd rather have gone quickly, in one fell swoop, and stayed there."

Another woman says:

"You're never satisfied. The ones I've seen dying in the hospital all say, 'Whatever state I'm in, I want to survive, go home, see my wife, my mother. I'd give anything to live a little longer.' "

A man says:

"You shut up. Women have seen nothing of the war."

The woman says:

"Seen nothing? Idiot! We have all the work and all the worry: children to feed, wounds to tend. Once the war is over, you men are all heroes. The dead: heroes. The survivors: heroes. The maimed: heroes. That's why you invented war. It's your war. You wanted it, so get on with it—heroes, my ass!"

Everybody starts talking and shouting. Near us, the old man says:

"Nobody wanted this war. Nobody, nobody."

We leave the cellar and decide to go home.

The moon lights the streets and the dusty road that leads to Grandmother's house.

We Expand Our Repertoire

We learn to juggle with fruit: apples, walnuts, apricots. First two, that's easy, then three, four, until we manage five.

We invent conjuring tricks with cards and cigarettes.

We also train ourselves in acrobatics. We can do cartwheels, somersaults, handsprings backward and forward, and we can walk on our hands with perfect ease.

We dress up in really old clothes way too big for us that we found in the attic trunk: loose-fitting, torn checked jackets and wide trousers, which we tie at the waist with string. We also found a hard, round black hat.

One of us sticks a red pepper on his nose, and the other a false mustache made out of corn silks. We get hold of some lipstick and draw our mouths out to our ears.

Dressed up as clowns, we go to the marketplace. That's where there are the most shops and the most people.

We begin our show by making a lot of noise with our harmonica and a hollow gourd made into a drum. When there are enough spectators around us, we juggle tomatoes or even eggs. The tomatoes are real tomatoes, but the eggs have been emptied and filled with fine sand. People don't know this, so they exclaim, laugh, and applaud when we pretend we've nearly dropped one.

We continue our show with conjuring tricks, and we end it with acrobatics.

While one of us keeps doing cartwheels and somersaults, the other makes the rounds of the spectators walking on his hands with the old hat between his teeth.

In the evening we do the cafés without our costumes.

We soon know all the cafés in the town, the cellars where the proprietor sells his own wine, the bars where you drink standing up, the smarter cafés frequented by well-dressed people and a few officers looking for girls to pick up.

People who drink part easily with their money. They also part easily with their confidences. We learn all kinds of secrets about all kinds of people.

Often people offer us drinks, and we are gradually getting used to alcohol. We also smoke the cigarettes people give us.

Wherever we go we are very successful. People think we have good voices; they applaud us and call us back several times.

Theater

Sometimes, if people are attentive, not too drunk and not too noisy, we put on one of our little dramas, for example, *The Story of the Poor Man and the Rich Man.*

One of us plays the poor man, the other the rich man.

The rich man is sitting at a table smoking. Enter the poor man:

"I've finished cutting up your wood, sir."

"Good. Exercise is very good for you. You look very well. Your cheeks are all red."

"My hands are frozen, sir."

"Come here! Show me! That's disgusting! Your hands are all chapped and covered with sores."

"They're chilblains, sir."

"You poor people are always getting disgusting illnesses. You're dirty, that's the trouble with you. Here, this is for your work."

He throws a pack of cigarettes to the poor man, who lights

101

one and starts to smoke it. But there's no ashtray where he's standing, near the door, and he doesn't dare approach the table. So he flicks the ash from his cigarette into the palm of his hand. The rich man, who would like the poor man to leave, pretends not to see that he needs an ashtray. But the poor man doesn't want to leave the premises so soon, because he is hungry. He says:

"It smells good in your house, sir."

"It smells of cleanliness."

"It also smells of hot soup. I haven't eaten anything all day."

"You should have. Myself, I'm dining out in a restaurant because I've given my cook the day off."

The poor man sniffs:

"It smells of good hot soup all the same."

The rich man shouts:

"It can't smell of soup here; nobody is making soup here; it must be coming from one of the neighbor's, or else you're just imagining it! You poor people think of nothing but your stomachs; that's why you never have any money; you spend all you earn on soup and sausages. You're pigs, that's what you are, and now you're dirtying my floor with your cigarette ashes! Get out of here, and don't let me see you again!"

The rich man opens the door and kicks the poor man, who sprawls on the sidewalk.

The rich man shuts the door, sits down in front of a plate of soup, and says, joining his hands:

"I give thanks to Thee, Lord Jesus, for all Thy blessings."

The Air Raids

When we arrived at Grandmother's, there were very few air raids in the Little Town. Now there are more and more of them. The sirens start to wail at all hours of the day and night, exactly as in the Big Town. People run for shelter, hide in cellars. Meanwhile, the streets are deserted. Sometimes the doors of houses and shops are left open. We take advantage of this to go in and quietly steal whatever we like.

We never hide in our cellar. Grandmother either. During the day, we keep doing whatever we're doing, and at night we go on sleeping.

Most of the time, the planes only fly over our town on their way to bomb the other side of the frontier. But sometimes a bomb falls on a house anyway. In which case we locate the spot by the direction of the smoke and go see what has been destroyed. If there's anything left to take, we take it.

We have noticed that the people in the cellar of a bombed

103

house are always dead. On the other hand, the chimney is almost always standing.

Sometimes, too, a plane goes into a dive to machine-gun people in the fields or in the street.

The orderly has taught us that we must be very careful when a plane is moving toward us, but that as soon as it is over our heads, the danger is past.

Because of the air raids, it is forbidden to light lamps at night unless the windows are completely blacked out. Grandmother thinks it is more practical not to light them at all. Patrols circulate all night to make sure the regulation is obeyed.

During a meal, we mention a plane we saw fall in flames. We also saw the pilot parachute from it.

"We don't know what happened to him, the enemy pilot."

Grandmother says:

"Enemy? They are friends, our brothers. They'll be here soon."

One day, we are out walking during an air raid. A terrified man dashes up to us:

"You shouldn't be out during air raids."

He grabs our arms and pulls us toward a door:

"Go in, get inside."

"We don't want to."

"It's a shelter. You'll be safe there."

He opens the door and pushes us in front of him. The cellar is full of people. Complete silence reigns there. The women are clutching their children to them.

Suddenly, somewhere, bombs go off. The explosions get nearer. The man who brought us to the cellar runs over to a pile of coal in one corner and tries to bury himself in it.

Several women snigger contemptuously. An elderly woman says:

"His nerves are shot. He's on leave because of it."

All of a sudden we find it difficult to breathe. We open the cellar door; a big fat woman pushes us back and shuts the door again. She shouts:

"Are you crazy? You can't go out now."

We say:

"People always die in cellars. We want to go out."

The fat woman leans against the door. She shows us her Civil Defense armband.

"I'm in charge here! You'll stay!"

We sink our teeth into her fleshy forearms; we kick her in the shins. She screams and tries to hit us. People laugh. In the end, all red with anger and shame, she says:

"Get out! Beat it! Go get yourselves killed outside! It'll be no great loss."

Outside, we can breathe. It's the first time we have been afraid.

The bombs continue to rain down.

The Human Herd

We have come to the priest's house to get our clean clothes.
We are eating bread and butter with the housekeeper in the
kitchen. We hear shouts coming from the street. We put down
our bread and butter and go out. People are standing in front
of their houses; they are looking in the direction of the station.
Excited children are running around shouting:

"They're coming! They're coming!"

At a bend in the road an army jeep full of foreign officers
appears. The jeep is moving slowly, followed by soldiers carrying their rifles on their shoulders. Behind them is a sort of
human herd. Children like us. Women like our mother. Old
men like the cobbler.

Two or three hundred of them pass by, flanked by soldiers.
A few women are carrying small children on their backs, on
their shoulders, or cradled against their breasts. One of them
falls; hands reach out to catch the child and the mother; they

must be carried, because a soldier has already pointed his rifle at them.

No one speaks, no one cries; their eyes are fixed on the ground. The only sound is the noise of the soldiers' hobnail boots.

Right in front of us, a thin arm emerges from the crowd, a dirty hand stretches out, a voice asks:

"Bread."

The housekeeper smiles and pretends to offer the rest of her bread; she holds it close to the outstretched hand, then, with a great laugh, brings the piece of bread back to her mouth, takes a bite, and says:

"I'm hungry too."

A soldier who has seen all this gives the housekeeper a slap on the behind; he pinches her cheek, and she waves to him with her handkerchief until all we can see is a cloud of dust against the setting sun.

We go back into the house. From the kitchen we can see the priest kneeling in front of the big crucifix in his room.

The housekeeper says:

"Finish your bread and butter."

We say:

"We aren't hungry anymore."

We go into the room. The priest turns around:

"Do you want to pray with me, my children?"

"We never pray, as you know very well. We want to understand."

"You cannot understand. You are too young."

"*You* are not too young. That's why we are asking you. Who are those people? Where are they being taken? Why?"

The priest gets up and comes toward us. Closing his eyes, he says:

"The Ways of the Lord are unfathomable."

He opens his eyes and places his hands on our heads:

"It is unfortunate that you were forced to witness such a spectacle. You are trembling all over."

"So are you, Father."

"Yes, I am old, I tremble."

"As for us, we're cold. We came here stripped to the waist. We're going to put on the shirts your housekeeper has washed."

We go into the kitchen. The housekeeper hands us our parcel of clean clothes. We each take a shirt. The housekeeper says:

"You're too sensitive. The best thing you can do is to forget what you've seen."

"We never forget anything."

She pushes us to the door:

"Off you go, and don't worry! None of that has anything to do with you. It'll never happen to you. Those people are only animals."

Grandmother's Apples

We run from the priest's house to the cobbler's house. His windowpanes are broken; his door is smashed in. Inside, everything has been ransacked. Filthy words are written on the walls.

An old woman is sitting on a bench in front of the house next door. We ask her:

"Has the cobbler gone away?"

"A long time ago, the poor man."

"He wasn't among those who went through town today?"

"No, the ones who went today came from somewhere else. In cattle trucks. Him, he was killed here, in his workshop, with his own tools. Don't worry. God sees everything. He will recognize His Own."

When we get home, we find Grandmother lying on her back in front of the garden gate, her legs apart, apples scattered all around her.

Grandmother doesn't move. Her forehead is bleeding.

We run to the kitchen, wet a cloth, and take the brandy down from the shelf. We put the wet cloth on Grandmother's forehead and pour brandy into her mouth. After a while she opens her eyes and says:

"More!"

We pour more brandy into her mouth.

She raises herself up on her elbows and starts shouting:

"Pick up the apples! What are you waiting for, sons of a bitch?"

We pick the apples up from the dusty road. We put them in her apron.

The cloth has fallen from Grandmother's forehead. Blood is trickling into her eyes. She wipes it away with a corner of her shawl.

We ask:

"Are you hurt, Grandmother?"

She sniggers:

"It'll take more than a blow from a rifle butt to kill me off."

"What happened, Grandmother?"

"Nothing. I was picking apples. I came to the gate to watch the procession. My apron slipped; the apples fell and rolled into the road. In the middle of the procession. That's no reason to hit someone."

"Who hit you, Grandmother?"

"Who do you think? You're not fools! They hit them too. They hit people in the crowd. But all the same there were some who were able to eat my apples!"

We help Grandmother get up. We take her into the house. She starts peeling the apples to make a compote, but she falls down, and we carry her to her bed. We take off her shoes. Her shawl slips off; a completely bald skull appears. We put her shawl back on. We stay by her bedside for a long time, holding her hands and watching her breathe.

The Policeman

We are having our breakfast with Grandmother. A man comes into the kitchen without knocking. He shows his police card.

Immediately, Grandmother starts shouting:

"I don't want the police in my house! I've done nothing!"

The policeman says:

"No, nothing, never. Just a few little poisonings here and there."

Grandmother says:

"Nothing was ever proved. You can't do anything to me."

The policeman says:

"Take it easy, Grandmother. We're not going to dig up the dead. We've got enough to do burying them."

"Then what do you want?"

The policeman looks at us and says:

"The acorn doesn't fall far from the oak."

Grandmother looks at us too:

112

"I should hope not. What have you been doing now, sons of a bitch?"

The policeman asks:

"Where were you yesterday evening?"

We answer:

"Here."

"You weren't hanging around the cafés as usual?"

"No. We stayed here because Grandmother had an accident."

Grandmother says very quickly:

"I fell going down to the cellar. The steps are all mossy, and I slipped. I banged my head. The kids brought me back up and looked after me. They stayed by my bedside all night."

The policeman says:

"You've got a bad bump there, I can see. You must be careful at your age. Very well. We're going to search the house. Come with me, all three of you. We'll start with the cellar."

Grandmother opens the cellar door, and we go down. The policeman moves everything, the sacks, the cans, the baskets, and the pile of potatoes.

Grandmother asks us in a whisper:

"What's he looking for?"

We shrug our shoulders.

After the cellar, the policeman searches the kitchen. Then Grandmother has to unlock her room. The policeman strips her bed. There is nothing in the bed or in the straw mattress, just a bit of cash under the pillow.

At the door of the officer's room, the policeman asks:

"What's in here?"

Grandmother says:

"It's a room I rent to a foreign officer. I don't have the key."

The policeman looks at the door to the attic:

"You don't have a ladder?"

Grandmother says:

"It's broken."

"How do you get up there?"

"I don't. Only the kids go up there."

The policeman says:

"Well, let's go, kids."

We climb up to the attic by the rope. The policeman opens the chest where we keep the things we need for our studies: Bible, dictionary, paper, pencils, and the Notebook in which everything is written. But the policeman hasn't come to read. He rummages through a pile of old clothes and blankets one more time, and we go down again. Back downstairs, the policeman looks around him and says:

"I obviously can't dig up the whole garden. Right. Come with me."

He takes us into the forest, to the edge of the big hole where we found the corpse. The corpse isn't there anymore. The policeman asks:

"Have you ever been here before?"

"No. Never. We would have been afraid to go so far."

"You've never seen this hole or a dead soldier?"

"No, never."

"When they found that dead soldier, his rifle, his cartridges, and his grenades were missing."

We say:

"He must have been very absentminded and careless, that soldier, to have lost all those things so indispensable to a soldier."

The policeman says:

"He didn't lose them. They were stolen from him after he died. You often come into the forest, don't you have any ideas on the matter?"

"No. No ideas at all."

"Yet someone certainly took that rifle, those cartridges, and those grenades."

We say:

"Who would dare to touch such dangerous things?"

The Interrogation

We are in the policeman's office. He is sitting at a table, we are standing in front of him. He gets paper and pencil. He is smoking. He asks us questions:

"How long have you known the priest's housekeeper?"

"Since the spring."

"Where did you meet her?"

"At Grandmother's. She came for potatoes."

"You deliver wood to the priest's house. How much are you paid for that?"

"Nothing. We take wood to the priest's house to thank the housekeeper for doing our washing."

"Is she nice to you?"

"Very nice. She makes bread and butter for us, cuts our nails and hair, and lets us have baths there."

"Like a mother, in fact. And the parish priest, is he nice to you?"

"Very nice. He lends us books and teaches us a lot of things."

"When did you last take wood to the priest's house?"

"Five days ago. On Tuesday morning."

The policeman walks up and down the room. He closes the curtains and turns on his desk lamp. He draws up two chairs and tells us to sit down. He shines the lamp in our faces:

"You're very fond of the housekeeper?"

"Yes, very."

"Do you know what's happened to her?"

"Has something happened to her?"

"Yes. Something horrible. This morning, as usual, she was lighting the fire, and the kitchen stove blew up. It hit her full in the face. She's in the hospital."

The policeman stops talking; we say nothing. He says:

"You have nothing to say?"

We say:

"If something blows up in your face, you're bound to end up in the hospital, or even in the morgue. She's lucky she isn't dead."

"She's disfigured for life!"

We are silent. The policeman too. He looks at us. We look at him. He says:

"You don't look particularly sad about it."

"We're glad she's alive. After such an accident!"

"It wasn't an accident. Someone hid an explosive in the firewood. A cartridge from an army rifle. We've found the case."

We ask:

"Why would anyone do that?"

"To kill her. Her or the priest."

We say:

"People are cruel. They like to kill. It's the war that has taught them that. And there are explosives lying around everywhere."

The policeman starts to shout:

"Stop trying to be clever! You're the ones who deliver wood to the priest's house! You're the ones who hang around all day in the forest! You're the ones who strip the corpses! You're capable of anything! You have it in your blood! Your Grandmother has a murder on her conscience too. She poisoned her husband. With her it's poison, with you it's explosives! Admit it, you little bastards! Admit it! It was you!"

We say:

"We aren't the only ones who deliver wood to the priest's house."

He says:

"That's true. There's also the old man. I've already questioned him."

We say:

"Anyone can hide a cartridge in a pile of wood."

"Yes, but not anyone can have cartridges. I'm not interested in your housekeeper! What I want to know is where the cartridges are. And the grenades? And the rifle? The old man has admitted everything. I've questioned him so well that he's admitted everything. But he couldn't show me where the cartridges, the grenades, and the rifle are. He's not the guilty one. It's you! You know where the cartridges, the grenades, and the rifle are. You know, and you're going to tell me!"

We don't respond. The policeman hits us. With both hands. Right and left. We are bleeding from the nose and mouth.

"Admit it!"

We say nothing. He goes white, he hits us over and over again. We fall off our chairs. He kicks us in the ribs, in the kidneys, in the stomach.

"Admit it! Admit it! It was you! Admit it!"

We can no longer open our eyes. We can no longer hear. Our bodies are covered with sweat, blood, urine, and excrement. We lose consciousness.

In Prison

We are lying on the hard dirt floor of a cell. Through a tiny barred window, a little light is coming in. But we don't know what time it is, or even if it is morning or afternoon.

We hurt all over. The slightest movement makes us fall back into semiconsciousness. Our vision is fuzzy, our ears are ringing, our heads are pounding. We are terribly thirsty. Our mouths are dry.

Hours go by this way. We don't speak. Later, the policeman comes in and asks us:

"Do you need anything?"

We say:

"Something to drink."

"Talk. Confess. And you'll have as much as you want to eat and drink."

We don't answer. He asks:

120

"Grandfather, do you want something to eat?"

Nobody answers. He goes out.

We realize we aren't alone in the cell. Carefully we raise our heads a little and see an old man lying huddled in a corner. Slowly we crawl over to him and touch him. He is stiff and cold. We crawl back to our place near the door.

It is already night when the policeman comes back with a flashlight. He shines it at the old man and says:

"Sleep well. Tomorrow morning you can go home."

He shines it at us too, straight in our faces, one after the other:

"Still nothing to say? It's all the same to me. I can wait. You'll either talk or die here."

Later that night the door opens again. The policeman, the orderly, and the foreign officer come in. The officer bends down and looks at us. He says to the orderly:

"Telephone the base for an ambulance!"

The orderly goes out. The officer examines the old man. He says:

"He's beaten him to death!"

He turns to the policeman:

"You'll pay dearly for this, you vermin! If you only knew how you'll pay for all this!"

The policeman asks us:

"What did he say?"

"He said that the old man is dead and that you'll pay dearly for it, you vermin!"

The officer strokes our foreheads:

"My poor little boys. How dare he hurt you, that filthy pig!"

The policeman says:

"What's he going to do to me? Tell him I've got children.
. . . I didn't know. . . . Is he your father or something?"

We say:

"He's our uncle."

"You should have told me. How could I have known?
Please forgive me. What can I do to . . ."

We say:

"Pray to God."

The orderly arrives with other soldiers. They put us on
stretchers and carry us out to the ambulance. The officer sits
beside us. The policeman, flanked by several soldiers, is taken
off in a jeep driven by the orderly.

At the army base, a doctor examines us immediately in a
big white room. He disinfects our wounds, gives us shots for
pain and tetanus. He also takes X-rays. We haven't broken
anything except a few teeth, but they're only baby teeth.

The orderly takes us back to Grandmother's. He puts us in
the officer's big bed and lies down on a blanket beside the bed.
In the morning, he goes to fetch Grandmother, who brings us
warm milk in bed.

When the orderly has left, Grandmother asks us:

"Did you confess?"

"No, Grandmother. We had nothing to confess."

"That's what I thought. And what happened to the policeman?"

"We don't know. But he certainly won't come back anymore."

Grandmother sniggers:

"Deported or shot, eh? The pig! We'll celebrate that. I'll go heat up the chicken I cooked yesterday. I haven't eaten any of it either."

At midday, we get up and go to the kitchen to eat.

During the meal, Grandmother says:

"I wonder why you wanted to kill her. You had your reasons, I suppose."

The Old Gentleman

Just after the evening meal, an old gentleman arrives with a girl who is bigger than us.

Grandmother asks him:

"What do you want?"

The old gentleman speaks a name, and Grandmother says to us:

"Go out. Go for a walk in the garden."

We go out. We circle the house and crouch down under the kitchen window. We listen. The old gentleman says:

"Have pity."

Grandmother replies:

"How can you ask me such a thing?"

The old gentleman says:

"You knew her parents. They entrusted her to me before they were deported. They gave me your address in case she was no longer safe with me."

Grandmother asks:

124

"You know what I'd be risking?"

"Yes, I know, but it's a matter of life and death."

"There's a foreign officer in the house."

"Precisely. No one will look for her here. All you'll have to say is that she's your granddaughter, the cousin of those two boys."

"Everyone knows I have no other grandchildren but those two."

"You can say she's from your son-in-law's family."

Grandmother sniggers:

"I've never even seen my son-in-law!"

After a long pause, the old gentleman goes on:

"I'm only asking you to feed the little girl for a few months. Till the end of the war."

"The war may go on for years."

"No, it won't last much longer now."

Grandmother starts to snivel:

"I'm just a poor old woman killing herself with work. How can I feed so many mouths?"

The old gentleman says:

"Here's all the money her parents had. And the family jewels. It's all yours if you'll save her."

A little later, Grandmother calls us in:

"This is your cousin."

We say:

"Yes, Grandmother."

The old gentleman says:

"You'll play together, the three of you, won't you?"

We say:

"We never play."

He asks:

"What do you do, then?"

"We work, we study, we do exercises."

He says:

"I understand. You're serious men. You don't have time to play. You'll look after your cousin, won't you?"

"Yes, sir. We'll look after her."

"Thank you."

Our cousin says:

"I'm bigger than you."

We answer:

"But there are two of us."

The old gentleman says:

"You're right. Two are much stronger than one. And you won't forget to call her 'cousin,' will you?"

"No, sir. We never forget anything."

"I'm depending on you."

Our Cousin

Our cousin is five years older than us. Her eyes are black. Her hair is reddish because of something called henna.

Grandmother tells us that our cousin is the daughter of Father's sister. We say the same thing to those who ask questions about our cousin.

We know that Father has no sister. But we also know that without this lie, our cousin's life would be in danger. And we've promised the old gentleman to look after her.

When the old gentleman has gone, Grandmother says:

"Your cousin will sleep with you in the kitchen."

We say:

"There's no more room in the kitchen."

Grandmother says:

"Straighten it out yourselves."

Our cousin says:

"I'm quite willing to sleep on the floor under the table if you give me a blanket."

We say:

"You can sleep on the seat and keep the blankets. We'll sleep in the attic. It's not very cold now."

She says:

"I'll come sleep in the attic with you."

"We don't want you. You must never set foot in the attic."

"Why?"

We say:

"You have a secret. We have one too. If you don't respect our secret, we won't respect yours."

She asks:

"Would you be capable of denouncing me?"

"If you go up to the attic, you die. Is that clear?"

She looks at us for a moment in silence, then she says:

"I see. You two little bastards are completely crazy. I'll never go up to your filthy attic, I promise."

She keeps her promise and never goes up to the attic. But everywhere else, she bothers us all the time.

She says:

"Bring me some raspberries."

We say:

"Go in the garden and get some yourself."

She says:

"Stop reading out loud. You're splitting my ears."

We go on reading.

She asks:

"What are you doing there, lying on the floor for hours without moving?"

We continue our immobility exercise even when she throws rotten fruit at us.

She says:

"Stop being so quiet, you're getting on my nerves!"

We continue our silence exercise without answering.

She asks:

"Why aren't you eating anything today?"

"It's our fasting day."

Our cousin doesn't work, doesn't study, doesn't do exercises. Often she stares at the sky, sometimes she cries.

Grandmother never hits our cousin. She never swears at her either. She doesn't ask her to work. She doesn't ask her to do anything. She never speaks to her.

The Jewels

The same evening our cousin arrives, we go and sleep in the attic. We take two blankets from the officer's room and lay hay on the floor. Before going to bed, we look through the holes. In the officer's room there is nobody. In Grandmother's room there is a light on, which doesn't happen very often.

Grandmother has taken the oil lamp from the kitchen and hung it over her dressing table. It's an old piece of furniture with three mirrors. The one in the middle is stationary, the other two move. You can adjust them to see yourself in profile.

Grandmother is sitting in front of the dressing table, looking at herself in the mirror. On her head, over her black shawl, she has placed something shiny. Around her neck hang several necklaces, her arms are covered with bracelets, her fingers with rings. She is talking to herself as she contemplates her reflection:

"Rich, rich. It's easy to be beautiful with all this. Easy. The

130

wheel turns. They're mine now, the jewels. Mine. It's only fair. How they shine, how they shine!"

Later, she says:

"And what if they return? What if they want them back? Once the danger is over, they forget. They don't know what gratitude is. They promise the moon and the stars, and then . . . No, no, they're already dead. The old gentleman will die too. He said I could keep everything. . . . But the girl . . . She saw everything, heard everything. She'll want them back, that's for sure. After the war, she'll claim them. But I don't want to give them back, I can't. They're mine. Forever.

"She'll have to die too. Then there'll be no proof. No one'll be any the wiser. Yes, the girl will die. She'll have an accident. Just before the end of the war. Yes, it will have to be an accident. Not poison. Not this time. An accident. A drowning in the stream. Hold her head under the water. Difficult. Push her down the cellar steps. Not high enough. Poison. There's only poison. Something slow. Small doses. An illness that eats away at her slowly, for months. There's no doctor. A lot of people die like that in wartime for lack of care."

Grandmother raises her fist and threatens her image in the mirror:

"You won't be able to do a thing to me! Not a thing!"

She sniggers. She takes off the jewelry, puts it in a canvas bag, and stuffs the bag in her straw mattress. She goes to bed, we do too.

Next morning, when our cousin has left the kitchen, we say to Grandmother:

"Grandmother, we have something to tell you."

"What now?"

"Pay close attention, Grandmother. We promised the old gentleman to look after our cousin. So nothing will happen to her. No accidents, no illnesses. Nothing. Or to us either."

We show her a sealed envelope:

"Everything is written here. We are going to give this letter to the priest. If anything happens to any of the three of us, the priest will open the letter. Do you understand, Grandmother?"

Grandmother looks at us, her eyes almost shut. She is breathing very heavily. She says very quietly:

"Sons of a bitch, a whore, and the devil! Cursed be the day you were born."

In the afternoon, when Grandmother goes off to work in her vineyard, we search her mattress. There is nothing in it.

Our Cousin and Her Lover

Our cousin is becoming serious. She doesn't bother us anymore. Every day she washes in the big tub we bought with the money we earned in the cafés. She washes her dress a lot, and her underpants too. While her clothes are drying, she wraps herself in a towel or lies in the sun with her underpants drying on top of her. She is very brown. Her hair covers her to her buttocks. Sometimes she turns over on her back and hides her breasts with her hair.

Toward evening, she goes off to town. She stays longer and longer in town. One evening, we follow her without her knowing.

Near the cemetery, she joins a group of boys and girls, all much older than us. They are sitting under the trees smoking. They've also got bottles of wine. They drink straight from the bottle. One of them keeps watch by the side of the path. If someone comes, the lookout sits quietly and whistles a well-known tune. The group disperses and hides in the bushes or behind the tombstones. When the danger is over, the lookout whistles a different tune.

The group talks in whispers about the war, and about desertions, deportations, resistance, and liberation.

According to them, the foreign soldiers who are in our country and who claim to be our allies are in fact our enemies, and those who will be here soon and win the war are not enemies but on the contrary our liberators.

They say:

"My father has gone over to the other side. He'll come back with them."

"*My* father deserted when war was declared."

"My parents joined the partisans. I was too young to go with them."

"Mine were taken away by those bastards. Deported."

"You'll never see them again, you know. Me either. They're all dead now."

"You can't be sure. There'll be survivors."

"And we'll avenge the dead."

"We were too young. Too bad. We couldn't do anything."

"It'll be over soon. *They* will be here any day now."

"We'll be waiting for them in the Town Square with flowers."

Late at night, the group breaks up. Everybody goes home.

Our cousin leaves with a boy. We follow her. They go into the little lanes around the castle and disappear behind a ruined wall. We can't see them, but we can hear them.

Our cousin says:

"Lie down on me. Yes, like that. Kiss me. Kiss me."

The boy says:

"You're really beautiful! I want you."

"Me too. But I'm afraid. What if I get pregnant?"

"I'll marry you. I love you. We'll get married after the Liberation."

"We're too young. We must wait."

"I can't wait."

"Stop! You're hurting me. You mustn't, darling, you mustn't."

The boy says:

"Yes, you're right. But touch me. Give me your hand. Touch me there, like that. Turn around. I want to kiss you there, there, while you touch me."

Our cousin says:

"No, don't do that. I'm ashamed. Oh! Go on, go on! I love you, I love you so much."

We go home.

The Blessing

We have to go back to the priest's house to return the books we've borrowed.

The door is opened by an old woman again. She lets us in and says:

"Father is expecting you."

The priest says:

"Sit down."

We put the books on his desk. We sit down.

The priest looks at us for a moment, then says:

"I've been waiting for you. You haven't come for a long time."

We say:

"We wanted to finish the books. And we've been very busy."

"And what about your bath?"

"We have all we need to wash ourselves now. We bought a tub, soap, scissors, and toothbrushes."

"With what? Where did you get the money?"

"With the money we earn playing music in the cafés."

"The cafés are places of perdition. Especially at your age."

We don't answer. He says:

"You haven't been for the blind woman's money either. It amounts to a considerable sum now. Take it."

He hands us the money. We say:

"Keep it. You have given enough. We took your money when it was absolutely necessary. Now we earn enough money to give some to Harelip. We have also taught her to work. We have helped her dig her garden and plant potatoes, beans, squash, and tomatoes. We have given her chicks and rabbits to raise. She looks after her garden and her animals. She doesn't beg anymore. She doesn't need your money anymore."

The priest says:

"Then take this money for yourselves. That way you will not have to work in the cafés."

"We like working in the cafés."

He says:

"I heard you were beaten and tortured."

We ask:

"What happened to your housekeeper?"

"She went to the front to care for the wounded. She died."

We say nothing. He asks:

"Would you like to confide in me? I am sworn to keep the secrets of the confessional. You have nothing to fear. You can confess."

We say:

"We have nothing to confess."

"You are wrong. Such a crime is very hard to bear. Confession will relieve you. God forgives all those who are sincerely sorry for their sins."

We say:

"We are sorry for nothing. We have nothing to be sorry for."

After a long silence, he says:

"I saw it all through the window. The piece of bread . . . But vengeance belongs to God. You have no right to do His work for Him."

We say nothing. He asks:

"Can I bless you?"

"If you want to."

He places his hands on our heads:

"Almighty God, bless these Thy children. Whatever their crime, forgive them. Poor lambs who have lost their way in an abominable world, themselves victims of our perverted times, they know not what they do. I beg Thee to save their child's souls, to purify them in Thy infinite goodness and mercy. Amen."

Then he says to us again:

"Come back and see me from time to time, even if you don't need anything."

Flight

From one day to the next, posters appear on the walls of the town. One poster shows an old man lying on the ground, his body pierced by the bayonet of an enemy soldier. A second shows an enemy soldier striking a child with another child, whom he is holding by the feet. Yet another shows an enemy soldier pulling at a woman's arm and tearing her blouse off with his other hand. The woman's mouth is open, and tears are streaming from her eyes.

The people who look at the posters are terrified.

Grandmother laughs and says:

"It's all lies. You mustn't be afraid."

People are saying that the Big Town has fallen.

Grandmother says:

"If they've crossed the Big River, nothing will stop them. They'll be here soon."

Our cousin says:

"Then I'll be able to go home."

One day, people say that the army has surrendered, that there is an armistice and the war is over. Next day, people say that there is a new government and the war is going on.

A lot of foreign soldiers arrive by train or truck. Soldiers from our country too. There are many wounded. When people ask the soldiers from our country questions, they reply that they don't know anything. They pass through town. They are going to the other country along the road that runs by the camp.

People say:

"They're running away. The country has collapsed."

Others say:

"They're withdrawing and regrouping behind the frontier. They'll stop them here. They'll never let the enemy cross the frontier."

Grandmother says:

"We'll see."

Many people pass by Grandmother's house. They too are going to the other country. They say they are leaving our country forever, because the enemy army is coming and will take its revenge. It will reduce our people to slavery.

There are people fleeing on foot with sacks on their backs, others pushing bicycles laden with various objects: a down quilt, a violin, a piglet in a cage, saucepans. Others are perched on horse-drawn carts: they are taking all their furniture with them.

Most of them are from our town, but some have come from further away.

One morning, the orderly and the foreign officer come to say goodbye.

The orderly says:

"It's all over. But it's better to be beaten than dead."

He laughs. The officer puts a record on the gramophone. We listen to it in silence, sitting on the big bed. The officer holds us tightly in his arms and cries.

"I'll never see you again."

We say:

"You'll have children of your own."

"I don't want any."

Then he says, pointing to the records and the gramophone:

"Keep these to remember me by. But not the dictionary. You'll have to learn another language."

The Charnel House

One night, we hear explosions, rifle volleys, and machine-gun fire. We go outside to see what is happening. A big fire is raging on the site of the camp. We think the enemy has arrived, but next day the town is silent; all we can hear is the distant rumble of cannons.

At the end of the road leading to the base, there is no sentry anymore. A thick cloud of smoke with a sickening smell rises up into the sky. We decide to go see.

We enter the camp. It is empty. There isn't a soul in sight. Some of the buildings are still burning. The stench is unbearable, but we hold our noses and keep going. A barbed-wire fence stops us. We climb a watchtower. We see four tall black pyres rising on a big square. We spot an opening, a gap in the fence. We come down from the watchtower and find the entry. It's a big iron gate, left open. Above it is written in the foreign language: "Transit Camp." We go in.

The black pyres we saw from above are burned bodies.

Some of them are thoroughly burned, only the bones remain. Others are barely blackened. There are many of these. Big and small. Adults and children. We think that they killed them first, then piled them up, poured gasoline over them, and set them on fire.

We vomit. We run out of the camp. We go home. Grandmother calls us in to eat, but we vomit again.

Grandmother says:

"You've been eating junk again."

We say:

"Yes, green apples."

Our cousin says:

"The camp has burned down. We ought to go see it. There can't be anybody left there."

"We've already been. There's nothing of interest."

Grandmother sniggers:

"The heroes didn't forget something? They took everything with them? They didn't leave anything useful at all? Did you take a good look?"

"Yes, Grandmother. We took a good look. There's nothing there."

Our cousin leaves the kitchen. We follow her. We ask her:

"Where are you going?"

"To town."

"Already? You usually don't go till evening."

She smiles:

"Yes, but I'm expecting someone. If you don't mind!"

Our cousin smiles at us again, then runs off toward town.

Our Mother

We are in the garden. An army jeep stops in front of the house. Our Mother gets out, followed by a foreign officer. They rush across the garden. Mother is holding a baby in her arms. She sees us and calls:

"Come along! Get into the jeep quickly. We're going. Hurry up. Leave everything and come!"

We ask:

"Whose baby is that?"

She says:

"It's your little sister. Come on! There's no time to waste."

We ask:

"Where are we going?"

"To the other country. Stop asking questions and come along."

We say:

"We don't want to go there. We want to stay here."

Mother says:

"I have to go there. And you're coming with me."

"No. We're staying here."

Grandmother comes out of the house. She says to Mother:

"What are you doing? What have you got there in your arms?"

Mother says:

"I've come for my sons. I'll send you money, Mother."

Grandmother says:

"I don't want your money. And I won't give the boys back."

Mother asks the officer to take us by force. We quickly climb up to the attic by the rope. The officer tries to catch us, but we kick him in the face. The officer swears. We pull the rope up.

Grandmother sniggers:

"You see, they don't want to go with you."

Mother shouts at us:

"I order you to come down immediately!"

Grandmother says:

"They never obey orders."

Mother starts to cry:

"Come, my darlings. I can't leave without you."

Grandmother says:

"Your foreign bastard isn't enough?"

We say:

"We're fine here, Mother. Go, and don't worry. We're really fine at Grandmother's."

We hear cannons and machine-gun fire. The officer takes Mother by the shoulders and leads her toward the car. But Mother pulls free:

"They're my sons, I want them! I love them!"

Grandmother says:

"I need them. I'm old. You can still have others—as we can see!"

Mother says:

"I beg you, don't keep them."

Grandmother says:

"I'm not keeping them. Hey, you boys, come down at once and go with your mother."

We say:

"We don't want to go. We want to stay with you, Grandmother."

The officer takes Mother in his arms, but she pushes him away. The officer goes and sits in the jeep and starts the engine. At precisely that moment, there is an explosion in the garden. Immediately afterward, we see Mother on the ground. The officer runs toward her. Grandmother tries to hold us back. She says:

"Don't look! Go back in the house!"

The officer swears, runs to his jeep, and drives off at top speed.

We look at Mother. Her guts are coming out of her belly. She is red all over. So is the baby. Mother's head is hanging in the hole made by the shell. Her eyes are open and still wet with tears.

Grandmother says:

"Go get the spade!"

We put a blanket at the bottom of the hole, we lay Mother on it. The baby is still pressed to her breast. We cover them with another blanket, then fill in the hole.

When our cousin comes back from town, she asks:
"Did something happen?"
We say:
"Yes, a shell made a hole in the garden."

The Departure of Our Cousin

All night we hear gunfire and explosions. At dawn, every-thing is suddenly quiet. We are sleeping in the officer's big bed. His bed has become our bed, and his room our room.

In the morning we go to the kitchen for breakfast. Grand-mother is standing in front of the stove. Our cousin is folding her blankets.

She says:

"I really slept badly."

We say:

"You'll sleep in the garden. There's no more noise, and it's warm."

She asks:

"Weren't you afraid last night?"

We shrug our shoulders and say nothing.

There's a knock at the door. A man in civilian clothes enters, followed by two soldiers. The soldiers have machine guns and are wearing a uniform we have never seen before.

Grandmother says something in the language she speaks when she's drinking her brandy. The soldiers answer. Grandmother flings her arms around their necks and kisses them one after the other as she goes on talking to them.

The civilian says:

"You speak their language, madam?"

Grandmother replies:

"It's my mother tongue, sir."

Our cousin asks:

"Are they here? When did they arrive? We wanted to welcome them in the Town Square with bouquets of flowers."

The civilian asks:

"Who's 'we'?"

"My friends and I."

The civilian smiles:

"Well, it's too late. They arrived last night. And I came just after them. I'm looking for a girl."

He speaks a name; our cousin says:

"Yes, that's me. Where are my parents?"

The civilian says:

"I don't know. My job is just to find the children on my list. First we'll go to a reception center in the Big Town. Then we'll try to find your parents."

Our cousin says:

"I have a friend here. Is he on your list too?"

She says the name of her lover. The civilian consults his list:

"Yes. He's already at army headquarters. You'll travel together. Get your things ready."

Our cousin joyfully packs her dresses and gathers all her toiletries together in her bath towel.

The civilian turns to us:

"And what about you? What are your names?"

Grandmother says:

"They're my grandsons. They'll stay with me."

We say:

"Yes, we'll stay with Grandmother."

The civilian says:

"I'd like to have your names all the same."

We tell him. He looks at his papers.

"You're not on my list. You can keep them, madam."

Grandmother says:

"What do you mean I can keep them? Of course I can keep them!"

Our cousin says:

"I'm ready. Let's go."

The civilian says:

"You're certainly in a hurry. You might at least thank this lady and say goodbye to these little boys."

Our cousin says:

"Little boys? Little bastards, you mean."

She gives us a big hug.

"I won't kiss you, I know you don't like that. Don't screw around too much. Take care."

She gives us an even bigger hug and starts crying. The civilian takes her by the arm and says to Grandmother:

"I thank you, madam, for everything you have done for this child."

We all go out together. In front of the garden gate is a jeep. The two soldiers sit in front, the civilian and our cousin in back. Grandmother shouts something. The soldiers laugh. The jeep moves off. Our cousin doesn't look back.

The Arrival of the New Foreigners

After our cousin has left, we go into town to see what's happening.

There is a tank at every street corner. On the Town Square, there are trucks, jeeps, motorcycles, sidecars, and everywhere lots of soldiers. In the Market Square, which is not paved, they are pitching tents and setting up open-air kitchens.

When we go by, they smile at us, they talk to us, but we can't understand what they're saying.

Apart from the soldiers, there is nobody in the streets. The doors of the houses are closed, the shutters drawn, the shop blinds lowered.

We go home and say to Grandmother:

"Everything is quiet in town."

She sniggers:

"They're resting for the moment, but this afternoon, you'll see!"

"What's going to happen, Grandmother?"

"They'll carry out searches. They'll go into everybody's house and ransack it. And they'll take whatever they like. I've lived through one war already, I know what happens. But we don't have anything to be afraid of: there's nothing to take here, and I know how to talk to them."

"But what are they looking for, Grandmother?"

"Spies, weapons, ammunition, watches, gold, women."

Sure enough, in the afternoon, the soldiers begin systematically searching the houses. If there is no answer, they fire a shot in the air, then batter down the door.

A lot of houses are empty. The residents have left for good or are hiding in the forest. These uninhabited houses are searched just like the others, along with all the stores and shops.

After the soldiers have gone, thieves invade the abandoned shops and houses. The thieves are mainly children and old men, and a few women too, those who are fearless or those who are poor.

We meet Harelip. Her arms are full of clothes and shoes. She says to us:

"Hurry up while there's still something left. This is the third time I've done my shopping."

We go into the Booksellers and Stationers, whose door is smashed in. There are only a few children inside, younger than us. They are taking pencils and colored chalk, erasers, pencil sharpeners, and schoolbags.

We take our time choosing what we need: a complete encyclopedia in several volumes, pencils, and paper.

In the street, an old man and an old woman are fighting over a smoked ham. They are surrounded by people laughing and urging them on. The woman scratches the old man's face, and in the end she goes off with the ham.

The thieves are guzzling stolen alcohol, picking fights with each another, smashing the windows of the houses and shops they've looted, breaking crockery, flinging to the floor whatever they don't need or can't carry off with them.

The soldiers are also drinking and returning to the houses, but this time to find women.

Everywhere we hear gunshots and the cries of women being raped.

On the Town Square, a soldier plays the accordion. Other soldiers dance and sing.

The Fire

For several days now, we haven't seen our neighbor in her garden. Nor have we met Harelip. We go and investigate.

The door of the shack is open. We enter. The windows are small. It is dark in the room, even though the sun is shining outside.

When our eyes get used to the darkness, we can make out our neighbor lying on the kitchen table. Her legs are dangling, her arms are covering her face. She doesn't move.

Harelip is lying on the bed. She is naked. Between her spread legs there is a dried pool of blood and sperm. Her eyelashes are stuck together forever, her lips are curled up over her black teeth in an eternal smile; Harelip is dead.

Our neighbor says:

"Go away."

We approach her and ask:

"You aren't deaf?"

"No. And I'm not blind either. Go away."

We say:

"We want to help you."

She says:

"I don't need help. I don't need anything. Go away."

We ask:

"What happened here?"

"You can see for yourself. She's dead, isn't she?"

"Yes. It was the new foreigners?"

"Yes. *She* called *them*. She went out on the road and waved at them to come in. There were twelve or fifteen of them. And as they took her, she kept shouting: 'Oh, I'm so happy, I'm so happy! Come, all of you, come on, another one, again, another one!' She died happy, fucked to death. But *I'm* not dead! I've been lying here without eating or drinking for I don't know how long. And death hasn't come. It never does come when you call it. It enjoys torturing us. I've been calling it for years and it pays no attention."

We ask:

"Do you really want to die?"

"What else could I want? If you'd like to do something for me, set fire to the house. I don't want anyone to find us like this."

We say:

"But you'll suffer terribly."

"Don't worry about that. Just set the fire, if you're capable of it."

"Yes, madam, we are capable of it. You can depend on us."

We slit her throat with a stroke of the razor, then we go and siphon some gasoline from an army vehicle. We pour the gasoline over both bodies and on the walls of the shack. We set fire to it and go home.

In the morning, Grandmother says:

"The neighbor's house burned down. They were both inside, her daughter and her. The girl must have left something on the fire, ninny that she is."

We go back to get the hens and the rabbits, but other neighbors have already taken them during the night.

The End of the War

For weeks now, we have seen them marching past Grandmother's house, the victorious army of the new foreigners, which we now call the army of the Liberators.

Tanks, cannons, armored cars, and trucks cross the frontier day and night. The front is moving further and further into the neighboring country.

In the opposite direction comes another procession: the prisoners of war, the conquered. Among them are many men from our own country. They are still wearing their uniforms, but they have been stripped of weapons and rank. They march, heads down, to the station, where they are sent off in trains. Where and for how long, nobody knows.

Grandmother says they are being taken very far away, to a cold, uninhabited country where they will be forced to work so hard that none of them will come back. They will all die of cold, exhaustion, hunger, and all kinds of diseases.

A month after our country has been liberated, the war is

over everywhere, and the Liberators move into our country, for good, people say. So we ask Grandmother to teach us their language. She says:

"How can I teach it to you? I'm not a teacher."

We say:

"It's simple, Grandmother. All you have to do is talk to us in that language all day, and in the end we'll understand."

Soon we know enough to act as interpreters between the local inhabitants and the Liberators. We take advantage of the fact to trade in articles that the army has plenty of, like cigarettes, tobacco, and chocolate, which we exchange for what the civilians have: wine, brandy, and fruit.

Money has no value anymore; everyone barters.

Girls sleep with soldiers in exchange for silk stockings, jewelry, perfume, watches, and other articles that the soldiers have stolen in the towns along their way.

Grandmother doesn't go to market with her wheelbarrow anymore. Instead well-dressed ladies come to Grandmother's and beg her to trade a chicken or a sausage for a ring or a pair of earrings.

Ration coupons are distributed. People start lining up in front of the butcher's and baker's as early as four in the morning. The other shops stay closed because they have nothing to sell.

Everybody is short of everything.

As for Grandmother and us, we have everything we need.

Later, we have our own army and government again, but our army and our government are controlled by our Liberators. Their flag flies over all the public buildings. Their leader's picture is displayed everywhere. They teach us their songs and their dances, they show us their films in our cinemas. In the schools, the language of our Liberators is compulsory, other foreign languages are forbidden.

It is strictly forbidden to criticize or make jokes about our Liberators or our new government. On the strength of a mere denunciation, anyone at all can be thrown into prison without trial, without sentence. Men and women disappear without anyone knowing why, and their families will never hear from them again.

The frontier has been rebuilt. It is now impassable.

Our country is surrounded by barbed wire; we are completely cut off from the rest of the world.

School Reopens

In the autumn, all the children go back to school, except us.

We say to Grandmother:

"Grandmother, we never want to go to school again."

She says:

"I should hope not. I need you here. And what more could you learn at school anyway?"

"Nothing, Grandmother, absolutely nothing."

Soon we receive a letter. Grandmother asks:

"What does it say?"

"It says that you are responsible for us and that we must report to the school."

Grandmother says:

"Burn the letter. I can't read, and you can't either. No one ever read that letter."

We burn the letter. Soon we get a second. It says that if we don't go to school, Grandmother will be punished by law. We burn that letter too. We say to Grandmother:

"Grandmother, don't forget that one of us is blind and the other deaf."

A few days later, a man turns up at our house. He says:

"I am the inspector of primary schools. You have in your house two children of compulsory school age. You have already received two warnings about this matter."

Grandmother says:

"You mean letters? I can't read. The children can't either."

One of us asks:

"Who is it? What's he saying?"

"He's asking if we can read. What's he like?"

"He's tall and looks mean."

We both shout:

"Go away! Don't hurt us! Don't kill us! Help!"

We hide under the table. The inspector asks Grandmother:

"What's the matter with them? What are they doing?"

Grandmother says:

"Oh! The poor things are afraid of everybody! They've lived through such terrible things in the Big Town. What's more, one of them is deaf and the other blind. The deaf one has to explain to the blind one what he sees, and the blind one has to explain to the deaf one what he hears. Otherwise, they don't understand anything."

Under the table, we yell:

"Help, help! It's blowing up! It's making too much noise! It's blinding my eyes!"

Grandmother explains:

"When someone frightens them, they hear things and see things that aren't there."

The inspector says:

"They have hallucinations. They should be treated in a hospital."

We yell even louder.

Grandmother says:

"Nothing could be worse! It was in a hospital that the misfortune happened. They were visiting their mother, who worked there. When the bombs fell on the hospital, they were there, they saw the wounded and the dead; they themselves were in a coma for several days."

The inspector says:

"Poor kids. Where are their parents?"

"Dead or missing. Who knows?"

"They must be a very heavy burden for you."

"What can you do? I'm all they have in the world."

Before leaving, the inspector shakes Grandmother's hand:

"You're a very brave woman."

We receive a third letter that says we are exempted from attending school because of our infirmity and our psychic trauma.

Grandmother Sells Her Vineyard

An officer comes to Grandmother's to ask her to sell her vineyard. The army wants to put up a building on her land for the frontier guards.

Grandmother asks:

"And what will you pay me with? Money is worth nothing."

The officer says:

"In exchange for your land, we'll install running water and electricity in your house."

Grandmother says:

"I don't need your electricity or your running water. I've always lived without."

The officer says:

"We could also take your vineyard without giving you anything in exchange. And that's what we're going to do if you don't accept our offer. The army needs your land. It is your patriotic duty to give it to us."

Grandmother opens her mouth to speak, but we intervene:

"Grandmother, you are old and tired. The vineyard gives you a lot of work and hardly brings anything in. On the other hand, the value of your house will increase a great deal with water and electricity."

The officer says:

"Your grandsons are more intelligent than you, Grandmother."

Grandmother says:

"You can say that again! So talk it over with them. Let them decide."

The officer says:

"But I need your signature."

"I'll sign whatever you like. Anyway, I can't write."

Grandmother starts to cry, gets up, and says to us:

"I'll leave it to you."

She goes off to her vineyard.

The officer says:

"Ah, she's very fond of her vineyard, the poor old woman. Well, is it a deal?"

We say:

"As you yourself have observed, that land has great sentimental value to her, and the army would certainly not want to usurp the hard-earned property of a poor old woman who, moreover, is a native of the country of our heroic Liberators."

The officer says:

"Ah, yes? She's a native . . ."

"Yes. She speaks their language perfectly. And we do too. And if you have any intention of committing an abuse . . ."

The officer says very quickly:

"No, no! What do you want?"

"In addition to the water and electricity, we want a bath-room."

"You don't say! And just where do you want this bath-room?"

We take him into our room and show him where we want our bathroom.

"Here, giving onto our room. Seven to eight square meters. Built-in bathtub, washbasin, shower, water heater, toilet."

He looks at us for a long time, then says:

"It can be done."

We say:

"We would also like a wireless set. We don't have one, and it's impossible to buy one."

He asks:

"And is that all?"

"Yes, that is all."

He bursts out laughing:

"You'll have your bathroom and your wireless. But I'd have been better off talking to your grandmother."

Grandmother's Illness

One morning, Grandmother doesn't come out of her room. We knock on her door, we call her, but she doesn't answer.

We go to the back of the house and break a pane of glass in her window so we can get into her room.

Grandmother is lying on her bed. She isn't moving. But she is breathing, and her heart is beating. One of us stays with her, the other fetches a doctor.

The doctor examines Grandmother. He says:

"Your Grandmother has had an attack of apoplexy, a cerebral hemorrhage."

"Is she going to die?"

"You can't tell. She's old, but her heart is sound. Give her these medicines three times a day. And she'll need someone to look after her."

We say:

"We'll look after her. What has to be done?"

"Feed her, wash her. She'll probably be permanently paralyzed."

The doctor leaves. We make a purée of vegetables and feed Grandmother with a small spoon. By evening, it smells very bad in her room. We lift her blankets: her straw mattress is full of excrement.

We get some straw from a peasant and buy babies' rubber pants and diapers.

We undress Grandmother, wash her in our bathtub, and make her a clean bed. She is so thin that the babies' pants fit her very well. We change her diapers several times a day.

A week later, Grandmother begins to move her hands. One morning, she greets us with a volley of insults:

"Sons of a bitch! Go roast a chicken! How do you expect me to get my strength back with your plant life and your purées? I want some goat's milk too! I hope you haven't neglected anything while I've been ill!"

"No, Grandmother, we haven't neglected anything."

"Help me get up, you good-for-nothings!"

"Grandmother, you must stay in bed, the doctor said so."

"The doctor, the doctor! That imbecile! Permanently paralyzed, indeed! I'll show him how paralyzed I am!"

We help her get up, accompany her to the kitchen, and sit her down on the seat. When the chicken is cooked, she eats it all herself. After the meal, she says:

"What are you waiting for? Make me a good stout stick, hurry up, you lazybones, I want to go see if everything is in order."

We run off to the forest, we find a suitable branch, and while she watches, we cut the stick to Grandmother's size. She promptly grabs it and threatens us:

"You'll be sorry if everything isn't in order!"

She goes out into the garden. We follow her at a distance. She goes into the privy, and we hear her muttering:

"Diapers! What an idea! They're completely mad!"

When she goes back to the house, we take a look in the privy. She has thrown the rubber pants and diapers down the hole.

Grandmother's Treasure

One evening, Grandmother says:

"Shut all the doors and windows tight. I want to talk to you, and I don't want anyone to hear us."

"Nobody ever comes this way, Grandmother."

"You know the frontier guards are always prowling around. And they're quite capable of listening at people's doors. And bring me a sheet of paper and a pencil."

We ask:

"You want to write something, Grandmother?"

She shouts:

"Do as you're told! Don't ask questions!"

We shut the windows and doors, we bring the paper and pencil. Sitting at the other end of the table, Grandmother draws something on the sheet of paper. She says in a whisper:

"This is where my treasure is hidden."

She hands us the sheet of paper. On it she has drawn a

169

rectangle, a cross, and under the cross, a circle. Grandmother asks:

"Do you understand?"

"Yes, Grandmother, we understand. But we knew already."

"What! What did you know already?"

We reply in a whisper:

"That your treasure is hidden under the cross on Grandfather's grave."

Grandmother is silent for a moment, then she says:

"I might have suspected as much. Have you known for a long time?"

"For a very long time, Grandmother. Ever since we saw you tending Grandfather's grave."

Grandmother breathes very heavily:

"There's no point in getting excited. Anyway, it's all yours. You're clever enough now to know what to do with it."

We say:

"For the moment, there's not much we can do with it."

Grandmother says:

"No. You're right. You must wait. Will you be able to wait?"

"Yes, Grandmother."

All three of us are silent for a moment, then Grandmother says:

"That isn't all. The next time I have an attack, I don't want any part of your bath, your rubber pants, or your diapers."

She gets up and rummages around on the shelf among her bottles. She comes back with a small blue flask:

"Instead of all your filthy medicines, you'll pour the contents of this flask into my first cup of milk."

We say nothing. She shouts:

"Do you understand, sons of a bitch?"

We say nothing. She says:

"Maybe you're afraid of the autopsy, you little brats? There won't be any autopsy. Nobody's going to make a fuss when an old woman dies after a second attack."

We say:

"We aren't afraid of the autopsy, Grandmother. We just think that you may recover a second time."

"No. I won't recover. I know it. So we must put an end to it as soon as possible."

We say nothing, Grandmother starts to cry:

"You don't know what it's like to be paralyzed. To see everything, hear everything, and not be able to move. If you aren't even capable of doing this simple little thing for me, then you're ingrates, vipers I have nursed in my bosom."

We say:

"Don't cry, Grandmother. We'll do it; if you really want us to, we'll do it."

Our Father

When our Father arrives, the three of us are working in the kitchen because it's raining outside.

Father stops in front of the door, arms folded, legs apart. He asks:

"Where's my wife?"

Grandmother sniggers:

"Well, well! So she really did have a husband."

Father says:

"Yes, I'm your daughter's husband. And these are my sons."

He looks at us and adds:

"You really have grown up. But you haven't changed."

Grandmother says:

"My daughter, your wife, entrusted the children to me."

Father says:

"She'd have done better to entrust them to someone else. Where is she? I've been told she went abroad. Is that true?"

Grandmother says:

"That's old news, all that. Where have you been all this time?"

Father says:

"I've been a prisoner of war. And now I want to find my wife again. Don't try to hide anything from me, you old witch."

Grandmother says:

"I really appreciate your way of thanking me for what I've done for your children."

Father shouts:

"I don't give a damn! Where's my wife?"

Grandmother says:

"You don't give a damn? About your children and me? All right, I'll show you where your wife is!"

Grandmother goes out into the garden, and we follow her. With her stick, she points to the flower bed that we have planted over Mother's grave:

"There! That's where your wife is. In the ground."

Father asks:

"Dead? From what? When?"

Grandmother says:

"Dead. From a shell. A few days before the end of the war."

Father says:

"It's forbidden to bury people just anywhere."

Grandmother says:

"We buried her where she died. And that isn't just any-where. It's my garden. It was also her garden when she was a little girl."

Father looks at the wet flowers and says:

"I want to see her."

Grandmother says:

"You shouldn't. The dead must not be disturbed."

Father says:

"In any case, she'll have to be buried in a cemetery. It's the law. Get me a spade."

Grandmother shrugs her shoulders:

"Get him a spade."

In the rain, we watch Father demolish our little flower garden, we watch him dig. He gets to the blankets, he pulls them away. A big skeleton is lying there, with a tiny skeleton pressed to its breast.

Father asks:

"What's that, that thing on her?"

We say:

"It's a baby. Our little sister."

Grandmother says:

"I did tell you to leave the dead in peace. Come and wash your hands in the kitchen."

Father doesn't answer. He stares at the skeletons. His face is wet with sweat, tears, and rain. He climbs laboriously out of the hole and walks off without turning around, his hands and clothes all muddy.

We ask Grandmother:

"What shall we do?"

She says:

"Fill the hole in again. What else can we do?"

We say:

"You go back into the warm, Grandmother. We'll take care of all this."

She goes in.

We carry the skeletons up to the attic in a blanket and

spread the bones out on straw to dry. Then we go down and fill in the hole where nobody is lying anymore.

Later, we spend months smoothing and polishing the skull and bones of our Mother and the baby, then we carefully reassemble the skeletons by attaching each bone to thin pieces of wire. When our work is done, we hang Mother's skeleton from one of the attic beams with the baby's skeleton clinging to her neck.

Our Father Comes Back

We don't see our Father again until several years later.

In the meantime, Grandmother has had a new attack, and we have helped her die as she asked us to do. She is now buried in the same grave as Grandfather. Before they opened the grave, we recovered the treasure and hid it under the bench in front of our window, where the rifle, the cartridges, and the grenades still are.

Father arrives one evening and asks:

"Where's your Grandmother?"

"She's dead."

"You live alone? How do you manage?"

"Very well, Father."

He says:

"I've come here in hiding. You must help me."

We say:

176

"We haven't heard from you in years."

He shows us his hands. He no longer has any fingernails. They have been torn out at the roots:

"I've just come out of prison. They tortured me."

"Why?"

"I don't know. For no particular reason. I'm a politically suspect person. I'm not allowed to practice my profession. I'm under constant surveillance. My apartment is searched regularly. It's impossible for me to live much longer in this country."

We say:

"You want to cross the frontier."

He says:

"Yes. You live here, you must know . . ."

"Yes, we know. The frontier is impassable."

Father lowers his head, looks at his hands for a moment, then says:

"There must be a weak spot somewhere. There must be a way of getting through."

"At the risk of your life, yes."

"I'd rather die than stay here."

"You must make up your own mind when you know all the facts, Father."

He says:

"I'm listening."

We explain:

"The first problem is to get as far as the first barbed wire without meeting a patrol or being seen from one of the watchtowers. It can be done. We know the times of the patrols and the positions of the watchtowers. The fence is one and a half meters high and a meter wide. You need two boards. One to climb onto the fence, the other to put on top so that you can stand up on it. If you lose your balance, you fall into the wire and you can't get out."

Father says:

"I won't lose my balance."

We go on:

"You have to retrieve the two boards and do the same thing at the next fence, seven meters further on."

Father laughs:

"It's child's play."

"Yes, but the space between the two fences is mined."

Father goes pale:

"Then it's impossible."

"No. It's a matter of luck. The mines are arranged in a zig-zag, in a *W*. If you follow a straight line, you only risk walking on one mine. And if you take big steps, you have almost a one in seven chance of avoiding it."

Father thinks for a moment, then says:

"I'll risk it."

We say:

"In that case, we are quite willing to help you. We'll go with you to the first fence."

Father says:

"Okay. Thanks. You wouldn't have something to eat, by any chance?"

We give him some bread and goat cheese. We also offer him some wine from Grandmother's old vineyard. We pour into his glass a few drops of the sleeping potion that Grandmother was so good at making out of plants.

We take Father into our room and say:

"Good night, Father. Sleep well. We'll wake you tomorrow."

We go to bed on the corner seat in the kitchen.

The Separation

Next morning, we get up very early. We make sure that Father is sleeping soundly.

We cut four boards.

We dig up Grandmother's treasure: gold and silver coins and a lot of jewelry. We put most of it into a linen sack. We also take a grenade each, in case we are surprised by a patrol. By getting rid of the patrol, we can gain time.

We make a reconnaissance tour near the frontier to locate the best place: a dead angle between two watchtowers. There, at the foot of a tall tree, we hide the linen sack and two of the boards.

We go back and eat. Later, we bring Father his breakfast. We have to shake him to wake him up. He rubs his eyes and says:

"It's been a long time since I slept so well."

We put the tray on his knees. He says:

"What a feast! Milk, coffee, eggs, ham, butter, jam! You just can't find these things in the Big Town. How do you do it?"

"We work. Eat up, Father. We won't have time to give you another meal before you leave."

He asks:

"I'm going this evening?"

We say:

"You're going right now. As soon as you're ready."

He says:

"Are you crazy? I refuse to cross that bitch of a frontier in broad daylight! They'll see us!"

We say:

"We have to see too, Father. Only stupid people try to cross the frontier at night. At night, the frequency of the patrols is four times greater and the area is continually swept by searchlights. On the other hand, the surveillance is relaxed around eleven in the morning. The frontier guards think that nobody would be crazy enough to try to get through at that hour."

Father says:

"You're absolutely right. I put myself in your hands."

We ask:

"Will you allow us to search your pockets while you eat?"

"My pockets? Why?"

"You mustn't be identified. If anything happens to you and they learn that you are our father, we'll be accused as accessories."

Father says:

"You think of everything."

We say:

"We have to think of our own safety."

We search his clothes. We take his papers, his identity card, his address book, a train ticket, some bills, and a photograph of Mother. We burn everything in the kitchen stove, except the photograph.

At eleven o'clock, we leave. Each of us carries a board.

Father carries nothing. We ask him just to follow us and make as little noise as possible.

We are getting near the frontier. We tell Father to lie down behind the big tree and not to move.

Soon, a few meters away from us, a two-man patrol passes by. We can hear them talking:

"I wonder what there'll be to eat."

"The same shit as usual."

"There's shit and shit. Yesterday it was disgusting, but it's good sometimes."

"Good? You wouldn't say that if you'd ever tasted my mother's soup."

"I've never tasted your mother's soup. Me, I never had a mother. I've never eaten anything but shit. In the army, at least, I eat well once in a while."

The patrol moves off. We say:

"Go on, Father. We have twenty minutes before the next patrol arrives."

Father puts the two boards under his arm, he moves forward, he places one of the boards against the fence, he climbs up.

We lie face down behind the big tree, we cover our ears with our hands, we open our mouths.

There is an explosion.

We run to the barbed wire with the other two boards and the linen sack.

Father is lying near the second fence.

Yes, there is a way to get across the frontier: it's to make someone else go first.

Picking up the linen sack, walking in the footprints and then over the inert body of our Father, one of us goes into the other country.

The one who is left goes back to Grandmother's house.

The Proof

Translated by David Watson

1

On his return to Grandmother's house, Lucas lies down by the garden gate in the shade of the bushes. He waits. An army truck pulls up in front of the border post. Some soldiers get out and lower a body wrapped in a camouflaged sheet to the ground. A sergeant comes out of the border post and gives a sign, and the soldiers open the sheet. The sergeant whistles.

"It'll be a real job identifying him! You've got to be crazy to try and cross that bitch of a border, and in broad daylight too!"

A soldier says, "You'd think people would realize it's impossible."

Another soldier says, "The people around here know that. It's the ones from elsewhere who try to get across."

The sergeant says, "Okay, let's go see the idiot across the road. Maybe he knows something."

Lucas goes into the house. He sits on the corner seat in the kitchen. He slices some bread, puts a bottle of wine and some

187

goat's cheese on the table. There is a knock. The sergeant and a soldier come in.

Lucas says, "I was expecting you. Sit down. Have some wine and cheese."

The soldier says, "Thanks."

He takes some bread and some cheese; Lucas pours the wine.

The sergeant says, "You were expecting us. Why?"

"I heard the explosion. After explosions someone always comes to ask if I saw anyone."

"And did you see anyone?"

"No."

"As usual."

"Yes, as usual. People don't come here to tell me they intend to cross the border."

The sergeant laughs. He takes some wine and cheese.

"You might have seen someone hanging around here, or in the forest."

"I saw no one."

"If you *had* seen someone, would you say so?"

"If I told you I would, you wouldn't believe me."

The sergeant laughs again. "I sometimes wonder why they call you the idiot."

"Me too. I simply have a nervous disorder due to suffering a psychological trauma as a child during the war."

The soldier asks, "What? What did he say?"

Lucas explains, "I'm a bit funny in the head because of the air raids. It happened when I was a child."

The sergeant says, "Your cheese is very good. Thank you. Come with us."

Lucas follows them. Pointing to the body, the sergeant says, "Do you know this man? Have you seen him before?"

Lucas gazes at the mangled body of his father. "He's beyond recognition."

"You can still recognize someone from his clothes, his shoes, or even his hands or hair."

Lucas says, "All I can tell is that he's not from this town. His clothes tell you that. No one wears such elegant clothes in this town."

The sergeant says, "Thank you. We knew that much already. We aren't idiots either. I'm asking you whether you have seen him before or noticed him anywhere."

"No. Nowhere. But I see his nails have been torn out. He's been in prison."

The sergeant says, "There's no torture in our prisons. It's strange that his pockets are completely empty. Not even a photo, or a key, or wallet. Yet you'd think he'd have an identity card, maybe even a pass giving him access to the border zone."

Lucas says, "He probably got rid of them in the forest."

"I think so too. He didn't want to be identified. I wonder who he was trying to protect. If by any chance you come across something when you're out picking mushrooms, you'll bring it to us, won't you, Lucas?"

"You can count on me, sergeant."

Lucas sits down on the bench in the garden and rests his head against the white wall of the house. The sun blinds him. He shuts his eyes.

"What do I do now?"

"Same as before. Keep getting up in the morning, going to bed at night, doing what has to be done in order to live."

"It will be a long time."

"Perhaps a whole lifetime."

The sounds of the animals wake Lucas. He gets up and goes to tend the livestock. He feeds the pigs, the hens, the rabbits. He rounds up the goats by the riverbank, brings them back, milks them. He carries the milk to the kitchen. He sits down on the corner seat and stays there until nightfall. Then he gets up, leaves the house, waters the garden. There is a full moon. When he goes back to the kitchen, he eats a bit of cheese and drinks some wine. He leans out of the window and throws up. He clears the table. He goes into Grandmother's room and opens the window to air it. He sits down in front of the dressing table and looks at himself in the mirror. Later Lucas opens his bedroom door. He looks at the double bed. He closes the door and goes off into town.

The streets are deserted. Lucas walks quickly. He stops in front of an open window with a light on. It is a kitchen. A family is eating the evening meal. A mother and three children around the table. Two boys and a girl. They are eating potato broth. The father isn't there. Perhaps he is at work, or in prison, or in a camp. Or else he never came back from the war.

Lucas walks past the noisy bars where, not long ago, he would sometimes play the harmonica. He doesn't go in, he keeps on walking. He goes down the unlit alleyways behind the castle, then follows the short dark street leading to the cemetery. He stops in front of the grave of Grandfather and Grandmother.

Grandmother died last year of her second stroke. Grandfather died a long time ago. The townspeople used to say he was poisoned by his wife.

Lucas's father died today trying to cross the border, and Lucas will never see his grave.

Lucas goes back home. He climbs up into the attic with the aid of a rope. There is a straw mattress, an old army blanket, a chest. Lucas opens the chest, takes out a large school notebook, and writes a few words. He closes the notebook. He lies down on the mattress.

Over his head, lit by the moonlight shining through the gable window, the skeletons of his mother and her baby hang from a beam.

Lucas's mother and little sister were killed by a shell five years ago, a few days before the end of the war, here in the garden of Grandmother's house.

Lucas is sitting on the garden bench. His eyes are closed. A horse-drawn wagon pulls up in front of the house. The noise wakes Lucas. Joseph, the market gardener, comes into the garden. Lucas looks at him.

"What do you want, Joseph?"

"What do I want? It was market day today. I waited for you until seven o'clock."

Lucas says, "Forgive me, Joseph. I forgot what day it was. If you like we can quickly load up the produce."

"Are you joking? It's two o'clock in the afternoon. I didn't come to load up, I came to ask if you still want me to sell your produce. If not, just say so. It's all the same to me. I'm only doing it as a favor to you."

"Of course, Joseph. I simply forgot that it was market day."

"It's not just today that you forgot. You also forgot last week, and the week before."

Lucas says, "Three weeks? I didn't realize."

Joseph shakes his head. "There's something not right with you. What have you done with your fruit and vegetables for the last three weeks?"

"Nothing. But I watered the garden every day, I think."

"You think? Let's take a look."

Joseph goes behind the house into the kitchen garden. Lucas follows him. The market gardener bends over the beds and swears.

"Jesus Christ! You've let it all rot. Look at those tomatoes on the ground, those overripe beans, those yellow cucumbers and black strawberries. What, are you crazy? Ruining all this good produce! You ought to be shot! You've destroyed this year's peas, and the apricots. We might just save the potatoes and the plums. Bring me a bucket!"

Lucas brings a bucket, and Joseph begins to gather up the potatoes, and the plums which have fallen into the grass. He says to Lucas, "Fetch another bucket and gather up the rotten stuff. Perhaps your pigs will eat it. God almighty! Your animals!"

Joseph rushes down to the farmyard. Lucas follows him. Joseph wipes his brow and says, "Thank God they're still alive. Give me a pitchfork so I can clean them out a bit. By what miracle did you remember the animals?"

"They don't let you forget. They cry out as soon as they're hungry."

Joseph works for several hours. Lucas helps him, following his orders. When the sun sets they go into the kitchen.

Joseph says, "For the love of God! I've never smelled such a stink! What on earth is it?" He looks around and notices a large bowl full of goat's milk. "The milk has turned. Take it out of here and throw it in the river."

Lucas obeys. When he comes back, Joseph has already aired the kitchen and washed down the tiles. Lucas goes down into the cellar and comes back with a bottle of wine and some bacon.

Joseph says, "We'll need some bread with that."

"I haven't got any."

Joseph gets up without a word and fetches a loaf of bread from his wagon.

"Here. I bought some after the market. We don't make our own anymore."

Joseph eats and drinks. He asks, "You aren't drinking? You're not eating either. What's wrong with you, Lucas?"

"I'm tired. I can't eat."

"Your face is pale beneath your tan. You're all skin and bones."

"It's nothing. It will pass."

Joseph says, "I suspected there was something bothering you. It must be a girl."

"No, it's not a girl."

Joseph winks at him. "Sure, I know what it's like to be young. But I'd be sorry to see a fine boy like you let himself go because of a girl."

"It's not because of a girl."

"What is it, then?"

"I don't know."

"You don't know? In that case you should go and see a doctor."

"Don't worry about me, Joseph. It'll pass."

"It'll pass, it'll pass. He neglects his garden, he lets the milk turn sour, he doesn't eat, he doesn't drink, and he thinks he can go on like that."

Lucas doesn't answer.

On his way out Joseph says, "Listen, Lucas. So you won't forget market day again, I'll get up an hour earlier, I'll come and wake you, and we can both load up the fruit, vegetables, and any animals you want to sell. Is that all right by you?"

"Yes. Thank you, Joseph."

Lucas gives Joseph another bottle of wine and accompanies him to his wagon.

As he whips the horse, Joseph shouts, "Take care, Lucas! Love can be fatal!"

Lucas is sitting on the garden bench. His eyes are closed. When he opens them again, he sees a little girl swinging on a branch of the cherry tree.

Lucas asks, "What are you doing there? Who are you?"

The little girl jumps to the ground. She fiddles with the pink ribbons on the ends of her braids. "Aunt Leonie wants you to go to the priest's house. He is all alone because Aunt Leonie can't work anymore. She's in bed at home, she won't get up again, she's too old. My mother doesn't have time to go to the priest's house, because she works at the factory like my father."

Lucas says, "I see. How old are you?"

"I don't know exactly. The last time it was my birthday I was five, but that was in the winter. Now it's already autumn, and I could go to school if I hadn't been born too late."

"It's already autumn?"

The little girl laughs.

"Didn't you know? It's been autumn for two days now, even though people think it's still summer because it's so warm."

"You know a lot!"

"Yes. My big brother teaches me everything. He's called Simon."

"And what are you called?"

"Agnes."

"That's a nice name."

"So is Lucas. I know you're Lucas because my aunt said, 'Go and fetch Lucas. He lives in the last house, opposite the border posts.' "

"Didn't the guards stop you?"

"They didn't see me. I went around the back."

Lucas says, "I'd like to have a little sister like you."

"Don't you have one?"

"No. If I had one I'd make her a swing. Do you want me to make you a swing?"

Agnes says, "I've got one at home, but I like to swing on other things better. It's more fun."

She jumps up, grabs the branch of the cherry tree, and swings on it, laughing.

Lucas asks, "Aren't you ever sad?"

"No, because one thing always makes up for another."

She jumps to the ground.

"You have to hurry to the priest's house. My aunt told me to tell you yesterday and the day before, and the day before that, but I forgot every day. She will scold me."

Lucas says, "Don't worry. I'll go this evening."

"Good. So now I'll go home."

"Stay awhile longer. Would you like to listen to some music?"

"What kind of music?"

"You'll see. Come."

Lucas takes the little girl in his arms. He goes into his room, puts the child down on the double bed, and puts a record on the old gramophone. Sitting on the ground next to the bed, his head resting on his arms, he listens.

Agnes asks, "Are you crying?"

Lucas shakes his head.

She says, "I'm scared. I don't like this music."

Lucas takes one of the little girl's legs in his hand. He squeezes it. She cries out, "You're hurting me! Let me go!"

Lucas loosens his grip.

When the record finishes, Lucas gets up to turn it over. The little girl has disappeared. Lucas listens to records until sunset.

That evening Lucas makes up a basket of vegetables, potatoes, eggs, cheese. He kills a chicken and cleans it. He also takes milk and a bottle of wine.

He rings the bell of the priest's house. No one answers. He goes in through the unlocked back door and puts the basket down in the kitchen. He knocks on the bedroom door. He goes in.

The priest, a tall, thin, old man, is sitting at his desk. He is playing chess, alone, by the light of a candle.

Lucas pulls up a chair, sits facing the priest, and says, "I'm sorry, Father."

The priest says, "I'll repay you a bit at a time for what I owe you, Lucas."

Lucas asks, "Have I not been here for a long time?"

"Not since the beginning of the summer. Don't you remember?"

"No. Who has been feeding you all this time?"

"Leonie has been bringing me a little soup each day. But she has been ill for the last few days."

Lucas says, "Forgive me, Father."

"Forgive you? For what? I haven't paid you in months. I have no money left. The State has broken links with the Church, and I am no longer paid for my work. I have to live off the donations of my flock. But people stay away from church for fear of disapproval. Only a few poor old women come to mass."

Lucas says, "If I didn't come, it wasn't because of the money you owe me. It's worse than that."

"What do you mean, 'worse than that'?"

Lucas lowers his head. "I completely forgot about you. I also forgot about my garden, the market, the milk, the cheese. I even forgot to eat. For months I've been sleeping in the attic. I was afraid to go into my room. It was only because a little girl, Leonie's niece, came today that I had the courage to go in. She also reminded me of my duty toward you."

"You have no duty, no obligation toward me. You sell your produce, you live from the proceeds. If I can't pay you it's right that you not supply me anymore."

"As I said, it's not because of the money. Try to understand."

"Tell me. I'm listening."

"I don't know how to go on living."

The priest gets up, takes Lucas's face in his hands. "What has happened to you, my child?"

Lucas shakes his head. "I can't explain. It's like an illness."

"I see. A sort of illness of the soul. Due to your tender age and, perhaps, your excessive solitude."

Lucas says, "Maybe. I will make a meal and we will eat together. I haven't eaten for a long time, either. When I try to eat, I just vomit. With you I might be able to manage it."

He goes to the kitchen, lights the fire, boils up the chicken with the vegetables. He sets the table, opens a bottle of wine.

The priest comes into the kitchen.

"As I said, Lucas, I can't pay you anymore."

"Nevertheless, you have to eat."

"Yes, but I don't need this banquet. A few potatoes and some corn would be enough."

Lucas says, "You will eat what I bring you, and we won't talk anymore about money."

"I can't accept."

"It is easier to give than to receive, is that it? Pride is a sin, Father."

They eat in silence. They drink wine. Lucas doesn't vomit. After the meal he does the washing up. The priest goes back into his room. Lucas joins him.

"I have to go now."

"Where are you going?"

"To walk around the streets."

"I could teach you to play chess."

Lucas says, "I don't think I could get interested. It's a complicated game that requires a lot of concentration."

"Let's try."

The priest explains the rules. They play a game. Lucas wins. The priest asks, "Where did you learn to play chess?"

"From books. But this is the first real game I've played."

"Will you play again sometime?"

Lucas comes every evening. The priest improves his strategies, and the games become interesting, even though Lucas always wins.

Lucas starts sleeping in his bedroom again, on the double bed. He doesn't forget market days, he doesn't let the milk go sour. He takes care of the animals, the garden, the house. He goes back into the forest to collect mushrooms and firewood. He takes up fishing again.

When he was a child, Lucas caught fish by hand or with a rod. Now he invents a system that diverts the fish from the mainstream into a pool where they are trapped. Then Lucas only needs to scoop them out in a net when he wants fresh fish.

In the evenings Lucas eats with the priest, plays a game or two of chess, then walks around the streets of the town.

One night he goes into the first bar he meets on his way. It used to be a well-kept café, even during the war. Now it is a dingy place, almost empty.

An ugly, weary waitress shouts from the counter, "How many?"

"Three."

Lucas sits at a table stained with red wine and cigarette ash. The waitress brings him three glasses of cheap red wine. She collects his money right away.

When he has finished his three glasses, Lucas gets up and leaves. He pushes on as far as the main square. He stops in front of the book and stationery store and stands gazing into the window: school notebooks, pencils, erasers, and a few books.

Lucas goes into the bar opposite.

It is a bit livelier, but it is even dirtier than the other bar. The floor is covered with sawdust.

Lucas sits next to the open door, the only form of ventilation in the place.

A group of border guards are sitting around a long table. They have girls with them. They are singing.

A ragged little old man comes and sits at Lucas's table.

"How about playing something, eh?"

Lucas shouts, "A half bottle and two glasses!"

The little old man says, "I wasn't scrounging a drink, I just wanted you to play. Like before."

"I can't play like before."

"I know. But play anyway. I'd like that."

Lucas pours the wine. "Drink."

He takes his harmonica out of his pocket and starts to play a sad song, a song about love and separation.

The border guards and the girls take up the tune. One of the girls comes and sits next to Lucas; she strokes his hair.

"Isn't he cute?"

Lucas stops playing. He gets up.

The girl laughs. "Touchy!"

Outside it is raining. Lucas goes into a third bar, orders another three glasses. When he starts playing, the customers' eyes turn to him, then back to their drinks. People come here to drink, not talk.

Suddenly, a large, well-built man, with one leg amputated, plants himself on his crutches in the middle of the room beneath the single bare light bulb and begins to sing a forbidden song.

Lucas accompanies him on the harmonica.

The other customers drink up quickly, and one after another leave the bar.

Tears run down the man's cheeks as he sings the last two lines of the song:

> *The people have already atoned*
> *For the past and the future.*

The next day Lucas goes to the book and stationery shop. He picks out three pencils, a pack of lined paper, and a thick notebook. When he comes to the cash register, the bookseller, a pale, obese man, says to him, "I haven't seen you for a long time. Have you been away?"

"No. I was just too busy."

"Your consumption of paper is most impressive. I sometimes wonder what it is you do with it."

Lucas says, "I like filling up blank sheets with pencil. It passes the time."

"You must have a mountain of them by now."

"I waste a lot. I use the spoiled pages to light the fire."

The bookseller says, "Unfortunately my other customers aren't as regular as you. Business is poor. Before the war, things were good. There were lots of schools around here. High schools, boarding schools, secondary schools. The students wandered through the streets in the evening having fun. There was also a musical conservatory, concerts and plays every week. Look out there now. Nothing but children and old people. A few workers, a few winegrowers. There are no more young people in this town. The schools have been moved to the interior of the country, all except the primary school. The young people, even those who aren't studying, move away, to towns that have some life. Our town is dead, empty. The border zone, sealed off, forgotten. Everyone knows everyone else in this town. Always the same faces. No outsiders can get in."

Lucas says, "There are the border guards. They're young."

"Yes, poor fellows. Locked away in their barracks, on patrol at night. Every six months they change them to keep them from forming contacts with the townspeople. This town has ten thousand inhabitants, plus three thousand foreign soldiers and two thousand of our own border guards. Before the war there were five thousand students, and tourists during the summer. The tourists came from the interior as well as from across the border."

Lucas asks, "The border was open?"

"Of course. The farmers from over there came to sell their produce here, the students went to the other side for village fairs. The train used to run to the next big town in the other country.

Now this town is the end of the line. Everybody off! And show your papers!"

Lucas asks, "You could come and go freely? You could travel abroad?"

"Of course. You've never known what that's like. Now you can't take a step without having to show your identity card. And the special permit for the border zone."

"What if you haven't got one?"

"It's better to have one."

"I haven't got one."

"How old are you?"

"Fifteen."

"You should have one. Even children get an identity card at school. What do you do when you leave town and then come back?"

"I never leave town."

"Never? You don't even go to the next town when you need to buy something you can't find here?"

"No. I haven't left this town since my mother brought me here six years ago."

The bookseller says, "If you want to avoid trouble, get yourself an identity card. Go to the town hall and explain your case. If anyone gives you trouble, ask for Peter N. Tell him Victor sent you. Peter comes from the same town as me. Up north. He has an important position in the Party."

Lucas says, "That's kind of you. But why should I have problems getting an identity card?"

"You never know."

* * *

Lucas goes into a large building near the castle. Flags hang from the facade. Numerous black plaques with gold lettering indicate the offices:

POLITICAL BUREAU OF THE REVOLUTIONARY PARTY

SECRETARIAT OF THE REVOLUTIONARY PARTY

ASSOCIATION OF REVOLUTIONARY YOUTH

ASSOCIATION OF REVOLUTIONARY WOMEN

FEDERATION OF REVOLUTIONARY TRADE UNIONS

Through the door a simple gray plaque with red letters:

COUNCIL INQUIRIES SECOND FLOOR

Lucas goes up to the second floor, knocks on a frosted window above which is written: "Identity cards."

A man in gray overalls opens the sliding window and looks at Lucas without speaking.

Lucas says, "Hello. I'd like to apply for an identity card."

"Renew, you mean. Your present one's expired?"

"No, I don't have one. I've never had one. Someone told me I'm supposed to have one."

The official asks, "How old are you?"

"Fifteen."

"Then you are supposed to have one. Give me your school card."

Lucas says, "I haven't got a card. Of any kind."

The official says, "That's not possible. If you are still at primary school you have your school card; if you are a student you have your student card; if you are an apprentice you have your apprenticeship card."

Lucas says, "I'm sorry. I haven't got any of those. I never went to school."

"How come? School is compulsory up to the age of fourteen."

"I was excused from school because of a psychological disorder."

"So what are you doing now?"

"I live off the produce from my garden. I also play music in bars at night."

The official says, "Ah, it's you. Lucas T., is that your name?"

"Yes."

"Who do you live with?"

"I live in Grandmother's house near the border. I live alone. Grandmother died last year."

The official scratches his head. "Listen, you're a special case. I'll have to check on this. I can't decide this on my own. You'll have to come back in a few days."

Lucas says, "Peter N. might be able to straighten it out."

"Peter N.? The Party Secretary? You know him?" He picks up the telephone.

Lucas tells him, "I was recommended by Victor."

The official hangs up and comes out of his office.

"Come on. We're going downstairs."

He knocks on a door marked SECRETARIAT OF THE REVOLUTIONARY PARTY. They go in. A young man is sitting behind a desk. The official hands him a blank card.

"It's about an identity card."

"I'll take care of it. Leave us."

The official leaves. The young man gets up and offers his hand to Lucas.

"Hello, Lucas."

"You know me?"

"Everyone in town knows you. I'm very pleased to be of service to you. Let's fill in your card. Last name, first name, address, date of birth. You're only fifteen? You're big for your age. Occupation? Shall I write 'musician'?"

Lucas says, "I also live off the produce from my garden."

"Then I'll write 'gardener.' It looks more responsible. Now let's see, brown hair, gray eyes . . . political allegiance?"

Lucas says, "Cross that out."

"All right. And here, what do you want me to write here—'Official assessment'?"

" 'Idiot,' if possible. I suffered a traumatic disorder. I'm not quite normal."

The young man laughs. "Not quite normal? Who would believe it? But you're right. An assessment like that could spare you a lot of inconvenience. Military service, for example. I'll write 'chronic psychological problems.' Does that suit you?"

Lucas says, "Yes, sir. Thank you, sir."

"Call me Peter."

Lucas says, "Thank you, Peter."

Peter comes close to Lucas and hands him his card. With his other hand he gently touches Lucas's face. Lucas closes his eyes. Peter kisses him lingeringly on the mouth, holding Lucas's head in his hands. He stays looking at Lucas's face for a moment, then he sits down at his desk.

"Excuse me, Lucas. I was moved by your beauty. I must be very careful. The Party does not forgive this sort of thing."

Lucas says, "No one will know about it."

Peter says, "You can't hide such a vice all your life. I won't stay long in this post. I'm only here because I deserted, gave myself up, and returned with the victorious army of our liberators. I was still a student when I was sent off to war."

Lucas says, "You should get married, or at least have a mistress to allay suspicion. You should find it easy to attract a woman. You are handsome, masculine. And you are sad. Women like sad men. What's more, you have a good position."

Peter laughs. "I have no desire to attract a woman."

Lucas says, "Nevertheless, there are perhaps women one can love, in some way."

"You know a lot for someone your age, Lucas!"

"I don't know anything. I'm just guessing."

"If you need anything at all, come and see me."

2

It is the final day of the year. A great cold from the north has gripped the earth.

Lucas goes down to the river. He will take some fish to the priest for the New Year's Eve supper.

It is already dark. Lucas is armed with a hurricane lamp and a pickax. He starts to break the ice covering the pool. Then he hears a child crying. He points his lamp in the direction of the sound.

A woman is sitting on the little bridge that Lucas built many years ago. The woman is wrapped in a blanket. She is watching the river bearing away blocks of snow and ice. Inside the blanket a baby is crying.

Lucas approaches and asks the woman, "Who are you? What are you doing here?"

She doesn't answer. Her large, black eyes stare into the light of the lamp.

Lucas says, "Come."

He wraps his right arm around her. He guides her toward the house, lighting the way ahead. The child is still crying.

In the kitchen it is warm. The woman sits down, uncovers her breast, and suckles the baby.

Lucas turns away. He warms up the remains of some vegetable soup.

The child sleeps on his mother's knee. The mother looks at Lucas.

"I wanted to drown him. I couldn't do it."

Lucas asks, "Do you want me to do it?"

"Do you think you could do it?"

"I've drowned mice, cats, puppies."

"A baby is a different matter."

"Do you want me to drown him or not?"

"No, not anymore. It's too late."

After a silence, Lucas says, "There's a spare room here. You can sleep here with your child."

She raises her dark eyes to Lucas. "Thank you. My name is Yasmine."

Lucas opens the door of Grandmother's room.

"Lay your child on the bed. We can leave the door open to warm the room. When you've eaten you can go and sleep next to him."

Yasmine places her child on Grandmother's bed. She comes back to the kitchen.

Lucas asks, "Are you hungry?"

"I haven't eaten since yesterday evening."

Lucas pours the soup into a bowl.

"Eat, then go to sleep. We'll talk tomorrow. I have to go now."

He goes back to the pool, scoops out two fish with the net, and goes off to the priest's house.

He prepares the meal as usual. He eats with the priest and they play a game of chess. Lucas loses for the first time.

The priest is cross.

"You are distracted this evening, Lucas. You're making stupid mistakes. Let's play again, and concentrate this time."

Lucas says, "I'm tired. I have to go home."

"You're going to hang around in the bars again."

"You are well informed, Father."

The priest laughs. "I see many old women. They tell me everything that happens in town. Don't make a face! Go on, enjoy yourself. It's New Year's Eve."

"I wish you a Happy New Year, Father."

The priest gets up, too; he places his hand on Lucas's head.

"God bless you. May His peace be with you."

Lucas says, "I'll never have peace within me."

"You must pray and hope, my child."

Lucas walks down the street. He goes past the noisy bars, doesn't stop, quickens his step. When he reaches the unlit lane that leads to Grandmother's house he is running.

He opens the kitchen door. Yasmine is still sitting on the corner seat. She has opened the door of the stove; she is looking into the fire. The bowl, full of cold soup, still stands on the table.

Lucas sits down opposite Yasmine.

"You haven't eaten."

"I'm not hungry. I'm still frozen."

Lucas takes a bottle of brandy from the shelf, pours out two glasses.

"Drink. It'll warm you up inside."

He drinks, and so does Yasmine. He pours again. They drink in silence. They hear the town bells ringing in the distance.

Lucas says, "It's midnight. A new year begins."

Yasmine lowers her head onto the table. She cries.

Lucas gets up, removes the blanket which is still wrapped round Yasmine. He strokes her long, shiny black hair. He strokes her breasts, which are swollen with milk. He unfastens her blouse, bends forward, and drinks her milk.

The next day Lucas goes into the kitchen. Yasmine is sitting on the bench with the baby on her knee.

She says, "I'd like to bathe my baby. After that I'll leave."

"Where would you go?"

"I don't know. I can't stay in this town after what has happened."

Lucas asks, "What has happened? Is it the child? There are other unmarried mothers in the town. Have your parents disowned you?"

"I haven't got any parents. My mother died giving birth to me. I lived with my father and with my aunt, my mother's sister. My aunt brought me up. When my father returned from the war he married her. But he didn't love her. He only loved me."

Lucas says, "I see."

"Yes. And when my aunt found out she denounced us. My father is in prison. I worked in the hospital as a cleaner until the birth. I left the hospital this morning. I knocked at the door of our house. My aunt wouldn't open it to me. She cursed me through the door."

Lucas says, "I know your story. I've heard the gossip in the bars."

"Yes, everyone talks about it. It's a small town. I can't stay here. I was going to drown the child, then go over the border."

"You can't cross the border. You'd step on a mine."

"I don't care if I die."

"How old are you?"

"Eighteen."

"You're too young to die. You could rebuild your life somewhere else. In another town, later, when your child has grown up. For now you can stay here as long as you want."

She says, "What about the people in town?"

"They'll stop gossiping. They'll shut up eventually. You don't have to face them. We're not in the town here. This is my home."

"You would keep me here with my child?"

"You can live in this room, you can use the kitchen, but you must never go into my room or up into the attic. You must never ask me any questions."

"I won't ask you any questions and I won't disturb you. I won't let the child disturb you either. I'll cook and clean up. I can do everything. At home I did the housework, because my aunt works in a factory."

Lucas says, "The water is boiling. You can prepare the bath."

Yasmine puts a basin on the table. She takes off the child's clothes and diaper. Lucas warms a bath towel over the stove. Yasmine washes the child. Lucas watches her.

He says, "He is deformed around the shoulders."

"Yes. His legs, too. They told me at the hospital. It's my fault. I wore a tight corset around my stomach to hide the pregnancy. He'll be crippled. If only I'd had the courage to drown him."

Lucas takes the bundle in his arms, looks at the little crumpled face.

"You shouldn't say things like that, Yasmine."

She says, "He will be unhappy."

"You are unhappy yourself, yet you are not crippled. He may not be any more unhappy than you, or anyone else."

Yasmine takes back the child, her eyes filling with tears.

"You are kind, Lucas."

"You know my name?"

"Everyone knows you in town. They say you're an idiot, but I don't believe that."

Lucas goes out. He comes back with some planks of wood.

"I'm going to build him a cradle."

Yasmine does the washing, prepares the meal. When the cradle is finished, they lay the child inside. They rock him.

Lucas asks, "What is he called? Have you given him a name yet?"

"Yes. At the hospital they needed one for the town hall records. I called him Mathias. It's my father's name. I couldn't think of another name."

"You loved him that much?"

"He was all I had."

That evening Lucas comes home from the priest's house without stopping at a bar. The fire is still alight in the stove. Through the open door Lucas hears Yasmine singing softly. He goes into Grandmother's room. Yasmine, in her chemise, is rocking the child near the window.

Lucas asks, "Why aren't you in bed yet?"

"I was waiting for you."

"You don't have to wait up for me. Usually I come home a lot later."

Yasmine smiles. "I know. You play in the bars."

Lucas approaches her. He asks, "Is he asleep?"

"For a long time. I just enjoy rocking him."

Lucas says, "Come to the kitchen. We don't want to wake him."

They sit opposite each other in the kitchen, drinking brandy in silence. Later, Lucas asks, "When did it start? Between your father and you?"

"Right away. As soon as he came back."

"How old were you?"

"Twelve."

"Did he rape you?"

Yasmine laughs. "Oh no! He didn't rape me. He just lay down beside me, held me against him, kissed me, stroked me, cried."

"Where was your aunt all this time?"

"Working at the factory, on shift work. When she worked the night shift my father slept with me in my bed. It was a narrow bed in a tiny room without a window. We were happy, the two of us, in that bed."

Lucas pours some brandy. He says, "Go on."

"I grew up. My father touched my breasts. He said, 'Soon you'll be a woman, you'll go off with some boy.' I said, 'No, I'll never leave.' One night, in my sleep, I took his hand and placed it between my legs. I squeezed his fingers and felt that pleasure for the first time. The following evening it was I who asked him to give me that wonderfully sweet pleasure again. He cried, he said he musn't, that it was wrong, but I insisted, I pleaded. So he leaned over my sex, he licked it, he sucked it, he kissed it, and I felt an even more intense pleasure than the first time.

"One evening he lay on top of me, he put his sex between my thighs. He said, 'Close your legs, close them tight, don't let me enter, I don't want to hurt you.'

"For years we made love this way, but one night I couldn't resist anymore. My desire for him was too strong. I spread my legs, I was completely open, he entered me."

She stops talking. She looks at Lucas, her large dark eyes shining, her fleshy lips parted. She uncovers a breast and asks, "Do you want to?"

Lucas grabs her by the hair, drags her into the bedroom, throws her onto Grandmother's bed, and bites her neck as he takes her.

During the following days Lucas goes back to the bars. He starts walking again through the empty streets of the town.

When he gets home, he goes straight to his room.

One evening, however, coming home drunk, he opens the door of Grandmother's room. It is illuminated by the light from the kitchen. Yasmine is asleep, as is the child.

Lucas undresses and climbs into Yasmine's bed. Yasmine's body is burning, Lucas's is frozen. She is facing the wall. He presses against her back, puts his sex between Yasmine's thighs.

She closes her thighs, she moans.

"Father, oh father!"

Lucas whispers in her ear, "Tighter. Grip tighter."

She struggles, she has trouble breathing. He penetrates her. She screams.

Lucas puts his hand over Yasmine's mouth, pulls the pillow over her head. "Be quiet. You'll wake the baby!"

She bites his fingers, sucks his thumb.

When it's over, they lie there for a few minutes, then Lucas gets up.

Yasmine cries.

Lucas goes into his room.

It is summer. The child is everywhere. In Grandmother's room, in the kitchen, in the garden. He crawls around on all fours.

He is hunchbacked, deformed. His legs are too thin, his arms too long, his body ill-proportioned.

He also comes into Lucas's room. He beats on the door with his little fists until Lucas opens it. He climbs onto the bed.

Lucas puts a record on the gramophone and the child rocks on the bed.

Lucas puts on another record and the child hides under the covers.

Lucas picks up a piece of paper, draws a rabbit, a chicken, a pig. The child laughs and kisses the paper.

Lucas draws a giraffe and an elephant. The child shakes his head and tears up the paper.

Lucas constructs a sandpit for the child. He buys him a spade, a watering can, and a wheelbarrow.

He makes him a swing. He builds him a car from a box and some wheels. He sits the child in the box and pulls him around. He shows him the fish. He lets him go inside the rabbit hutch. The child tries to stroke the rabbits, but the rabbits run off crazily in all directions.

The child cries.

Lucas goes into town and buys a teddy bear.

The child looks at the bear. He takes it, talks to it, shakes it, and throws it at Lucas's feet.

Yasmine picks up the bear. She strokes it. "He's a nice bear. He's a lovely little teddy bear."

The child looks at his mother and bangs his head against the floor of the kitchen. Yasmine puts the bear down and takes the child in her arms. The child starts bawling. He pummels his mother's head and kicks her in the stomach. Yasmine lets him down, and the child hides under the table until evening.

That evening, Lucas brings back a tiny kitten he has saved

from Joseph's pitchfork. Standing on the kitchen floor, the little animal mews and trembles all over.

Yasmine places a bowl of milk in front of it. The cat continues mewing.

Yasmine places the cat in the child's cradle.

The child climbs into his cradle, lies down next to the little cat, cuddles up to it. The cat struggles and claws the child on the face and hands.

A few days later, the cat eats everything it is given and sleeps in the cradle at the child's feet.

Lucas asks Joseph to get him a little dog.

One day, Joseph turns up with a black puppy with long curly hair. Yasmine is hanging out the washing in the garden; the child is having a nap. Yasmine knocks on Lucas's door. She shouts, "Someone to see you!"

She hides in Grandmother's room.

Lucas goes out to meet Joseph. Joseph says, "Here's the dog I promised you. It's a sheepdog from the plains. It'll be a good guard dog."

Lucas says, "Thank you, Joseph. Come in and have a glass of wine."

They go into the kitchen; they drink some wine. Joseph asks, "Won't you introduce me to your wife?"

Lucas says, "Yasmine is not my wife. She had nowhere to go, so I took her in."

Joseph says, "The whole town knows her story. She's a fine-looking girl. The puppy is for her child, I presume."

"Yes, for Yasmine's child."

Before leaving, Joseph says, "You're very young to be taking care of a woman and a child, Lucas. It's a big responsibility."

Lucas says, "That's my business."

Once Joseph has gone, Yasmine comes out. Lucas is holding the little dog in his arms.

"Look what Joseph brought for Mathias."

Yasmine says, "He saw me. Did he say anything?"

"Yes. He thinks you're very beautiful. You're wrong to worry about what people might think about us, Yasmine. You should come with me into town one day to buy yourself some clothes. You've been wearing the same dress since you got here."

"One dress is enough. I don't need another one. I won't go into town."

Lucas says, "Come on, let's show Mathias the dog."

The child is underneath the kitchen table with the cat.

Yasmine says, "Mathi, it's for you. It's a present."

Lucas sits on the corner seat with the dog. The child climbs onto his knees. He looks at the dog, pulls back the hair covering its muzzle. The dog licks the child's face. The cat hisses at the dog and runs away into the garden.

It is getting progressively colder. Lucas says to Yasmine, "Mathias needs warm clothes. So do you."

Yasmine says, "I can knit. I'll need some wool and some needles."

Lucas buys a basket of balls of wool and several pairs of needles for knitting different thicknesses. Yasmine knits pullovers, socks, scarves, gloves, hats. With the leftover wool she makes up patchwork blankets. Lucas praises her.

Yasmine says, "I can also sew. At home I had my mother's old sewing machine."

"Do you want me to go and fetch it?"

"You'd be brave enough to go to my aunt's house?"

Lucas sets off with the wheelbarrow. He knocks at the door of Yasmine's aunt. A youthful-looking woman comes to the door.

"What do you want?"

"I've come to collect Yasmine's sewing machine."

She says, "Come in."

Lucas goes into a very clean kitchen. Yasmine's aunt stares at him.

"So you're the one. Poor boy. You're only a child."

Lucas says, "I'm seventeen."

"And she will soon be nineteen. How is she?"

"Well."

"And the child?"

"Also very well."

After a silence she says, "I heard that the child was born deformed. It is God's punishment."

Lucas asks, "Where is the sewing machine?"

The aunt opens a door to a narrow room without a window.

"Everything that belongs to her is here. Take it."

There is a sewing machine and a wicker basket. Lucas asks, "There was nothing else here?"

"Her bed. I burned it."

Lucas carries the sewing machine and the basket to the wheelbarrow. He says, "Thank you, madame."

"You're welcome. Good riddance."

It rains a lot. Yasmine sews and knits. The child has to play indoors. He spends the day under the table with the dog and the cat.

The child can already say a few words, but he can't walk yet. When Lucas tries to stand him upright, he struggles free, crawls away on all fours, and escapes under the table.

Lucas goes to the bookseller's. He picks out some large sheets of white paper, some colored pencils, and some picture books.

Victor asks, "You have a child?"

"Yes. But he's not mine."

Victor says, "There are so many orphans. Peter was asking after you. You should go and see him."

Lucas says, "I'm very busy."

"I understand. With a child. At your age."

Lucas goes home. The child is asleep on a rug under the kitchen table. In Grandmother's room Yasmine is sewing. Lucas puts the packet down next to the child. He goes into the bedroom and kisses Yasmine on the neck, and Yasmine stops sewing.

The child draws. He draws the dog and the cat. He also draws other animals. He draws trees, flowers, the house. He also draws his mother.

Lucas asks him, "Why don't you ever draw me?"

The child shakes his head and hides under the table with his books.

On Christmas Eve, Lucas chops down a Christmas tree in the forest. He buys some colored glass balls and some candles. In Grandmother's room he decorates the tree with Yasmine's help. The presents go under the tree: material and a pair of warm boots for Yasmine, a thick sweater for Lucas, books and a rocking horse for Mathias.

Yasmine roasts a duck in the oven. She cooks potatoes, cabbage, beans. The biscuits were made some days ago.

When the first star appears in the sky, Lucas lights the candles on the tree. Yasmine comes into the room with Mathias in her arms.

Lucas says, "Go and get your presents, Mathias. The books and the horse are for you."

The child says, "I want the horse. He's nice, the horse."

He tries unsuccessfully to climb on the horse's back. He cries.

"The horse is too big. Lucas did it. He's a nasty Lucas. He made the horse too big for Mathi."

The child cries and bangs his head against the floor of the bedroom. Lucas picks him up; he shakes him.

"The horse isn't too big. It's Mathias who is too small because he won't stand up. Always on all fours like an animal! You're not an animal!"

He is holding the child's chin to force him to look into his eyes. He says firmly, "If you don't walk now you will never walk. Never, do you understand?"

The child starts bawling. Yasmine grabs him from Lucas.

"Leave him alone! He'll walk soon enough."

She sits the child on the horse's back. She holds him upright.

Lucas says, "I have to go. Put the child to bed and wait for me. I won't be long."

He goes into the kitchen. He cuts the roast duck in two, puts half on a warm plate, surrounds it with vegetables and potatoes, and wraps the plate in a cloth. The meal is still warm when he arrives at the priest's house.

After they have eaten, Lucas says, "I'm sorry, Father, I have to go home. I'm expected."

The priest says, "I know, my son. To be honest, I'm surprised you came this evening. I know that you live in sin with a sinful woman, and with the fruit of her immoral love. That child isn't even baptized, although he bears the name of one of our saints."

Lucas is silent.

The priest says, "Come to mass, both of you, if only for this evening."

Lucas says, "We can't leave the child alone."

"Then come yourself."

Lucas says, "You're talking down to me, Father."

"Forgive me, Lucas. I was carried away by my anger. But it's because I think of you as my own son, and I fear for your immortal soul."

Lucas says, "Treat me as your son, Father. It pleases me. But you know very well I never go to church."

Lucas goes home. All the lights in Grandmother's house are out. The cat and the dog are asleep in the kitchen. The other half of the roast duck stands uneaten on the table.

Lucas tries to go into the bedroom. The door is locked. He knocks. Yasmine doesn't answer.

Lucas goes into town. Candles burn in the windows. The bars are closed. Lucas wanders through the streets for a long time, then he goes into the church. The big church is cold, almost empty. Lucas leans against the wall next to the door. Far off, at the other end of the church, the priest conducts mass at the altar.

Lucas feels a hand on his shoulder. Peter says, "Come on, Lucas. Let's go."

Outside he asks, "What were you doing there?"

"What about you, Peter?"

"I followed you. I saw you as I was leaving Victor's."

Lucas says, "I feel lost in this town when the bars are closed."

"I feel lost here all the time. Come back to my place to warm yourself up before you go home."

Peter lives in a beautiful house in the main square. There are deep armchairs, bookcases covering the walls; it is warm. Peter brings out the brandy.

"I have no friends in this town apart from Victor, who is kind and cultured, but rather boring. He never stops complaining."

Lucas goes to sleep. At daybreak, when he wakes up, Peter is still there, sitting opposite, watching him.

The following summer the child stands upright. Clinging to the dog's back, he shouts, "Lucas! Look! Look!"

Lucas rushes in. The child says, "Mathi is bigger than the dog. Mathi can stand."

The dog moves away, the child falls. Lucas takes him in his arms, he lifts him over his head, he says, "Mathias is bigger than Lucas!"

The child laughs. The next day, Lucas buys him a tricycle.

Yasmine says to Lucas, "You spend too much money on toys."

Lucas says, "The tricycle will help his legs develop."

By autumn the child is walking with confidence, but with a pronounced limp.

One morning, Lucas says to Yasmine, "After lunch, bathe the child and dress him in clean clothes. I'm taking him to a doctor."

"To a doctor? Why?"

"Can't you see he's limping?"

Yasmine replies, "It's a miracle he's even walking."

Lucas says, "I want him to walk like everyone else."

Yasmine's eyes fill with tears. "I accept him as he is."

When the child has been washed and dressed, Lucas takes him by the hand.

"We're going for a long walk, Mathias. When you feel tired, I'll carry you."

Yasmine asks, "You're going to walk across town with him, all the way to the hospital?"

"Why not?"

"People will look at you. You could bump into my aunt."

Lucas doesn't answer.

Yasmine continues, "If they want to keep him, you won't let them, will you, Lucas?"

Lucas says, "What a question!"

When he comes back from the hospital, Lucas says simply, "You were right, Yasmine."

He locks himself in his room, listens to records. When the child beats on his door, he doesn't open it.

That evening, after Yasmine has put the child to bed, Lucas comes into Grandmother's room. As on every other evening he sits beside the cradle and tells Mathias a story. When he finishes the story, he says, "Your cradle will soon be too small for you. I'll have to make you a bed."

The child says, "We'll keep the cradle for the dog and the cat."

"Yes, we'll keep the cradle. I'll also build you some shelves for the books you already own and all the ones I'm going to buy you."

The child says, "Tell me another story."

"I have to go to work."

"People don't work at night."

"I work all the time. I have to earn lots of money."

"What's money for?"

"To buy the things we need, the three of us."

"Clothes and shoes?"

"Yes. And toys, books, and records."

"Toys and books, that's good. Go to work."

Lucas says, "And you go to sleep, so you can grow bigger."

The child says, "I'll never grow bigger, you know that. The doctor said so."

"You misunderstood, Mathias. You will grow. Not as quickly as the other children, but you will grow."

The child asks, "Why not as quickly?"

"Because everyone is different. You won't be as big as the others, but you'll be more intelligent. Your size isn't important. Only intelligence matters."

Lucas goes out. But instead of going into town he goes down to the river. He sits on the damp grass and stares into the dark, muddy water.

3

Lucas says to Victor, "These children's books are all the same. The stories in them are stupid. They're not good enough for a child of four."

Victor shrugs his shoulders. "What can I do? It's the same for adults. Look. Novels written to the greater glory of the regime. You'd think there weren't any writers left in our country."

Lucas says, "Yes, I know those novels. They're not worth the paper they're printed on. What has happened to the old books?"

"Banned. Disappeared. Pulled out of circulation. You might find some at the library, if it still exists."

"A library here in this town? I never knew there was one. Where is it?"

"The first street on the left after the castle. I can't tell you the name of the street, it keeps changing all the time. They're constantly renaming all the streets."

Lucas says, "I'll find it."

The street that Victor described is empty of people. Lucas

waits. An old man comes out of a house. Lucas asks him, "Do you know where the library is?"

The old man points to an old, gray, dilapidated building.

"It's there. But not for much longer, I think. It seems like they're moving out. Every week a truck arrives to take away a load of books."

Lucas goes into the gray building. He goes down a long, dark corridor, which ends at a glass-paneled door with a rusted plaque reading PUBLIC LIBRARY.

Lucas knocks. A woman's voice replies, "Come in!"

Lucas enters a huge room lit by the setting sun. A gray-haired woman is sitting behind a desk. She asks, "What do you want?"

"I'd like to borrow some books."

The woman takes off her glasses and looks at Lucas.

"Borrow some books? Since I've been here no one has come to borrow books."

"Have you been here long?"

"For two years. It's my job to put this place in order. I have to sort out the books and eliminate any that are on the index."

"What happens then? What do you do with them?"

"I put them in boxes and they are taken off to be pulped."

"Are there many books on the index?"

"Almost all of them."

Lucas looks at the large boxes filled with books.

"It's a sad job you've got."

She asks, "Do you like books?"

"I've read all the priest's books. He has a lot, but some of them aren't very interesting."

She smiles. "I can believe that."

"I've also read the ones you can buy in the shops. They are even less interesting."

She smiles again. "What sort of books would you like to read?"

"The books on the index."

She puts her glasses back on. She says, "I'm sorry, that's impossible. Go away now."

Lucas doesn't move. She repeats, "I told you to go away."

Lucas says, "You look like my mother."

"In her younger days, I trust."

"No. My mother was younger than you when she died."

She says, "Forgive me. I'm sorry."

"My mother still had dark hair. You have gray hair and you wear glasses."

The woman gets up. "It's five o'clock. I'm closing."

Out in the street Lucas says, "I'll walk with you. Let me carry your basket. It looks very heavy."

They walk in silence. Near the station, at a small, low house, she stops.

"I live here. Thank you. What is your name?"

"Lucas."

"Thank you, Lucas."

She takes back her basket. Lucas asks, "What's inside it?"

"Charcoal briquettes."

The next day, late in the afternoon, Lucas returns to the library. The gray-haired woman is sitting at her desk.

Lucas says, "You forgot to lend me a book yesterday."

"I told you it's impossible."

Lucas takes a book from one of the big boxes.

"Let me take just one. This one."

She raises her voice. "You haven't even looked at the title. Put that book back in the box and leave!"

Lucas puts the book back in the box.

"Don't get angry. I won't take a book. I'll wait till you close."

"You'll do no such thing! Get out of here, you damn trouble-maker! It's disgraceful, at your age!" She starts sobbing. "When will they stop spying on me, watching me, suspecting me?"

Lucas leaves the library. He sits on the steps of the house opposite. He waits. Shortly after five o'clock the woman comes out, smiling.

"Forgive me. I'm so afraid. Afraid all the time. Of everyone."

Lucas says, "I won't ask you for any more books. I came back only because you remind me of my mother." He takes a photo from his pocket. "Look."

She looks at the photo. "I can't see any resemblance. Your mother is young, beautiful, elegant."

Lucas asks, "Why do you wear flat-heeled shoes, and that colorless dress? Why do you go around like an old woman?"

She says, "I'm thirty-five years old."

"My mother was that old in the photo. You could at least dye your hair."

"My hair went white in the space of a single night. It was the night *they* hanged my husband for high treason. That was three years ago."

She hands her basket to Lucas.

"Walk with me."

Outside her house, Lucas asks, "Can I come in?"

"No one comes into my house."

"Why?"

"I don't know anyone in this town."

"You know me now."

She smiles. "Yes. Come in, Lucas."

In the kitchen, Lucas says, "I don't know your name. I don't want to call you 'madame.' "

"My name is Clara. You can carry the basket into the bedroom and empty it next to the stove. I'll make some tea."

Lucas empties the charcoal briquettes into a wooden box. He goes to the window; he sees the small, overgrown garden, and beyond that a railway embankment infested with weeds.

Clara comes into the room.

"I forgot to buy sugar."

She puts a tray on the table. She comes up to Lucas.

"It's quiet here. There are no trains anymore."

Lucas says, "It's a nice house."

"It's a civil service house. It used to belong to some people who fled the country."

"The furniture too?"

"The furniture in this room, yes. The furniture in the other room is mine. My bed, my desk, my bookcase."

Lucas asks, "Can I see your room?"

"Another time, perhaps. Come and drink your tea."

Lucas takes a sip of bitter tea, then says, "I have to go, I've got work to do. But I could come back later."

She says, "No, don't come back. I go to bed very early to save on charcoal."

When Lucas gets home, Yasmine and Mathias are in the kitchen. Yasmine says, "The little one wouldn't go to bed without you. I've already fed the animals, and I've milked the goats."

Lucas tells Mathias a story. Then he goes to the priest's house. Finally he goes back to the little house on Station Street. There are no lights on.

Lucas waits in the street. Clara comes out of the library. She hasn't got her basket. She says to Lucas, "Surely you don't intend to wait for me every day?"

"Why not? Does it bother you?"

"Yes. It's stupid and pointless."

Lucas says, "I'd like to walk back with you."

"I haven't got my basket. Besides, I'm not going straight home. I've got some shopping to do."

Lucas asks, "Can I come around later this evening?"

"No!"

"Why not? It's Friday today. You don't have to work tomorrow. You don't have to go to bed early."

Clara says, "That's enough! Don't interest yourself in me, or the time I go to bed. Stop waiting for me and following me like a little dog."

"So I won't see you until Monday?"

She sighs and shakes her head. "Not on Monday, not on any day. Stop pestering me, Lucas, please. What do you want from me?"

Lucas says, "I like seeing you. Even in your old dress and with your gray hair."

"Don't be impertinent!"

Clara turns on her heel and heads off in the direction of the main square. Lucas follows her.

Clara goes into a clothes shop, then into a shoe shop. Lucas waits a long time. Then she goes into a grocery shop. She is fully laden as she sets off down the road to Station Street. Lucas catches up with her.

"Let me help you."

Clara speaks without stopping. "Don't bother me! Go away! Don't let me see you again!"

"Very well, Clara. You won't see me again."

Lucas goes home. Yasmine says to him, "Mathias is already in bed."

"Already? Why?"

"I think he's sulking."

Lucas goes into Grandmother's room.

"Are you asleep, Mathias?"

The child doesn't answer. Lucas leaves the room. Yasmine asks, "Will you be back late this evening?"

"It's Friday."

She says, "We make enough from the garden and the animals. You should stop playing in the bars, Lucas. It's not worth spending the whole night there for the few pennies you earn."

Lucas doesn't answer. He does his evening chores and goes to the priest's house.

The priest says, "We haven't played chess for ages."

Lucas says, "I'm very busy at the moment."

He goes into town, enters a bar, plays the harmonica. He drinks. He drinks in all the bars in town, and goes back to Clara's house.

At the kitchen window there is a crack of light through the curtains. Lucas walks around the block, then comes back along the railway line. He goes into Clara's garden. On this side the curtains are thinner; Lucas makes out two silhouettes in the room where he was yesterday. A man paces up and down in the room. Clara is leaning on the stove. The man approaches her, withdraws, approaches her again. He is speaking. Lucas hears his voice but can't make out the words.

The two silhouettes join. They stay like that a long time. They separate. The light goes on in the bedroom. The living room is now empty.

When Lucas goes to the other window, the light goes out.

Lucas goes back to the front of the house. Hidden in the shadows, he waits.

Early in the morning a man leaves Clara's house and walks off quickly. Lucas follows him. The man goes into one of the houses in the main square.

Back home, Lucas goes into the kitchen for a drink of water. Yasmine comes out of Grandmother's room.

"I waited for you all night. It's six o'clock in the morning. Where were you?"

"In the street."

"What's wrong, Lucas?"

She reaches out a hand to touch his face. Lucas brushes it away, walks out of the kitchen, and locks himself in his room.

On Saturday evening, Lucas goes from one bar to another. The people are drunk and generous.

Suddenly, through a cloud of smoke, Lucas sees her. She is sitting alone, near the entrance; she is drinking red wine. Lucas sits at her table.

"Clara! What are you doing here?"

"I couldn't sleep. I wanted to be with people."

"These people?"

"Any people. I can't stay in the house alone, always alone."

"You weren't alone yesterday evening."

Clara doesn't reply, she pours some wine, she drinks. Lucas takes the glass from her hands.

"You've had enough!"

She laughs. "No. I've never had enough. I want to drink and go on drinking."

"Not here! Not with them!"

Lucas grips Clara's wrist. She looks at him, she murmurs, "I was looking for you."

"You didn't want to see me."

She doesn't reply; she turns her head away.

The customers are demanding some music.

Lucas throws some coins onto the table. "Come!"

He takes Clara by the arm, he leads her to the exit. Remarks and rude laughter follow them out.

Outside, it is raining. Clara staggers; she trips on her high heels. Lucas virtually has to carry her.

In her room, she falls onto the bed. She shivers. Lucas takes off her shoes and covers her up. He goes into the other room. He lights a fire in the stove that warms up the two rooms. He makes some tea in the kitchen. He brings two cups.

Clara says, "There's some rum in the kitchen cupboard."

Lucas brings the rum. He pours some into the cups.

Clara says, "You're too young to drink."

Lucas says, "I'm twenty. I learned to drink at the age of twelve."

Clara closes her eyes. "I'm almost old enough to be your mother."

Later she says, "Stay here. Don't leave me alone."

Lucas sits at the desk, he looks around the room. Apart from the bed, there is only the big desk and a small shelf of books. He looks at the books. They are of no interest; he is familiar with them.

Clara sleeps. Her arm is hanging out of the bed. Lucas takes hold of the arm. He kisses the back of the hand, then the palm. He licks it, running his tongue up to her elbow. Clara doesn't move.

It is warm now. Lucas pulls back the eiderdown. Clara's body lies before him, white and black. While Lucas was in the kitchen, Clara took off her skirt and sweater. Now Lucas takes off her black stockings, her black suspenders, her black bra. He covers up her white body with the eiderdown. Then he burns her underwear in the stove in the next room. He pulls up an armchair and settles down next to the bed. He notices a book on the ground. He looks at it. It is an old, worn-out book. The flyleaf bears the library stamp. Lucas reads. The hours pass.

Clara begins to moan. Her eyes remain closed, her face is covered with sweat. She tosses her head from side to side on the pillow and mutters incomprehensibly.

Lucas goes into the kitchen, dampens a cloth and lays it on Clara's forehead. Her mutterings turn into screams.

Lucas shakes her to wake her up. She opens her eyes.

"In the desk drawer. Tranquilizers. A white box."

Lucas finds the tranquilizers. Clara takes two with the remains of the cold tea. She says, "It's nothing. It's always the same nightmare."

She closes her eyes. When her breathing becomes regular, Lucas leaves. He takes the book.

He walks slowly in the rain through the deserted streets to Grandmother's house, on the other side of town.

On Sunday afternoon, Lucas goes back to Clara's house. He knocks on the kitchen door.

Clara asks, "Who is it?"

"It's me, Lucas."

Clara opens the door. She looks pale. She is wearing an old red dressing gown.

"What do you want?"

Lucas says, "I was passing by. I just wondered if you were all right."

"Yes, I feel fine."

Her hand, which holds the door, is trembling.

Lucas says, "Forgive me. I was afraid."

"Of what? You don't need to be afraid on my account."

Lucas whispers, "Clara, please, let me in."

Clara shakes her head. "You're very persistent, Lucas. Come in, then, and have some coffee."

They sit in the kitchen, they drink coffee.

Clara asks, "What happened last night?"

"You don't remember?"

"No. I've been receiving treatment since the death of my husband. The medication I'm on sometimes has a disastrous effect on my memory."

"I brought you home from the bar. If you're under medication you should stay off alcohol."

She buries her face in her hands. "You can't imagine what I've been through."

Lucas says, "I know the pain of separation."

"The death of your mother."

"And something else besides. The loss of a brother who was as one with me."

Clara raises her head. She looks at Lucas.

"We too, Thomas and I, we were a single being. *They* killed him. Did they also kill your brother?"

"No. He went away. He went across the border."

"Why didn't you go with him?"

"One of us had to stay behind to look after the animals, the garden, Grandmother's house. We also had to learn to live without each other. Alone."

Clara rests her hand on Lucas's.

"What is his name?"

"Claus."

"He'll come back. Thomas will never come back."

Lucas gets up. "Do you want me to light the fire in the room? Your hands are frozen."

Clara says, "That would be nice. I'll make some pancakes. I haven't eaten anything today."

Lucas cleans the stove. There is no trace of the black underwear. He lights the fire and comes back into the kitchen.

"There's no charcoal left."

Clara says, "I'll go and get some from the cellar." She picks up a tin bucket.

Lucas says, "Let me do it."

"No! There's no light. I know my way."

Lucas sits in the armchair in the living room. He takes Clara's book out of his pocket. He reads.

Clara brings in the pancakes.

Lucas asks, "Who is he, your lover?"

"You spied on me?"

Lucas says, "It was for him that you bought the black underwear, it was for him that you wore high heels. You should have dyed your hair while you were at it."

Clara says, "That's none of your business. What are you reading?"

Lucas hands her the book.

"I borrowed it from you yesterday. I liked it very much."

"You had no right to take it away with you. I have to return it to the library."

"Don't be angry, Clara. I'm sorry."

Clara turns away.

"What about my underwear? Did you borrow that, too?"

"No. I burned it."

"You burned it? What gave you the right?"

Lucas gets up.

"I think it's best if I leave."

"Yes, go on. They're expecting you."

"Who's expecting me?"

"A wife and child, by all accounts."

"Yasmine is not my wife."

"She's been living with you for four years with her child."

"He's not my child, but he belongs to me now."

On Monday, Lucas waits opposite the library. Evening comes and Clara does not appear. Lucas goes into the old, gray building, walks down the long corridor, knocks at the glass-paneled door. There is no answer; the door is locked.

Lucas runs to Clara's house. He enters without knocking, goes into the kitchen, then the living room. The door to the bedroom is half open. Lucas calls, "Clara?"

"Come in, Lucas."

Lucas goes into the room. Clara is in bed. Lucas sits on the edge of the bed, takes Clara's hand. It is burning hot. He touches her forehead.

"I'll go get a doctor."

"No, it's not worth it. It's only a chill. I've got a headache and a sore throat, that's all."

"Do you have any medicine for aches and fever?"

"No, nothing. I'll see how I feel tomorrow. For now just light the fire and make some tea."

While drinking the tea she says, "Thank you for coming, Lucas."

"You knew I'd come back."

"I hoped so. It's awful being ill when you're on your own."

Lucas says, "You'll never be alone again, Clara."

Clara presses Lucas's hand against her cheek. "I've treated you badly."

"You treated me like a dog. It doesn't matter."

He strokes Clara's hair, which is wet with perspiration.

"Try to sleep. I'll go get some medicine and come back."

"The pharmacy is probably already closed."

"I'll make them open up."

Lucas runs to the main square. He rings the bell of the only pharmacist in town. He rings several times. Finally a small window opens in the wooden door. The pharmacist asks, "What do you want?"

"Medicine for fever and aches. It's urgent."

"Do you have a prescription?"

"I haven't had the time to see a doctor."

"That doesn't surprise me. The problem is that it's more expensive without a prescription."

"That doesn't matter."

Lucas takes a bill from his pocket. The pharmacist brings him a bottle of tablets.

Lucas runs to Grandmother's house. Yasmine and the child are in the kitchen. Yasmine says, "I've already taken care of the animals."

"Thank you, Yasmine. Could you take the priest his meal tonight? I'm in a hurry."

Yasmine says, "I don't know the priest. I don't want to see him."

"You only have to leave the basket on the kitchen table."

Yasmine is silent; she looks at Lucas.

Lucas turns to Mathias. "This evening Yasmine will tell you a story."

The child says, "Yasmine can't tell stories."

"Well, you tell her one. And you can draw me a nice picture."

"Yes, a nice picture."

Lucas goes back to Clara. He dissolves two tablets in a glass of water, he takes it to Clara.

"Drink it."

Clara obeys. Soon she is asleep.

Lucas goes down into the cellar with his flashlight. In the corner there is a small pile of charcoal, and there are sacks lined along the wall. Some of the sacks are open; others are tied up with string. Lucas looks in one of the sacks: it is full of potatoes. He unties the string on another sack: it contains charcoal briquettes. He tips the contents of the sack onto the floor; four or five briquettes and two dozen books fall out. Lucas picks out a book and puts the others back in the sack. He goes back upstairs with the book and the bucket of charcoal.

Sitting beside Clara's bed, he reads.

The next morning, Clara asks, "You stayed here all night?"

"Yes. I slept very well."

He makes some tea, gives Clara the tablets, relights the fire. Clara takes her temperature. She is still feverish.

Lucas says, "Stay in bed. I'll come back at noon. What would you like to eat?"

She says, "I'm not hungry. But can I ask you to go to the council office to tell them I'm out sick?"

"I will. Don't worry."

Lucas goes to the council office. Then he goes home, kills a chicken, and boils it up with some vegetables. At noon, he takes some soup to Clara. She drinks a little.

Lucas says to her, "I went down into the cellar yesterday for the charcoal. I saw the books. You carried them in your basket, didn't you?"

She says, "Yes. I couldn't bear the thought of *them* destroying them all."

"Will you allow me to read them?"

"Read all you want. But be careful. I'm risking imprisonment."

"I know."

In the late afternoon, Lucas goes home. There's nothing to do in the garden at this time of year. Lucas sees to the animals, then listens to records in his room. The child knocks; Lucas lets him in.

The child climbs onto the double bed. He asks, "Why is Yasmine crying?"

"She's crying?"

"Yes. Nearly all the time. Why?"

"Hasn't she told you why?"

"I'm afraid to ask her."

Lucas turns away to change the record.

"She's probably crying for her father, who is in prison."

"What's prison?"

"It's a big building with bars in the windows. They lock people up there."

"Why?"

"For all sorts of reasons. They say that they are dangerous. My father was also locked up."

The child raises his large, dark eyes to Lucas.

"Could they lock you up as well?"

"Yes, me as well."

The child sniffs, his little lip trembles.

"And me?"

Lucas lifts him onto his knees, he kisses him.

"No, not you. They don't lock up children."

"But when I grow up?"

Lucas says, "Things will have changed by then and no one will be locked up anymore."

The child is silent for a moment, then asks, "The ones who are locked up will never be able to get out of prison!"

Lucas says, "They will get out someday."

"Yasmine's father as well?"

"Yes, of course."

"And she'll stop crying?"

"Yes, she'll stop crying."

"And will your father get out too?"

"He already got out."

"Where is he?"

"He's dead. He had an accident."

"If he hadn't got out, he wouldn't have had an accident."

Lucas says, "I have to go now. Go back to the kitchen, and don't talk to Yasmine about her father. You'll make her cry even more. Be nice and obedient to her."

Standing in the kitchen doorway, Yasmine asks, "You're going out, Lucas?"

Lucas halts at the garden gate. He doesn't answer.

Yasmine says, "I'd just like to know if I have to go to the priest's house myself again."

"If you would, Yasmine. I haven't got the time."

Lucas spends his nights by Clara's side until Friday.

On Friday morning Clara says, "I feel better. I'll go back to work on Monday. You don't have to spend your nights here. You've given me so much of your time."

"What do you mean, Clara?"

"I'd like to be alone this evening."

"*He* is coming! Is that it?"

She lowers her eyes and doesn't reply.

Lucas says, "You can't do this to me!"

Clara looks Lucas in the eyes. "You reproached me for acting like an old woman. You were right. I'm still young."

Lucas asks, "Who is he? Why does he only come on Fridays? Why doesn't he marry you?"

"He's already married."

Clara cries.

Lucas asks, "Why are you crying? I should be the one who's crying."

In the evening, Lucas goes to the bar. After closing time, he walks around the streets. It is snowing. Lucas stops in front of Peter's house. The windows are dark. Lucas rings; no one answers. Lucas rings again.

A window opens. Peter asks, "Who's there?"

"It's me. Lucas."

"Stay there, Lucas. I'm coming."

The window closes and soon the door opens. Peter says, "Come in, lost soul."

Peter is in his dressing gown. Lucas says, "I woke you. I'm sorry."

"It's not important. Sit down."

Lucas sits in a leather armchair.

"I can't face going home in this cold. It's too far, and I've had too much to drink. Can I sleep here?"

"Of course, Lucas. Take my bed. I'll sleep on the sofa."

"I prefer the sofa. So I can leave when I wake up without disturbing you."

"As you wish, Lucas. Make yourself comfortable. I'll fetch a blanket."

Lucas takes off his jacket and his boots. He lies down on the sofa. Peter returns with a thick blanket. He lays it over Lucas and puts some cushions under his head. He sits down next to him on the sofa.

"What's wrong, Lucas? Is it about Yasmine?"

Lucas shakes his head. "Everything at home is fine. I just wanted to see you."

Peter says, "I don't believe you."

Lucas takes Peter's hand and presses it to his abdomen. Peter pulls his hand away. He gets up.

"No, Lucas. Don't come into this world of mine."

He goes to his room, closes the door.

Lucas waits. A few hours later he gets up. He opens the door quietly, approaches Peter's bed. Peter is asleep. Lucas leaves the room, closes the door, pulls on his boots, picks up his jacket, checks to see that his weapons are still in the pocket, and leaves the house without a sound. He goes to Station Road. He waits outside Clara's house.

A man leaves the house. Lucas follows him, then passes him on the other side of the street. To get home, the man has to go past a small park. There Lucas hides himself behind some bushes. He wraps the large red scarf knitted by Yasmine around his head, and when the man arrives, he stands up in front of him. He recognizes him. It is one of the doctors from the hospital who examined Mathias.

The doctor says, "Who are you? What do you want?"

Lucas grabs the man by the lapel of his coat, pulls a razor from his pocket.

"If you go to see her again I'll cut your throat."

"You're insane! I've just been on night duty at the hospital."

"Don't bother lying. I'm not joking. I'm capable of anything. Today is just a warning."

Lucas takes a stocking full of gravel from his jacket pocket and strikes the man on the head with it. The man falls senseless to the icy ground.

Lucas goes back to Peter's, lies down on the sofa, and goes to sleep. Peter wakes him at seven o'clock with some coffee.

"I came to check on you earlier. I thought you had gone home."

Lucas says, "I haven't moved from here all night. It's important, Peter."

Peter looks at him long and hard. "I understand, Lucas."

Lucas goes home. Yasmine says to him, "A policeman came. You have to go to the police station. What has happened, Lucas?"

Mathias says, "They are going to lock Lucas up in prison. And Lucas will never come home."

The child snickers. Yasmine grabs his arm and slaps him. "Will you shut up?"

Lucas grabs the child from Yasmine and takes him in his arms. He wipes the tears from his face.

"Don't be afraid, Mathias. They won't lock me up."

The child stares Lucas straight in the eyes. He stops crying. He says, "Too bad."

Lucas presents himself at the police station. He is shown the way to the commissioner's office. Lucas knocks and enters. Clara and the doctor are sitting with a policeman.

The commissioner says, "Hello, Lucas. Sit down."

Lucas sits on a chair next to the man he knocked out a few hours previously.

The commissioner asks, "Do you recognize your attacker, doctor?"

"I wasn't attacked, I told you. I slipped on the ice."

"And you fell on your back. Our officers found you lying on your back. It's strange that you have a lump on your forehead."

"I probably fell forward, then turned over as I began to regain consciousness."

The commissioner says, "Of course. You claim that you were on night duty at the hospital. According to our information you left the hospital at nine o'clock in the evening, and you spent the night with this lady."

The doctor says, "I didn't want to compromise her."

The commissioner turns to Lucas. "The lady's neighbors have seen you enter her house on numerous occasions."

Lucas says, "I've been doing her shopping for her for some time. Especially last week when she was ill."

"We know that you didn't go home last night. Where were you?"

"I was too tired to go home. When the bars closed I went to a friend's house and spent the night there. I left at half past seven."

"Who is this friend? A drinking buddy, I suppose."

"No. He's the Party Secretary."

"You claim you spent the night at the Party Secretary's house?"

"Yes. He made me some coffee at seven o'clock this morning."

The commissioner leaves the room.

The doctor turns to Lucas, stares at him. Lucas returns his gaze. The doctor looks at Clara. Clara looks out of the window.

The doctor stares straight ahead; he says, "I haven't brought charges against you, even though I recognize you perfectly. It was some border guards on patrol who found me and brought me here, like a common drunk. This is all very unfortunate for me. I ask you for your total discretion. I am an internationally renowned psychiatrist. I have children."

Lucas says, "Your only solution is to leave this town. It's a small town. Sooner or later, everyone will know. Even your wife."

"Is that a threat?"

"Yes."

"I've been assigned to this godforsaken hole. It's not for me to decide where I go."

"It doesn't matter. Ask for a transfer."

The commissioner comes in with Peter. Peter looks at Lucas, then at Clara, then at the doctor. The commissioner says, "Your alibi is confirmed, Lucas."

He turns to the doctor. "I think we'll leave it there, doctor. You slipped while returning from the hospital. The case is closed."

The doctor asks Peter, "Can I see you on Monday at your office? I wish to leave this town."

Peter says, "Certainly. You can count on my help."

The doctor gets up, offers Clara his hand. "I'm sorry."

Clara turns her head away. The doctor leaves the room, saying, "Thank you, gentlemen."

Lucas says to Clara, "I'll walk you home."

Clara goes out ahead of him without saying a word.

Lucas and Peter also leave the commissioner's office. Peter watches Clara leave. "So it was because of her."

Lucas says, "Do everything you can, Peter, to get this man transferred. If he stays in this town he's a dead man."

Peter says, "I believe you. You're crazy enough to do it. Don't worry. He'll leave. But if she loved him, do you realize what you've done to her?"

Lucas says, "She doesn't love him."

It is already almost noon when Lucas gets home from the police station.

The child says, "They didn't lock you up?"

Yasmine says, "I hope it was nothing serious."

Lucas says, "No. Everything is all right. They needed me as a witness to a fight."

Yasmine says, "You'd better go and see the priest. He's stopped eating. He hasn't touched anything I took him yesterday or the day before."

Lucas takes a bottle of goat's milk and goes to the priest's house. The congealed food stands on the kitchen table. The stove is cold. Lucas crosses an empty room and enters the bedroom without knocking. The priest is in bed.

Lucas asks, "Are you ill?"

"No, I'm just cold. I'm always cold."

"I brought you enough wood. Why don't you warm yourself up?"

The priest says, "I have to economize. On wood and everything else."

"You're just too lazy to light the fire."

"I am old, I don't have enough strength left."

"You don't have enough strength because you don't eat."

"I have no appetite. Since you no longer bring the meals, I have no appetite."

Lucas hands him his dressing gown. "Get dressed and come to the kitchen."

He helps the old man into his dressing gown, he helps him to walk to the kitchen, he helps him to sit on the bench. He pours him a cup of milk. The priest drinks.

Lucas says, "You can't go on living on your own. You are too old."

The priest puts his cup down. He looks at Lucas.

"I'm leaving, Lucas. My superiors have recalled me. I'm going to retire to a monastery. There won't be a priest in this town anymore. The priest from the neighboring town will come once a week to celebrate mass."

"It's a sensible decision. I'm happy for you."

"I will miss this town. I've been here for forty-five years."

After a silence, the priest continues. "You have taken care of me all these years as if you were my own son. I would like to thank you. But how can I repay you for so much love and so much goodness?"

"Don't thank me. There is no love and no goodness in me."

"That's what you think, Lucas. I'm convinced of the contrary. You have suffered a wound from which you have not yet recovered."

Lucas is silent. The priest continues. "I feel that I am leaving you during a particularly difficult time in your life, but I will be with you in spirit and I will pray always for the salvation of your soul. You have taken the wrong course. I sometimes wonder where you will end up. Your passionate and tortured nature can drive you to the worst extremes. But I live in hope. God's mercy is infinite."

The priest gets up and takes Lucas's face in his hands. " 'Remember now thy Creator in the days of thy youth, while the evil days come not, nor the years draw nigh, when thou shalt say, I have no pleasure in them. . . .' "

Lucas lowers his head; his forehead rests on the priest's chest.

" 'While the sun, or the light, or the moon, or the stars, be not darkened, nor the clouds return after the rain. . . .' It's Ecclesiastes."

The priest's frail body shakes with sobbing. "Yes. You recognized it. You still remember. When you were a child you knew entire pages of the Bible by heart. Do you still find the time to read it sometimes?"

Lucas frees himself. "I've got a lot of work. And I have other books to read."

The priest says, "I understand. I also know that my sermons bore you. Go now, and don't come back. I'm leaving tomorrow on the first train."

Lucas says, "I wish you a peaceful retirement, Father."

He goes home. He says to Yasmine, "The priest is going away tomorrow. There's no need to take him food anymore."

The child asks, "Is he leaving because you don't love him anymore? Yasmine and me, we'll leave too if you don't love us anymore."

Yasmine says, "Be quiet, Mathias!"

The child cries out, "She's the one who said it! But you do love us, don't you, Lucas?"

Lucas takes him in his arms. "Of course, Mathias."

At Clara's house the fire is burning in the living-room stove. The bedroom door is open.

Lucas goes into the room. Clara is in bed, with a book in her hands. She looks at Lucas, shuts the book, puts it on the bedside table.

Lucas says, "I'm sorry, Clara."

Clara throws back the quilt covering her. She is naked. She continues staring at Lucas.

"It's what you wanted, isn't it?"

"I don't know. I really don't know, Clara."

Clara switches off the bedside lamp. "What are you waiting for?"

Lucas lights the desk lamp, points it at the bed. Clara closes her eyes.

Lucas kneels by the bed, opens Clara's legs, then the lips of her vulva. A thin trickle of blood comes out. He bends forward; he licks and drinks the blood. Clara moans; her hands grasp Lucas's hair.

Lucas gets undressed, lies on top of Clara, enters her, cries out. Later, Lucas gets up, opens the window. Outside it is snowing. Lucas returns to the bed. Clara takes him in her arms. Lucas shivers. She says, "Calm yourself."

She strokes Lucas's hair, his face. He asks, "You're not angry with me about him?"

"No. It's better that he left."

Lucas says, "I knew you didn't love him. You were so unhappy last week when I saw you in the bar."

Clara says, "I met him at the hospital. It was he who took care of me when I had another depression during the summer. The fourth since Thomas died."

"Do you often dream of Thomas?"

"Every night. But only of his execution. Never of Thomas happy, alive."

Lucas says, "I see my brother everywhere. In my room, in the garden, walking beside me in the street. He speaks to me."

"What does he say?"

"He says he is living in mortal solitude."

Lucas goes to sleep in Clara's arms. In the middle of the night he enters her again, softly, slowly, as if in a dream.

From then on, Lucas spends all his nights at Clara's.

The winter is very cold this year. The sun doesn't appear for five months. An icy mist lies stagnant on the deserted town. The ground is frozen, the river too.

In the kitchen of Grandmother's house, the fire is on all the time. The firewood runs out quickly. Every afternoon, Lucas goes into the forest to find wood, which he sets to dry next to the stove.

The kitchen door is left open to warm the room of Yasmine and her child. Lucas's room is not heated.

When Yasmine sews or knits in the room, Lucas sits with the child on the large rug made by Yasmine that covers the kitchen floor, and they play together with the dog and the cat. They look at picture books; they draw. Lucas teaches Mathias to count on an abacus.

Yasmine prepares the evening meal. They all sit on the corner seat in the kitchen. They eat potatoes, dried beans, or cabbage. The child doesn't like this food and eats little. Lucas makes him jam tarts.

After the meal, Yasmine washes up. Lucas carries the child into the bedroom, undresses him, puts him to bed and tells him a story. When the child falls asleep, Lucas goes off to Clara's house on the other side of town.

4

On Station Road the chestnut trees are in bloom. Their white petals lie so deep on the ground that Lucas can't even hear the sound of his footsteps. He is coming back from Clara's house, late at night.

The child is sitting on the corner seat in the kitchen. Lucas says, "It's only five o'clock. Why are you up so early?"

The child asks, "Where is Yasmine?"

"She's gone to the big city. She was bored here."

The child's dark eyes open wide. "Gone? Without me?"

Lucas turns away, he lights the fire in the stove.

The child asks, "Is she coming back?"

"No, I don't think so."

Lucas pours some goat's milk into a pan, which he sets to boil.

The child asks, "Why didn't she take me with her? She promised to take me with her."

Lucas says, "She thought you'd be better off here with me, and I agreed."

The child says, "I'm not better off here with you. I'd be better off anywhere else with her."

Lucas says, "A big city is no fun for a child. There are no gardens or animals."

The child says, "But my mother's there."

He looks out of the window. When he turns around his little face is contorted with sorrow.

"She doesn't love me because I'm crippled. That's why she left me here."

"That's not true, Mathias. She loves you with all her heart. You know that."

"Then she will come back to get me."

The child pushes away his cup, his plate, and leaves the kitchen. Lucas goes to water the garden. The sun is rising.

The dog is asleep beneath a tree. The child approaches him with a stick. Lucas watches the child. The child lifts the stick and hits the dog. The dog runs off howling. The child looks at Lucas.

"I don't like animals. I don't like gardens either."

With his stick the child starts thrashing the greens, the tomatoes, the pumpkins, the beans, the flowers. Lucas watches him without saying a word.

The child goes back to the house, he gets into Yasmine's bed. Lucas follows him, he sits on the edge of the bed.

"Are you so unhappy about staying with me? Why?"

The child stares at the ceiling. "Because I hate you."

"You hate me?"

"Yes, I've always hated you."

"I didn't know. Can you tell me why?"

"Because you're big and handsome, and because I thought Yasmine loved you. But if she's gone, it's because she didn't love you either. I hope you're as unhappy as I am."

Lucas puts his head in his hands.

The child asks, "Are you crying?"

"No, I'm not crying."

"But you're sad because of Yasmine?"

"No, not because of Yasmine. I'm sad because of you, because you're sad."

"Is that right? Because of me? That's nice." He smiles. "However, I'm just a little cripple, and she's beautiful."

After a silence the child asks, "Where is your mother?"

"She's dead."

"Was she too old? Is that why she died?"

"No. She died because of the war. She was killed by a shell, together with her baby, who was my little sister."

"Where are they now?"

"The dead are nowhere and everywhere."

The child says, "They're in the attic. I've seen them. The big bone thing and the little bone thing."

Lucas asks in a low voice, "You went up into the attic? How did you get up there?"

"I climbed. It's easy. I'll show you."

Lucas is silent. The child says, "Don't be afraid, I won't tell anyone. I don't want them to take them away. I like them."

"You like them?"

"Yes. Especially the baby. It's smaller and uglier than me. And it will never grow. I didn't know it was a girl. You can't tell when it's just those bone things."

"Those things are called skeletons."

"Yes. Skeletons. I've also seen some in the big book on top of your bookcase."

Lucas and the child are in the garden. A rope hangs from the attic, just within the reach of Lucas's outstretched arm. He says to the child, "Show me how you climb up."

The child pulls the nearby garden bench under the window of Lucas's room. He climbs onto the bench, jumps and grabs the rope, stops it swinging by pressing his feet against the wall, and uses his arms and legs to hoist himself up to the attic door. Lucas follows him. They sit on a mattress, looking at the skeletons hanging from a beam.

The child asks, "Didn't you keep your brother's skeleton?"

"Who told you I had a brother?"

"No one. I've heard you talking to him. You talk to him, and he's nowhere and everywhere, so he must be dead as well."

Lucas says, "No, he's not dead. He's gone to another country. He will return."

"Like Yasmine. She'll return too."

"Yes, both my brother and your mother."

The child says, "That's the only difference between the dead and those who go away, isn't it? Those who aren't dead will return."

Lucas says, "But how do we know they aren't dead when they're away?"

"We can't know."

The child is silent for a moment, then asks, "What did you feel when your brother went away?"

"I didn't know how to go on living without him."

"And do you know now?"

"Yes. Since you came here, I know."

The child opens the chest.

"What are these notebooks in the chest?"

Lucas closes the chest.

"It's nothing. Thank God you can't read yet!"

The child laughs. "Oh yes I can. I can read if it's printed. Look."

He opens the chest and takes out Grandmother's old Bible. He reads words, entire phrases.

Lucas asks, "Where did you learn to read?"

"From books, of course. From mine and yours."

"With Yasmine?"

"No, on my own. Yasmine doesn't like reading. She said she'd never send me to school. But I'll be going soon, won't I, Lucas?"

Lucas says, "I could teach you everything you need to know."

The child says, "School is compulsory from the age of six."

"Not for you. You can get a dispensation."

"Because I'm a cripple, you mean? I don't want your dispensation. I want to go to school like the other children."

Lucas says, "If you want to go, you can. But why do you want to?"

"Because I know I'll be the best at school, the most intelligent."

Lucas laughs. "And the most vain, no doubt. I always hated school. I pretended to be deaf so I wouldn't have to go."

"You did that?"

"Yes. Listen, Mathias. You may come up here whenever you want. You may also go into my room, even when I'm not there. You may read the Bible, the dictionary, the entire encyclopedia if you wish. But you must never read the notebooks, you son of a bitch."

He adds, "Grandmother called us that: sons of a bitch."

"Who's 'us'? You and who else? You and your brother?"

"Yes. My brother and me."

They climb down from the attic, they go into the kitchen. Lucas prepares the meal. The child asks, "Who'll do the dishes, the washing, the clothes?"

"We will. Together. You and I."

They eat. Lucas leans out the window, he throws up. He turns around, his face bathed in sweat. He loses consciousness and falls to the floor of the kitchen.

The child cries, "Don't do that, Lucas, don't do that!"

Lucas opens his eyes. "Don't cry, Mathias. Help me to get up."

The child pulls him by the arm. Lucas clings to the table. He staggers out of the kitchen, he sits on the garden bench. The child stands before him, looking at him.

"What's wrong, Lucas? You were dead for a moment!"

"No, I just felt faint because of the heat."

The child asks, "It doesn't matter that she left, does it? It's not so serious, is it? You won't die because of that?"

Lucas doesn't answer. The child sits at his feet, hugs his legs, lays his head with its dark, curly hair on Lucas's knees.

"Maybe I'll be your son later."

When the child goes to sleep, Lucas goes back into the attic. He takes the notebooks from the chest, wraps them in a jute cloth, and goes into town.

He rings at Peter's.

"I'd like you to keep these for me, Peter."

He puts the packet on the living-room table.

Peter asks, "What is it?"

Lucas pulls open the cloth. "Some school notebooks."

Peter shakes his head. "It's like Victor said. You write. You buy huge quantities of paper and pencils. For years now, pencils, lined paper, and large school notebooks. Are you writing a book?"

"No, not a book. I simply make notes."

Peter feels the weight of the notebooks. "Notes! Half a dozen thick notebooks."

"It accumulates over the years. Even so, I reject a lot. I only keep what's absolutely necessary."

Peter asks, "Why do you want to hide them? Because of the police?"

"The police? Of course not! It's because of the child. He's beginning to learn to read and he gets into everything. I don't want him to read these notebooks."

Peter smiles. "And you don't want the child's mother to read them either, do you?"

Lucas says, "Yasmine is no longer living with me. She's gone away. She has always dreamed of going to the big city. I gave her some money."

"And she left her child with you?"

"I insisted on keeping him."

Peter lights a cigarette and looks at Lucas without speaking.

Lucas asks, "Can you keep these notebooks here, yes or no?"

"Of course I can."

Peter wraps up the notebooks, carries them into his bedroom. When he comes back he says, "I've hidden them under my bed. I'll find a better hiding place tomorrow."

Lucas says, "Thank you, Peter."

Peter laughs. "Don't thank me. Your notebooks interest me."

"You intend to read them?"

"Of course. If you don't want me to read them you should take them to Clara."

Lucas gets up. "Certainly not! Clara reads everything there is to read. But I could give them to Victor."

"In which case I would read them at Victor's. He can't refuse me anything. Anyway, he's leaving soon. He's going back to his hometown to live with his sister. He intends to sell his house and the shop."

Lucas says, "Give me the notebooks back. I'll bury them somewhere in the forest."

"Yes, bury them. Or better still, burn them. It's the only way of preventing people from reading them."

Lucas says, "I have to keep them. For Claus. These notebooks are for Claus. For him alone."

Peter turns on the radio. He fiddles with the dial until he finds some soft music.

"Sit down, Lucas, and tell me, who is Claus?"

"My brother."

"I didn't know you had a brother. You've never mentioned him. Nobody has, not even Victor, and he's known you since childhood."

Lucas says, "My brother has been living on the other side of the border for several years."

"How did he get across the border? It's supposed to be impossible."

"He got across, that's all."

After a silence, Peter asks, "Do you keep in touch with him?"

"What do you mean, keep in touch?"

"What everyone means. Do you write to him? Does he write to you?"

"I write to him every day in the notebooks. Undoubtedly he does the same."

"But don't you get any letters from him?"

"He can't send letters from over there."

"Lots of letters arrive from the other side of the border. Your brother hasn't written since he left? He hasn't given you his address?"

Lucas shakes his head. He gets up again.

"You think he's dead, don't you? Well, Claus isn't dead. He's alive and he will return."

"Yes, Lucas. Your brother will return. As for the notebooks, I could have promised not to read them, but you wouldn't have believed me."

"You're right, I wouldn't have believed you. I knew you wouldn't be able to prevent yourself from reading them. I knew when I came here. So read them. I'd rather it were you than Clara or anyone else."

Peter says, "That's something else I don't understand: your relationship with Clara. She's much older than you."

"Age doesn't matter. I'm her lover. Is that all you wanted to know?"

"No, that's not all. I knew that already. But do you love her?"

Lucas opens the door.

"I don't know the meaning of that word. No one does. I didn't expect that sort of question from you, Peter."

"Nevertheless, you will be asked that sort of question many times in the course of your life. And sometimes you will be obliged to answer it."

"And you, Peter? One day you will also be obliged to answer certain questions. I've been to some of your political meetings. You make speeches, the audience applauds. Do you really believe in what you say?"

"I have to believe it."

"But in your deepest self, what do you think?"

"I don't think. I can't allow myself the luxury. I've lived with fear since I was a child."

* * *

Clara is standing in front of the window, looking out into the garden engulfed in darkness. She doesn't turn around when Lucas comes into the room.

She says, "The summer is frightening. It is in the summer that death is closest. Everything dries out, suffocates, comes to a standstill. It's already been four years since they killed Thomas. In August, very early in the morning, at dawn. They hanged him. The disturbing thing is that they start again every year. At dawn, when you go home, I go to the window and I see them. They are starting again, but you can't kill the same person over and over."

Lucas kisses Clara on the neck.

"What's wrong, Clara? What's wrong with you today?"

"Today I received a letter. An official letter. It's there on my desk, you can read it. It exonerates Thomas, proclaims his innocence. I never doubted his innocence. They write: 'Your husband was innocent. We killed him by mistake. We killed many people by mistake, but at present everything is being sorted out. We apologize and promise that such mistakes will not be allowed to happen in the future.' They murder and they exonerate. They apologize, but Thomas is dead! Can they bring him back to life? Can they wipe out that night when my hair went white, when I went mad?

"That summer night I was alone in our apartment, in Thomas's and my apartment. I'd been alone there for several months. Since they had imprisoned Thomas no one wanted to visit me, no one could, no one dared. I was already used to being alone, it wasn't unusual that I was alone. I didn't sleep, but that wasn't unusual either. What was unusual was that I didn't cry that night. The previous evening the radio announced the execution of a number of people for high treason. Among the names I clearly heard Thomas's name. At three o'clock in the morning, the time of the executions, I looked at the clock. I kept looking at it until seven o'clock, then I went to my job in a large library in the capital. I sat at my desk. I was in charge of the reading room. One after the other my colleagues came up. I heard them whisper, 'She's come!' 'Have you seen her hair?' I left the library, I walked around the streets until evening, I got lost, I didn't know which part of town I was in, even though I knew the town well. I came home in a taxi. At three o'clock in the morning I looked out the window, and I saw them: they were hanging Thomas from the front of the building opposite. I screamed. Some neighbors came. An ambulance took me to the hospital. And now they say it was just a mistake. Thomas's murder, my illness, the months in the hospital, my white hair were just a mistake. Well, let them bring me Thomas alive, smiling. The Thomas who took me in his arms, who stroked my hair, who held my face in his warm hands, who kissed me on the eyes, the ears, the mouth."

Lucas takes Clara by the shoulders, he turns her to face him.

"Will you never stop talking to me about Thomas?"

"Never. I'll never stop talking about Thomas. And you? When will you start talking to me about Yasmine?"

Lucas says, "There's nothing to say. Especially since she's no longer here."

Clara punches and scratches Lucas on the face, the neck, the shoulders. She cries, "She's no longer here? Where is she? What have you done with her?"

Lucas drags Clara onto the bed, he lies on top of her.

"Calm down. Yasmine has gone to the big city, that's all."

Clara grips Lucas in her arms.

"They will separate me from you as they separated me from Thomas. They will put you in prison, take you away."

"No, that's all over. Forget Thomas, the prison, and the rope."

At dawn, Lucas gets up.

"I have to go home. The child wakes up early."

"Yasmine left her child here?"

"He's crippled. What would she have done with him in a big city?"

Clara says, "How could she have left him?"

Lucas says, "She wanted to take him. I forbade her."

"Forbade her? By what right? He's her child. He belongs to her."

Clara watches Lucas get dressed. She says, "Yasmine left because you didn't love her."

"I helped her when she was in trouble. I never promised her anything."

"You've never promised me anything either."

Lucas goes home to prepare breakfast for Mathias.

Lucas goes into the bookshop. Victor asks him, "Do you need any paper or pencils, Lucas?"

"No. I'd like to talk to you. Peter said that you wanted to sell your house."

Victor sighs. "These days nobody has enough money to buy a house with a shop."

Lucas says, "I'd like to buy it."

"You, Lucas? With what, my boy?"

"By selling Grandmother's house. The army has offered a good price for it."

"I'm afraid it wouldn't be enough, Lucas."

"I also own a good plot of land. And other things besides. Very valuable things that I inherited from Grandmother."

Victor says, "Come and see me this evening at the apartment. I'll leave the front door open."

That evening, Lucas goes up the narrow, dark stairway that leads to the apartment above the bookshop. He knocks at the door, below which there is a crack of light.

Victor shouts, "Come in, Lucas!"

Lucas enters a room filled with a thick cloud of cigar smoke, in spite of the open window. The ceiling is stained a dirty brown color, the net curtains are yellowed. The room is crammed with old furniture, divans, sofas, small tables, lamps, trinkets. The walls are covered with paintings, etchings, the floor with layers of threadbare rugs.

Victor is sitting next to the window at a table covered with a red plush tablecloth. On the table are boxes of cigars and cigarettes. Ashtrays of all shapes and sizes full of cigarette butts stand next to glasses and a half-empty carafe of yellow liquid.

"Come in, Lucas. Sit down and have a drink."

Lucas sits down; Victor pours him a drink, drinks up his own glass, refills it.

"I wish I could offer you a better brandy than this, some of the stuff my sister brought on her last visit, for example, but I'm afraid there's none left. My sister came in July. It was very warm, if you remember. I don't like the heat, I don't like summer. A cool, wet summer, fine, but these dog days make me feel positively ill.

"When she came my sister brought me a liter of apricot brandy such as we drink at home in the country. My sister probably thought the bottle would last all year, or at least until Christmas. In fact I'd already drunk half the bottle by the first evening. I was ashamed, so I hid the bottle, then I went to buy a bottle of cheap brandy—it's all you can get in the shops—and used it to top off my sister's bottle, which I left out in an obvious place, there on the sideboard in front of you.

"So by drinking the cheap brandy every evening in secret, I was able to fool my sister by showing her the level in her bottle hardly going down at all. Once or twice, for appearance's sake, I would pour a small glass of this brandy, which I pretended to appreciate, even though it was already quite diluted.

"I waited patiently for my sister to go. Not that she was in the way, quite the opposite. She made my meals, she darned my socks, mended my clothes, cleaned the kitchen and everything else that was dirty. So she was useful, and what's more, we would have pleasant chats over a good meal after I closed the shop. She slept in the small room here at the side. She went to bed early and slept soundly. I had the whole night to myself to walk up and down in my room and in the kitchen and the corridor.

"You must realize, Lucas, that my sister is the person I love most in the world. Our father and mother died when we were young, me especially, since I was still a child. My sister was a little older, five years older. We lived with various relatives, uncles and aunts, but I assure you it was really my sister who brought me up.

"My love for her hasn't diminished in all this time. You will never know the joy I felt when I saw her getting off the train. I hadn't seen her for twelve years. There was the war, poverty, the border zone. When she managed to save enough money for the journey, for instance, she couldn't get a permit for the zone, and so on. For my part, I never have very much ready cash, and I can't just close up the bookshop when I want. And she can't simply walk out on her clients. She's a dressmaker, and even when times are hard women need a dressmaker. Especially during the hard times when they can't afford to buy new clothes. My sister had to work miracles during the hard times. Turning their dead husbands' trousers into short skirts, their nightgowns into blouses, and as for the children's clothes, any old bit of material would do.

"When my sister finally managed to get enough money and the necessary papers and permits, she wrote to tell me she was coming."

Victor gets up, looks out the window.

"It must be ten o'clock by now."

Lucas says, "No, not yet."

Victor sits down again, pours a drink, lights a cigar.

"I waited for my sister at the station. It was the first time I had ever waited for someone at that station. I was ready to wait for several trains if necessary. My sister arrived on the very last train. She had been traveling all day. Of course I recognized her immediately, but she was so different from the image I had of her in my memory! She had become really small. She had always been petite, but not that much. Her—I have to admit—grumpy face was now lined with hundreds of tiny wrinkles. In a word, she had really aged. Naturally, I said nothing, I kept these observations to myself. She, on the other hand, started crying and said, 'Oh, Victor! You've changed so much! I hardly recognize you. You've put on weight, you've lost your hair, you've let yourself go.'

"I carried her cases. They were heavy, stuffed with jam, sausages, apricot brandy. She unpacked it all in the kitchen. She had even brought some beans from her garden. I tasted the brandy straight away. While she was cooking the beans I drank about a quarter of the bottle. After washing up she came to join me in my room. The windows were wide open, it was very hot. I kept on drinking. I constantly went over to the window, smoked cigars. My sister talked about her awkward clients, her difficult, solitary life. I listened to her while drinking brandy and smoking cigars.

"The window opposite lit up at ten o'clock. The man with white hair appeared. He was chewing something. He always eats at that hour. At ten o'clock in the evening he sits at his window and eats. My sister was still talking. I showed her her room and said to her, 'You must be tired. You've had a long journey. Go and rest.' She kissed me on both cheeks, went into the small bedroom at the side, got into bed, and slept, I suppose. I kept on drinking, walking up and down smoking cigars. Now and then I looked out the window. I saw the white-haired man leaning out of his window. I heard him ask the infrequent passersby, 'What time is it? Could you tell me the time, please?' Someone in the street answered, 'It's twenty past eleven.'

"I slept very badly. The silent presence of my sister in the other room disturbed me. The next morning, I heard the insomniac asking the time again, and someone replying, 'It's quarter to seven.' Later, when I got up, my sister was already working in the kitchen; the window opposite was closed.

"What do you think of that, Lucas? My sister, whom I haven't seen for twelve years, comes to visit me, and I can't wait for her to go to bed so I can observe the insomniac across the street in peace—the fact is, he's the only person who interests me, even though I love my sister above all.

"You're saying nothing, Lucas, but I know what you're thinking. You think I'm mad, and you're right. I'm obsessed by this old man who opens his window at ten o'clock at night and closes it again at seven o'clock in the morning. He spends the whole night at his window. I don't know what he does after that. Does he sleep, or does he have another room or a kitchen where he spends the day? I never see him in the street, I never see him during the day, I don't know him and I've never asked anyone anything about him. You're the first person I've talked to about him. What does he think about all night, leaning out of his window? How can we know? By midnight the street is completely empty. He can't even ask the time from the passersby. He can't do that until six or seven in the morning. Does he really need to know the time? Is it possible he doesn't own a watch or an alarm clock? In that case how does he manage to appear at his window at precisely ten o'clock in the evening? There are so many questions I ask myself about him.

"One evening, after my sister had already left, the insomniac spoke to me. I was at my window. I was looking out for the storm clouds that had been forecast for days. The old man spoke to me from across the street. He said, 'You can't see the stars. The storm is coming.' I didn't reply. I looked elsewhere, left and right up the street. I didn't want to strike up an acquaintance. I ignored him.

"I sat in a corner of my room where he couldn't see me. I realize now that if I stay here I'll do nothing but drink, smoke, and watch the insomniac through the window, until I become an insomniac myself."

Victor looks out the window and collapses into his armchair with a sigh. "He's there. He's there and he's watching me. He's waiting for a chance to strike up a conversation with me. But I won't let him, he might as well give up, he won't have the last word."

Lucas says, "Calm down, Victor. Maybe he's just a retired night watchman who got used to sleeping during the day."

Victor says, "A night watchman? Perhaps. It makes no difference. If I stay here, he'll destroy me. I'm already half mad. My sister noticed. Before she got on the train she said, 'I'm too old to make such a long and tiring journey again. We should make a decision, Victor, otherwise I'm afraid we might never see each other again.' I asked, 'What kind of decision?' She said, 'Your business is failing, I can see that much. You sit all day in the shop and never get any customers. At night you walk up and down in the apartment and in the morning you're exhausted. You drink too much—you've drunk nearly half the brandy I brought you. If you go on like that you'll become an alcoholic.'

"I didn't tell her that during her stay I had drunk six other bottles of brandy as well as the bottles of wine we opened at each meal. I didn't tell her about the insomniac either, of course. She continued, 'You look terrible, you have rings round your eyes, you're pale and overweight. You eat too much meat, you get no exercise, you never go out, you lead an unhealthy life.' I said, 'Don't worry about me. I feel fine.' I lit a cigar. The train was late. My sister turned her head away in disgust. 'You smoke too much. You never stop smoking.'

"I didn't tell her that two years ago the doctors discovered that I had an arterial disease caused by nicotine poisoning. My right iliac artery is blocked, there is no circulation, or hardly any, in my left leg. I get pains in my hip and my calf, and I have no feeling in the big toe of my left foot. The doctors gave me medicine, but there will be no improvement if I don't stop smoking and don't start getting exercise. But I have no desire to stop smoking. In fact I'm totally lacking in willpower. You can't expect an alcoholic to have willpower. So if I want to stop smoking, I will first of all have to stop drinking.

"I sometimes think that I should give up smoking, and then right away I light up a cigar or a cigarette, and I think while I'm smoking it that if I don't stop smoking it will soon mean the end of all circulation in my left leg, which will bring about gangrene, which in turn will mean amputation of my foot or the whole leg.

"I said nothing about any of this so as not to worry my sister, but she was worried anyway. As she got on the train she said,

'Sell the bookshop and come live with me in the country. We can live on next to nothing, in the house we grew up in. We can go for walks in the forest. I'll take care of everything. You'll stop smoking and drinking and you can write your book.'

"The train left. I went home, I poured myself a glass of brandy, and wondered what book she was talking about.

"That evening I took a sleeping pill, along with my usual medicine for my circulation, and I drank all the brandy left in my sister's bottle, about half a liter. In spite of the sleeping pill I woke up very early the next morning, with a total lack of sensation in my left leg. I was bathed in perspiration, my heart was pounding, my hands were shaking, I was immersed in a foul and fearful anguish. I checked the time on my alarm clock. It had stopped. I dragged myself to the window. The old man opposite was still there. I called across the empty street, 'Could you tell me the time, please? My watch has stopped.' He turned away, as if consulting a clock, before replying, 'It is half past six.' I was going to get dressed but found that I already was. I had slept in my clothes and my shoes. I went down into the street, I went to the nearest grocery. It was still closed. I walked up and down in the street while I waited. The manager arrived, he opened the shop, he served me. I bought the first bottle of brandy I saw, went home. I drank a few glasses, my anguish disappeared, the man across the street had closed his window.

"I went down to the bookshop, I sat down at the counter. There were no customers. It was still summer, the school holidays, no one needed books or anything else. Sitting there, looking at the books on the shelves, I remembered my book, the book my sister mentioned, the book I had been intending to write since I was a young man. I wanted to become a writer, to write books, that was the dream of my youth, and we often talked about it together, my sister and I. She believed in me, I also believed in myself, but less and less until finally I completely forgot this dream of writing books.

"I'm only fifty years old. If I stop smoking and drinking, or rather drinking and smoking, I can still write a book. Not books, but a single book, perhaps. I am convinced, Lucas, that every human being is born to write a book, and for no other reason. A work of genius or mediocrity, it doesn't matter, but he who writes nothing is lost, he has merely passed through life without leaving a trace.

"If I stay here I will never write a book. My only hope is to sell the house and the shop and go live with my sister. She will keep me from drinking and smoking, we will lead a healthy life, she will take care of everything, I will have nothing else to do except write my book, once I'm rid of the alcoholism and the nicotine poisoning. You yourself, Lucas, are writing a book. About whom, about what, I don't know. But you write. Since you were a child you have never stopped buying sheets of paper, pencils, notebooks."

Lucas says, "You're right, Victor. Writing is the most important thing. Name your price. I'll buy the house and the bookshop. We can close the deal in a few weeks."

Victor asks, "The valuables you mentioned—what are they?"

"Gold and silver coins. And jewels as well."

Victor smiles. "Do you want to inspect the house?"

"That's not necessary. I'll make whatever changes are needed. These two rooms will be enough for the two of us."

"There were three of you, if I remember correctly."

"There are only two of us now. The child's mother has gone away."

*　　*　　*

Lucas says to the child, "We're moving. We'll be living in town, in the main square. I bought the bookshop."

The child says, "That's good. I'll be closer to school. But when Yasmine comes back, how will she find us?"

"In a town this size she'll find us easily."

The child asks, "Will we not have a garden and animals anymore?"

"We'll have a little garden. We'll keep the dog and the cat, and some chickens for the eggs. We'll sell the other animals to Joseph."

"Where will I sleep? There's no Grandmother's room there."

"You'll sleep in a little room next to mine. We'll be right next to each other."

"Without the animals and the produce from the garden, what will we live off?"

"We'll live off the bookshop. I'll sell pencils, books, paper. You can help me."

"Yes, I'll help you. When are we moving?"

"Tomorrow. Joseph is coming with his wagon."

Lucas and the child settle into Victor's house. Lucas repaints the rooms. They are light and clean. Lucas installs a bathroom in the small room next to the kitchen.

The child asks, "Can I have the skeletons?"

"Of course not. What if someone came into your room?"

"No one will come into my room. Except Yasmine when she comes back."

Lucas says, "All right. You can have the skeletons. But all the same we'll hide them behind a curtain."

Lucas and the child clear the garden, which was neglected by Victor. The child points to a tree.

"Look at that tree, Lucas. It's completely black."

Lucas says, "It's a dead tree. It should be cut down. The other trees are losing their leaves, but that one is dead."

Often in the middle of the night the child wakes up, rushes into Lucas's room, into his bed, and if Lucas isn't there, he waits for him in order to tell him his nightmares. Lucas lies down next to the child, and holds his little, thin body tightly until the child stops trembling.

The child tells him his nightmares, always the same ones, which recur regularly to haunt his nights.

One of these dreams is the river dream. The child, lying on the surface of the water, lets himself be carried off by the stream while watching the stars. The child is happy, but slowly something approaches, something frightening, and suddenly that thing, the child doesn't know what it is, explodes and screams and howls and blinds.

Another dream is the dream of the tiger lying next to the child's bed. The tiger appears to be asleep; it seems soft and gentle, and the child has a great desire to stroke it. The child is afraid, but his desire to stroke the tiger grows and the child can no longer resist this desire. His fingers touch the tiger's silky fur, and the tiger, with a swipe of its paw, rips his arm off.

Another dream is the dream of the desert island. The child is there playing with his wheelbarrow. He fills it with sand, transports the sand somewhere else, empties it again, and so on, for a long time. Then suddenly it is dark, it is cold, there is no one, anywhere, only the stars shine in their infinite solitude.

Another dream. The child wants to go back to Grandmother's house. He walks in the streets, but he does not know the streets in the town. He gets lost, the streets are deserted, the house is no longer where it should be, nothing is in the right place, Yasmine is calling for him, she is crying, but the child does not know which street, which alley to take in order to find her.

The most terrible dream is the dream of the dead tree, the black tree in the garden. The child is looking at the tree and the tree stretches out its bare branches toward the child. The tree says, "I am nothing but a dead tree, but I love you just as much as I did when I was alive." The tree speaks with Yasmine's voice, the child approaches, and the blackened, dead branches embrace him and strangle him.

Lucas chops down the dead tree, he saws it up and makes a bonfire in the garden.

When the fire goes out, the child says, "Now it is nothing but a pile of ashes."

He goes to his room. Lucas uncorks a bottle of brandy. He drinks. He is overcome with nausea. He goes back into the garden and he throws up. A plume of white smoke still rises from the black ashes, but then large raindrops begin to fall, and the shower finishes off the work of the fire.

Later, the child finds Lucas in the wet grass, in the mud. He shakes him.

"Get up, Lucas. You have to come in. It's raining. It's dark. It's cold. Can you walk?"

Lucas says, "Leave me here. Go inside. Tomorrow everything will be all right."

The child sits down next to Lucas; he waits.

The sun rises. Lucas opens his eyes.

"What happened, Mathias?"

The child says, "It's just a new nightmare."

5

The insomniac continues to appear at his window every evening at ten o'clock. The child is already in bed. Lucas leaves the house. The insomniac asks him the time, Lucas tells him. Then he goes to Clara's house. At dawn, when he comes home, the insomniac asks him the time again; Lucas tells him and goes to bed. A few hours later the light goes out in the insomniac's room and the pigeons take over his windowsill.

One morning, when Lucas comes home, the insomniac calls out, "Excuse me!"

Lucas says, "It is five o'clock."

"I know. I'm not interested in the time. It's just my way of starting a conversation with people. I just wanted to tell you that the child was very restless last night. He woke up about two o'clock, he went into your bedroom several times, he spent ages looking out the window. He even went out into the street, down to the bar, then he came back and went to bed, I suppose."

"Does he do that often?"

"He often wakes up, yes. Nearly every night. But it's the first time I've seen him leave the house during the night."

"Even during the day he never leaves the house."

"I think he was looking for you."

Lucas goes up to the apartment. The child is sleeping soundly in his bed. Lucas looks out the window. The insomniac asks, "Everything in order?"

"Yes. He's asleep. What about you? Do you never sleep?"

"I doze off now and again, but I never really sleep. I haven't slept for eight years."

"What do you do during the day?"

"I go for walks. When I feel tired I go and sit in a park. I spend most of my time in parks. It's there that I sometimes doze off for a few minutes, sitting on a bench. Would you like to come with me sometime?"

Lucas says, "Now, if you like."

"Fine. I'll feed my pigeons and come right down."

They walk down the deserted streets of the sleeping town toward Grandmother's house. The insomniac stops by a few square meters of yellow grass with two old trees spreading out their bare branches.

"Here's my park. The only place I can manage a moment's sleep."

The old man sits on the solitary bench next to a dried-up fountain covered in moss and mildew.

Lucas says, "There are nicer parks in town."

"Not for me."

He lifts his walking stick and points to large, beautiful house. "We used to live there, my wife and I."

"Is she dead?"

"She was killed by several shots from a revolver three years after the end of the war. One evening at ten o'clock."

Lucas sits down next to the old man.

"I remember her. We used to live by the border. When we came home from town we used to stop here to have a drink of water and rest. When your wife saw us from her window she would come down and bring us large lumps of potato sugar. I've never eaten it since. I remember her smile and her accent, and also her murder. The whole town talked about it."

"What did they say?"

"They said she was killed so they could nationalize the three textile factories that belonged to her."

The old man says, "She inherited those factories from her father. I worked there as an engineer. I married her and she stayed here. She loved this town very much. But she retained her nationality, and they were forced to kill her. It was the only solution. They killed her in our bedroom. I heard the gunshots from the bathroom. The assassin got in and out by the balcony. She was shot in the head, the chest, and the stomach. The inquiry concluded that it was an embittered employee who did it for revenge and then fled across the border."

Lucas says, "The border was already sealed, even then, and a worker wouldn't have owned a revolver."

The insomniac closes his eyes; he is silent.

Lucas asks, "Do you know who is living in your house now?"

"It's full of children. Our house has been turned into an orphanage. But you must get back, Lucas. Mathias will soon be waking up and you must open the bookshop."

"You're right. It's already half past seven."

* * *

Sometimes Lucas goes back to the park to chat with the insomniac. The old man talks about the past, about the happy times with his wife.

"She was always laughing. She was happy, carefree as a child. She loved the fruits, the flowers, the stars, the clouds. At sunset she would go out onto the balcony to look at the sky. She claimed that nowhere else in the world were sunsets as wonderful as in this town, were the colors in the sky so brilliant and beautiful."

The man closes his bloodshot eyes, heavy with sleeplessness. He continues in a different tone of voice, "After her murder, the authorities requisitioned the house and everything in it: all my wife's furniture, crockery, books, jewelry, clothes. All they let me take away was a suitcase with a few clothes. They told me I should leave town. I lost my job at the factory. I had no work, no house, and no money.

"I went to see a friend, a doctor, the same one I telephoned the night of the murder. He gave me some money for a train ticket. He said, 'Never come back to this town. It's a wonder they let you live.'

"I took the train, I arrived in the next town. I sat down in the waiting room in the station. I still had enough money to go farther, maybe even to the capital. But there was nothing for me to do in the capital, or in any other town. I bought a ticket at the booking office and came back here. I knocked at the door of a small house opposite the bookshop. I knew all the workers in our factories. I knew the woman who opened the door. She didn't ask any questions. She told me to come in, she led me to a room. 'You can stay here as long as you like, sir.'

"She is an old woman, she lost her husband, her two sons, and her daughter during the war. Her daughter was only seventeen.

She died at the front, where she had signed up as a nurse after being disfigured in a horrible accident. My landlady never speaks about it, and in fact she hardly speaks at all anymore. She leaves me alone in my room, which looks out onto the street. She herself lives in a smaller room which looks out onto the garden. The kitchen is also in back. I can use it when I want, and there is always something hot on the stove. Every morning I find my shoes polished, my shirts washed and ironed, lying over the back of a chair in the corridor outside my door. My landlady never comes into my room, and I see her rarely. We don't keep the same hours. I don't know what she lives on. On her war widow's pension and her garden, I suppose.

"A few months after I moved in I went to the council office to look for any sort of work. The officials sent me from one office to another. They were afraid to make a decision about me, I was an object of suspicion because of my marriage to a foreigner. Finally, it was the Party Secretary, Peter, who took me on as a handyman. I was a caretaker, a window cleaner, a sweeper of dust, dead leaves, and snow. Thanks to Peter I am now entitled to a retirement pension like everyone else. I didn't have to beg, and I can end my days in the town where I was born and where I have spent my whole life.

"I left my first wages on the kitchen table. It was a paltry amount, but to my landlady it was a lot of money, too much, according to her. She left half of it on the table, and we went on like that: I leave my small pension next to her plate every month; she leaves exactly half of it next to mine."

A woman wrapped in a large shawl comes out of the orphanage. She is thin and pale; her huge eyes shine in her bony face. She stops in front of the bench, looks at Lucas, smiles, and says to the old man, "I see you've found yourself a friend."

"Yes, a friend. This is Lucas, Judith. He runs the bookshop in the main square. Judith is in charge of the orphanage."

Lucas gets up. Judith shakes his hand.

"I should buy some books for the children, but I'm overwhelmed with work and my budget is very tight."

Lucas says, "I can send some books around with Mathias. How old are your children?"

"Between five and ten. Who is Mathias?"

The old man says, "Lucas is looking after an orphan."

Lucas says, "Mathias isn't an orphan. His mother has gone away. He's mine now."

Judith smiles. "My children aren't all orphans either. Mostly their fathers are unknown and they have been abandoned by their mothers, who are rape victims or prostitutes."

She sits down next to the old man, rests her head on his shoulder, closes her eyes.

"We'll need the heating soon, Michael. If the weather doesn't change we'll start the stoves on Monday."

The old man holds her close to him.

"Fine, Judith. I'll be there at five o'clock on Monday morning."

Lucas looks at the woman and the man, holding each other tight, their eyes closed, in the damp cold of an autumn morning, in the complete silence of a forgotten little town. He starts to tiptoe away, but Judith shivers, opens her eyes, gets up.

"Stay, Lucas. The children will be waking up. I have to make their breakfast." She kisses the old man on the forehead.

"Until Monday, Michael. See you, Lucas, and thanks in advance for the books."

She goes back to the house. Lucas sits down again.

"She is very beautiful."

"Very beautiful, yes." The insomniac laughs. "At first, she was suspicious of me. She saw me here every day, sitting on this bench. Maybe she took me for a pervert. One day she came and sat next to me and asked me what I was doing here. I told her everything. It was at the beginning of last winter. She asked me to help her with the heating in the rooms, she couldn't manage it alone, she only has a sixteen-year-old to help in the kitchen. There's no central heating in the building, just stoves in each room, seven of them. If you only knew what joy I felt to be able to go back into our house, our rooms! And also to be able to help Judith. She's had her trials. Her husband disappeared during the war, she herself was deported, she's been to hell and back. I mean that literally. There was a real fire behind those doors, lit by human beings to burn the bodies of other human beings."

Lucas says, "I know what you're talking about. I saw things like that with my own eyes, right here in this town."

"You must have been very young."

"I was no more than a child. But I forgot nothing."

"You will forget. Life is like that. Everything goes in time. Memories blur, pain diminishes. I remember my wife as one remembers a bird or a flower. She was the miracle of life in a world where everything seemed light, easy, and beautiful. At first I came here for her, now I come for Judith, the survivor. This might seem ridiculous to you, Lucas, but I'm in love with Judith. With her strength, her goodness, her kindness toward these children who aren't hers."

Lucas says, "I don't think it's ridiculous."

"At my age?"

"Age is irrelevant. The essential things matter. You love her and she loves you as well."

"She's waiting for her husband to return."

"Many women are waiting for or mourning their husbands who are disappeared or dead. But you just said, 'Pain diminishes, memories blur.' "

The insomniac raises his eyes to Lucas.

"Diminish, blur, I said, not disappear."

That same morning, Lucas picks out some children's books. He puts them in a box and says to Mathias, "Can you take these books to the orphanage next to the park on the way to Grandmother's house? It's a big house with a balcony, there's a fountain in front."

The child says, "I know the one."

"The principal is called Judith. Give her these books from me."

The child goes off with the books, but returns soon after. Lucas asks, "What did you think of Judith and the children?"

"I didn't see Judith and the children. I left the books outside the door."

"You didn't go in?"

"No. Why should I go in? So they can keep me?"

"What? What are you saying, Mathias!"

The child locks himself in his room. Lucas stays in the bookshop until closing time, then makes the evening meal, which he eats alone. He has a shower and is just getting dressed when the child comes quickly out of his room.

"Are you going out, Lucas? Where do you go to every evening?"

Lucas says, "I go to work. You know that."

The child lies on Lucas's bed. "I'll wait for you here. If you worked in the bars you would come home at closing time, at midnight. But you come home much later."

Lucas sits on a chair in front of the child. "Yes, Mathias, you're right. I do come home later. I go and see some friends after the bars close."

"Which friends?"

"You don't know them."

The child says, "I'm alone every night."

"You should be asleep at night."

"I would sleep if I knew you were here, in your room, asleep as well."

Lucas lies down next to the child. He kisses him.

"Did you really think I sent you to the orphanage so that they could keep you? How could you think such a thing?"

"I didn't really think that. But when I arrived at the door, I was afraid. You never know. Yasmine promised she would never leave me. Don't send me there again. I don't like going toward Grandmother's house."

Lucas says, "I understand."

The child says, "Orphans are children who don't have any parents. I don't have any parents."

"You do. You have your mother, Yasmine."

"Yasmine is gone. And what about my father? Where is he?"

"I'm your father."

"But the other one, the real one?"

Lucas is silent for a moment before replying, "He died before you were born, in an accident, like mine."

"Fathers always die in an accident. Will you have an accident too?"

"No. I'll be careful."

Lucas and the child work in the bookshop. The child takes books out of a box and hands them to Lucas, who is standing on a stepladder setting them on the shelves of the bookcase. It is a rainy autumn morning.

Peter comes into the shop. He is carrying a hooded falcon. The rain is dripping down his face onto the floor. From under his falcon he takes a packet wrapped up in jute cloth.

"Here, Lucas. I've brought them back. I can't keep them. It's not safe at my house anymore."

Lucas says, "You look pale, Peter. What happened?"

"Don't you read the newspapers? Don't you listen to the radio?"

"I never read newspapers and I only listen to old records."

Peter turns to the child. "Is this Yasmine's child?"

Lucas says, "Yes, this is Mathias. Say hello to Peter, Mathias. He's a friend."

Mathias stares at Peter in silence.

Peter says, "Mathias has already said hello with his eyes."

Lucas says, "Go and feed the animals, Mathias."

The child lowers his eyes, rummages about in the box of books. "It isn't time to feed the animals."

Lucas says, "You're right. Stay here and tell me if a customer comes in. Let's go upstairs, Peter."

They go up to Lucas's room.

Peter says, "That child has amazing eyes."

"Yes, he has Yasmine's eyes."

Peter gives Lucas the packet.

"There are pages missing from your notebooks, Lucas."

"I know, Peter. As I said, I make corrections, I cross things out. I delete anything that isn't indispensable."

"You correct, you cross out, you delete. Your brother Claus won't understand a word."

"Claus will understand."

"I understood too."

"Is that why you brought them back? Because you think you understood everything?"

Peter says, "What happened has nothing to do with your notebooks, Lucas. It's more serious than that. Our country is in the throes of an uprising. A counterrevolution. It began with intellectuals writing things they shouldn't have. Then it was taken up by the students. Students are always willing to sow the seeds of unrest. They organized a demonstration that degenerated into a riot against the forces of order. But it all began to get out of hand when the workers and even a part of the army joined up with the students. Yesterday evening, soldiers were distributing arms to irresponsible individuals. There are people shooting at each other in the capital, and it's now spreading to the provinces and the peasants."

Lucas says, "That covers every level of society."

"Except one. The class I belong to."

"You are greatly outnumbered by those who are against you."

"Indeed. But we have powerful friends."

Lucas is silent. Peter opens the door.

"We probably won't see each other again, Lucas. Let's part on good terms."

Lucas asks, "Where are you going?"

"Party officials have to place themselves under the protection of the foreign army."

Lucas gets up, holds Peter by the shoulders, and looks him in the eyes.

"Tell me, Peter! Aren't you ashamed?"

Peter grabs Lucas's hands and presses them to his face. He closes his eyes and says quietly, "Yes, Lucas. I am very ashamed." Tears escape from his closed eyes.

Lucas says, "No. Stop that. Get hold of yourself."

Lucas accompanies Peter to the street. He watches the dark silhouette walking away in the rain, head lowered, toward the station.

When Lucas comes back to the bookshop, the child says to him, "He's handsome. When is he coming back?"

"I don't know, Mathias. Maybe never."

That evening, Lucas goes to Clara's. He goes into the house, where all the lights are out. Clara's bed is cold and empty. Lucas lights the bedside lamp. On the pillow is a note from Clara: "I have gone to avenge Thomas."

Lucas goes home. He finds the child in his bed. He says, "I'm sick of finding you in my bed every night. Go to your room and get some sleep."

The child's lip trembles. He sniffs. "I heard Peter say that people are shooting at each other in the capital. Do you think Yasmine is in danger?"

"Yasmine isn't in danger, don't worry."

"You said that Peter might never come back. Do you think he'll die?"

"No, I don't think so. But Clara, definitely."

"Who's Clara?"

"A friend. Go to bed, Mathias, and sleep. I'm very tired."

In the little town hardly anything happens. The foreign flags are removed from public buildings, along with the effigies of Party officials. A parade passes through town with the old national flags, singing the old national anthem and other old songs, recalling another revolution in another century.

The bars are packed. People talk, laugh, sing louder than usual.

Lucas listens to the radio continually, until the day when classical music replaces the news broadcast.

Lucas looks out the window. In the main square stands a foreign army tank.

Lucas goes out to buy a pack of cigarettes. All the shops are closed. He has to go to the railway station. He passes other tanks along the way. The gun barrels turn in his direction, track him. The streets are deserted, the windows are shut, the shutters closed. But the station and the surrounding area are full of soldiers and border guards without weapons. Lucas approaches one of them: "What's going on?"

"I don't know. We've been demobilized. Did you want to catch a train? There are no trains for civilians."

"I didn't want to catch a train. I just wanted to buy some cigarettes. The shops are closed."

The soldier hands Lucas a pack of cigarettes. "You're not allowed inside the station. Take this pack and go home. It's dangerous out on the streets."

Lucas goes home. The child is still awake; they listen to the radio together. Lots of music and a few short speeches. "We have won the revolution. The people are victorious. Our government has asked for the help of our great protectors against the enemies of the people." And again: "Remain calm. Gatherings of more than two people are forbidden. The sale of alcohol is forbidden. Restaurants and bars will remain closed until further notice. All individual journeys by train or bus are forbidden. Observe the curfew. Do not leave the house after nightfall."

More music, then instructions and threats: "Work must begin again in the factories. Any workers who do not turn up at their place of work will be laid off. Saboteurs will be brought up before special tribunals. They will face the death sentence."

The child says, "I don't understand. Who won the revolution? And why is everything forbidden? Why are they so evil?"

Lucas switches off the radio. "We won't listen to the radio anymore. There's no point."

There is still some resistance, fighting, strikes. There are also arrests, imprisonments, disappearances, executions. Two hundred thousand panic-stricken inhabitants leave the country.

A few months later, silence, calm, and order reign once more.

Lucas rings at Peter's door. "I know you're back. Why are you hiding from me?"

"I'm not hiding from you. I just thought you wouldn't want to see me. I was waiting for you to make the first move."

Lucas laughs. "I've made it. Basically, things are just like before. The revolution has achieved nothing."

Peter says, "History will be the judge of that."

Lucas laughs again. "Such grand words. What's got into you, Peter?"

"Don't laugh. I've been through a serious crisis. First I resigned from the Party, then I let myself be persuaded into taking up my old position in this town. I like this town very much. It has a hold on my soul. Once you've lived here you can't not come back. And besides, Lucas, there's you."

"Is that a declaration of love?"

"No. Of friendship. I know I can't expect anything from you on that score. What about Clara? Has she come back?"

"No, Clara hasn't come back. Someone else has already moved into her house."

Peter says, "There were thirty thousand deaths in the capital. They even fired on a march where there were women and children. If Clara participated in anything . . ."

"She certainly participated in everything that was going on in the capital. I think she has rejoined Thomas, and that is for the best. She never stopped talking about Thomas. She thought only of Thomas, loved only Thomas, was ill because of Thomas. One way or another she would have died for Thomas."

After a silence, Peter says, "Many people crossed the border during the troubled period when it was left unguarded. Why didn't you take advantage of it to rejoin your brother?"

"I didn't consider it for a moment. How could I leave the child all on his own?"

"You could have taken him with you."

"You don't set off on an adventure like that with a child his age."

"You can set off anywhere, anytime, with whoever you want, if you want to badly enough. The child is just an excuse."

Lucas lowers his head. "The child has to stay here. He's waiting for his mother to come back. He wouldn't have come with me."

Peter doesn't answer. Lucas raises his head and looks at him. "You're right. I don't want to go find Claus. It's up to him to come back. He's the one who went away."

Peter says, "Someone who doesn't exist can't come back."

"Claus exists and he will come back!"

Peter goes up to Lucas and grabs him by the shoulder. "Calm down. You have to face facts. Neither your brother nor the child's mother will ever come back, and you know it."

Lucas mumbles, "Claus will."

He falls forward off his chair, he hits his head on the edge of the low table; he slumps onto the carpet. Peter pulls him onto the sofa, he wets a cloth and wipes Lucas's face, which is bathed in sweat. When Lucas comes to, Peter gives him a drink and lights him a cigarette.

"I'm sorry, Lucas. We won't talk about this again."

Lucas asks, "What were we talking about?"

"What about?" Peter lights another cigarette. "About politics, of course."

Lucas laughs. "It must have been pretty boring for me to fall asleep on your sofa."

"Yes, that's right, Lucas. You've always found politics boring, haven't you?"

The child is six and a half. On the first day of school Lucas wants to accompany him, but the child prefers to go on his own. When he comes home at noon, Lucas asks him whether everything went all right. The child says that everything went all right.

In the days that follow the child says that everything is going well at school. But one day he returns with a wound on his cheek. He says that he fell. Another day his right hand bears some red marks. The next day the nails on this hand all turn black, with the exception of the thumbnail. The child says that he jammed his fingers in a door. For weeks afterward, he has to write with his left hand.

One evening the child comes home with his mouth all split and swollen. He is unable to eat. Lucas doesn't ask questions, he pours some milk into the child's mouth, then places a sock filled with sand, a pointed stone, and a razor on the table. He says, "These were our weapons when we had to defend ourselves against the other children. Take them. Defend yourself!"

The child says, "There were two of you. I'm on my own."

"Even on your own you have to learn how to defend yourself."

The child looks at the objects on the table. "I can't. I could never hit anyone, hurt anyone."

"Why not? They hit you and hurt you."

The child looks Lucas in the eyes.

"Physical wounds don't matter when I receive them. But if I had to inflict them on someone else, that would wound me in a way I couldn't bear."

Lucas asks, "Do you want me to talk to your teacher?"

The child says, "Definitely not! I forbid it! Don't ever do that, Lucas! Have I complained? Have I asked for your help? Your weapons?"

He sweeps the defensive tools off the table. "I'm stronger than all of them, braver, and above all, more intelligent. That's all that matters."

Lucas throws the stone and the sock full of sand into the garbage. He closes the razor, puts it in his pocket. "I still carry it on me, but I don't use it anymore."

When the child has gone to bed, Lucas goes into his room and sits down on the edge of his bed. "I won't meddle in your affairs any more, Mathias. I won't ask any more questions. When you want to leave school, just tell me."

The child says, "I'll never leave school."

Lucas asks, "Tell me, Mathias, do you cry sometimes when you're alone?"

The child says, "I'm used to being alone. I never cry, you know that."

"Yes, I know. But you never laugh either. When you were small you laughed all the time."

"That must have been before Yasmine died."

"What are you saying, Mathias? Yasmine isn't dead."

"She is dead. I've known for a long time. Otherwise she would have come back."

After a silence, Lucas says, "Even after Yasmine left, you still laughed, Mathias."

The child looks at the ceiling. "Yes, maybe. Before we left Grandmother's house. We should never have left Grandmother's house."

Lucas takes the child's face in his hands. "Perhaps you're right. Perhaps we shouldn't have left Grandmother's house."

The child closes his eyes. Lucas kisses him on the forehead. "Sleep well, Mathias. When you feel too much pain, too much sorrow, and you don't want to talk to anyone, write it down. It will help you."

The child answers, "I've already written it down. I've written down everything. Everything that has happened since we've been here. My nightmares, the school, everything. I've got a big notebook like you. You've got lots, I've only got one, only a slim one so far. I'll never let you read it. You forbade me to read yours, I forbid you to read mine."

At ten o'clock in the morning an old bearded man comes into the bookshop. Lucas has seen him before. He is one of his best customers. Lucas gets up and asks with a smile, "What can I do for you, sir?"

"I have everything I need, thank you. I came to talk to you about Mathias. I'm his teacher. I have written to you on numerous occasions to ask you to come and see me."

Lucas says, "I never received your letters."

"Yet you've signed them."

The teacher takes three envelopes from his pocket and hands them to Lucas. "Isn't that your signature?"

Lucas examines the letters. "Yes and no. It's a good forgery of my signature."

The teacher smiles as he takes back the letters. "That's the conclusion I came to also. Mathias doesn't want me to speak with you. I decided to come and see you during school hours. I left an older pupil in charge of the class during my absence. This visit can remain our secret, if you wish."

Lucas says, "Yes, I think that would be best. Mathias has forbidden me to talk to you."

"He's very proud, arrogant even. He is also by far the most intelligent pupil in the class. Nevertheless, the only advice I can offer you is to withdraw him from school. I can sign the necessary papers."

Lucas says, "Mathias doesn't want to leave school."

"If only you knew what he goes through! The cruelty of the other children is beyond belief. The girls make fun of him. They call him 'spider,' 'hunchback,' 'bastard.' He sits on his own in the front row, no one wants to sit next to him. The boys hit him, kick him, punch him. The boy behind him slammed the desk shut on his fingers. I have intervened many times, but that just aggravates the situation. The other children can't stand the fact that Mathias knows everything, that he's best at everything. They are jealous of him and they are making his life unbearable."

Lucas says, "I know it, even though he never talks to me."

"No, he never complains. He doesn't even cry. He has considerable strength of character. But he can't go on suffering so much humiliation forever. Withdraw him from school and I will come every evening to give him lessons here. It would be a real pleasure for me to work with such a gifted child."

Lucas says, "Thank you, but it's not up to me. Mathias insists on going to school normally, like the other children. For him, leaving school would mean recognizing his difference, his infirmity."

The teacher says, "I understand. However, he *is* different, and one day he will have to accept it."

Lucas is silent. The teacher browses through the books on the shelves.

"These premises are very spacious. What would you say to setting out a few tables and chairs to make a reading room for the children? I could bring you some secondhand books, I've got plenty that I don't know what to do with. Then the children whose parents don't own books, and there are lots of them, believe me, could come and read in peace here for an hour or two."

Lucas stares at the teacher. "You think that might improve the relations between Mathias and the other children, don't you? Yes, it's worth a try. It's probably a good idea."

6

It is ten o'clock at night. Peter rings at Lucas's house. Lucas throws him the front-door key from the window. Peter comes up and enters the room. "Am I disturbing you?"

"Not at all. On the contrary. I was looking for you, but you had disappeared. Even Mathias was worried about you."

Peter says, "That's nice. Is he asleep?"

"He's in his room, but how do I know if he's asleep or doing something else? He wakes up at all hours of the night and starts reading, writing, thinking, studying."

"Can he hear us?"

"He can if he wants to, yes."

"In that case I'd rather you came to my place."

"Fine."

At his house, Peter opens the windows in all the rooms. He collapses into an armchair. "This heat is unbearable. Fix yourself a drink and sit down. I've just come from the station. I've been traveling all day. I had to change trains four times and wait ages for the connections."

Lucas pours a drink. "Where have you been?"

"To my hometown. I was summoned there by the local magistrate concerning Victor. He strangled his sister in a fit of *delirium tremens.*"

Lucas says, "Poor Victor. Did you see him?"

"Yes, I saw him. He's in an insane asylum."

"How is he?"

"Very well, very calm. His face is a bit puffed up because of the medication he's on. He was happy to see me. He asked about you, and the shop, and the child. He sends his greetings."

"And what did he say about his sister?"

"He said quietly, 'It's done now, we can't change it.' "

Lucas asks, "What will become of him?"

"I don't know. They haven't had the trial yet. I think he'll spend the rest of his days in the asylum. Victor doesn't belong in a prison. I asked if there was anything I could do for him. He said to send him a regular supply of writing materials. 'Paper and pencils are all I need. Here I can finally write my book,' he said."

"Yes, Victor wanted to write a book. He told me when I bought the bookshop. In fact, that's the reason he sold it."

"Yes, and he's already started writing." Peter takes a pile of typewritten sheets from his briefcase. "I read them on the train. Take them home, read them, and bring them back to me. He typed them next to his sister's body. He strangled his sister and then sat at his desk to write. They were found like that, in Victor's room, the sister strangled, stretched out on the bed, Victor typing, drinking brandy, smoking cigars. It was some of his sister's clients who called the police the next day. On the day of the crime, Victor left the house, drew some money from the bank, went to buy some brandy, cigarettes, and cigars. He told the clients who had an appointment for a fitting and were waiting outside the door that his sister was feeling poorly because of the heat and didn't want to be disturbed. The clients, obstinate and no doubt impatient to have their new dresses, came back the next day, knocked at the door, spoke to the neighbors, decided that the whole thing was a bit strange, and finally went to contact the police. The police forced the door open and found Victor blind drunk, quietly typing away at his manuscript. He let himself be led away without resistance, taking the finished sheets along with him. Read them. There are a lot of errors, but they're readable, and very interesting."

Lucas goes home with Victor's manuscript and starts to copy it out into his notebook during the night:

It is August 15; the heat wave has lasted three weeks now. The heat is unbearable indoors as well as outside. You can't get away from it. I don't like the heat, I don't like summer. A wet, cool summer, fine, but these dog days have always made me feel positively ill.

I have just strangled my sister. She is lying on my bed. I have covered her with a sheet. In this heat her body will soon start smelling. No matter. I'll report it later. I've locked the front door, and if anyone knocks I won't answer. I've also closed the windows and pulled the shutters.

I've lived with my sister for almost two years. I sold the bookshop and house I owned in a little town far away near the border. I came to live with my sister in order to write a book. I thought I would be unable to do it in the little town far away because of the solitude that threatened to make me ill and turn me into an alcoholic. I thought that here, with my sister taking care of the housework, the meals, and the clothes, I would lead a healthy, regular life, which would at last allow me to write the book that I've always wanted to write.

Unfortunately, the calm and quiet life I'd anticipated quickly turned into hell on earth.

My sister watched over me, spied on me constantly. Right from my arrival she forbade me to drink or smoke, and whenever I returned from an errand or a walk she would kiss me affectionately, solely, I realized, in order to detect the smell of drink or tobacco on my breath.

I abstained from drink for several months, but I was quite incapable of giving up smoking as well. I smoked in secret like a schoolboy. I would buy a cigar or a pack of cigarettes and go off for a walk in the forest. On the way back I would chew pine needles or suck mints to get rid of the smell. I also smoked at night with the window open, even in winter.

Many times I sat down at my desk with some sheets of paper, but my mind was a complete blank.

What could I write about? Nothing happened in my life, nothing ever had happened in my life or in the world around me. Nothing worth writing about. And my sister disturbed me all the time; she came into my room on the slightest pretext. She brought me tea, dusted the furniture, put away my clean clothes in the wardrobe. She would also lean over my shoulder to see how my writing was coming along. Because of this I had to fill in sheet after sheet, and since I didn't know what to write on them, I copied out excerpts from books, any books. Sometimes my sister would read a phrase over my shoulder that pleased her, and would encourage me with a contented smile.

There was no chance of her seeing through my deceit, for she never read herself; she possibly never read a book in her life. She never had the time—since childhood she has worked from morning till night.

In the evening she made me come into the sitting room. "You've worked enough for one day. Let's chat for a while."

As she talked, she did her sewing, either by hand or on her old pedal-driven sewing machine. She talked about her neighbors, her clients, about dresses and fabrics, about how tired she felt, and all the sacrifices she had made to ensure the success of the work of her brother, me, Victor.

I had to sit there, without being able to smoke or drink, listening to this drivel. When finally she went to her room, I went to my own, lit a cigar or a cigarette, picked up a sheet of paper, and filled it with insults directed at my sister, her narrow-minded clients, and her stupid dresses. I hid the sheet among the others containing random excerpts from some book or other.

For Christmas my sister gave me a typewriter.

"Your manuscript is already quite thick. You'll soon be reaching the end of your book, I imagine. Then you'll need to type it up. You took typing lessons at business school, and even if you've forgotten some of it through lack of practice you'll soon pick it up again."

I was in the depths of despair, but in order to please my sister I sat down straight away at my desk and, somewhat clumsily, began copying out various pages, themselves copied from some book or other. My sister watched me, nodding her head with satisfaction.

"You're not too bad at it, Victor. I'm surprised, you're actually quite good. You'll soon be typing as quickly as you used to."

When I was alone, I reread what I had typed. It was nothing but a series of typing errors and misprints.

A few days later, on my way back from my "constitutional," I went into a local bar. I only wanted a cup of tea to warm myself up a bit, for my hands and feet were cold and completely numb because of my poor circulation. I sat at a table next to the stove, and when the waiter asked me what I wanted I said, "Tea." Then I added, "With some rum in it."

I don't know why I said that; I didn't intend to say it, but I did nevertheless. I drank my tea with rum and ordered another rum, without the tea this time, and then a third rum after that.

I looked around anxiously. It isn't a big town, and almost everyone knows my sister. If she found out from one of her clients or neighbors that I'd been in a bar! But I saw only the faces of tired, indifferent, distracted men, and my anxiety subsided. I had another rum and left the bar. I was a bit unsure on my feet. I hadn't drunk for several months, and the alcohol had gone straight to my head.

I didn't dare go home. I was afraid of my sister. I wandered around the streets for a while, then I went into a shop to buy some mints. I put two in my mouth immediately. When I went to pay, without knowing why, without wanting to say it, I casually told the assistant, "I'll also have a bottle of plum brandy, two packs of cigarettes, and three cigars."

I put the bottle in the inside pocket of my overcoat. Outside it was snowing. I felt perfectly happy. I was no longer afraid of going home, no longer afraid of my sister. When I arrived back at the house she called out from the room which serves as her workshop. "I've got a rush job, Victor. Your supper is in the oven. I'll eat later."

I ate quickly in the kitchen, retired to my room, and locked the door. It was the first time I had dared to lock my door. When my sister tried to come into my room, I shouted, I dared to shout,

"Don't disturb me! I've had some brilliant ideas! I must get them on paper before I lose them."

My sister replied humbly, "I didn't want to disturb you. I just wanted to wish you good night."

"Good night, Sophie!"

She didn't leave.

"I had this very demanding client. She wanted her dress finished for the New Year. I'm sorry you had to eat on your own, Victor."

"It doesn't matter," I replied nicely. "Go to bed, Sophie, it's late."

After a silence she asked, "Why have you locked the door, Victor? You didn't need to lock it. That wasn't really necessary."

I drank a mouthful of brandy to calm myself. "I don't want to be disturbed. I'm writing."

"That's good. Very good, Victor."

I drank the bottle of brandy—it was only a half-liter—smoked two cigars and numerous cigarettes. I threw the butts out the window. It was still snowing. The snow covered the butts and the empty bottle, which I had also thrown out the window, out into the street.

The next morning my sister knocked at my door. I didn't answer. She knocked again. I shouted, "Let me sleep!"

I heard her go.

I didn't get up until two o'clock in the afternoon. My sister and her meal were waiting for me in the kitchen. This was our conversation:

"I reheated the meal three times."

"I'm not hungry. Make me some coffee."

"It's two o'clock. How can you sleep so long?"

"I was writing till five o'clock this morning. I am an artist. I have the right to work when I want, whenever I feel inspired. Writing is not the same as sewing. Get that into your head, Sophie."

My sister looked at me admiringly. "You're right, Victor, I'm sorry. Will it soon be finished, your book?"

"Yes, soon."

"How wonderful! It will be a very fine book, if the bits I've read are anything to go on."

I thought, "Stupid cow!"

I drank more and more; I became careless. I left packs of cigarettes in the pocket of my overcoat. My sister brushed and cleaned it in order to search the pockets. One day she came into my room brandishing a half-empty pack. "You're smoking!"

I answered defiantly, "Yes, I'm smoking. I can't write without smoking."

"You promised me you'd stop!"

"I also promised myself. But then I realized that I couldn't write if I didn't smoke. It was a moral dilemma, Sophie. If I stop smoking, I also stop writing. I decided that it was better to carry on smoking and writing than to live without writing. I've nearly finished my book. You should leave me in peace, Sophie, to finish my book and not worry about whether I smoke or not."

My sister was impressed by this. She went out and came back with an ashtray, which she placed on my desk.

"Go ahead and smoke. It's not so bad if it's for your book. . . ."

As for drinking, I adopted the following tactic. I bought liter bottles of brandy in different parts of town, taking care not to go into the same shop twice in a row. I would bring the bottle home in the inside pocket of my overcoat and hide it in the umbrella stand in the corridor, and when my sister went out or went to bed

I would grab the bottle, lock myself in my room, and smoke and drink late into the night.

I avoided bars, I came home sober from my walks, and everything was going fine between my sister and me until the spring of this year, when Sophie began to get impatient.

"Won't you ever finish that book, Victor? This can't go on. You never get up before two o'clock in the afternoon, you look terrible, you'll make yourself ill, and me besides."

"I've finished it, Sophie. I now have to correct it and type it up. It's a big job."

"I never thought it would take so much time to write a book."

"A book's not the same as a dress, Sophie, remember that."

Summer came. I suffered terribly from the heat. I spent the afternoons in the forest, lying under the trees. Sometimes I slept and had confused dreams. One day I was awakened by a storm, a huge storm. It was August 14. I left the forest as quickly as my bad leg would allow. I sought shelter in the first bar along the way. It was a workingmen's bar. Everyone was glad about the storm, as it hadn't rained for several months. I ordered a lemonade. They all laughed, and one of them offered me a glass of red wine. I accepted. Then I ordered a bottle and offered it around. And so we carried on as the rain continued to fall. I ordered one bottle after another. I felt exceptionally good, surrounded by this warm camaraderie. I spent all the money I had on me. My companions gradually drifted away, but I didn't want to go home. I felt alone; I didn't have a home to go to. I didn't know where to go. I would have liked to have gone back to my house, my bookshop, in the faraway little town that was my ideal place. I knew now, for certain, that I should never have left that border town to live with my sister, whom I had hated since childhood.

The bartender said, "Closing time!"

Out on the street my left leg, the bad one, gave out under me, and I fell over.

I don't remember the rest. I woke up bathed in sweat in my bed. I didn't dare leave my room. Slowly it all began to come back to me. The vulgar, laughing faces in a local bar . . . later, the rain, the mud . . . the uniforms of the policemen who brought me home . . . my sister's horrified expression . . . the insults I hurled at her . . . the policemen's laughter . . .

The house was silent. Outside, the sun was shining again; the heat was suffocating.

I got up, took my old suitcase from under the bed, and started packing my clothes. It was the only solution. Leave here as soon as possible. My head was spinning. My eyes, my mouth, my throat felt raw. I felt dizzy and had to sit down. I decided I would never make it to the station in this state. I rummaged around in the wastepaper basket, found a virtually full bottle of brandy. I drank from the bottle. I felt better. I touched the back of my head. I had a painful bump behind my left ear. I picked up the bottle, lifted it to my mouth, and my sister came into the room. I put the bottle down, and I waited. My sister also waited. There was a long silence. She finally broke it, speaking in a weird, calm voice.

"What have you got to say to me?"

"Nothing," I said.

She screamed, "It's so easy! It would be, wouldn't it! He's got nothing to say! He is picked up by the police, blind drunk, lying in the mud, and he has nothing to say!"

I said, "Let me be. I'm leaving."

She snorted, "So I see, you've packed your case. But where will you go, you stupid fool, where will you go without money?"

"I've still got some money in the bank from the sale of the bookshop."

"Oh, really? I ask myself how much money you have left. You sold off the bookshop for a pittance, and the little money you made from it you've squandered on drink and cigarettes."

Of course I had never told her about the gold and silver pieces and the jewelry I received as well, which were also deposited in the bank. I simply replied, "I've got enough left to go away."

She said, "And what about me? *I* haven't been paid. I've fed you, housed you, taken care of you. Who'll repay me for all that?"

I fastened up my case. "I'll pay you. Let me leave."

Suddenly much softer, she said, "Don't be childish, Victor. I'll give you a last chance. What happened yesterday evening was just an accident, a relapse. It will all be different when you've finished your book."

I asked, "What book?"

She picked up my "manuscript." "This book, your book."

"I didn't write a single word of it."

"There are nearly two hundred pages of typescript."

"Yes, two hundred pages copied from other books."

"Copied? I don't understand."

"You'll never understand anything. I copied these two hundred pages from books. I didn't write a single word of it."

She looked at me. I raised the bottle and drank. A long drink. She shook her head. "I don't believe you. You're drunk. You're talking nonsense. Why would you do that?"

I snickered. "To make you believe I was writing. You disturb me, you spy on me constantly, you prevent me from writing; seeing you, your very presence in this house, prevents me from writing. You destroy everything, degrade everything, annihilate all creativity, life, freedom, inspiration. Since childhood you've done nothing but watch over me, guide me, annoy me, since childhood!"

She remained silent for a moment, then she said, she recited, staring down at the floor, the threadbare carpet, "I sacrificed everything for your work, your book. My own work, my clients, my last years. I walked on tiptoe so as not to disturb you. And you haven't written a single word during the two years you've been here? You do nothing but eat, drink, and smoke! You're nothing but a good-for-nothing cheat, a drunk, and a parasite! I told all my clients that your book was about to appear! And you've written nothing? I'll be the laughingstock of the whole town! You've brought dishonor on my house! I should have left you wallowing in your dirty little town and your filthy bookshop. You lived there, alone, for more than twenty years, so why didn't you write a book there where I wasn't disturbing you, where no one was disturbing you? Why? Because you couldn't even write one word of a third-rate book, no matter where you were or how you were living."

I kept on drinking while she was talking, and then heard my own voice answer her from afar, as if coming from the next room. I told her she was right, that I wouldn't be able, was not able to write anything at all as long as she was still alive. I reminded her of our childhood sexual experiences, which she'd initiated, being older than me by several years, and which had shocked me more deeply than she could ever imagine.

My sister replied that they were just childish games, and that it was in bad taste to bring them up again, especially since she had remained a virgin and had had no interest in "that" for a long time.

I said I knew "that" didn't interest her, she was happy to stroke the hips and breasts of her clients, I had watched her during fittings, I'd seen the pleasure she took in touching her young clients, beautiful as she had never been; depraved was all she had ever been.

I told her that because of her ugliness and her hypocritical puritanism, she had never been able to interest any man. So she turned instead to her clients and used taking measurements and smoothing out the material as a pretext for touching the young, beautiful women who ordered dresses from her.

My sister said, "You're going too far, Victor. That's enough!"

She grabbed the bottle, my bottle of brandy, she smashed it over the typewriter, the brandy spilled out over the desk. My sister came toward me, holding the neck of the broken bottle.

I stood up, pinned her arm back, twisted her wrist; she dropped the bottle. We fell onto the bed, and I lay on top of her. I gripped her skinny throat in my hands, and when she stopped struggling, I ejaculated.

The next day Lucas takes Victor's manuscript back to Peter.

A few months later, Peter goes back to his hometown to take part in the trial. He is away for several weeks. On his return he calls in at the bookshop, strokes Mathias's hair, and says to Lucas. "Come and see me this evening."

Lucas says, "Sounds like bad news, Peter."

Peter shakes his head. "Don't ask any questions now. See you later."

When Peter leaves, the child turns to Lucas. "Has something bad happened to Peter?"

"Not to Peter, but to one of his friends, I'm afraid."

The child says, "It's the same thing, it's maybe even worse."

Lucas holds Mathias close. "You're right. Sometimes it's worse."

When he gets to Peter's, Lucas asks, "Well?"

Peter drinks the glass of brandy he has just poured in a single gulp. "Well? Sentenced to death. Executed yesterday by hanging. Drink up!"

"You're drunk, Peter!"

Peter raises the bottle, examines the level of the liquid, snickers. "You're right, I've already drunk half a bottle. I'm taking over where Victor left off."

Lucas gets up. "I'll come back another time. It's no use talking to you in this state."

Peter says, "On the contrary. I can't talk about Victor unless I'm in this state. Sit down. Here, this belongs to you. Victor sends it to you." He pushes a small linen bag over to Lucas.

Lucas asks, "What is it?"

"Gold coins and jewelry. Some money as well. Victor didn't have enough time to spend it. He said, 'Give this all back to Lucas. He paid too much for the house and the bookshop. As for you, Peter, I leave you my house, the house of my sister and our parents. We don't have any heirs, neither my sister nor I have an heir. Sell this house, it is cursed. It has had a curse on it since our childhood. Sell it, and go back to the little town far away, that wonderful place I never should have left.' "

After a silence, Lucas says, "You thought Victor would receive a lighter sentence. You even hoped he would avoid prison and live out his days in an asylum."

"I was wrong, that's all. I couldn't know that the psychiatrists would judge Victor responsible for his actions, nor that Victor would act like a fool at his trial. He showed no remorse, no regret, no contrition. He just kept on repeating, 'I had to do it, I had to kill her. It was the only way I could write my book.' The jury deemed that no one had a right to kill someone solely because that person was preventing him from writing a book. They also declared that it would be too easy to have a few drinks, kill an honest person, and get away with it. They concluded that Victor was a selfish, perverse individual who was a danger to society. Apart from me all the witnesses gave evidence against him in favor of his sister, who led an honorable, exemplary life, and was appreciated by everyone, particularly her clients."

Lucas asks, "Were you able to see him apart from the trial?"

"After the sentence, yes. I was allowed to go into his cell and stay as long as I wanted. I kept him company up to the end."

"Was he afraid?"

"Afraid? I don't think that's the right word. At first he didn't believe it, he couldn't believe it. Was he expecting a pardon, a miracle? I don't know. The day he wrote and signed his will he certainly had no illusions. The final evening he said to me, 'I know I'm going to die, Peter, but I don't understand it. Instead of just one corpse, my sister's, there will now be a second, mine. But who needs a second corpse? Certainly not God, he has no use for our bodies. Society? It would gain a book or two by letting me live, instead of gaining an extra corpse which would benefit no one.' "

Lucas asks, "Did you go to the execution?"

"No. He asked me to, but I said no. You think I'm a coward, don't you?"

"Not for the first time. But I understand."

"Would you have gone?"

"If he had asked me, yes, I would have gone."

7

The bookshop has been converted into a reading room. Some children have already got into the habit of going there to read or draw; others come in at random when they are cold or tired from having been out playing too long in the snow. These children stay a quarter of an hour or so, just long enough to get warm and flip through some picture books. There are also those who peer through the shop window and then run away when Lucas comes out to invite them in.

Now and then Mathias comes down from the apartment, sits down with a book next to Lucas, goes back up after an hour or two, and returns for closing time. He doesn't mix with the other children. When they have left, Mathias rearranges the books, empties the wastepaper basket, places the chairs on the tables, and wipes down the floor. He also keeps accounts: "They've stolen another seven colored pencils, three books, and they've wasted dozens of sheets of paper."

Lucas says, "It's nothing, Mathias. If they asked I'd give them these things for free. They're shy, they prefer to take things in secret. It's not important."

Late one afternoon, while everyone is reading in silence, Mathias slides a note to Lucas. It says, "Look at that woman!" Outside the window, in the darkness of the street, the shadowy figure of a woman, a faceless silhouette, is looking into the brightly lit bookshop. Lucas gets up and the shadow disappears.

Mathias whispers, "She follows me everywhere. At recess she watches me over the playground fence. She walks behind me on the way home from school."

Lucas asks, "Does she speak to you?"

"No. Once, a few days ago, she offered me an apple, but I didn't take it. Another time, when four other boys were holding me down in the snow and were about to undress me, she scolded them and hit them. I ran away."

"She's not evil, then. She defended you."

"Yes, but why? She has no reason to defend me. And why does she follow me? Why does she watch me? Her look scares me. Her eyes scare me."

Lucas says, "Don't pay any attention, Mathias. Many women lost their children during the war, so they get attached to another child who reminds them of the one they lost."

Mathias snickers. "I'd be surprised if I reminded anyone of her child."

That evening, Lucas rings at the door of Yasmine's aunt. She opens the window. "What do you want?"

"To talk to you."

"I haven't time. I have to go to work."

"I'll wait for you."

When she comes out of the house, Lucas says, "I'll walk with you. Do you often work at night?"

"One week in three. Like everybody else. What do you want to talk about? My job?"

"No. About the child. I just want to ask you to leave him alone."

"I've done nothing to him."

"I know. But you follow him, you watch him. It bothers him. Do you understand?"

"Yes. Poor little thing. She left him."

They walk silently down the empty, snow-covered street. The woman hides her face in her scarf; her shoulders shake with her silent sobbing.

Lucas asks, "When will your husband be freed?"

"My husband? He's dead. Didn't you know?"

"No. I'm sorry."

"Officially he committed suicide. But I heard from someone who knew him inside, who's now been released, that it wasn't suicide. It was his cellmates who killed him because of what he did to his daughter."

They reach the front of the large textile factory, which is lit up by neon lights. From all sides shivering, shadowy figures hurry in and disappear through the metal gate. Even out here the noise of the machines is deafening.

Lucas asks, "If your husband weren't dead, would you take him back?"

"I don't know. He wouldn't have dared come back to this town in any case. I think he would have gone to the capital to look for Yasmine."

The factory siren goes. Lucas says, "I'll let you go. You'll be late."

The woman raises her pale, youthful face; she has the brilliant, dark eyes of Yasmine.

"Now that I'm on my own, I could maybe, if you like, if you wanted, take the child in."

Lucas screams louder than the factory siren. "Take Mathias? Never! He's mine, mine alone! I forbid you to go near him, watch him, talk to him, or follow him!"

The woman retreats toward the factory gate. "Calm down. Have you gone mad? It was only a suggestion."

Lucas turns on his heels and runs back to the bookshop. He leans against the wall of the house and waits for his heartbeat to slow down.

A young girl enters the bookshop, comes up to Lucas, smiles. "Don't you recognize me, Lucas?"

"Should I?"

"Agnes."

Lucas tries to think. "I'm sorry, Miss, I don't recall."

"But we're old friends. I once came to your house to listen to music. I suppose I was only six at the time. You wanted to make me a swing."

Lucas says, "I remember. Your Aunt Leonie sent you."

"That's right. She's dead now. This time it's the factory manager who sent me to buy some picture books for the children in the day-care center."

"You work at the factory? You should still be at school."

Agnes blushes. "I'm fifteen. I left school last year. I don't work at the factory, I'm a kindergarten teacher. The children call me Miss."

Lucas laughs. "I called you Miss as well."

She hands Lucas a bill. "Give me some books, and also some paper and pencils for drawing."

Agnes comes by often. She browses at length among the books

on the shelves, she sits with the children, she reads and draws with them.

The first time that Mathias sees her he says to Lucas, "She's a very beautiful woman."

"A woman? She's just a kid."

"She's got breasts, she's not a kid anymore."

Lucas looks at Agnes's breasts, enhanced by a red sweater.

"You're right, Mathias, she does have breasts. I hadn't noticed."

"What about her hair? She has lovely hair. Look how it shines in the light."

Lucas looks at Agnes's long blond hair shining in the light.

Mathias continues, "Look at her dark eyelashes."

Lucas says, "It's eyeshadow."

"Her mouth."

"Lipstick. At her age she shouldn't be wearing makeup."

"You're right, Lucas. She'd be beautiful even without makeup."

Lucas laughs. "And at your age you shouldn't be eyeing the girls."

"I don't look at the girls in my class. They're stupid and ugly."

Agnes gets up. She climbs the stepladder to get a book. She is wearing a short skirt that reveals her garter belt and black stockings, which have a run in them. Noticing this, she wets her index finger and tries to stop the run with the saliva. To do this she must bend down, revealing white panties decorated with pink flowers—little girl's panties.

One evening, she stays until closing time. She says to Lucas, "I'll help you tidy up."

Lucas says, "Mathias does the tidying. He's good at it."

Mathias says to Agnes, "If you helped me I'd finish quicker, then I could make you some pancakes with jam, if you like them."

Agnes says, "Everybody likes pancakes with jam."

Lucas goes up to his room. A little while later, Mathias calls him. "It's ready, Lucas."

They eat pancakes with jam in the kitchen, they drink tea. Lucas doesn't speak. Agnes and Mathias laugh a lot. After the meal, Mathias says, "You'll have to walk Agnes home. It's dark outside."

Agnes says, "I can go on my own. I'm not afraid of the dark."

Lucas says, "Come on. I'll walk with you."

When they reach her house, Agnes asks, "Aren't you coming in?"

"No."

"Why not?"

"You're just a child, Agnes."

"No, I'm not a child anymore. I'm a woman. You wouldn't be the first to come into my bedroom. My parents aren't home. They're at work. Even if they were here . . . I have my own room and I can do what I like."

Lucas says, "Good night, Agnes. I have to go."

Agnes says, "I know where you're going. Down to that alley where the soldiers' girls are."

"That's right. But that's no concern of yours."

The next day, Lucas says to Mathias, "Before you invite someone to eat with us you should ask my opinion."

"Don't you like Agnes? Too bad. She's in love with you. It's obvious. It's because of you that she comes so often."

Lucas says, "You've got a fertile imagination, Mathias."

"Wouldn't you like to marry her?"

"Marry her? What an idea! No, certainly not."

"Why not? Are you still waiting for Yasmine? She won't come back."

Lucas says, "I don't want to marry anyone."

It is spring. The back door to the garden is open. Mathias is tending to his plants and his animals. He has a white rabbit, several cats, and the black dog that Joseph gave him. He is looking forward to the birth of some chicks being hatched out by a hen in the chicken coop.

Lucas is watching over the room where the children are bent over their books, absorbed in their reading.

A small boy raises his eyes, smiles at Lucas. He has blond hair, blue eyes. It's the first time he has been here. Lucas can't tear his eyes away from the child. He sits behind the counter, opens a book, and continues watching the unknown child. He feels a sudden, sharp pain in his left hand, which is resting on the book. A pair of compasses is stuck in the back of his hand. Half paralyzed by the intensity of the pain, Lucas turns slowly to Mathias.

"Why did you do that?"

Mathias hisses between his teeth, "I don't want you looking at him!"

"I wasn't looking at anyone."

"Yes you were! Don't lie to me! I saw you looking at him. I don't want you looking at him like that."

Lucas pulls out the compasses. He presses his handkerchief over the wound.

"I'm going upstairs to put some antiseptic on this."

When he comes back down the children have all gone. Mathias has pulled down the metal shutter in front of the door.

"I told them we were closing early today."

Lucas takes Mathias in his arms, carries him to the apartment, and puts him on the bed.

"What's the matter with you, Mathias?"

"Why were you looking at him, the blond boy?"

"He reminded me of someone."

"Someone you loved?"

"Yes. My brother."

"You mustn't love anyone else but me, not even your brother."

Lucas is silent.

Mathias continues, "There's no point in being intelligent. It's better to be beautiful and blond. If you got married, you could have children like him, the blond boy, like your brother. You'd have real children of your own, beautiful and blond, who aren't crippled. I'm not your son. I'm Yasmine's son."

Lucas says, "You are my son. I don't want any other children." He shows Mathias his bandaged hand. "You hurt me, you know."

The child says, "And you hurt me, only you don't know it."

Lucas says, "I didn't want to hurt you. You must know one thing, Mathias: the only person in the world I care about is you."

The child says, "I don't believe you. Only Yasmine really loved me, and she's dead. I've told you that lots of times."

"Yasmine isn't dead. She just went away."

"She wouldn't have left without me, so she's dead." The child continues. "We must close down the reading room. What made you open a reading room in the first place?"

"I did it for you. I thought it would help you make friends."

"I don't want friends. I never asked you for a reading room. In fact, I'm asking you to close it."

Lucas says, "I'll close it. I'll tell the children tomorrow evening that the weather is nice enough to read and draw outside."

The little blond boy returns the next day. Lucas doesn't look at him. He stares at the lines, the letters in a book.

Mathias says, "You don't dare look at him. But you're dying to, all the same. You've been reading that page for the last five minutes."

Lucas closes the book and buries his face in his hands.

Agnes comes into the library. Mathias runs to meet her, she gives him a kiss. Mathias asks, "Why did you stop coming?"

"I haven't had time. I've been on a teacher training course in the next town. I wasn't home very often."

"But now you'll stay here, in our town?"

"Yes."

"Will you come and eat pancakes with us this evening?"

"I'd love to, but I have to look after my brother. Our parents are at work."

Mathias says, "Bring him with you, your little brother. There will be enough pancakes to eat. I'll go and make the batter."

"And I'll tidy up the shop for you."

Mathias goes up to the apartment. Lucas says to the children, "You can take the books that are out on the tables. The sheets of paper as well, and a box of colored pencils each. You shouldn't be cooped up in here in this weather. Go and read and draw in your gardens or in the park. If you need anything you can come and see me."

The children leave. Finally only the little blond boy is left, sitting quietly at his desk. Lucas asks him softly, "What about you? Aren't you going home?"

The child doesn't answer. Lucas turns to Agnes.

"I didn't know he was your brother. I knew nothing about him."

"He's shy. His name is Samuel. I suggested he come here, now that he's learning to read. He's the youngest. My brother Simon has been working at the factory for five years. He is a truck driver."

The blond child gets up and takes his sister's hand. "Are we going to eat pancakes with the man?"

Agnes says, "Yes, let's go up. Mathias will need some help."

They go up the stairs leading to the apartment. In the kitchen Mathias is mixing batter.

Agnes says, "Mathias, meet my little brother. He's called Samuel. I'm sure you'll be good friends. You're more or less the same age."

Mathias's eyes open wide, he drops the wooden spoon, he leaves the kitchen.

Agnes turns to Lucas. "What's wrong?"

Lucas says, "Mathias has probably gone to look for something in his room. Start cooking the pancakes, Agnes. I'll be back in a moment."

Lucas goes into Mathias's room. The child is lying on his eiderdown. He says, "Leave me alone. I want to sleep."

"You invited them, Mathias. It's bad manners."

"I invited Agnes. I didn't know he was her brother."

"I didn't know either. Make an effort for Agnes's sake, Mathias. You like Agnes, don't you?"

"And you like her brother. When I saw you all come into the kitchen I knew you were a real family. Beautiful, blond parents with their beautiful, blond child. I haven't got a family. I haven't got a mother or a father. I'm not blond. I'm ugly and crippled."

Lucas holds him tight. "Mathias, my little boy. You're my whole life."

Mathias smiles. "Fine. Let's eat."

In the kitchen the table is set, and there is a large pile of pancakes in the middle.

Agnes talks a lot, gets up frequently to serve the tea. She pays the same attention to her little brother as to Mathias.

"Jam? Cheese? Chocolate?"

Lucas watches Mathias. He eats little and never takes his eyes off the blond child. The blond child eats a lot. He smiles at Lucas when their eyes meet, he smiles at his sister when she hands him something; but when his blue eyes encounter Mathias's dark stare, he lowers his gaze.

Agnes washes up with Mathias. Lucas goes to his room.

Mathias calls him later. "Time to walk Agnes and her brother home."

Agnes says, "We're really not afraid to walk home on our own."

Mathias insists. "It's good manners. Walk them home."

Lucas walks them home. He bids them good night and goes to sit on the bench in the insomniac's park.

The insomniac says, "It's half past three. At eleven o'clock the child lit a fire in his room. I took the liberty of calling out to him, something I wouldn't normally do. I was worried that he might set fire to something. I asked the child what he was doing, but he told me not to worry, he was just burning the rough notes from his homework in a metal pail in front of the window. I asked him why he didn't use the stove to burn his papers. He said he didn't want to go to the kitchen to do it. The fire went out shortly after, and I didn't see the child or hear any sound after that."

Lucas goes up the stairs, enters his room, then the child's room. In front of the window there is a metal pail containing some burned paper. The child's bed is empty. On the pillow lies a blue notebook, closed. On the white label is written: MATHIAS'S NOTEBOOK. Lucas opens the notebook. There are only a few empty sheets and the edges of ripped-out pages. Lucas pulls open the dark red curtain. Alongside the skeleton of his mother and her baby hangs the little body of Mathias, already cold.

The insomniac hears a long scream. He goes down into the street, rings at Lucas's door. There is no reply. The old man goes up the stairs, enters Lucas's room, sees another door, opens it. Lucas is lying on the bed, clutching the child's body against his chest.

"Lucas?"

Lucas doesn't answer. His eyes stare wide open at the ceiling.

The insomniac goes back down into the street, he goes to call on Peter. Peter opens a window.

"What's going on, Michael?"

"Lucas needs you. Something terrible has happened. Come."

"Go home, Michael. I'll take care of everything."

He goes up to Lucas's apartment. He sees the metal pail, the two bodies stretched out on the bed. He pulls open the curtain, discovers the skeletons and, on the same hook, the end of a rope cut with a razor. He turns back to the bed, gently pushes the child's body away, and slaps Lucas on the face.

"Snap out of it!"

Lucas closes his eyes. Peter shakes him.

"Tell me what happened!"

Lucas says, "It's Yasmine. She's taken him from me."

Peter says firmly, "Don't ever say that again to anyone else but me, Lucas. Do you understand? Look at me!"

Lucas looks at Peter.

"Yes, I understand. What do I do now, Peter?"

"Nothing. Stay where you are. I'll bring you some tranquilizers. I'll take care of the formalities."

Lucas hugs Mathias's body.

"Thank you, Peter. I don't need any tranquilizers."

"No? Well, try to cry at least. Where are your keys?"

"I don't know. Maybe I left them in the front door."

"I'll lock up. You mustn't go out in this state. I'll be back."

Peter finds a bag in the kitchen, unhooks the skeletons, slips them into the bag, and takes them away with him.

Lucas and Peter walk behind Joseph's wagon, which is carrying the child's coffin.

At the cemetery a gravedigger sits on a mound of earth eating some bacon with onions.

Mathias is buried in the grave of Lucas's grandmother and grandfather.

When the gravedigger has filled in the hole, Lucas himself plants the cross, on which is engraved MATHIAS and two dates. The child lived seven years and four months.

Joseph asks, "Can I give you a lift, Lucas?"

Lucas says, "Go home, Joseph, and thank you. Thank you for everything."

"There's no point in staying here."

Peter says, "Come, Joseph. I'll go back with you."

Lucas hears the wagon depart. He sits down by the grave. The birds are singing.

A woman dressed in black comes by silently and places a bouquet of violets at the foot of the cross.

Later, Peter comes back. He touches Lucas on the shoulder.

"Come. It will soon be dark."

Lucas says, "I can't leave him here on his own at night. He's afraid of the dark. He's still so little."

"No, now he's not afraid anymore. Come, Lucas."

Lucas gets up, he stares at the grave. "I should have let him go with his mother. I made a fatal mistake, Peter, in wanting to keep the child at any price."

Peter says, "Every one of us commits a fatal mistake sometime in his life. When we realize it, the damage is already done."

They go back down into town. Outside the bookshop Peter asks, "Do you want to come to my place, or would you rather go in?"

"I'd rather go in."

Lucas goes in. He sits at his desk, looks at the closed door of the child's room, opens a school notebook, and writes, "Everything is fine with Mathias. He is always first at school, and he doesn't have nightmares anymore."

Lucas closes the notebook. He leaves the house, goes back to the cemetery, and sleeps on the child's grave.

At dawn, the insomniac comes to wake him.

"Come, Lucas. Time to open the bookshop."

"Yes, Michael."

8

Claus arrives by train. The little station hasn't changed, but there is now a bus for the passengers.

Claus doesn't take the bus. He goes on foot to the town center. The chestnut trees are in blossom; the street is as quiet and empty as it used to be.

Claus stops in the main square. There is a large three-story building in place of the simple, low houses. It is a hotel. Claus goes in and asks the receptionist, "When was this hotel built?"

"About ten years ago, sir. Would you like a room?"

"I don't know yet. I'll come back in a few hours. Could I leave my case here?"

"Please do."

Claus continues walking, he goes across town, passes the last of the houses, takes an unpaved road that leads to a playing field. Claus crosses the field and sits on the grass next to the river. Later, some children start playing ball. Claus asks one of them, "Has this playing field been here long?"

The child shrugs his shoulders. "The field? It's always been here."

Claus goes back to town. He goes up to the castle, then the cemetery. He searches for ages but can't find the grave of Grandmother and Grandfather. He goes back down into town. He sits on a bench in the main square. He watches the people doing their shopping, coming home from work, going for walks or bicycle rides. There are only a few cars. When the shops close, the square empties, and Claus goes back into the hotel.

"I'll take a room, please."

"For how many nights?"

"I don't know yet."

"Can I have your passport, sir?"

"Here."

"Are you a foreigner? Where did you learn to speak our language so well?"

"Here. I spent my childhood in this town."

She looks at him. "It must have been a long time ago."

Claus laughs. "Do I look that old?"

The young woman blushes. "No, no, I didn't mean that. I'll give you our best room, they're almost all empty. The season hasn't started yet."

"Do you get many tourists?"

"In summer, lots. I also recommend our restaurant, sir."

Claus goes up to his room on the second floor. Its two windows look out onto the square.

Claus eats in the deserted restaurant and goes back to his room. He opens his case, puts his clothes in the dresser, pulls up a chair to one of the windows, and looks out onto the empty street. On the other side of the square, the old houses have remained intact. They have been restored, repainted pink, yellow, blue, and green. The ground floor of each is occupied by a shop: a grocer, a souvenir shop, a dairy, a bookshop, a boutique. The bookshop is in the blue house where it used to be when Claus was a child and went there to buy paper and pencils.

The next day, Claus goes back to the playing field, the castle, the cemetery, the station. When he feels tired, he goes into a bar; he sits in a park. Later in the afternoon, he comes back to the main square. He goes into the bookshop.

A man with white hair sits at the counter, reading by the light of a desk lamp. The shop is in darkness. There are no customers. The white-haired man gets up.

"Excuse me, I forgot to turn on the lights."

The room and window lights come on. The man asks, "Can I help you?"

Claus says, "Please don't bother. I'm just looking."

The man takes off his glasses. "Lucas!"

Claus smiles. "You know my brother! Where is he?"

The man repeats, "Lucas!"

"I'm Lucas's brother. I'm called Claus."

"Don't joke, Lucas, please."

Claus takes his passport from his pocket. "See for yourself."

The man examines the passport. "That doesn't prove anything."

Claus says, "I'm sorry, I have no other means of proving my identity. I am Claus T. and I've come to look for my brother, Lucas. You know him. He has certainly told you about me, his brother Claus."

"Yes, he often talked to me about you, but I must admit I never believed you really existed."

Claus laughs. "Whenever I spoke to people about Lucas, they didn't believe me either. Rather funny, don't you think?"

"No, not really. Come, let's sit down over there."

He points to a low table and some armchairs at the back of the shop, in front of the French windows opening onto the garden.

"If you're not Lucas, I had better introduce myself. I am called Peter. Peter N. But if you aren't Lucas, why did you come here, to this particular place?"

Claus says, "I arrived yesterday. First I went to Grandmother's house, but it's no longer there. There's a playing field there instead. I came in here because this used to be a book and stationery shop when I was a child. We often came here to buy paper and pencils. I can still remember the man who ran it, a pale, fat man. I was hoping to find him here."

"Victor?"

"I don't know his name. I never did."

"He was called Victor. He's dead."

"Of course. He was getting on a bit even then."

"That's right."

Peter looks at the garden disappearing in the darkness.

Claus says, "I naively expected to find Lucas in Grand-mother's house after all these years. Where is he?"

Peter continues looking out into the dark. "I don't know."

"Is there anyone in this town who might know?"

"No, I don't think so."

"Did you know him well?"

Peter looks Claus straight in the eyes. "As well as you can know anyone."

Peter leans across the table, grips Claus's shoulders. "Stop it,

Lucas, stop this play-acting! It's pointless! Aren't you ashamed to be doing this to me?"

Claus frees himself, gets up. "I can see you were very close, you and Lucas."

Peter falls back into his chair. "Yes, very. Forgive me, Claus. I knew Lucas when he was fifteen. At the age of thirty he disappeared."

"Disappeared? You mean he left this town?"

"The town and maybe even the country. Then he returns today with a different name. I always thought that play on words with your names was stupid."

"Our grandfather had that double name, Claus-Lucas. Our mother, who had a great deal of affection for her father, gave us these two names. It's not Lucas standing here before you, Peter, it's Claus."

Peter gets up. "Very well, Claus. In that case I must give you something that your brother Lucas left with me. Wait here."

Peter goes up to the apartment. He comes back shortly after with five large school notebooks.

"Here. These are meant for you. He had a lot more to start with, but he took them back, corrected them, erased everything that wasn't indispensable. If he'd had the time I think he would have eliminated everything."

Claus shakes his head. "No, not everything. He would have kept what was essential. For me."

He takes the notebooks, he smiles. "At last, here is the proof of Lucas's existence. Thank you, Peter. Has anyone read them?"

"Apart from me, no."

"I'm staying at the hotel across the way. I'll be back."

Claus reads all night, occasionally raising his eyes to look at the street.

Above the bookshop the light stays on for a long time in two of the three windows in the apartment. The third stays dark.

In the morning, Peter raises the metal shutter of the shop. Claus goes to bed. After noon, Claus leaves the hotel. He has a meal in one of the bars in town where they serve hot dishes all day.

The sky is overcast. Claus goes back to the playing field, sits next to the river. He stays there until night falls and it begins to rain. When Claus arrives back at the main square the bookshop is already closed. Claus rings at the front door of the apartment. Peter leans out of the window.

"The door is open. I was expecting you. Just come up."

Claus finds Peter in the kitchen. There are pans boiling on the stove.

Peter says, "The meal isn't ready yet. I've got some brandy. Would you like some?"

"Yes. I've read the notebooks. What happened afterward? After the death of the child?"

"Nothing. Lucas kept on working. He opened the shop in the morning, he closed it at night. He served his customers without saying a word. He hardly ever spoke. Some people thought he was mute. I often came to see him. We played chess in silence. He played badly. He didn't read or write anymore. I think he ate very little and hardly slept. The light was on all night in his room, but he wasn't in. He went walking in the dark streets of the town and in the cemetery. He said that the best place to sleep was the grave of someone you'd loved."

Peter is silent; he pours the drinks.

Claus says, "And then? Go on, Peter."

"Five years later, in the course of the work being done to lay out the playing field, I heard that the body of a woman had been discovered buried in the riverbank, near your grandmother's house. I told Lucas about it. He thanked me, and the next day he disappeared. No one has seen him since. On his desk he left a letter entrusting the house and the bookshop to me. The saddest thing about this story, you see, Claus, was that Yasmine's body was never identified. The authorities botched the whole affair. There are bodies in the ground everywhere in this unhappy land since the war and the revolution. This body could have been any woman who had tried to cross the border and stepped on a mine. Lucas wouldn't have been questioned."

Claus says, "He could come back now. There's the statute of limitations."

"Yes, I suppose so. After twenty years there is a statute of limitations." Peter looks Claus in the eyes. "That's right, Claus. Lucas could come back now."

Claus counters Peter's gaze. "Yes, Peter. Lucas will probably come back."

"They say that he's hiding in the forest and that he roams the streets of the town after dark. But that's just talk."

Peter shakes his head. "Come to my room, Claus. I'll show you Lucas's letter."

Claus reads: "I entrust the house and the bookshop that forms part of it to Peter N.—on the condition that he maintain the premises *in their present state*—until my return or, failing that, the return of my brother Claus T. Signed: Lucas T."

Peter says, "He underlined 'in their present state.' Now, whether you are Claus or Lucas, this house belongs to you."

"Listen, Peter, I'm only here for a short time, on a thirty-day visa. I'm a foreign citizen, and as you know, foreigners are not allowed to own any property here."

Peter says, "But you can accept the profits from the bookshop which I've been depositing in a bank every month for the last twenty years."

"What do you live on, then?"

"I have a government pension, and I rent out Victor's house. I only take care of the bookshop for you two. I keep careful accounts, you can check them."

Claus says, "Thank you, Peter. I don't need the money, and I don't wish to check the accounts. I came back only to see my brother."

"Why didn't you ever write to him?"

"We decided to separate. It had to be a total separation. The border wasn't enough. We needed silence as well."

"Yet you came back. Why?"

"The test has lasted long enough. I'm tired and ill. I want to see Lucas again."

"You know that you won't see him again."

A woman's voice calls from the next room.

"Is there someone there, Peter? Who is it?"

Claus looks at Peter. "You've got a wife? You're married?"

"No, it's Clara."

"Clara? She isn't dead?"

"We thought she was, yes. But she was just in prison. Shortly after Lucas disappeared she came back. She had no job and no money. She was looking for Lucas. I let her stay at my place, that is, here. She has the small room, the child's room. I take care of her. Do you want to see her?"

"Yes, I'd like to see her."

Peter opens the door of the room.

"Clara, a friend has come to see us."

Claus goes into the room. Clara is sitting in a rocking chair in front of the window, with a blanket over her knees and a shawl around her shoulders. She is holding a book, but she's not reading it. She is staring into space through the gap in the window. She is rocking.

Claus says, "Hello, Clara."

Clara doesn't look at him; she recites in a monotonous voice, "It's raining as usual. Fine, cold rain, falling on the houses, the trees, the graves. When they come to see me the rain trickles over their distorted faces. They look at me and the cold grows more intense. My walls no longer protect me. They never protected me. Their solidity is mere illusion, their whiteness is stained."

Her voice changes suddenly. "I'm hungry, Peter! When do we eat? With you the meals are always late."

Peter returns to the kitchen.

Claus says, "It's me, Clara."

"You?"

She looks at Claus, holds out her arms to him. He kneels down at her feet, rests his head on her knees. Clara strokes his hair. Claus takes Clara's hand, presses it against his cheek, against his lips. A thin, wizened hand, covered with the marks of old age.

She says, "You left me alone for a long time, too long, Thomas."

Tears run down her face. Claus wipes them away with his handkerchief.

"I'm not Thomas. Have you no memory of Lucas?"

Clara closes her eyes, shakes her head, "You haven't changed, Thomas. You've aged a little, but you are still the same. Kiss me."

She smiles, revealing her toothless gums.

Claus draws back, stands up. He goes to the window, looks out to the street. The main square is empty and dark in the rain. Only the lighted entrance of the hotel is visible in the dark.

Clara starts rocking again. "Go away. Who are you? What are you doing in my room? Why doesn't Peter come? I want to eat and go to bed. It's late."

Claus leaves Clara's room, he finds Peter in the kitchen. "Clara is hungry."

Peter carries a tray in to Clara. When he comes back he says, "She likes her food. I take her a tray three times a day. Fortunately, she sleeps a lot because of her medication."

"She must be a burden to you."

Peter serves up stew with some pasta. "No, not really. She doesn't bother me. She treats me as if I were her valet, but I don't mind. Eat up, Claus."

"I'm not hungry. Does she ever go out?"

"Clara? No. She doesn't like to, and in any case she would just get lost. She reads a lot and likes looking at the sky."

"What about the insomniac? His house must have been opposite, there where the hotel is now."

Peter gets up. "Yes, that's right. I'm not hungry either. Come, let's go out."

They walk down the street. Peter points out a house. "That's where I lived at that time. On the second floor. If you're not too tired, I can show you where Clara used to live."

"I'm not tired."

Peter stops in front of a two-story building on Station Road.

"This is it. This house will soon be demolished, like nearly all the houses on this street. They are too old and unsanitary."

Claus shivers. "Let's go back. I'm frozen."

They part in front of the hotel entrance. Claus says, "I've been to the cemetery several times, but I can't find Grandmother's grave."

"I'll show you tomorrow. Come to the bookshop at six o'clock. It will still be light."

In an abandoned part of the cemetery, Peter sticks his umbrella in the ground.

"Here's the grave."

"How can you be so sure? There's nothing here but weeds. No cross, nothing. You could be mistaken."

"Mistaken? If only you knew how many times I came here looking for your brother Lucas. Even afterward, later, when he was no longer here. This spot has been the end of an almost daily walk for me."

They go back into town. Peter attends to Clara, then they drink brandy in what used to be Lucas's room. The rain falls on the windowsill, drips into the room. Peter goes to get a cloth to mop up the water.

"Tell me about yourself, Claus."

"There's nothing to tell."

"Over there, is life easier?"

Claus shrugs his shoulders. "It's a society based on money. There is no place for questions about life. I've spent thirty years in mortal solitude."

"Did you never have a wife, a child?"

Claus laughs. "Women, yes. Lots of women. No children."

After a silence he asks, "What did you do with the skeletons, Peter?"

"I put them back in their place. Do you want to see them?"

"We mustn't disturb Clara."

"We don't need to cross the room. There's another door. Don't you remember?"

"How could I remember?"

"You might have noticed as you went past. It's the first door on the left as you come to the landing."

"No, I didn't notice."

"The door does blend in with the wallpaper."

They enter a small space separated from Clara's room by a thick curtain. Peter switches on a flashlight, illuminating the skeletons.

Claus whispers, "There are three of them."

Peter says, "You don't need to whisper. Clara won't wake up. She takes strong sedatives. I forgot to tell you that Lucas dug up Mathias's body two years after the burial. He told me that it was easier for him, he was tired of spending his nights at the cemetery to keep the child company."

Peter shines the flashlight on a mattress beneath the skeletons.

"That's where he slept."

Claus touches the mattress, the gray army blanket that covers it.

"It's warm."

"What's on your mind, Claus?"

"I'd like to sleep here, just for one night. Do you mind, Peter?"

"This is your home."

Report drawn up by the authorities of the town of K. for the attention of the embassy of D.

Re: request for the repatriation of your citizen Claus T., presently held in the prison of the town of K.

Claus T., aged fifty, holder of a valid passport and a thirty-day tourist visa, arrived in this town on April 2 of this year. He rented a room in the only hotel in town, the Grand Hotel in the main square.

Claus T. spent three weeks in the hotel, behaving like a tourist, walking around town, visiting historic sights, having his meals in the hotel restaurant, or in other restaurants in town.

Claus T. often visited the bookshop opposite the hotel to buy paper and pencils. Conversant in the local language, he chatted readily with the bookseller, Mrs. B., and with other persons in public places.

After three weeks, Claus T. asked Mrs. B. if she would rent

him the two rooms above the bookshop on a monthly basis. As he offered a good price, Mrs. B. gave up the two-room apartment and went to stay with her daughter, who lives nearby.

Claus T. requested an extension to his visa on three occasions, which was granted without difficulty. However, his fourth request for an extension was refused in August. Claus T. disregarded this refusal, and owing to negligence on the part of our employees, the matter rested there until the month of October. On October 30, in the course of a routine identity check, our local police established that Claus T.'s papers were no longer in order.

At this point, Claus T. had run out of money. He owed two months' rent to Mrs. B. He was hardly eating. He went from bar to bar playing the harmonica. Drunkards bought him drinks. Mrs. B. brought him a little soup each day.

During his interrogation, Claus T. claimed to have been born in our country, and to have spent his childhood in our town, at his grandmother's house, and declared his wish to remain here until the return of his brother Lucas T. The said Lucas does not appear in any of the records of the town of K. Neither does Claus T.

We request you to settle the enclosed invoice (fine, administrative costs, rent for Mrs. B.) and to repatriate Claus T. on your own responsibility.

Signed, on behalf of the authorities of the town of K.: I.S.

Postscript

We have naturally, for reasons of security, examined the manuscript in the possession of Claus T. He claims that this manuscript proves the existence of his brother Lucas, who wrote the major part of it himself, Claus himself having merely added the last few pages, chapter number eight. However, the manuscript is in the same handwriting from beginning to end, and the sheets of paper show no signs of age. The entire text was written in one sequence, by the same person, over a period of time not exceeding six months, that is, by Claus T. himself during his stay in our town.

As for the content of the text, this can only be a fiction, since neither the events described nor the characters portrayed ever existed in the town of K., with the sole exception of one person, the supposed grandmother of Claus T., whom we have traced. This woman did in fact own a house on the present site of our playing field. Deceased without heir thirty-five years ago, she appears in our records under the name Maria Z., wife of V.

It is possible that during the war she was entrusted with the care of one or more children.

The Third Lie

Translated by Marc Romano

Part One

I am in prison in the small town of my childhood.

It's not a real prison but a cell in the basement of the local police station, a building no different from the rest of the buildings in town. It too is a single-storied house.

My cell must have been a laundry room at one time; its door and window look out onto the courtyard. Window bars have been installed on the inside in a way that makes it impossible to reach through and break the glass. A toilet in the corner is concealed by a curtain. Against one wall are four chairs and a table bolted to the floor; on the opposite wall are four collapsible beds. Three of them are still folded up.

I am alone in my cell. There aren't many criminals in this town, and when there is one he is immediately brought to the neighboring town, the regional seat, twelve miles away.

I'm not a criminal. I'm here because my papers are not in order; my visa has expired. I've also run into debt.

In the morning my guard brings me breakfast—milk, coffee, bread. I drink some coffee and then shower. My guard finishes

343

my breakfast and cleans my cell. The door is left open; I can go out into the courtyard if I want. The courtyard is enclosed by high walls covered with ivy and wild vines. Behind one of these walls, the one to the left as you leave my cell, is a school playground. I hear the children laughing, playing, and shouting during recess. The school was there when I was a child, as I recall, although I never went. The prison was here, on the other hand, as I also recall because I went there once.

For one hour in the morning and one hour in the evening I walk around the courtyard, a habit I developed during my child-hood, when at the age of five I had to learn how to walk again.

This annoys my guard, because while I'm doing it I don't speak a word and don't hear the questions he asks me.

I pace with my eyes to the ground, my hands behind my back, turning and following the line of the walls. The ground is paved, but grass grows in the gaps between the stones.

The courtyard is almost square. Fifteen paces long, thirteen paces wide. Supposing I take three-foot strides, the courtyard's area must be 195 square yards. But my stride is probably not that long.

In the middle of the courtyard is a round table with two garden chairs; against the back wall is a wooden bench.

It is by sitting on that bench that I am able to see the greatest amount of my childhood sky.

The bookseller came to visit me on the very first day, bringing my personal effects and some vegetable soup. She continues to show up every day around noon with soup. I tell her I'm well fed here, that my guard brings me a full meal twice a day from the restaurant across the street, but she keeps coming with her soup. I eat a little out of politeness and I pass the pot to my guard, who finishes it.

I apologize to the bookseller for the mess that I left in the apartment.

She says, "Don't mention it. My daughter and I have already cleaned everything up. Mostly there was a lot of paper. I burned every sheet that was crumpled or thrown in the wastebasket. I left the others on the table, but the police came and took them."

I remain silent for a moment and then say, "I still owe you two months' rent."

She laughs. "I asked you far too much for that little apartment. But if you mean it, you can pay me when you come back. Next year, maybe."

I say, "I don't think I'll be coming back. My embassy will pay."

She asks me if there is anything I want, and I say, "Yes, paper and pencils. But I have no money."

She says, "I should have thought of it myself."

I say to her, "Thank you. The embassy will reimburse you for everything."

She says, "You're always going on about money. I wish you'd talk about something else. What are you writing, for instance?"

"What I write is absolutely meaningless."

She insists. "What I want to know is whether you write things that are true or things that are made up."

I answer that I try to write true stories but that at a given point the story becomes unbearable because of its very truth, and then I have to change it. I tell her that I try to tell my story but all of a sudden I can't—I don't have the courage, it hurts too much. And so I embellish everything and describe things not as they happened but the way I wish they had happened.

She says, "Yes. There are lives sadder than the saddest of books."

I say, "Yes. No book, no matter how sad, can be as sad as a life."

After a silence she asks, "Your limp, is it from an accident?"

"No, from an illness when I was very small."

She adds, "You can hardly even notice it."

I laugh.

I have things to write with again, but I haven't got anything to drink or any cigarettes either, aside from the two or three my guard offers me after dinner. I request an interview with the chief of police, who sees me immediately. His office is upstairs. I go. I sit down in a chair across from him. He has red hair and his face is covered with red spots. A game of chess is set up on the table in front of him. The policeman looks at the board, advances a pawn, jots the move down in a notebook, and raises his pale blue eyes.

"What do you want? The inquiry isn't over yet. It will be several weeks, a month, perhaps."

I say, "I'm not in any hurry. I'm very comfortable here. Except that I need one or two little things."

"Such as?"

"The embassy wouldn't mind if you added a bottle of wine and two packs of cigarettes a day to my prison tab."

He says, "It probably wouldn't. But that would be bad for your health."

I say, "Do you know what happens to alcoholics when they're forced to stop drinking?"

He says, "No, and I don't give a damn."

I say, "There's a risk of delirium tremens. I could die at any moment."

"No kidding."

He turns his eyes back to the board. I tell him, "The black knight."

He keeps staring at the board. "Why? I don't understand."

I advance the knight. He notes it down in his book. He ponders for a long time, then picks up his rook.

"No."

He sets down the rook and looks at me. "You play? Well?"

"I don't know. It's been a long time. But at any rate I'm better than you."

He turns redder than his spots. "I only started three months ago. And without anyone to teach me. Could you give me a few lessons?"

I say, "Gladly. But don't get angry when I win."

He says, "I'm not interested in winning. What I want is to learn."

I stand up. "Bring your set whenever you want. Ideally in the morning. The mind then is sharper than it is in the afternoon or evening."

"Thank you," he says.

He looks at the board; I wait, then cough. "What about the wine and cigarettes?"

He says, "No problem. I'll give the orders. You'll have your cigarettes and wine."

I leave the policeman's office. I go back downstairs and into the courtyard. I sit on the bench. The autumn is very mild this year. The sun sets and the sky takes on colors—orange, yellow, violet, red, and others for which there are no names.

For around two hours almost every day I play chess with the policeman. The games are long; the policeman thinks a lot, notes everything down, and always loses.

Every afternoon, after the bookseller has put away her knitting and gone off to reopen her shop, I also play cards with my guard. The card games in this country are unlike anything anywhere else. Although they are simple and there is a large element of chance to them, I always lose. We play for money, and since I don't have any my guard writes my losses down in a ledger. After every game he laughs loudly and repeats, "I'm screwed! I'm screwed!"

He is a young newlywed and his wife is expecting a baby in a few months. He often says, "If it's a boy and you're still here, I'll forgive your debt."

He talks a lot about his wife, telling me how pretty she is, especially now that she has gained weight and her buttocks and breasts have almost doubled in size. He also tells me in detail about how they met, about their "going together," their lovers' walks in the forest, her resistance, his victory, and their quick marriage, which became urgent because of the baby on the way.

But what he talks about in even greater detail and with even more pleasure is last night's dinner—how his wife prepared it, with which ingredients in what way and for how long, because "the longer it simmers the better it is."

The policeman does not speak, does not relay anything. The only disclosure he has made is that he replays, by himself and based on his notes, all of our games—once during the afternoon in his office, once again at home that night. I asked him if he was married and he replied with a shrug, "Married? Me?"

The bookseller relays nothing either. She says she has nothing to say, that she has raised two children and that she has been a widow for six years, that's all. When she asks me questions about my life in the other country, I answer by saying I have even less to tell than she, since I have raised no children and have never had a wife.

One day she says to me, "We're about the same age."

I protest: "I'd be surprised. You seem much, much younger than me."

She blushes. "Come on, I'm not fishing for compliments. What I meant was, if you grew up in this town we must probably have gone to the same school."

I say, "Yes, only me, I never went to school."

"That's impossible. School was mandatory even then."

"Not for me. I was mentally retarded at the time."

She says, "It's impossible to talk seriously with you. You're always joking."

I am seriously ill. I have known this for exactly one year today.

It began in the other country, in my adoptive country, one morning at the beginning of November. At five.

Outside it is still night. I am having trouble breathing. An intense pain keeps me from inhaling. The pain starts in my chest and spreads to my sides, back, shoulders, arms, throat, neck, jaws. As though a huge hand were trying to crush the upper part of my body.

Stretching out my arm slowly, switching on the bedside lamp.

Gingerly sitting up. Waiting. Rising. Getting to the desk, to the telephone. Sitting down on the chair. Calling for an ambulance. No! No ambulances. Waiting.

Going to the kitchen, making coffee. Not hurrying. Taking no deep breaths. Inhaling and exhaling slowly, softly, calmly.

After my coffee, showering, shaving, brushing my teeth. Returning to the bedroom, getting dressed. Waiting eight hours

351

and then calling not an ambulance but a taxi and my regular doctor.

He sees me on an emergency basis. He listens to me, takes an X ray of my lungs, examines my heart, measures my blood pressure.

"Get dressed."

We are now face-to-face in his office.

"Do you still smoke? How much? Do you still drink? How much?"

I answer truthfully. I don't think I have ever lied to him. I know that he doesn't give a damn, neither about my health nor my illness.

He writes in my file and looks at me. "You're doing everything you can to kill yourself. That concerns only you. It has been ten years since I formally forbade you to smoke or drink. You keep on doing both. But if you want to live another few years, you have to stop immediately."

I ask, "What do I have?"

"Cardiac angina, probably. It was to be expected. But I'm no heart specialist."

He hands me a piece of paper. "I am referring you to a well-known cardiologist. Take this to his clinic for a more in-depth examination. The sooner the better. Meanwhile, take these in case of pain."

He hands me a prescription. I ask, "Will they operate on me?"

He says, "If there's still time."

"If there isn't?"

"You could have a heart attack at any moment."

I go to the nearest pharmacy and am given two vials of pills. One of them contains ordinary painkillers; on the other I read, "Trinitrine. For cardiac angina. Active ingredient: Nitroglycerine."

I go home, take a pill from each vial, and lie down on my bed. The pain quickly disappears and I fall asleep.

I walk through the streets in the town of my childhood. It is a ghost town; the doors and windows of the houses are shut and the silence is complete.

I reach a wide older street lined by wooden houses and tumbledown barns. The ground is dusty and it feels good to walk barefoot through the dust.

There is, however, a strange tension in the air.

I turn around and see a puma at the other end of the street. A beautiful animal, khaki-colored and golden, whose silken fur shines under the burning sun.

Suddenly everything is on fire. The houses and barns burst into flames but I must continue down the burning street because the puma too has begun to walk and follows me at some distance, with majestic slowness.

Where to turn? There's no way out. It's either fire or teeth.

Maybe at the end of the street?

It has to end somewhere, this street, all of them do, flowing into a square, another street, fields, the open countryside, unless the street happens to be a dead end, which must be the case here and is.

I can feel the puma's breath very close behind me. I don't dare turn around but I can go no farther; my feet are rooted to the ground. I wait in horror for the puma to leap onto my back, ripping me from shoulders to thighs, clawing my head, my face.

But the puma passes me by; it walks on complacently and lies at the feet of a child at the end of the street, a child who wasn't there before but is now, and it strokes the puma lying at its feet.

The child says to me, "He isn't mean. He belongs to me. Don't be scared of him. He doesn't eat people, he doesn't eat meat. He just eats souls."

There are no more flames; the fire has gone out and the street is only soft ashes cooling.

I ask the child, "You're my brother, aren't you? Were you waiting for me?"

The child shakes his head. "No, I have no brother and I'm not waiting for anyone. I am the guardian of eternal youth. The one waiting for his brother is sitting on a bench in Central Square. He's very old. Perhaps he's waiting for you."

I find my brother sitting on a bench in Central Square. When he sees me, he stands. "You're late. We must hurry."

We climb up to the cemetery and sit down on the yellow grass. Everything around us is decaying: the crosses, the trees, the bushes, the flowers. My brother scratches at the earth with his cane and white worms emerge.

My brother says, "Not everything is dead. Those are alive."

The worms writhe. The sight of them gladdens me. I say, "As soon as you begin to think, you can no longer love life."

My brother raises my chin with his cane. "Don't think. Look— have you ever seen such a beautiful sky?"

I look up. The sun sets over the town.

I answer, "No, never. Nowhere else."

We walk side by side to the castle. We come to a stop in the courtyard at the base of the battlements. My brother climbs the rampart and, when he reaches the top, starts to dance to a music that seems to come from underground. He dances, flailing his arms toward the sky, toward the stars, toward the full and rising moon. A thin silhouette in his long black coat, he advances along the ramparts, dancing, while I follow him from below, running and shouting: "No! Don't! Stop it! Come down! You'll fall!"

He comes to a halt above me. "Don't you remember? We used to climb over the rooftops and we were never afraid of falling."

"We were young, we didn't feel the height. Come down!"

He laughs. "Don't be scared. I won't fall; I can fly. I fly over the town every night."

He raises his arms, jumps, and crashes onto the courtyard stones at my feet. I lean over him, take his bald head, his wrinkled face into my hands, and I cry.

His face decomposes, his eyes disappear, and in my hands there is now nothing but an anonymous and disintegrating skull that flows through my fingers like fine sand.

I wake up in tears. My room is lit by the dusk; I have slept for most of the day. I change out of my sweat-damp shirt and wash my face. Looking at myself in the mirror, I wonder when I last cried. I cannot remember.

I light a cigarette and sit down at the window, watching night settle on the town. Under my window is an empty garden, its lone tree already leafless. Farther away are houses, windows lighting up in greater and greater numbers. There are lives behind those windows, calm and normal and peaceful lives. Couples, children, families. I also hear the faraway sound of cars. I wonder why people drive, even at night. Where are they going, and why?

Death will obliterate everything soon.

It frightens me.

I am afraid of dying, but I will not go to the hospital.

I spent most of my childhood in a hospital. My memories of that time are very vivid. I can see my bed among some twenty other beds, my closet in the corridor, my wheelchair, my crutches, the torture room with its swimming pool and devices. The treadmills on which you were forced to trudge endlessly, supported by a harness; the rings from which you had to dangle, the exercise cycles you had to keep pedaling even though you were screaming with pain.

I remember the suffering and also the smells, medicines mixed with blood, sweat, piss, and shit.

I also remember the injections, the nurses' white blouses, the questions without answers, and most of all the waiting. Waiting for what? Healing, probably, but also perhaps for something else.

I was told later that I came to the hospital in a coma, the result of a serious illness. I was four years old, and the war started.

I no longer know what there had been before the hospital.

The white house with green shutters on a quiet street, the kitchen in which my mother sang, the yard in which my father chopped wood—was it once a reality, the perfect happiness in the white house, or had I merely hallucinated it or dreamed it up during the long nights of five years spent in a hospital?

And he who lay in the other bed in the little room, who breathed at the same rhythm as me, the brother whose name I still believe I know, was he dead or had he never existed?

One day we changed hospitals. The new one was called "Rehabilitation Center," but it was still a hospital. The rooms, beds, closets, and nurses were the same, and the agonizing exercises continued.

A huge park surrounded the center. We were allowed to leave the building to splash around in a pool of mud—the more mud you got on yourself, the happier the nurses were. We were also allowed to ride the longhair ponies that bore us gently on their backs all over the park.

At six I began school in a little room in the hospital. Eight to twelve of us, depending on the state of our health, took the lessons provided by a teacher.

The teacher did not wear a white blouse, but short, narrow skirts with lively colored blouses and high-heeled shoes. Nor did she have her hair up in a bun; it flowed freely over her shoulders, and its color was like that of the chestnuts that fell from the trees in the park in the month of September.

My pockets were filled with those shiny fruits. I used them to bombard the nurses and supervisors. At night I threw them at the beds of anyone who whined or cried, to make them shut up. I also lobbed them at the panes of a greenhouse where an old gardener grew the salads we were forced to eat. Very early one morning I left a few dozen of these chestnuts in front of the director's door so that she would tumble down the staircase, but she just fell on her fat buttocks and didn't even break a bone.

At this point I no longer used a wheelchair but walked on crutches, and I was told that I was making a lot of progress.

I went to class from eight in the morning until noon. After lunch I had to nap, but instead of sleeping I read books the teacher lent me or that I borrowed from the director when she wasn't in her office. In the afternoon I did my exercises like everyone else; in the evening I had to do homework.

I finished my homework quickly and then I wrote letters. To the teacher. I never gave them to her. To my parents, to my brother. I never sent them. I didn't know their address.

Almost three years passed this way. I no longer needed crutches; I could walk with a cane. I knew how to read, write, and do arithmetic. We weren't given grades, but I often got the gold star that was stuck up beside our names on the wall. I was especially strong at mental arithmetic.

The teacher had a room at the hospital, but she didn't always sleep there. She went into town in the evening and didn't come back until morning. I asked her if she wanted to take me with her, and she answered that it was impossible, that I wasn't allowed to leave the center, but she promised to bring me chocolate. She gave me the chocolate secretly because there wasn't enough for everybody.

One evening I said to her, "I've had enough sleeping with the other boys. I'd like to sleep with a woman."

She laughed. "You'd like to sleep in the girls' room?"

"No. Not with girls. With a woman."

"Which woman?"

"Well, with you. I'd like to sleep in your room, in your bed."

She kissed me on the eyelids. "Little boys your age should sleep alone."

"Do you sleep alone too?"

"Yes, me too."

One afternoon she appeared under my hiding place, which was high up in a walnut tree whose branches formed a comfortable sort of seat where I could read and from which the town was visible.

The teacher said to me, "Tonight, when everyone's asleep, you can come to my room."

I didn't wait until everyone was asleep. I might well have waited until morning. They were never all asleep at the same time. There were those who cried, those who went to the bathroom ten times a night, those who climbed into each other's beds to do things, those who talked until dawn.

I gave my usual whacks to the crybabies, then I went to see the little blond paralytic who doesn't move and doesn't speak. All he does is look at the ceiling, or the sky if he is brought outside, and smile. I took his hand, held it to my face, and then placed my hands against his face. He looked at the ceiling and smiled.

I left the dormitory and went into the teacher's room. She wasn't there. I lay down in her bed. It smelled nice. I fell asleep. When I woke up in the middle of the night she was lying beside me, her arms crossed over her face. I uncrossed her arms, put them around me, pressed myself against her, and stayed that way, awake, until morning.

Some of us received letters, which the nurses handed out or read to the recipients if they were unable to do so themselves. Afterward, when they asked me, I read their letters to them again. Generally I read the exact opposite of what the letters actually said. The results were, for instance: "Our dear child, whatever you do, don't get well. We're getting along just fine without you. We don't miss you at all. We hope that you'll remain where you are, because the last thing we want is a cripple in the house. Still, we send you a couple of kisses, and be good, because the people taking care of you are very good. We couldn't do as much for you. We're lucky that someone else is doing the job for us, since there is no place for you in this family, where everyone else is healthy. Your parents, sisters, and brothers."

The person I read the letter to said, "That's not how the nurse read my letter."

I said, "She read it differently because she didn't want to hurt your feelings. I read what the letter really says. I think you have a right to know the truth."

He said, "I have the right, yes, but I don't like the truth. The nurse was right to read it differently."

He cried.

Many of us also got packages. Cakes, cookies, ham, sausages, jam, honey. The director said that these packages had to be shared among everyone. Still, some of the children hid food in their beds or closets.

I went up to one of these children and asked, "You're not afraid that it might be poisoned?"

"Poisoned? Why?"

"Parents prefer a dead child to a crippled one. Haven't you ever thought about that?"

"No, never. You're a liar. Get lost."

Later I saw the child throwing his package out with the center's garbage.

Some parents also came to see their children. I waited for them at the front door of the center. I asked them the reason for their visit and the name of their child. When they answered I said, "I'm so sorry. Your child died two days ago. You haven't received our letter yet?"

After that I ran off quickly to hide.

The director called me in. She asked, "Why are you so nasty?"

"Nasty? Me? I don't know what you're talking about."

"You know very well what I'm talking about. You told a child's parents that he was dead."

"So? Wasn't he dead?"

"No, and you're perfectly aware of the fact."

"I must have gotten the names mixed up. They all sound the same."

"Except yours, right? But no child died this week."

"No? Well, I must have been thinking of last week."

"Yes, obviously. But I am advising you to make no more mistakes about names, or weeks. And I forbid you from talking to parents and visitors. I also forbid you from reading letters to the children who can't read."

I said, "I was only trying to be helpful."

She said, "I forbid you from being helpful to anyone. Do you understand me?"

"Yes, Madame Director, I understand. But no one should complain if I won't help them up stairs, if I don't pick them up when they fall down, if I don't explain their sums to them, if I don't correct the spelling in their letters. If you forbid me from being of help, forbid them from asking me for it."

She looked at me for a long time and then said, "Fine. Get out."

I left her office and saw a child crying because he had dropped his apple and couldn't pick it up. I walked past him and said, "You can cry but that won't get you your apple back, you oaf."

He asked me from his wheelchair, "Couldn't you please bring it to me?"

I said, "You're going to have to do it yourself, idiot."

That evening the director came into the dining hall. She made a speech and at the end of it she said that no one should ask favors of anyone but the nurses, the teacher, or, as a last resort, her.

As a consequence of all this I had to go twice weekly into the little room next to the infirmary, where a very old woman sat in a big armchair with a thick cover over her knees. I had already heard about her. The other children who went into the room said that the old woman was very nice and grandmotherly and that it was pleasant to be there, lying down on a cot or sitting at a table and drawing whatever you wanted. You could also look at picture books and you could say whatever you pleased.

The first time I went we didn't say anything to each other except good morning. Afterward I grew bored—none of her books interested me, I didn't want to draw—so I paced from the door to the window and from the window to the door.

After a while she asked me, "Why do you constantly pace like that?"

I stopped and replied, "I have to exercise my weak leg. I pace whenever I can, when I don't have anything else to do."

She smiled a wrinkled smile. "It seems to be doing very well, that leg."

"Not well enough."

I threw my cane onto the bed, took a few steps, and fell down by the window.

"See how well it's doing?"

I crawled back and retrieved my cane. "When I can do without this, I'll be better."

I didn't go the next few times I was meant to. They looked for me everywhere but couldn't find me. I was deep in the garden, up in the branches of my walnut tree. Only the teacher knew about my hiding place.

The final time the director herself brought me to the little room just after the midday meal. She shoved me inside and I fell onto the bed. I didn't stir. The old woman asked me questions.

"Do you remember your parents?"

I answered, "No, not at all. How about you?"

She kept on with her questions.

"What do you think about at night before falling asleep?"

"Sleeping. And you?"

She asked me: "You told some parents that their child had died. Why?"

"To make them happy."

"Why?"

"Because they're happier knowing that their child is dead and not a cripple."

"How do you know that?"

"I just know, that's all."

The old woman asked me again: "Do you do these things because your own parents never come to see you?"

I said to her, "What business is that of yours?"

She continued: "They never write to you. They don't send you packages. And so you avenge yourself on the other children."

I rose from the bed and said, "Yes, and on you too."

I hit her with my cane, then fell.

She screamed.

She kept screaming and I kept hitting her, right there from the floor where I had fallen. My blows struck only her legs and knees.

Nurses came in, drawn by the screams. They pinned me and brought me to a little room like the first one, only here there was no desk, no bookshelf, just a bed and nothing else. There were also bars on the windows and the door was locked from the outside.

I slept briefly.

When I awoke I pounded on the door, kicked the door, shouted. I cried out for my things, my homework, my books.

No one answered.

In the middle of the night the teacher came into my room and lay down beside me on the narrow bed. I buried my face in her hair and suddenly I was seized by a fit of trembling. It shook my whole body; hiccups came out of my mouth, my eyes filled with water, my nose ran. I sobbed helplessly.

There was less and less food at the center; the park had to be turned into a vegetable garden. Everyone who could worked under the gardener's direction. We planted potatoes, beans, carrots. I was sorry I was no longer confined to a wheelchair.

More and more often we also had to go down into the basement because of air raid warnings, which came almost every night. The nurses carried in their arms those who couldn't walk. Amid piles of potatoes and bags of coal I found the teacher, pressed myself against her, and told her not to be afraid.

When the bomb hit the center we were in class; there had been no warning. Bombs started falling everywhere around us. The other pupils hid under the tables but I stayed where I was; I had just been reciting a poem. The teacher threw herself over me, knocking me to the ground; I couldn't see anything, and she was suffocating me. I tried to push her off, but she grew heavier and heavier. A thick, warm, salty liquid flowed into my eyes, my mouth, down my throat, and I fell unconscious.

I woke up in a gymnasium. A nun was wiping my face with a damp cloth, and she was saying to someone, "This one isn't hurt, I think."

I began to throw up.

Everywhere in the gymnasium people were lying down on straw mattresses. Children and adults. Some were crying; others weren't moving, and it was hard to tell if they were alive or dead. I looked for the teacher among them but couldn't find her. The little blond paralytic wasn't there either.

The next day they interrogated me, asking me my name, who my parents were, my address, but I blocked my ears and didn't answer the questions, didn't say a word. Then they thought I was a deaf-mute and left me alone.

I was given a new cane, and one morning a nun took me by the hand. We went to the station, got onto a train, and came to another town. We crossed it by foot until we reached the very last house, right next to the forest. The sister left me there with an old peasant woman whom I later learned to call "Grandmother."

She called me "son of a bitch."

I am sitting on a bench at the station. I am waiting for my train. I am almost an hour early.

From here I can see the whole town, the town where I have lived for nearly forty years.

At one time, when I first came, it was a charming small town with a lake, forest, low old houses, and many parks. Now it is cut off from the lake by a highway, its forest has been decimated, its parks have disappeared, and tall buildings have made it ugly. Its narrow old streets are packed with cars, even on the sidewalks. The old bistros have been replaced by soulless restaurants and fast-food places where people eat quickly, sometimes even standing up.

I look at this town for the last time. I will never come back; I do not want to die here.

I didn't say good-bye or farewell to anyone. I don't have friends here, much less girlfriends. My many mistresses must be married,

367

housewives, and no longer so young now. It has been a long time since I last recognized one on the street.

My best friend, Peter, who had been my tutor in my youth, died of a heart attack two years ago. His wife, Clara, who had been my first mistress, killed herself a long time before that; she couldn't face the prospect of old age.

I go leaving no one and nothing behind me. I have sold everything. It wasn't much. My furniture was worth nothing, my books even less. I got a little money for my old piano and my few paintings, but that's all.

The train arrives and I get in. I have only one suitcase. I am leaving here with little more than I came with. In this rich and free country I have made no fortune.

I have a tourist visa for my native land, a visa that expires in only one month but that can be renewed. I hope my money will last me for a few months, perhaps a year. I have also stocked up on medications.

Two hours later I arrive at a large metropolitan train station. More waiting, and then I take a night train on which I have reserved a berth—a low berth, since I know that I will not sleep and that I will often get up to smoke a cigarette.

For the time being I am alone.

Slowly the compartment fills. An old woman, two young girls, a man of about my age. I go out into the corridor to smoke and look at the night. At around two I go to bed, and I think I sleep a little.

Early in the morning we come to another large station. Three hours of waiting, which I spend at the canteen, drinking coffee.

This time the train I board is from my native country. There are very few travelers. The seats are uncomfortable, the windows dirty, the ashtrays full, the floor black and sticky, the toilets almost unusable. No restaurant car or even bar car. The travelers take out their lunches and eat, leaving greasy paper and empty bottles on the windowsills or throwing them to the floor under the seats.

Only two of the travelers speak the language of my country. I listen but say nothing.

I look out the window. The countryside changes. We leave the mountains and come onto a plain.

My pains start again.

I swallow my medications without water. I didn't think to bring a drink with me and I am repelled at the thought of asking for one from the other travelers.

I close my eyes. I know that we are approaching the border.

We're there. The train stops, and border guards, customs officials, and policemen come aboard. I am asked for my papers and they are given back to me with a smile. On the other hand, the two travelers who speak the language of the country are lengthily questioned and their bags are searched.

The train moves off; at each stop now, the only people who get on are from this country.

My little town is on another line than that of the trains coming from abroad. I reach the neighboring town, which is farther into the country and bigger. I could make my connection immediately; I am shown the small red train, only three cars long, that leaves for the little town on the hour from Track One. I watch the train pull out.

I leave the station, get into a taxi, and have myself taken to a hotel. I go up to my room, get in bed, and fall asleep immediately.

When I awake I draw the curtains from my window. It faces west. Over there, behind my little town's mountain, the sun is setting.

Every day I go to the station and watch the red train come and leave again. Then I take a walk around town. At night I drink at the hotel bar or at another bar in town, surrounded by strangers.

My room has a balcony. I often sit there now that it's getting warmer. From there I look at an immense sky of the sort I haven't seen for forty years.

I walk farther and farther in the town; I even leave it and go out into the countryside.

I skirt a wall of stone and steel. Behind it a bird sings and I glimpse the bare branches of chestnut trees.

The cast-iron gate is open. I enter and sit down on the big moss-covered boulder just inside the wall. We used to call this boulder the "black" rock even though it was never black but rather gray or blue, and now it is completely green.

I look at the park and recognize it. I also recognize the big building at its far end. The trees may be the same, but the birds probably aren't. So many years have passed. How long does a tree live? A bird? I have no idea.

And how long do people live? Forever, it seems to me, since I see the center's director approaching.

She asks me, "What are you doing here, sir?"

I rise and say, "I am only looking, Madame Director. I spent five years of my childhood here."

"When?"

"About forty years ago. Forty-five. I recognize you. You were the director of the Rehabilitation Center."

She cries out, "What nerve! For your information, sir, I wasn't even born forty years ago, but I can spot perverts from a mile away. Leave or I will call the police."

I go, return to my hotel, and drink with a stranger. I tell him about what happened with the director. "Obviously they're not the same person. The other one must have died."

My new friend raises his glass. "Conclusion: Either directors across the ages all look alike, or they live for a really long time.

Tomorrow I'll go to your center with you. You can see it again for as long as you want."

The next day the stranger picks me up at the hotel. He drives me to the center. Just before we turn in, at the gate, he says to me, "You know, the old woman you saw, it really was her. Only she's no longer director here or anywhere else. I looked into it. Your center is now an old folk's home."

I say, "I'd just like to see the dormitory. And the garden."

The walnut tree is there, but it seems stunted to me. It will die soon.

I say to my companion, "It's going to die, my tree."

He says, "Don't be sentimental. Everything dies."

We enter the building. We walk down the corridor and go into the room that belonged to me and so many other children forty years ago. I stop at the threshold and look. Nothing has changed. A dozen beds, white walls, the white beds empty. They always are at this hour.

I take the stairs at a run and open the door to the room where I had been locked up for several days. The bed is still there, in the same place. Perhaps it's even the same bed.

A young woman shows us out and says, "Everything here was bombed out. But it was all rebuilt. Just like before. Everything is like it was before. It's a very beautiful building and it must not be altered."

My pains come back one afternoon. I return to the hotel, take my medications, pack my bags, pay my bill, and call a taxi.

"To the station."

The taxi stops in front of the station and I say to the driver, "Please go buy me a ticket for the town of K. I'm ill."

The driver says, "That's not my job. I brought you to the station. Get out. I want nothing to do with a sick man."

He puts my suitcase down on the sidewalk and opens my door. "Out. Get out of my car."

I hand my wallet with its foreign money to him. "I beg you."

The driver goes into the station building, comes back with my wallet, helps me out of the car, takes me by the arm, carries my suitcase, accompanies me to Track One, and waits for the train with me. When it comes he helps me in, sets my suitcase down beside me, and asks the conductor to look after me.

The train leaves. There is almost no one in the other compartments. Smoking is forbidden.

I close my eyes and my pain fades away. The train stops nearly every ten minutes. I know that I once made this journey forty years ago.

The train had stopped before it arrived at the station in the little town. The nun grabbed my arm and shook me but I didn't move. She jumped out of the train, ran, and lay down in a field. All the passengers had run out and lain down in the fields. I was alone in the compartment. Planes flew over us and strafed the train. When silence returned the nun returned too. She slapped me and the train started moving again.

I open my eyes. We will arrive soon. I can already see the silver cloud over the mountain, and then the castle walls and the bell towers of many churches appear.

On the twenty-second of the month of April, after an absence of forty years, I am again in the small town of my childhood.

The station hasn't changed. Except that it's cleaner, even flower-filled, with the local flowers whose name I don't know and that I have never seen anywhere else.

There is also a bus, which pulls out filled with the few travelers from the train and workers from the factory across the street.

I don't take the bus. I stay here, in front of the station, my suitcase on the ground, and I look at the avenue of chestnut trees along Station Street, which leads into town.

"May I carry your suitcase, sir?"

A child of about ten is standing before me.

He says, "You've missed the bus. There won't be another one for half an hour."

I say to him, "No matter. I'll walk."

He says, "Your suitcase is heavy."

He picks up my suitcase and doesn't let go. I laugh. "Yes, it's heavy. You won't be able to carry it very far, that I know. I've done your sort of work before."

The child sets the suitcase down. "Really? When?"

"When I was your age. A long time ago."

"And where was that?"

"Here. In front of this station."

He says, "I can carry this suitcase. No problem."

I say, "Fine, but give me ten minutes' head start. I want to walk alone. And take your time, I'm in no hurry. I'll wait for you at the Black Garden. If it still exists."

"Yes, sir, it exists."

The Black Garden is a small park at the end of the avenue of chestnuts, and there's nothing black in it except the cast-iron fence that encloses it. There I sit on a bench and wait for the child. He soon arrives, puts my suitcase down on another bench across from me, and sits, out of breath.

I light a cigarette and ask, "Why do you do this?"

He says, "I want to buy a bike. A dirt bike. Would you give me a cigarette?"

"No. No cigarettes for you. I'm dying because of cigarettes. Do you want to die of cigarettes too?"

He says to me, "We're all dying of one thing or another. That's what all the experts say, anyway."

"What else do they say, the experts?"

"That the world is fucked. And that there's nothing to do about it. It's too late."

"Where have you heard all this?"

"Everywhere. At school. Especially on television."

I toss away my cigarette. "You're not getting a cigarette, no matter what."

He says to me, "You're mean."

I say, "Yes, I'm mean. So? Is there a hotel somewhere in this town?"

"Sure, there are a couple. You don't know? And you seem to know the town so well."

I say, "When I lived here there weren't any hotels. Not one."

He says, "That must have been a long time ago then. There's a brand-new hotel on Central Square. It's called the Grand Hotel because it's the biggest."

"Let's go."

In front of the hotel the child sets down my suitcase.

"I can't go in, sir. The woman at the reception desk knows me. She'll tell my mother."

"What? That you carried my suitcase?"

"Yes. My mother doesn't want me carrying suitcases."

"Why?"

"I don't know. She doesn't want me doing it. She just wants me to study."

I ask: "Your parents—what do they do?"

He says, "I don't have parents. Only a mother. No father, I've never had one."

"And what does she do, your mother?"

"She works right here at the hotel. She cleans the floors twice a day. But she wants me to have an education."

"An education as what?"

"That she couldn't say, since she doesn't know what educated people do. She thinks professor or doctor, I guess."

I say, "Good. How much for carrying the suitcase?"

He says, "It's up to you, sir."

I give him two coins.

"That enough?"

"Yes, sir."

"No, sir, that's not enough. Don't tell me you've carried that heavy suitcase all the way from the station for as little as that."

He says, "I take what I'm given, sir. I don't have the right to charge more. And then there are poor people. Sometimes I end up carrying suitcases for free. I like the work. I like waiting at the station. I like seeing the people who arrive. The people from here, I know them all by sight. I like seeing the people who come from other places. Like you. You've come from far away, haven't you?"

"Yes, very far. Another country."

I give him a banknote and enter the hotel.

I choose a corner room from which I can see the whole square, the church, the grocery store, the shops, the bookseller's.

It's nine at night and the square is empty. Lights are on in the houses. Blinds are being lowered, shutters closed, curtains pulled; the town is going to bed.

I settle down at one of the windows in my room and watch the square, the houses, late into the night.

During my childhood I often dreamed of living in one of the houses on Central Square — it didn't matter which one — but most of all the blue house where there was and still is a bookseller's.

But the only one I lived in when I was here was the ramshackle one belonging to Grandmother, far from the center of town, at its very limits, near the frontier.

At Grandmother's I worked from morning till night, as she did herself. She fed me and housed me, but she never gave me money, which I needed to buy soap, toothpaste, clothes, and shoes. So at night I came to town and played the harmonica in bars. I sold the wood that I gathered in the forest along with mushrooms and chestnuts. I also sold eggs that I stole from Grandmother, as well as fish, which I quickly learned to catch. I also did all sorts of work for anyone who would pay. I delivered messages, letters, and packages; people trusted me because they thought I was a deaf-mute.

In the beginning I didn't speak, not even to Grandmother, but soon I had to talk numbers in order to sell my wares.

I spent much time at night on Central Square. I looked through the window of the bookseller-stationer's, at the white paper, the school notebooks, the erasers, the pencils. All of it was too expensive for me.

To make a bit more money, whenever I could I went to the station and waited for travelers. I carried their suitcases.

377

And so I was able to buy paper, a pencil and eraser, and a big notebook in which I wrote down my first lies.

Several months after the death of Grandmother some people came into the house without knocking. They were three men, one in the uniform of a border guard. The other two were in civilian dress. One of these two didn't say anything but only noted things down. He was young, almost as young as I. The other had white hair. It was he who questioned me.

"How long have you lived here?"

I say, "I don't know. Since the hospital was bombed."

"Which hospital?"

"I don't know. The center."

The man in the uniform interrupts. "He was already here when I took command of this unit."

The civilian asks, "When was that?"

"Three years ago. But he was here before that."

"How do you know?"

"It's obvious. He worked around the house like someone who had always been here."

The white-haired man turns to me. "Are you related to Mrs. V., née Maria Z.?"

I say, "She was my grandmother."

He asks me, "Do you have documents proving the relationship?"

I say, "No, I don't have any papers. All I have are the sheets I buy at the bookseller's."

He says, "This is the situation. Take this down!"

The younger civilian writes: "Mrs. V., née Maria Z., is deceased without heirs, and so all her possessions, house, and lands will become state property belonging communally to the town of Z., which will make use of them as it deems fit."

The men stand up and I ask them, "What should I do?"

They look at one another. The uniformed man says, "You must leave."

"Why?"

"Because this place doesn't belong to you."

I ask, "When do I have to leave?"

"I don't know."

He looks at the white-haired man in civilian clothes, who says, "We'll inform you soon enough. How old are you?"

"Fifteen, nearly. I can't leave before the tomatoes ripen."

He says, "Of course, the tomatoes. You're only fifteen? Well, then, there's no problem."

I ask, "Where should I go?"

He is silent for a moment and looks at the man in uniform; the man in uniform looks back at him. The civilian lowers his eyes. "Don't worry. You'll be taken care of. Above all, don't be scared."

The three men go outside. I follow them, walking on the grass to make no noise.

The border guard says, "Can't you leave him alone? He's a good little fellow and he works hard."

The man in civilian dress says, "That's beside the point. The law is clear. The property of Mrs. V. belongs to the commune. Your little fellow has been living on it illegally for almost two years."

"And who's been harmed by it?"

"No one. But come on—why are you defending that little good-for-nothing?"

"For three years I've watched him tending his garden and his animals. He's not a good-for-nothing, in any case no more than you are."

"You dare call me a good-for-nothing?"

"I didn't say that. All I said is that he's no more of one than you are. And anyway I don't give a damn. Not about you, not about him. In three weeks I'll be out of the service and tending my own garden. You, sir, will have a soul on your conscience if you turn that child out into the street. Good night, and sleep well."

The civilian says, "We won't be turning him out. We'll take care of him."

They leave. Several days later they come back. The same man with the white hair and the young man; they have brought a woman with them. She is older and wears eyeglasses; she looks like the director at the center.

She says to me, "Listen to me carefully. We don't want to hurt you; we want to take care of you. You're coming with us to a nice house where there are children like you."

I say to her, "I'm not a child anymore. I don't want to be taken care of. And I don't want to go to a hospital either."

She says, "It isn't a hospital. You'll be able to study there."

We're in the kitchen. The woman speaks but I don't listen. The white-haired man speaks too. I don't listen to him either.

Only the young man who writes everything down doesn't speak; he doesn't even look at me.

As she leaves, the woman says, "Don't worry. We're on your side. Everything will be better soon. We won't abandon you; we're going to take care of you. We're going to rescue you."

The man adds, "You can stay here for the summer. The demolition will begin at the end of August."

I'm scared, scared of going to a house where I will be taken care of, where I will be rescued. I must leave here. I ask myself where I could go.

I buy a map of the country and one of the capital. Every day I go to the station and consult the schedule. I ask how much tickets are to this or that town. I only have a very little bit of money and don't want to use what Grandmother left me. She had warned me: "No one must know that you have all this. You'll be questioned, locked up, and everything will be taken from you. And never tell the truth. Pretend you don't understand the questions. If people take you for an idiot, so much the better."

Grandmother's legacy is buried under the bench in front of the house, a canvas bag that contains jewels, gold pieces, and money. If I tried to sell it all, I would be accused of having stolen it.

It was at the station that I met the man who wanted to cross the border.

It is night. The man is there, in front of the station, his hands in his pockets. The other travelers are already gone. Station Square is deserted.

The man signals me to come closer and I walk toward him. He has no luggage.

I say, "Usually I carry travelers' bags. But I see that you don't have any."

He says, "No, I don't."

I say, "If I could be of some other service. I can see that you're a stranger in town."

"And how can you tell I'm a stranger?"

I say, "No one in town wears clothes like yours. And everyone in our town has the same face. A face that's recognized and familiar. You can tell who people from our town are even if you don't know them personally. When a stranger comes he's immediately spotted."

The man looks around us. "Do you think I've been spotted already?"

"Absolutely. But if your papers are in order it won't matter much. You'll present them at the police station tomorrow morning, and you can stay as long as you like. There's no hotel, but I can show you to houses where they rent out rooms."

The man says, "Follow me."

He sets off toward town, but instead of taking the main road he veers off to the right, onto a small dusty road, and sits down between two bushes. I sit down beside him and ask, "Are you trying to hide? Why?"

He asks me, "Do you know the town well?"

"Yes, perfectly."

"The border?"

"That too."

"Your parents?"

"I don't have any."

"They're dead?"

"I don't know."

"Whose house do you live at?"

"Mine. It's Grandmother's house. She's dead."

"With anyone else?"

"Alone."

"Where's your house?"

"At the other end of town. Near the border."

"Could you put me up for one night? I have a lot of money."

"Yes, I can put you up."

"Do you know a way we can get to your house without being seen?"

"Yes."

"Let's go. I'll follow you."

We walk in the fields behind the houses. Sometimes we have to clamber over fences and gates and cross gardens and private yards. Night has fallen, and the man behind me makes no noise.

When we reach Grandmother's house I congratulate him: "Even at your age you had no trouble following me."

He laughs. "At my age? I'm only forty, and I fought in the war. I learned how to get through towns without making noise."

After some time he adds, "You're right. I'm old now. My youth was swallowed up by the war. Do you have anything to drink?"

I set some brandy on the table and say, "You want to cross the border, don't you?"

He laughs again. "How did you guess? Do you have anything to eat?"

I say, "I can make you a mushroom omelet. I also have goat's cheese."

He drinks while I make dinner.

We eat. I ask him, "How did you make it into the frontier zone? You need a special permit to come to our town."

He says, "I have a sister who lives here. I asked permission to visit her and it was granted."

"But you're not going to see her."

"No. I don't want to make trouble for her. Here, burn all this in your stove."

He gives me his identity card and other papers. I throw everything into the fire.

I ask, "Why do you want to leave?"

"That's not your business. Show me the way, that's all I ask. I'll give you all the money I have."

He puts banknotes on the table.

I say, "It's no great sacrifice to leave that much behind. Anyway it's not worth anything on the other side."

He says, "But here, for a young fellow like you, it's worth quite a bit."

I throw the bills into the fire.

"You know, I don't need money that much. I have everything I want here."

We watch the money burn. I say, "You can't cross the frontier without risking your life."

The man says, "I know."

I say, "You should also know that I could turn you in right now. There's a border post right across from my house, and I collaborate with them. I'm an informer."

Very pale, the man says, "An informer, at your age?"

"Age has nothing to do with it. I've turned in a number of people who wanted to cross the frontier. I see and report on everything that goes on in the forest."

"But why?"

"Because sometimes they send in plants to see if I inform on them or not. Until now I was forced to report them whether they were plants or not."

"Why until now?"

"Because tomorrow I'm crossing the frontier with you. I want to get out of here too."

A little before noon the next day we cross the frontier.

The man walks in front and doesn't have a hope. Near the second barrier a land mine goes off and takes him with it. I walk behind him and risk nothing.

I watch the empty square until late into the night. When I finally go to bed, I dream.

I go down to the river; my brother is there, sitting on the bank, fishing. I sit down beside him.

"You getting many?"

"No. I was waiting for you."

He stands and packs up his rod. "It's been a long time since there were fish here. There isn't even water anymore."

He reaches for a rock and throws it at the other rocks in the dried-up river.

We walk toward town. I stop in front of a house with green shutters. My brother says, "Yes, it was our house. You recognized it."

I say, "Yes, but it wasn't here before. It was in another town."

My brother corrects me: "In another life. And now it's here and it's empty."

We reach Central Square.

385

In front of the bookshop door two little boys are sitting on the stairs that lead up to the living quarters.

My brother says, "Those are my sons. Their mother is gone."

We go into the kitchen. My brother makes the evening meal. The children eat in silence, not raising their eyes.

I say, "They're happy, your sons."

"Very happy. I'm going to put them to bed."

When he returns he says, "Let's go to my room."

We go into the large room and my brother retrieves a bottle hidden behind the books on the shelves.

"This is all that's left. The barrels are empty."

We drink. My brother strokes the red plush tablecloth.

"You see, nothing's changed. I kept everything. Even this hideous tablecloth. Tomorrow you can move in to the house."

I say, "I don't want to. I'd rather play with your children."

My brother says, "My children don't play."

"What do they do?"

"They are preparing to make it through life."

I say, "I made it through life and haven't found anything."

My brother says, "There's nothing to find. What were you looking for?"

"You. It's because of you that I came back."

My brother laughs. "Because of me? You know very well that I'm just a dream. You must accept that. There is nothing anywhere."

I am cold and stand up.

"It's late. I have to go back."

"Go back? Where?"

"To the hotel."

"What hotel? You're at home here. I'm going to introduce you to our parents."

"Our parents? Where are they?"

My brother points at the brown door that leads into the other half of the apartment.

"There. They're asleep."

"Together?"

"As ever."

I say, "They shouldn't be woken up."

My brother says, "Why not? They'll be overjoyed to see you after all these years."

I step backward toward the door.

"No, no, I don't want to see them again."

My brother grabs my arm. "You don't want to, you don't have to. I see them every day. You should see them at least once, just once!"

My brother pulls me toward the brown door; with my free hand I grab a very heavy glass ashtray from the table and hit him on the back of the neck with it.

My brother's forehead slams into the door and he falls. There is blood on the floor all around his head.

I leave the house and sit on a bench. An enormous moon lights the empty square.

An old man stops in front of me and asks for a cigarette. I offer him one, as well as a light.

He stays there, standing in front of me, smoking his cigarette.

After a few moments he asks, "So, then, you killed him?"

I say, "Yes."

The old man says, "You did what you had to do. That's good. Few people do what must be done."

I say, "It was because he wanted to open the door."

"You did well. It was good that you stopped him. You had to kill him. With that everything falls into order, the order of things."

I say, "But he won't be here anymore. Order doesn't mean much to me if he isn't here anymore."

The old man says, "On the contrary. From now on he'll always be with you wherever you go."

The old man moves off; he rings at the door of a little house and goes in.

When I wake up the square has already been busy for quite some time. People are moving around it on foot or by bicycle. There are very few cars. The shops are open, including the book-seller's. The hotel corridors are being vacuumed.

I open my door and call out to the cleaning woman: "Could you bring me a cup of coffee?"

She turns around; it is a young woman with very black hair.

"I'm not allowed to serve the guests, sir, I'm just a cleaning woman. We don't have room service. There's a restaurant and a bar."

I go back into my room, brush my teeth, shower, then climb back in under the covers. I'm cold.

There is a knock at the door. The cleaning woman comes in and sets a tray down on the night table.

"You can pay for the coffee at the bar whenever you like."

She lies down beside me on the bed and offers me her lips. I turn my head away.

"No, my lovely one. I'm old and ill."

She stands and says, "I have very little money. The work I do is very badly paid. I'd like to give my son a dirt bike as a birthday present. And I have no husband."

"I understand."

I give her a banknote without knowing if it is too little or too much; I still haven't figured out the prices of things here.

Around three in the afternoon I go out.

I walk slowly. Nevertheless, after half an hour I come to the end of the town. Where Grandmother's house used to be there is a very well-maintained athletic field. Children are playing on it.

For a long time I sit on the riverbank, then I return to town. I pass through the old section, the little streets around the castle; I climb up to the cemetery but cannot find Grandmother's grave.

Every day I walk like this for hours on end through every part of town. Especially through the narrow streets where the houses have sunk into the earth and their windows are at ground level. Sometimes I sit in a park or on the low walls of the castle or on a tomb in the cemetery. When I'm hungry I go into a little bistro and eat what it has to offer. Then I drink with the workers. No one recognizes me, no one remembers me.

One day I go into the bookseller's to buy paper and pencils. The fat man of my childhood is no longer there; now it is a woman who runs the place. She is sitting and knitting in an armchair near the French door that looks out onto the garden. She smiles at me.

"I know you. I see you going in and out of the hotel every day. Except for when you return too late and I'm already asleep. I live above the bookshop and like to look at the square at night."

I say, "Me too."

She asks, "Are you vacationing here? For very long?"

"Yes, vacationing. In a way. I'd like to spend as much time here as possible. It depends on my visa as well as on my money."

"Your visa? You're a foreigner? You don't look it."

"I spent my childhood in this town. I was born in this country. But I've been abroad for a very long time."

She says, "There are a lot of foreigners here now that the country is free. Those who went away after the revolution come back to visit, but more than anything it's the curious ones, the tourists. You'll see, when the nice weather sets in they'll come by the busload. That'll be the end of our peace and quiet."

In fact the hotel is increasingly filled. Saturdays are dance nights; sometimes the dances last until four in the morning. I can stand neither the music nor the shouts and laughter of the people amusing themselves. So I stay out in the streets, sitting down on a bench with a bottle of wine I have bought earlier in the day, and wait.

One night a small boy sits down next to me.

"Can I stay here next to you, mister? I get a little scared at night."

I recognize his voice. It's the child who carried my suitcase when I arrived. I ask him, "What are you doing out so late?"

He says, "I'm waiting for my mother. When there are parties she has to stay to help serve and to do the dishes."

"So? All you have to do is stay home and sleep quietly."

"I can't sleep quietly. I'm afraid something will happen to my mother. We live far away from here and I can't let her walk alone. There are men who attack women walking alone at night. I saw it on television."

"And children aren't attacked?"

"No, not really. Just women. Especially if they're pretty. I could defend myself. I can run very fast."

We wait. Slowly silence descends inside the hotel. A woman comes out, the one who brings me coffee in the morning. The little boy runs to her and they go off together, hand in hand.

Other staff members come out of the hotel and quickly fade into the distance.

I climb up to my room.

The next day I go see the bookseller.

"It's impossible for me to stay in the hotel any longer. It's too crowded and there's too much noise. Would you know of anyone who might rent me a room?"

She says, "Come live at my place. Here, upstairs."

"I would be disturbing you."

"No, not at all. I'll live at my daughter's, it's not far from here. You'd have the whole floor. Two rooms, a kitchen, and a bathroom."

"For how much?"

"How much do you pay at the hotel?"

I tell her. She smiles.

"Those are tourist prices. I'd let you live here for half that much. I'd even clean up for you after I closed the shop. You're always out then anyway, so I wouldn't disturb you. Would you like to see the apartment?"

"No, I'm sure it will be fine. When could I move in?"

"As early as tomorrow, if you like. All I have to do is collect my clothes and my things."

The next day I pack my suitcase and settle my bill at the hotel. I arrive at the bookseller's just before it closes. The bookseller hands me a key.

"That's the key to the front door. It's possible to get up to the apartment directly from the store, but you'll be using the other door, the street door. I'll show you."

She closes the shop. We climb up a narrow staircase lighted by two windows that look onto the garden. The bookseller explains to me, "The door to the left is the bedroom, across from the bathroom. The second door is the living room, from which you can also pass through into the bedroom. The kitchen is at the end. There's a refrigerator. I've left some food in it."

I say, "I only need coffee and wine. I eat my meals in bars."

She says, "That's not very healthy. The coffee is on the shelf and there's a bottle of wine in the fridge. I'll go now. I hope you like it here."

She leaves. I immediately open the bottle of wine; I'll lay in a supply tomorrow. I go into the living room. It's a big room, simply furnished. Between its two windows is a large table covered with a red plush cloth. I immediately cover it with my papers and pencils. Then I go into the bedroom, which is narrow and has only a single window, or rather a French door that leads out onto a little balcony.

I lift my suitcase onto the bed and put my clothes away in the empty closet.

I do not go out that night. I finish the bottle of wine and settle in front of one of the living room windows in a deep armchair. I watch the square, and then I go to sleep in a bed that smells like soap.

When I get up around ten o'clock the next morning I find two newspapers on the kitchen table and a pot of vegetable soup on the stove. The first thing I do is make myself some coffee, which I drink while reading the newspapers. I have the soup later, around four in the afternoon, before going out.

The bookseller does not disturb me. I only see her when I pay a visit downstairs. When I'm out she cleans the apartment, taking away my dirty laundry as well and bringing it back washed and ironed.

Time passes quickly. I have to appear in the neighboring town, the regional capital, to have my visa renewed. A young woman stamps my passport RENEWED FOR ONE MONTH. I pay and thank her. She smiles at me: "Tonight I'll be at the bar of the Grand Hotel. There'll be a lot of foreigners there; you might run into some compatriots."

I say, "Yes, perhaps I'll come."

I immediately take the red train back home to my town.

The following month the young woman is less amiable; she stamps my passport without saying a word. The third time she crisply warns me that a fourth time will be impossible.

Toward the end of summer I have almost run out of money; I am forced to economize. I buy a harmonica and play in bars, as I did in my childhood. The patrons offer me drinks. As for meals, I am content with the bookseller's vegetable soups. In September and October I am no longer able to pay my rent. The bookseller does not ask me for it; she continues to clean, to do my laundry, to bring me soup.

I don't know how I'll get by, but I don't want to return to the other country; I must stay here, I must die here, in this town.

My pains have not reappeared since my arrival despite my excessive consumption of alcohol and tobacco.

On the thirtieth of October I celebrate my birthday with my drinking friends in the town's more popular bars. They all pay for me. Couples dance to the sound of my harmonica. Women kiss me. I am drunk. I begin to talk about my brother the way I always do when I've drunk too much. Everybody in town knows my story: I'm looking for my brother who I lived with here, in this town, until I was fifteen. It is here that I must find him; I am waiting for him and know that he will come when he hears that I have returned from abroad.

All this is a lie. I know very well that I was already alone in this town, with Grandmother, that even then I only fantasized that there were two of us, me and my brother, in order to endure the unbearable solitude.

The bar quiets down somewhat around midnight. I no longer play, I just drink.

A scruffy old man sits down in front of me. He drinks from my glass. He says, "I remember you both very well, your brother and you."

I say nothing. Another man, a younger one, brings a liter of wine to my table. I ask for a clean glass. We drink.

The younger man asks me, "What would you give me if I found your brother?"

I tell him, "I have no more money."

He laughs. "But you can wire for money from abroad. All foreigners are rich."

"Not me. I couldn't even buy you a drink."

He laughs. "It doesn't matter. Another liter, on me."

The waitress brings more wine and says, "That's the last one. I can't serve you anymore. If we don't close up we'll get into trouble with the police."

The old man continues to drink next to us, saying from time to time, "Yes, I knew you well, you two, you were already pretty wild in those days. Yes, yes."

The younger man says to me, "I know that your brother is hiding in the forest. I've sometimes seen him off in the distance. He's made clothes out of army blankets and he goes barefoot even in winter. He lives on herbs, roots, chestnuts, and small animals. He has long gray hair and a gray beard. He has a knife and matches, and he smokes cigarettes that he rolls himself, which proves that he must come into town sometimes at night. Maybe the girls who live on the other side of the cemetery and who sell their bodies know him. One of them at least. Perhaps she sees him secretly and gives him what he needs. We could organize a search. If we all look for him we could trap him."

I stand up and hit him.

"Liar! That isn't my brother. And if you want to trap anyone, count me out."

I hit him again and he falls from his chair. I tip over the table and keep screaming: "He's not my brother!"

The waitress shouts in the street: "Police! Police!"

Someone must have telephoned because the police arrive very quickly. Two of them. On foot. The tavern falls silent. One of the policemen asks, "What's going on? This place should have closed up long ago."

The man I hit whimpers, "He hit me."

Several people point at me: "It was him."

The policeman picks the man up. "Stop complaining. You're not even scratched. And you're plastered as usual. You'd better go home. You'd all better go home."

He turns to me. "I don't know you. Show me your papers."

I try to escape but the people around me grab me. The policeman digs through my pockets and finds my passport. He studies it for a long time and says to his colleague, "His visa is expired. Has been for months. We'll have to bring him in."

I struggle but they put handcuffs on me and lead me out onto the street. I stagger and am having trouble walking, so they practically carry me all the way to the station. There they take off my handcuffs, lie me down on a bed, and leave, shutting the door behind them.

The next morning a police officer questions me. He is young, his hair is red, and his face is covered with red spots.

He says to me, "You have no right to remain in our country. You must leave."

I say, "I don't have money for the train. I don't have any money at all."

"I'll notify your embassy. They'll repatriate you."

I say, "I don't want to leave. I have to find my brother."

The officer shrugs. "You can come back whenever you want. You could even move here permanently, but there are rules for that. They'll explain to you at your embassy. As for your brother, I'll look into the matter. Do you have any information about him that could help us?"

"Yes, I have a manuscript written in his own hand. It's on the living room table in my apartment above the bookseller's."

"And how did you come into possession of this manuscript?"

"Someone left it in my name at the reception desk."

He says, "Odd, very odd."

One morning in November I am summoned to the policeman's office. He tells me to sit and hands me my manuscript.

"Here, I'm giving it back to you. It's just fiction, and it has nothing to do with your brother."

We are silent. The window is open. It's raining and cold. At last the officer speaks. "Even as far as you're concerned we haven't found anything in the municipal archives."

I say, "Naturally. Grandmother never declared me. And I never went to school. But I know that I was born in the capital."

"The archives there were totally destroyed by the bombing. They're coming for you at two this afternoon."

He added that very quickly.

I hide my hands under the table because they are shaking.

"At two? Today?"

"Yes, I'm sorry. It's so sudden. But I repeat, you can come back whenever you like. You can come back permanently. Many emigrants have. Our country currently belongs to the free world. Soon you won't even need a visa."

I tell him, "That will be too late for me. I have a bad heart. I came back because I wanted to die here. As for my brother, perhaps he never existed."

The officer says, "Yes, that's probably true. If you keep going on about him people will think you're insane."

"Is that what you think too?"

He shakes his head. "No, I only think you're confusing reality with fiction. Your fiction. I also feel that you should return to your country, think things over, and then come back. Permanently perhaps. That's what I hope for you, and for me."

"Because of our chess games?"

"No, not just that."

He stands and extends his hand.

"I won't be here when you leave, so I'll say good-bye to you now. Return to your cell."

I return to my cell. My guard says to me, "It looks like you're leaving today."

"Yes, so it seems."

I lie down on my bed and wait. At noon the bookseller arrives with her soup. I tell her I have to go. She cries. She pulls a sweater out of her bag and says, "I knitted you this. Put it on, it's cold out."

I put on the sweater and say, "Thank you. I still owe you two months' rent. I hope the embassy will pay it."

She says, "Who cares? You're coming back, aren't you?"

"I'll try."

She leaves in tears. She has to open her shop.

My guard and I are sitting in my cell. He says, "It's funny to think that you won't be here tomorrow. But you'll come back, of course. Meanwhile, I'm canceling your debt."

I say, "No, absolutely not. I'll pay you as soon as the embassy people come."

He says, "No, no, it was all just for fun. And I cheated."

"Ah, so that's why you always won."

"Don't hold it against me. I just can't help cheating."

He sniffles and wipes his nose.

"You know, if I have a son I'll give him your first name."

I tell him, "Give him my brother's name instead, Lucas. That would make me happiest."

He thinks.

"Lucas? That's a nice name. I'll talk it over with my wife. Maybe she won't object. Anyway, it's not up to her. I'm the one who decides in my house."

"I'm sure of it."

A policeman comes to collect me from my cell. My guard and I go out into the courtyard, where there is a well-dressed man with a hat, tie, and umbrella. The stones in the courtyard glisten in the rain.

The man from the embassy says, "A car is waiting for us. I've already taken care of your debts."

He speaks in a language that I shouldn't understand but do anyway. I motion to my guard.

"I owe that man a certain amount. It's a debt of honor."

"How much?"

He pays, takes me by the arm, and leads me to a big black car parked in front of the house. A chauffeur in a visored cap opens the doors.

The car pulls away. I ask the man from the embassy if we can stop for a minute in front of the bookseller's on Central Square, but he just looks at me uncomprehendingly and I realize that I have spoken to him in my old language, the language of this country.

The chauffeur drives quickly; we pass the square, we're already on Station Street, and soon my little town is well behind us.

It's hot in the car. Through the window I watch the villages parade by, the fields and poplars and acacias, my country's landscape beaten by the rain and the wind.

I suddenly turn to the man from the embassy. "This isn't the road to the border. We're going in the opposite direction."

He says, "First we're taking you to the embassy in the capital. You'll cross the border several days from now, by train."

I close my eyes.

The child crosses the frontier.

The man goes first; the child waits. There is an explosion. The child approaches. The man is lying near the second barrier. Then the child makes his move. Walking in the man's footsteps, then over his motionless body, he reaches the other side and hides behind some bushes.

A squad of border guards arrives in a four-wheel-drive vehicle. There is a sergeant and several soldiers. One of them says, "The poor fuck."

Another: "What rotten luck. He almost made it."

The sergeant cries out, "Stop your chatter. We have to collect the body."

The soldiers say:

"What's left of it."

"Why?"

The sergeant says: "Identification. Orders are orders. The body must be retrieved. Any volunteers?"

The soldiers look at one another.

"The land mines. We might not make it."

"So what. It's your duty. Bunch of cowards."

One soldier raises his hand. "I'll go."

"Bravo. Go to it, son. The rest of you move back."

The soldier walks slowly up to the shattered body, then breaks into a run. He passes by the child without seeing him.

The sergeant screams: "The bastard! Shoot him! Fire!"

The soldiers do not shoot.

"He's on the other side. We can't shoot over there."

The sergeant raises his rifle. Two foreign border guards appear on the other side. The sergeant lowers his weapon and hands it to a soldier. He walks up to the corpse, hoists it onto his back, returns, and drops it to the ground. He wipes his face with the sleeve of his uniform. "You'll pay for this, you sons of bitches. You're all nothing but a pile of shit."

The soldiers wrap the body in a tarpaulin and put it in the back of their vehicle. They drive off. The two foreign border guards go away too.

The child remains where he is, not moving a muscle. He falls asleep. Early in the morning he is awakened by the singing of birds. He clutches his coat and rubber boots to himself and heads toward the village. He comes across two border guards, who ask him, "Hey, you. Where are you coming from?"

"The other side of the frontier."

"You crossed it? When?"

"Yesterday. With my father. But he fell. He stayed on the ground after the explosion and the soldiers from over there came and took him away."

"Yes, we were there. But we didn't see you. The soldier who deserted didn't see you either."

"I hid. I was scared."

"How come you speak our language?"

"I learned it from soldiers during the war. You think they'll make my father better again?"

The guards lower their eyes. "Definitely. Come with us. You must be hungry."

The guards bring the child to the village and ask one of their wives to take care of him.

"Give him something to eat, then bring him to the police station. Tell them that we'll come at eleven to make a report."

The woman is fat and blond, her face red and smiling.

She asks the child, "You like milk and cheese? Lunch isn't ready yet."

"Yes, ma'am, I like everything. I'll eat anything."

The woman serves him.

"No, wait, go wash up first. At least your face and hands. I'll get your clothes nice and clean, but I guess you don't have anything to change into."

"No, ma'am."

"I'll lend you one of my husband's shirts. It'll be too big for you, but that doesn't matter. Just roll up the sleeves. Here's a towel. The bathroom is right there."

The child takes his coat and rubber boots into the bathroom with him. He washes, returns to the kitchen, eats bread and cheese and drinks milk. He says, "Thank you, ma'am."

She says, "You're well brought up and polite. And you speak our language very well. Did your mother stay on the other side?"

"No, she died during the war."

"Poor little thing. Come, we have to go to the commissioner's. Don't be scared, the policeman's nice, he's a friend of my husband's."

At the station she tells the policeman, "Here's the son of the man who tried to cross yesterday. My husband will come by at eleven. I'd be glad to look after the child while they're coming to a decision. Perhaps he'll have to be sent back because he's a minor."

The policeman says, "We'll see. In any case I'll send him back to you for lunch."

The woman leaves and the policeman hands the child a questionnaire.

"Fill it out. If you don't understand any of the questions, ask me."

When the child hands the questionnaire back the policeman reads it out loud: "Full name, Claus T. Age eighteen. You're not very big for your age."

"It's because I was ill as a child."

"Do you have an identity card?"

"No, nothing. My father and I burned all our papers before we left."

"Why?"

"I don't know. Something about being caught. My father told me to do it."

"Your father stepped on a land mine. If you'd been walking with him you'd have been blown up too."

"I didn't walk with him. He told me to wait until he was on the other side, then to follow him at a distance."

"Why did you cross in the first place?"

"It was my father who wanted to. They were putting him in prison all the time and watching him. He didn't want to live there anymore. And he took me with him because he didn't want me to be alone."

"Your mother?"

"She died in a bombing during the war. Afterward I lived with my grandmother, but she died too."

"So you don't have anyone left over there. No one who will call for you to be returned. Except the authorities, if you committed any crime."

"I haven't committed any crimes."

"Good. All we have to do now is wait for my superiors to decide. For the time being you're not allowed to leave the village. Here. Sign this paper there."

The child signs the statement, in which there are three lies.

The man he crossed the frontier with was not his father.

The child is not eighteen, but fifteen.

His name is not Claus.

Some weeks later a man from the city comes to the border guard's house. He says to the child, "My name is Peter N. I will take care of you from now on. Here is your identity card. All it needs is your signature."

The child looks at the card. His birthdate has been moved back three years, his first name is "Claus," and his nationality is "None."

The very same day Peter and Claus take the bus to the city. Along the way Peter asks questions:

"What did you do before, Claus? Were you a student?"

"A student? No. I worked in my garden, tended my animals, played my harmonica in bars, carried travelers' bags for them."

"And what would you like to do in the future?"

"I don't know. Nothing. Why is it so necessary to do anything?"

"One has to make a living."

"That I know. I've always done that. I'm happy to do any sort of work to make a little money."

"A little money? Through any sort of work? You could get a scholarship and go to school."

"I don't want to go to school."

"And yet you should, even just a little bit, to learn the language better. You speak it well enough, but you also have to know how to read and write it. You'll live in a youth house with other students. You'll have your own room. You'll take language courses and after that we'll see."

Peter and Claus spend the night at a hotel in a big city. In the morning they take a train to a smaller city situated between a forest and a lake. The youth house is on a steep street in the middle of a garden near the center of town.

A couple, the director of the house and his wife, meet them. They bring Claus to his room. The window looks out onto the park.

Claus asks, "Who takes care of the garden?"

The director's wife says, "I do, but the children help out a great deal."

Claus says, "I'll help you too. Your flowers are very pretty."

The director's wife says, "Thank you, Claus. You'll be completely free here, but you have to be back in at eleven every night at the latest. You'll clean your own room. You can borrow a vacuum cleaner from the super."

The director says, "If you have any problems, talk to me."

Peter says, "You'll be comfortable here, won't you, Claus?"

Claus is also shown the dining room, the showers, and the common room. He is introduced to the boys and girls there.

Later Peter shows Claus the town, then brings him to his house.

"You can find me here if you need me. This is my wife, Clara."

The three of them have lunch together, then spend the afternoon shopping for clothes and shoes.

Claus says, "I've never had this many clothes in my life."

Peter smiles. "You can throw away your old coat and boots. You'll be getting some money each month for school expenses and pocket money. If you need anything more, tell me. Your board and tuition are paid for, of course."

Claus asks, "Who's giving me all this money? You?"

"No, I'm just your tutor. The money comes from the state. Since you have no parents, the state is obligated to take care of you until you're in a position to make a living on your own."

Claus says, "I hope that will happen as soon as possible."

"In a year you'll decide if you want to go to school or take an apprenticeship."

"I don't want to go to school."

"We'll see, we'll see. Have you no ambition at all, Claus?"

"Ambition? I don't know. All I want is peace to write."

"To write? What? You want to be a writer?"

"Yes. You don't have to go to school to be a writer. You just have to know how to write without too many mistakes. I want to learn how to write in your language properly, but that's all I need."

Peter says, "Writing is no way to earn a living."

Claus says, "No, I know. But I can work during the day and quietly write at night. That's what I did at Grandmother's."

"What? You've already written something?"

"Yes. I've filled a couple of notebooks. They're wrapped up in my old coat. When I've learned to write your language, I'll translate them and show them to you."

They are in his room at the youth house. Claus unties the string around his old coat. He sets five school notebooks on the table. Peter opens them one after the other.

"I'm very curious to know what's in these notebooks. Is it a journal of some kind?"

Claus says, "No, it's all lies."

"Lies?"

"Yes. Made-up things. Stories that aren't true but might be."

Peter says, "Hurry up and learn to write our language, Claus."

We arrive at the capital around seven in the evening. The weather has grown worse; it's cold and the raindrops have turned into ice crystals.

The embassy building is in the middle of a large garden. I am brought to a well-heated room with a double bed and a bathroom. It's like a suite in a luxury hotel.

A waiter brings me a meal. I eat very little of it. The meal is not like the kind to which I grew reaccustomed in the little town. I set the tray down outside my door. A man is seated in the corridor a few yards away.

I shower and brush my teeth with a brand-new toothbrush I found in the bathroom. I also find a comb and, on my bed, a pair of pajamas. I go to bed.

My pains come back. I wait for a while but they become unbearable. I get up, look through my suitcase, find my medications, take two pills, and return to bed. Instead of going away the pains intensify. I drag myself to the door and open it; the

411

man is still sitting there. I say to him, "A doctor, please. I'm ill. My heart."

He picks up a telephone hung on the wall next to him. I don't remember what happens next; I faint. I wake up in a hospital bed.

I stay in the hospital for three days. I undergo all sorts of examinations. At last the cardiologist comes to see me.

"You can get up and dress. You're going back to the embassy."

I ask, "You're not going to operate on me?"

"No operation is necessary. Your heart is perfectly sound. Your pains are the result of anxiety and nervousness and a profound depression. Don't take any more trinitrine, just the sedatives I've prescribed for you."

He extends his hand to me. "Don't be afraid. You still have a very long time to live."

"I don't want to live much longer."

"As soon as you're out of your depression you'll change your mind."

A car returns me to the embassy. I am brought into an office. A smiling young man with curly hair motions me toward a leather armchair.

"Have a seat. I'm happy that everything went well at the hospital. But that's not why I called you here. You're looking for your family, and for your brother in particular, are you not?"

"Yes, my twin brother. But not very hopefully. Have you found something? I was told that the archives were destroyed."

"I didn't need the archives. I simply looked in the phone book. There's a man in this city whose name is the same as yours. The same last name as well as first name."

"Claus?"

"Yes, Klaus T., with a 'K.' So it obviously can't be your brother. But he might be related to you and could give you some information. Here is his address and telephone number in case you'd like to contact him."

I take the address and say, "I don't know. I'd like to see the street he lives on and his house first."

"I understand. We can spin by around five-thirty. I'll come with you. Without valid papers you can't go out alone."

We cross the city. It is already almost night. In the car the curly-haired man says to me, "I did some research on your homonym. He's one of this country's most important poets."

I say, "The bookseller who rented me her apartment never mentioned it. And yet she must have known his name."

"Not necessarily. Klaus T. writes under a pen name, Klaus Lucas. He's said to be a misanthrope. He's never seen in public and nothing is known about his private life."

The car stops in a narrow street between two rows of single-storied houses surrounded by gardens.

The curly-haired man says, "There — number eighteen. This is it. It's one of the prettiest parts of the city. Also the quietest and most expensive."

I say nothing. I look at the house. It is somewhat set back from the street. A few steps lead from the garden to the front door. The green shutters are open on the four windows that look out onto the street. A light is on in the kitchen, and a blue light soon appears in the two living room windows. For the moment the study remains dark. The other part of the house, the part that looks out over the courtyard in the back, is invisible from here. There are three more rooms there: the parents' bedroom, the children's room, and a guest bedroom that Mother used mostly as a sewing room.

In the courtyard there was sort of a shed for firewood, bikes, and our larger toys. I remember two red tricycles and wooden scooters. I also recall hoops that we rolled down the street with sticks. A huge kite leaned against one of the walls. In the courtyard there was a swing with two seats hanging side by side. Our mother pushed us, and we tried to swing up into the branches of the walnut tree that may still be there behind the house.

The man from the embassy asks me, "Does all this remind you of anything?"

I say, "No, nothing. I was only four at the time."

"Do you want to try right now?"

"No, I'll call tonight."

"Yes, that would be best. He's not a man who readily receives visitors. It might be impossible for you to see him."

We return to the embassy. I go up to my room. I place the number beside the telephone. I take a sedative and open the window. It's snowing. The flakes make a watery sound as they fall on the yellow grass and black earth of the garden. I lie down on the bed.

I walk through the streets of an unfamiliar town. It's snowing and growing darker and darker. The streets I am following become less and less well lit. Our old house is on one of the last streets. Farther off it is already the countryside. A completely lightless night. There is a bar across from the house. I go in and order a bottle of wine. I am the only customer.

The windows of the house light up all at once. I see shadows moving through the curtains. I finish the bottle, leave the bar, cross the street, and ring at the garden door. No one answers; the bell isn't working. I open the cast-iron gate; it isn't locked. I climb the five steps that lead to the door on the veranda. I ring again. Two times, three times. A man's voice asks from behind the door, "Who is it? What do you want? Who are you?"

I say, "It's me, Claus."

"Claus? Claus who?"

"Don't you have a son named Claus?"

"Our son is here, inside the house. With us. Leave."

The man moves away from the door. I ring again, knock, cry out, "Father, Father, let me in. I made a mistake. My name is Lucas. I'm your son Lucas."

A woman's voice says, "Let him in."

The door opens. An old man says to me, "Come in, then."

He leads me into the living room and sits down in an armchair. A very old woman is seated in another. She says to me, "So, you claim to be our son Lucas? Where were you until now?"

"Abroad."

My father says, "Yes, abroad. And why have you come back now?"

"To see you, Father. You both, and Klaus too."

My mother says, "Klaus didn't go away."

Father says, "We looked for you for years."

Mother continues, "After that we forgot you. You shouldn't have come back. It's upsetting everyone. We lead quiet lives and we don't want to be upset."

I ask, "Where is Klaus? I want to see him."

Mother says, "He's in his room. As usual. He's sleeping. He mustn't be woken up. He's only four, he needs his sleep."

Father says, "Nothing proves that you're Lucas. Go away."

I don't hear them anymore; I leave the living room, open the door to the children's room, and switch on the ceiling light. Sitting up in his bed, a little boy looks at me and begins to cry. My parents run in. Mother takes the little boy in her arms and rocks him.

"Don't be afraid, little one."

Father grabs my arm, pulls me across the living room and the veranda, opens the door, and shoves me down the stairs.

"You woke him up, you idiot. Get lost."

I fall, my head strikes a step, I bleed, I lie there in the snow.

The cold awakens me. The wind and snow are coming into my room and the floor under the window is wet.

I shut the window, fetch a towel from the bathroom, and sponge up the puddle. I tremble and my teeth chatter. It's hot in the bathroom; I sit on the edge of the tub, take another sedative, and wait for my shivering to stop.

It's seven in the evening. I am brought a meal. I ask the waiter if I can have a bottle of wine.

He says, "I'll go see."

He brings the bottle several minutes later.

I say, "You can clear away the tray."

I drink. I pace around my room. From the window to the door, from the door to the window.

At eight I sit down on the bed and dial my brother's telephone number.

Part Two

It is eight o'clock when the telephone rings. Mother has already gone to bed. I'm watching television, a detective movie, as I do every night.

I spit the biscuit I am eating into a paper napkin. I can finish it later.

I pick up the telephone. I don't say my name, just "Hello."

A man's voice at the other end says, "This is Lucas T. I'd like to speak to my brother, Klaus T."

I am silent. Sweat runs down my back. Finally I say, "There's some sort of mistake. I have no brother."

The voice says, "Yes you do. A twin brother. Lucas."

"My brother died a long time ago."

"No, I'm not dead. I'm alive, Klaus, and I'd like to see you again."

"Where are you? Where have you been?"

"I lived abroad for a long time. I'm here right now, in the capital, at the embassy of D."

419

I inhale deeply and say in one breath, "I don't think you're my brother. I see no one and don't want to be disturbed."

He insists. "Five minutes, Klaus. I'm asking you for five minutes. I'm leaving the country in two days and not coming back."

"Come tomorrow. But not before eight in the evening."

He says, "Thank you. I'll be at our house—I mean at your house—at eight-thirty."

He hangs up.

I wipe my forehead. I return to the television. I can no longer follow the movie. I throw the rest of my biscuit in the trash can. I can't eat anymore. "At our house." Yes, it was our house once, but that was a long time ago. Now it's my house and everything here belongs to me alone.

I quietly open the door to Mother's bedroom. She is asleep. She's so small you'd think she was a child. I brush the gray hair off her face, kiss her on the forehead, and stroke her wrinkled hands on the bed cover. She smiles in her sleep, squeezes my hand, and murmurs, "My little one. There you are."

Then she says the name of my brother: "Lucas, my little Lucas."

I leave the room, get a bottle of strong alcohol from the kitchen, and settle in the study to write, as I do every night. This study used to be our father's; I haven't changed anything, not the old typewriter, not the uncomfortable wooden chair, not the lamp, not the pencil holder. I try to write but I can only cry and think about the thing that has ruined all of our lives.

Lucas will come tomorrow. I know it's him. I knew it was him from the very first ring. My telephone almost never rings. I had it installed for Mother, in case of emergencies, to order in when I don't have the strength to go to the market or when her condition doesn't allow me to leave.

Lucas will come tomorrow. How to make sure that Mother doesn't find out? That she doesn't wake up during Lucas's visit? Get her out of here? Escape? Where? How? What excuse to give Mother? We've never left here. Mother doesn't want to leave. She thinks it's the only place where Lucas could find us again when he comes.

And it is in fact here that he has found us.

If it's really him.

It's really him.

I don't need any proof. I know. I knew, I have always known, that he wasn't dead, that he would come back.

But why now? Why this late? Why after an absence of fifty years?

I have to protect myself. I have to protect Mother. I don't want Lucas to destroy our peace, our routine, our happiness. I do not want our lives turned upside down. Neither Mother nor I could bear Lucas starting to root around in our past, reviving memories, asking Mother questions.

At all costs I must fend off Lucas, keep him from reopening that terrible wound.

It is winter. I must save coal. I take the edge off the cold in Mother's room with an electric heater that I turn on an hour before she goes to bed and turn off when she has fallen asleep, then turn on again an hour before she wakes up.

As far as I'm concerned, the heat of the kitchen stove and a bit of coal for the living room stove are enough. I wake up early to light the kitchen stove, and once it has produced enough embers I take some into the living room stove. I add a few lumps of coal and in half an hour it's warm in there too.

Late at night, when Mother is already asleep, I open the study door and the heat from the living room immediately flows in. It's a small room and warms up quickly. It is there that I change into my pajamas and bathrobe before starting to write. That way, after I have finished writing all I have to do is go to my room and climb into bed.

Tonight I pace around the house. I stop several times in the kitchen. Then I go into the children's room. I look at the garden. The bare branches of the walnut tree brush against the window. A fine snow settles in thin, frosted layers on the branches and on the ground.

I walk from one room into the other. I've already opened the study door; it is there that I will see my brother. I will close the door as soon as my brother comes, the cold be damned; I do not want Mother to hear us or for our conversation to wake her.

What will I say if that happens?

I will say, "Go back to bed, Mother, it's only a journalist."

And to the other one, to my brother, I will say, "It's only my mother-in-law, Antonia. She's been living at our house for a few years, ever since she was widowed. She's not completely right in the head. She confuses everything, gets things mixed up. She sometimes thinks that she's my real mother because she raised me."

I must keep them from seeing each other or they will recognize each other. Mother will recognize Lucas. And if Lucas doesn't recognize Mother, she will say when she recognizes him, "Lucas, my son!"

I want no "Lucas, my son!" Not anymore. It would be too easy.

Today, while Mother was taking her nap, I moved all the watches and clocks in the house forward by an hour. Luckily night falls early this time of year. It's already dark at five in the afternoon.

I make Mother's dinner an hour early. Carrot puree with potatoes, meatloaf, and crème caramel for dessert.

I set the kitchen table and go call Mother from her room. She comes into the kitchen and says, "I'm not hungry yet."

I say, "You're never hungry, Mother. But you have to eat."

She says, "I'll eat later."

I say, "Later everything will be cold."

She says, "All you have to do is reheat it. Or maybe I won't eat at all."

"I'll make you some herbal tea to whet your appetite."

Into her tea I dissolve one of the sleeping pills she usually takes. I put another next to her cup.

Ten minutes later Mother falls asleep in front of the television. I pick her up, carry her to her room, undress her, and put her to bed.

I go back into the living room. I turn down the television and mute its screen. I reset the hands on the alarm clock in the kitchen and on the living room clock.

I still have time to eat before my brother arrives. In the kitchen I have a bit of carrot puree and meatloaf. Mother has difficulty chewing despite the dentures I had made for her not too long ago. Her digestion isn't very good either.

When I've finished eating I do the dishes and put the leftovers in the refrigerator; there's just enough for tomorrow's lunch.

I settle down in the living room. I put two glasses and a bottle of brandy out on the little table next to my armchair. I drink and wait. At eight o'clock on the dot I check on Mother. She's sleeping deeply. The detective movie begins and I try to watch it. Around eight-twenty I give up on the movie and take up a post by the kitchen window. The light inside is off and it's impossible to see me from outside.

At eight-thirty exactly a big black car pulls up in front of the house and parks on the sidewalk. A man gets out, walks up to the gate, and rings.

I return to the living room and say into the intercom, "Come in. The door is open."

I turn on the veranda light, sit back down in my armchair, and my brother comes in. He is thin and pale and walks toward me with a limp; a portfolio case is tucked under his arm. Tears come into my eyes, and I rise and stretch out my hand to him. "Welcome."

He says, "I won't disturb you for long. A car is waiting for me."

I say, "Come into my study. It will be quieter in there."

I leave the television sound on. If Mother wakes up she will hear the detective show, as is usual every night.

My brother asks, "You're not switching off the television?"

"No. Why? We cannot hear it in the study."

I take the bottle and the two glasses. I sit down behind my desk and motion to a chair across from me.

"Have a seat."

I pick up the bottle.

"A glass?"

"Yes."

We drink. My brother says, "This was our father's study. Nothing has changed. I remember the lamp, the typewriter, the furniture, the chairs."

I smile. "What else do you remember?"

"Everything. The veranda and the living room. I know where the kitchen is, the children's room, the parents' room."

I say, "That is not so difficult. All these houses are modeled on the same pattern."

He goes on: "There was a walnut tree outside the window of the children's room. Its branches touched the glass, and a swing hung from it. With two seats. We kept our scooters and tricycles in the shed at the back of the courtyard."

I say, "There are still toys there, but not the same ones. These ones belong to my grandchildren."

We are silent. I refill the glasses. When he sets his down Lucas asks, "Tell me, Klaus, where are our parents?"

"Mine are dead. As for yours, I do not know."

"Why so formal with me, Klaus? I'm your brother, Lucas. Why don't you want to believe me?"

"Because my brother is dead. I would be very happy to see your papers, if you wouldn't mind."

My brother pulls a foreign passport out of his pocket and hands it to me. He says, "Don't believe too much of it. There are one or two errors in it."

I examine the passport.

"So you are called Claus, with a 'C.' Your date of birth is not the same as mine, and yet Lucas and I were twins. You are three years older than I am."

I hand him back his passport. My brother's hands are shaking, as is his voice.

"When I crossed the frontier I was fifteen. I gave a false birthdate to seem older, of legal age, in fact. I didn't want to be put under a guardianship."

"And the first name? Why the change in first names?"

"Because of you, Klaus. When I filled out the questionnaire at the border guards' office I thought of you, of your name, which had been with me for the whole length of my childhood. So instead of Lucas I wrote Claus. You did the same thing when you published your poems under the name Klaus Lucas. Why Lucas? In memory of me?"

I say, "In memory of my brother, actually. But how do you know I publish poems?"

"I write too, but not poems."

He opens his portfolio and takes out a large schoolboy's notebook, which he places on the table.

"This is my last manuscript. It's unfinished. I won't have time to complete it. I'm leaving it for you. You'll finish it. You have to finish it."

I open the notebook but he stops me with a gesture.

"No, not now. When I'm gone. There's something important I'd like to know. How did I get my wound?"

"What wound?"

"A wound close to the spinal column. A bullet wound. How did I get it?"

"How would you suppose me to know? My brother, Lucas, did not have a wound. He had a childhood illness. Poliomyelitis, I believe. I was no more than four or five when he died and cannot remember exactly. All I know is what I was told later on."

He says, "Yes, exactly. For a long time I too thought I had had a childhood illness. That's what I was told. But later I learned that I had been wounded by a bullet. Where? How? The war had only just started."

I remain silent and shrug. Lucas persists: "If your brother is dead, he must have a grave. His grave, where is it? Can you show me?"

"No, I cannot. My brother is buried in a mass grave in the town of S."

"Oh yes? And Father's grave, and Mother's grave, where are they? Can you show me?"

"No, I cannot do that either. My father did not come back from the war, and my mother is buried with my brother, Lucas, in the town of S."

He asks, "So then I didn't die of poliomyelitis?"

"My brother didn't, no. He died in the middle of a bombing. My mother had just gone with him to the town of S., where he was to be treated at the rehabilitation center. The center was bombed and neither my brother nor my mother ever came back."

Lucas says, "If they told you that, they lied to you. Mother never went with me to the town of S. She never went there to see me. I had lived at the center with my alleged childhood illness for several years before it was bombed. And I wasn't killed in the bombing. I survived."

I shrug again. "You, yes. My brother, no. Nor my mother."

We look each other in the eye and I don't turn away.

"As you can see, we are talking about two different fates. You will have to pursue your investigation elsewhere."

He shakes his head. "No, Klaus, and you know it very well. You know I'm your brother, Lucas, but you deny it. What are you afraid of? Tell me, Klaus, what?"

I reply, "Nothing. What could I be afraid of? Were I convinced that you are my brother, I would be the happiest of men for having found you again."

He asks, "Why would I come find you if I weren't your brother?"

"I have no idea. There is also your appearance."

"My appearance?"

"Yes. Look at me and look at you. Is there the slightest physical resemblance between us? Lucas and I were true twins and looked perfectly alike. You are a head shorter and weigh sixty pounds less than me."

Lucas says, "You're forgetting my illness, my infirmity. It's a miracle that I learned to walk again."

I say, "Let us move on. Tell me what became of you after the bombing."

He says, "Since my parents didn't reclaim me, I was sent to live with an old peasant woman in the town of K. I lived with her and worked for her until I left for abroad."

"And what did you do abroad?"

"All sorts of things, and then I wrote books. And you, Klaus, how did you survive after the death of Mother and Father? From what you tell me, you were orphaned very young."

"Yes, very young. But I was fortunate. I spent only a few months at an orphanage. A kindly family took me in. I was very happy with them. It was a large family with four children, of which I married the eldest daughter, Sarah. We had two children, a girl and a boy. At present I am a grandfather, a very happy grandfather."

Lucas says, "It's odd. When I first came in, I had the impression that you lived alone."

"I am alone at the moment, that is true. But only until Christmas. I have pressing work to complete. A collection of new poems to prepare. After that I will rejoin my wife, Sarah, my children, and my grandchildren in the town of K., where we will all spend the holidays together. We have a house there that my wife inherited from her parents."

Lucas says, "I've lived in the town of K. I know the place very well. Where's your house?"

"Central Square, across from the Grand Hotel, next to the bookseller's."

"I've just spent several months in the town of K. In fact I lived right above the bookseller's."

I say, "What a coincidence. It is a very pretty town, would you not agree? I often spent vacations there when I was a child, and my grandchildren like it very much. Especially the twins, my daughter's children."

"Twins? What are their names?"

"Klaus and Lucas, obviously."

"Obviously."

"For the time being my son has only one child, a little girl named Sarah after her grandmother, my wife. But my son is still young and he too may have other children."

Lucas says, "You're a happy man, Klaus."

I reply, "Yes, very happy. You too, I suppose, have a family."

He says, "No. I've always lived alone."

"Why?"

Lucas says, "I don't know. Perhaps because no one ever taught me how to love."

I say, "That is a shame. Children bring one a great deal of joy. I cannot imagine my life without them."

My brother stands up. "They're waiting for me in the car. I don't want to disturb you any longer."

I smile. "You haven't disturbed me. So, are you going to return to your adoptive country?"

"Of course. I have nothing more to do here. Farewell, Klaus."

I rise. "I will see you out."

At the garden gate I extend my hand to him. "Good-bye, sir. I hope that in the end you find your true family. I wish you much luck."

He says, "You keep in role to the very end, Klaus. Had I known you were so hard-hearted I would never have tried to find you. I sincerely regret that I came."

My brother climbs into the big black car, which starts up and drives him away.

While climbing the veranda stairs I slip on the icy steps and fall; my forehead slams into one of the stone edges, and the blood flowing into my eyes mixes with my tears. I want to remain lying here until I freeze and die but I can't; I have to take care of Mother tomorrow morning.

I enter the house and go into the bathroom; I wash my wound, disinfect it, bandage it, and then I return to the study to read my brother's manuscript.

The next morning Mother asks, "How did you hurt yourself, Klaus?"

I say, "On the stairs. I went down to make sure the gate was locked. I slipped on the ice."

Mother says, "You probably had too much to drink. You're a drunk, an incompetent, and an oaf. Haven't you made my tea yet? Unbelievable! And the house is cold too. Couldn't you get up half an hour earlier so that when I wake up I find the house warm and my tea made? You're a layabout, a good-for-nothing."

I say, "Here's the tea. In a few minutes the house will be warm, you'll see. The truth is, I didn't go to bed at all; I wrote all night long."

She says, "Again? The gentleman prefers to write all night long instead of worrying about the heat and the tea. You should write during the day, working like everyone else, not at night."

I say, "Yes, Mother. It would be better to work during the day. But at the printing press I got used to working nights. I can't help it. Anyway there are too many things to distract me during the day. There are errands to do, meals to make, but especially the street noise."

Mother says, "And there's me, isn't there? Say it, say it outright, that it's me who disturbs you. You can only write once your mother is in bed and asleep, right? You're always in such a hurry to see me off to bed at night. I understand. I've understood for quite a while."

I say, "It's true, Mother, I have to be completely alone when I write. I need silence and solitude."

She says, "As far as I can tell I'm neither very noisy nor very obtrusive. Just say the word and I won't come out of my room anymore. Once I'm in my grave I won't bother you any longer, you won't have to run errands or make the meals anymore, you'll have nothing to do but write. There at least I'll find my son Lucas, who was never mean to me, who never wished me dead and gone. I'll be happy there, and no one will yell at me for anything."

I say, "Mother, I'm not yelling at you, and you don't disturb me in the least. I'm happy to run errands and make meals, but I need the night to write in. My poems have been our only income since I left the printing press."

She says, "Precisely. You should never have left. The printing press was a normal, reasonable job."

I say, "Mother, you know very well that I was forced to leave my job because of illness. I couldn't go on without ruining my health completely."

Mother doesn't answer; she sits down in front of the television. But she starts in again at the evening meal.

"The house is falling to bits. The downspout has come loose and the water pours out all over the garden; it'll come down inside the house soon. Weeds are taking over the garden and the rooms are all black with smoke from your cigarettes. The kitchen is yellow with it, as are the living room windows. Let's not even talk about the study or the children's room, which are both filthy with smoke. One can't even breathe in this house, not even in the garden, where the flowers have been killed off by the pestilence from inside."

I say, "Yes, Mother, calm down, Mother. There are no flowers in the garden because it's winter. I'll have the bedrooms and kitchen repainted. I'm glad you reminded me. By spring I'll have everything repainted and the downspout fixed."

After taking her sleeping pill Mother calms down and goes to bed.

I sit in front of the television, watching a detective movie as I do every night, and drink. Then I go into my study, reread the last pages of my brother's manuscript, and begin to write.

There were always four of us at table: Father, Mother, and the two of us.

Mother sang all day long in the kitchen, the garden, and the courtyard. She also sang us to sleep at night in our room.

Father did not sing. He whistled sometimes while chopping wood for the kitchen stove, and we listened to his typewriter as he wrote in the evening and sometimes until late at night.

It was a sound as pleasant and comforting as music, as Mother's sewing machine, as the noise of the dishes being done, the singing of blackbirds in the garden, the wind in the leaves of the wild vine on the veranda or in the branches of the walnut tree in the courtyard.

The sun, the wind, night, the moon, the stars, the clouds, rain, snow—everything was a miracle. We were afraid of nothing, neither shadows nor the stories adults told among themselves. Stories of war. We were four years old.

One night Father comes home dressed in a uniform. He hangs his coat and belt on the rack near the living room door. There is a revolver holstered on his belt.

433

During dinner Father says, "I must go to another town. War has been declared and I've been called up."

We say, "We didn't know you were a soldier, Father. You're a journalist, not a soldier."

He says, "In wartime all men are soldiers, even journalists. Especially journalists. I have to observe and describe what happens at the front. It's called being a war correspondent."

We ask, "Why do you have a revolver?"

"Because I'm an officer. Soldiers have rifles, officers revolvers."

Father says to Mother, "Put the children to bed. I have something to talk to you about."

Mother says to us, "Off to bed. I'll come tell you a story. Say good-bye to your father."

We kiss Father and then go to our room, but we immediately come back. We sit silently in the hallway just behind the living room door.

Father says, "I'm going to go live with her. It's war and I have no time to waste. I love her."

Mother asks, "What about the children?"

Father says, "She's expecting a child as well. That's why I couldn't remain silent."

"Do you want a divorce?"

"It's not the time for that. After the war we'll see. Meanwhile I'm going to recognize the baby. I might not make it back alive. One never knows."

Mother asks, "You don't love us anymore?"

Father says, "That's beside the point. I'll keep on taking care of the boys and you. But I also love another woman. Can't you understand?"

"No. I can't understand and I don't want to."

We hear a gunshot. We open the living room door. It is Mother who has fired. She has Father's revolver in her hand. She is still shooting. Father is on the ground and Mother keeps on shooting. Beside me Lucas falls too. Mother throws down the revolver, shrieks, and kneels next to Lucas.

I run out of the house and down the street shouting "Help!" Some people grab me, bring me back to the house, try to calm me. They also try to calm Mother, but she keeps shrieking, "No, no, no!"

The living room is filled with people. The police arrive as well as two ambulances. They bring us all to the hospital.

In the hospital they give me an injection to make me fall asleep because I am still shouting.

The next day the doctor says, "He's fine. He wasn't hurt. He can go home."

The nurse says, "Go home where? There's no one at his house. And he's only four."

The doctor says, "Go see the social worker."

The nurse brings me to an office. The social worker is an old woman with her hair in a bun. She asks me questions:

"Do you have a grandmother? An aunt? A neighbor who's fond of you?"

I ask, "Where's Lucas?"

She says, "Here, in the hospital. He's hurt."

I say, "I want to see him."

She says, "He's unconscious."

"What does that mean?"

"He can't talk right now."

"Is he dead?"

"No, but he must rest."

"And my mother?"

"Your mother's fine. But you can't see her either."

"Why? Is she hurt too?"

"No, she's sleeping."

"And my father's asleep too?"

"Yes, he's sleeping too."

She strokes my hair.

I ask, "How come they're all asleep and I'm not?"

She says, "That's how it is. These things happen sometimes. A whole family goes to sleep and the one who doesn't is left all alone."

"I don't want to be alone. I want to sleep too, like Lucas, like Mother, like Father."

She says, "Someone has to stay awake to wait for them and to take care of them when they come back, when they wake up."

"They'll all wake up?"

"Some of them, yes. At least we hope so."

We are quiet for a moment. She says, "You don't know anyone who could look after you while we wait?"

I ask, "Wait for what?"

"For when one of them comes back."

I say, "No, no one. And I don't want to be looked after. I want to go home."

She says, "You can't live in your house by yourself at your age. If you don't have anyone, I have to send you to an orphanage."

I say, "I don't care. If I can't live at our house I don't care where I go."

A woman comes into the office and says, "I've come for the little boy. I want to take him home with me. He doesn't have anyone else. I know his family."

The social worker tells me to go for a walk in the corridor. There are people in the corridor sitting on benches, talking. They're almost all dressed in bathrobes.

They say:

"How horrible."

"It's a pity, such a nice family."

"She was in the right."

"Men. That's men for you."

"They're a disgrace, these young women."

"And the war breaking out and all."

"There really are other things to worry about."

The woman who said "I want to take him home with me" comes out of the office. She says to me, "You can come with me. My name is Antonia. And you? Are you Lucas or Klaus?"

I offer my hand to Antonia. "I'm Klaus."

We get on a bus and then walk. We come to a little room where there is a big bed and a smaller one, a crib.

Antonia says to me, "You're still little enough to sleep in that bed, aren't you?"

I say, "Yes."

I lie down in the crib. There's just enough room; my feet touch the bars.

Antonia goes on, "The little bed is for the baby I'm expecting. It will be your little brother or sister."

I say, "I already have a brother. I don't want another one. Nor a sister either."

Antonia is lying on the big bed and says, "Come, come next to me."

I get out of my bed and go up to hers. She takes my hand and puts it on her stomach. "Can you feel it? It's moving. It will be with us soon."

She pulls me against herself in the bed and holds me.

"I hope that he'll be as handsome as you."

Then she puts me back in the little bed.

Each time Antonia held me I could feel the baby moving, and I thought it was Lucas. I was wrong. It was a little girl who came out of Antonia's stomach.

I am sitting in the kitchen. The two old women told me to stay here. I hear Antonia's cries. I do not move. The two old women come in from time to time to heat water and to say to me, "Sit there quietly."

Later one of the old women tells me, "You can go in."

I go into the room; Antonia holds her arms out, hugs me, and laughs. "It's a little girl. Look. A pretty little girl. Your sister."

I look inside the crib. A little crimson-colored thing is screaming. I hold her hand, count, and stroke her fingers one by one. She has ten. I stick her left thumb in her mouth and she stops crying.

Antonia smiles at me. "We'll call her Sarah. Do you like that name?"

I say, "Yes, the name doesn't matter. It isn't important. She's my little sister, isn't she?"

"Yes, your own little sister."

"And Lucas's too?"

"Yes, Lucas's too."

Antonia starts to cry. I ask her, "Where will I sleep now that the little bed is taken?"

She says, "In the kitchen. I asked my mother to make a bed for you in the kitchen."

I ask, "I can't sleep in your room anymore?"

Antonia says, "It's better for you to sleep in the kitchen. The baby will cry a lot and wake everyone up all night long."

I say, "If she cries and bothers you, all you have to do is put her thumb in her mouth. The left thumb, like me."

I go back into the kitchen. There's only one old woman there, Antonia's mother. She gives me honey sandwiches to eat. She makes me drink some milk. Then she says, "Get into bed, my little one. Choose whichever one you like best."

There are two mattresses on the floor with pillows and blankets. I choose the mattress under the window; that way I can look at the stars and the sky.

Antonia's mother lies down on the other mattress. Before going to sleep she prays: "Lord almighty, help me. The child doesn't even have a father. My daughter with a fatherless child! If my husband even knew! I lied to him. I hid the truth from him. And the other child, which isn't even hers. And this whole sad business. What must I do to save this sinner?"

Grandmother mumbles and I fall asleep, happy to be near Antonia and Sarah.

Antonia's mother rises early in the morning. She sends me off to run errands at a neighborhood store. All I have to do is hand over a list and give them money.

Antonia's mother cooks the meals. She bathes the baby and changes it several times a day. She does the laundry, which she hangs on cords over our heads in the kitchen. She mumbles the whole time. Prayers, maybe.

She does not stay long. Ten days after Sarah's birth she leaves with her suitcase and her prayers.

I'm happy all alone in the kitchen. In the morning I get up early to fetch bread and milk. When Antonia wakes up I go into her room with a bottle for Sarah and coffee for Antonia. Sometimes I give Sarah her bottle; afterward I can watch her being bathed, and I try to make her laugh with the toys that we have bought for her, Antonia and I.

Sarah becomes prettier and prettier. She grows hair and teeth, she knows how to laugh, and she has learned to suck her left thumb.

Unfortunately, Antonia has to go back to work because her parents no longer send her money.

Antonia goes away every evening. She works in a nightclub where she sings and dances. She comes back late at night and in the morning she is tired; she can't take care of Sarah.

A neighbor comes every morning; she gives Sarah her bath, then sets her down with her toys in her pen in the kitchen. I play with her while the neighbor makes lunch and washes the laundry. After doing the dishes the neighbor leaves, and after that I look after everything if Antonia is still asleep.

In the afternoon I take Sarah for walks in her carriage. We go to parks where there are playgrounds; I let Sarah run around in the grass or play in the sand, and I balance her on swings.

When I am six years old I have to go to school. Antonia comes with me on the first day. She speaks with the teacher and then leaves me there alone. When class is over I run home to see if everything's all right and to take Sarah for a walk.

We go farther and farther afield, and it is because of this, completely by chance, that I find myself on my street, the street where I lived with my parents.

I don't mention it to Antonia or anyone else. But each day I walk by the house with green shutters, stop for a moment, and cry. Sarah cries with me.

The house is abandoned. The shutters are closed, the chimney makes no smoke. The front yard is taken over by weeds; in the back, in the courtyard, the nuts have almost certainly fallen from the tree and no one has gathered them.

One evening when Sarah's asleep I leave the house. I run through the streets noiselessly and in total darkness. The lights in the town are out because of the war; the windows of the houses have been carefully blacked out. The light of the stars is enough, and all the streets, all the alleys have been engraved in my head.

I climb the fence, go around the house, and sit at the foot of the walnut tree. In the grass my hands touch nuts that are hard and dry. I fill my pockets. The next day I come back with a sack and gather as many nuts as I can carry. When she sees the sack in the kitchen Antonia asks me, "Where did these nuts come from?"

I say, "From our garden."

"What garden? We don't have a garden."

"The garden of the house where I lived before."

Antonia takes me on her knees. "How did you find it? How do you even remember? You were only four years old at the time."

I say, "And now I'm eight. Tell me, Antonia, what happened? Where did they all go? What happened to them? Mother, Father, Lucas?"

Antonia cries and squeezes me very tight. "I hoped you'd forget about all that. I've never spoken to you about it because I wanted you to forget everything."

I say, "I haven't forgotten anything. Every night when I look at the sky I think about them. They're all up there, aren't they? They're all dead."

Antonia says, "No, not all of them. Only your father. Yes, your father is dead."

"And my mother, where is she?"

"In a hospital."

"And my brother, Lucas?"

"In a house of rehabilitation. In the town of S., near the border."

"What happened to him?"

"A bullet ricocheted into him."

"What bullet?"

Antonia pushes me off and stands up. "Leave me alone, Klaus. Leave me alone, I beg you."

She goes into the room, lies down on the bed, and keeps sobbing. Sarah starts to cry too. I pick her up and sit on the edge of Antonia's bed.

"Don't cry, Antonia. Tell me everything. It would be better if I knew everything. I'm big enough now to know the truth. Asking oneself questions is worse than knowing."

Antonia takes Sarah, lays her down beside her, and says to me, "Lie down on the other side. Let's let her fall asleep. She mustn't hear what I'm going to tell you."

We remain there, the three of us, lying on the bed for a long time in silence. Antonia strokes Sarah's hair and mine by turns. When we hear Sarah breathing regularly we know she has fallen asleep. Antonia, looking up at the ceiling, begins to speak. She tells me that my mother killed my father.

I say, "I remember the gunshots and the ambulances. And Lucas. Did my mother shoot Lucas too?"

"No, Lucas was wounded by a stray bullet. It hit him right next to the spine. He was unconscious for months and it was thought that he'd be crippled forever. Now there's a hope that he'll heal completely."

I ask, "Is Mother in the town of S. too, like Lucas?"

Antonia says, "No, your mother is here, in this town, in a psychiatric hospital."

I ask, "Psychiatric? What does that mean? Is she sick or is she insane?"

Antonia says, "Insanity is an illness like any other."

"Can I go see her?"

"I don't know. You shouldn't. It's too sad."

I think for a moment and then ask, "Why did my mother go insane? Why did she kill my father?"

Antonia says, "Because your father loved me. He loved us both, me and Sarah."

I say, "Sarah wasn't born yet. So it was because of you. Everything happened because of you. Without you the happiness of the house with green shutters would have lasted through the war, even after the war. Without you my father wouldn't be dead, my mother wouldn't be insane, my little brother wouldn't be a cripple, and I wouldn't be alone."

Antonia says nothing. I leave the room.

I go to the kitchen and take the money Antonia has set aside for groceries. Every night she leaves the money for the next day's groceries on the kitchen table. She never asks me for receipts.

I leave the house. I walk to a big wide street trafficked by buses and streetcars. I ask an old lady who is waiting for the bus on a corner: "Excuse me, ma'am, which is the bus that goes to the station?"

"Which station, my little one? There are three of them."

"The closest."

"Take streetcar number five, then bus number three. The conductor will tell you where to transfer."

I come to an immense station filled with people. Everyone is jostling, shouting, swearing. I get into the line waiting in front of the ticket booth. We move slowly. When at last it's my turn I say, "A ticket for the town of S."

The man says, "The train to S. doesn't leave from here. You have to go to South Station."

445

I get on more buses and streetcars. It's night when I reach South Station and there are no more trains to S. until tomorrow morning. I go to the waiting room and find a seat on a bench. There are a lot of people, it smells bad, and the pipe and cigarette smoke stings my eyes. I try to sleep, but as soon as I close my eyes I see Sarah alone in the room, Sarah coming into the kitchen, Sarah crying because I'm not there. She is left alone all night because Antonia has to go to work and I'm sitting in a waiting room on my way to another town, the town where my brother, Lucas, lives.

I want to go to the town where my brother lives and I want to find him; then we will go look for my mother together. Tomorrow morning I will go to the town of S. I will.

I can't sleep. I find ration cards in my pockets; without them Antonia and Sarah will have nothing to eat.

I must go back.

I run. My gym shoes make no noise. In the morning I am near where we live; I line up for bread, then for milk, and go home.

Antonia is sitting in the kitchen. She takes me in her arms. "Where were you? Sarah and I cried all night long. You must never leave us again."

I say, "I won't leave you again. Here's the bread and the milk. Some of the money's not there. I went to the station. Then another station. I wanted to go to the town of S."

Antonia says, "We'll go there soon, together. We'll find your brother again."

I say, "I would also like to see my mother."

One Sunday afternoon we go to the psychiatric hospital. Antonia and Sarah wait in the reception room. A nurse leads me into a little visiting room furnished with a table and a couple of armchairs. Under the window is a small table with green plants on it. I sit and wait.

The nurse comes back holding the arm of a woman in a bathrobe whom she helps sit down in one of the armchairs.

"Say hello to your mother, Klaus."

I look at the woman. She is fat and old. Her half-gray hair is pulled back and fastened behind her head with a bit of string. I notice this when she turns around to take a long look at the closed door. Then she asks the nurse, "And Lucas? Where is he?"

The nurse answers, "Lucas couldn't come, but Klaus is here. Say hello to your mother, Klaus."

I say, "Good day, ma'am."

She asks, "Why are you alone? Why isn't Lucas with you?"

The nurse says, "Lucas will come too, soon."

Mother looks at me. Big tears start to roll down from her pale blue eyes. She says, "Lies. Always lies."

Her nose runs. The nurse wipes it. Mother lets her head fall to her chest. She says nothing more and doesn't look at me again.

The nurse says, "We're tired, we're going back to bed. Do you want to kiss your mother, Klaus?"

I shake my head and stand up.

The nurse says, "You can find your way back to the reception room on your own, can't you?"

I say nothing and leave the room. I walk by Antonia and Sarah without a word, leave the building, and wait outside the door. Antonia holds me by the shoulder and Sarah takes my hand, but I shrug them off and put my hands in my pockets. We walk to the bus station without saying a word.

When Antonia leaves for work that evening I say, "The woman I saw is not my mother. I'm not going to go see her again. It's you who should go see her to realize what you've done."

She asks, "Will you never be able to forgive me, Klaus?"

I don't answer. She adds, "If you knew how much I love you."

I say, "You shouldn't. You aren't my mother. It's my mother who should love me, but she loves only Lucas. And it's your fault."

The front line approaches. The town is bombed night and day. We spend a lot of time in the basement. We've brought down mattresses and bed covers. At first our neighbors come too, but one day they disappear. Antonia says they've been deported.

Antonia is out of work. The nightclub where she sang doesn't exist anymore. The school is closed. It's very hard to find food, even with ration cards. Luckily Antonia has a friend who sometimes comes and brings us bread, condensed milk, biscuits, and chocolate. At night the friend stays with us since he can't go home because of the curfew. On those nights Antonia sleeps with me in the kitchen. I hold her and speak to her about Lucas, who we will find again soon, and we fall asleep looking at the stars.

One morning Antonia wakes us early. She tells us to dress warmly, to put on several shirts and sweaters, our coats, and several pairs of socks since we're going on a long trip. She fills two suitcases with the rest of our clothes.

Antonia's friend comes for us in a car. We put the suitcases in the trunk. Antonia sits up front, Sarah and I in the back.

The car stops at the entrance to a cemetery almost across from our old house. The friend stays in the car; Antonia walks quickly, pulling Sarah and me by the hand.

We stop in front of a grave with a wooden cross upon which my father's name is written—a double name made up of mine and my brother's: Klaus-Lucas T.

Among several faded bouquets on the grave, one, of white carnations, is almost fresh.

I say to Antonia, "My mother used to plant carnations all over the garden. They were my father's favorite flower."

Antonia says, "I know. Say good-bye to your father, children."

Sarah says sweetly, "Good-bye, Father."

I say, "He wasn't Sarah's father. He was only our father, Lucas and me."

Antonia says, "I've already explained it to you. Didn't you understand? Too bad. Come, we have no time to waste."

We return to the car, which drives us to South Station. Antonia says thank you and good-bye to her friend.

We line up in front of the ticket booth. It's only then that I dare to ask Antonia, "Where are we going?"

She says, "To my parents'. But first we're going to stop in the town of S. to take your brother Lucas with us."

I hold her hand and kiss her. "Thank you, Antonia."

She withdraws her hand. "Don't thank me. I only know the name of the town; I can't remember what the rehabilitation center was called."

When Antonia pays for the tickets I realize that with the grocery money I couldn't have afforded my trip to the town of S.

The trip is uncomfortable. There are too many people; everyone is fleeing from the front. We have only one seat for the three of us; the one who sits takes Sarah on his knees while the other remains standing. We exchange places several times during the trip, which should have taken five hours but lasts more than twelve because of air raids. The train stops in the open countryside; the travelers get out and lie down in the fields. Whenever it happens I stretch my coat out on the ground, lay

Sarah down on it, and crouch over her to protect her from bullets, bombs, and shrapnel.

We arrive at the town of S. late at night. We take a hotel room. Sarah and I immediately get into the big bed; Antonia goes back down to the bar to ask for information and does not return until morning.

Now she has the address of the center where Lucas should be. We go the following day.

It's a building in the middle of a park. Half of it has collapsed. It is empty. We see the bare walls blackened by smoke.

The center was bombed three weeks ago.

Antonia makes inquiries. She questions the local authorities and tries to find survivors from the center. She finds the director's address. We go see her.

She says, "I remember little Lucas very well. He was the worst resident in the house. Always making trouble, always getting on people's nerves. A truly unbearable child, and incorrigible. No one ever came to see him, no one was interested in him. If I remember rightly, there was some sort of family tragedy. There is no more I can tell you."

Antonia insists: "Did you see him again after the bombing?"

The director says, "I myself was wounded in the bombing, but no one cares about me. A lot of people come to talk to me, asking questions about their children. But no one cares about me. And I spent two weeks in the hospital after the bombing. The shock, you understand. I was responsible for all those children."

Antonia asks again: "Think back. What can you tell us about Lucas? Did you see him again after the bombing? What happened to the surviving children?"

The director says, "I didn't see him again. I tell you, I was hurt too. The children who were still alive were sent back home. The dead were buried in the town cemetery. Those who weren't dead and whose addresses were unknown were sent away. To villages, to farms, to small towns. Those people are meant to return the children after the war."

Antonia consults the list of the town's dead.

She says to me, "Lucas isn't dead. We'll find him."

We get back on the train. We come to a little station; we walk to the center of town. Antonia carries the sleeping Sarah in her arms. I carry the suitcases.

We stop at Central Square. Antonia rings a doorbell and an old woman answers the door. I already know the old woman. It's Antonia's mother. She says, "God be praised! You're safe and sound. I was terribly scared. I prayed for you constantly."

She takes my face in her hands.

"And you came with them?"

I say, "I had no choice. I have to look after Sarah."

"Of course you have to look after Sarah."

She squeezes me, kisses me, then takes Sarah in her arms.

"How pretty you are, how big you are!"

Sarah says, "I'm sleepy. I want to sleep with Klaus."

We're put to bed in the same room, the room Antonia slept in when she was a child.

Sarah calls Antonia's parents Grandmother and Grandfather; I call them Aunt Mathilda and Uncle Andreas. Uncle Andreas is a priest, and he wasn't called up because he is ill. His head shakes all the time as though he's constantly saying "no."

Uncle Andreas takes me for walks through the streets in the little town, sometimes until dusk. He says, "I'd always wished for a son. A boy would have understood my love for this town. He would have understood the beauty of these streets, these houses, that sky. Yes, the beauty of this sky that is to be found nowhere else. Look. There are no names for the colors of that sky."

I say, "It's like a dream."

"A dream, yes. I had only one daughter. She left early, very young. She came back with a little girl and with you. You're not her son, nor my grandson, but you're the boy I've been waiting for."

I say, "But I have to go back to my mother when she's better, and I also have to find my brother, Lucas."

"Yes, of course. I hope you find them. But if you don't, you can stay with us forever. You can study and then choose the occupation that pleases you. What would you like to do when you grow up?"

"I'd like to marry Sarah."

Uncle Andreas laughs. "You can't marry Sarah. You're brother and sister. Marriage between you is impossible. It's against the law."

I say, "So I'll just live with her. No one can forbid me from keeping on living with her."

"You'll meet many other young girls you'll want to marry."

I say, "I don't think so."

Soon it becomes dangerous to walk in the streets, and at night it's forbidden to go out. What to do during the air-raid warning and bombings? During the day I give lessons to Sarah. I teach her to read and write and I make her do math exercises. There are a lot of books in the house. In the attic there are even children's books and Antonia's schoolbooks.

Uncle Andreas teaches me to play chess. When the women go to bed we begin a game and play late into the night.

At first Uncle Andreas always wins. When he begins to lose, he also loses his taste for the game.

He says to me, "You're too good for me, my boy. I don't want to play anymore. I don't want anything; all my desires have left me. I don't even have interesting dreams anymore, only boring ones."

I try to teach Sarah to play chess, but she doesn't like it. She gets tired and annoyed; she prefers simpler parlor games, and above all that I read her stories, it doesn't matter which ones, even a story I've read twenty times already.

When the war moves off into the other country, Antonia says, "We can go home to the capital."

Her mother says, "You'll starve to death. Leave Sarah here for a while. At least until you find work and a decent place to live."

Uncle Andreas says, "Leave the boy here too. There are good schools in our town. When we find his brother, we'll take him in too."

I say, "I have to return to the capital to find out what happened to my mother."

Sarah says, "If Klaus goes back to the capital, I'm going too."

Antonia says, "I'm going alone. As soon as I've found an apartment I'll come get you."

She kisses Sarah and then me. She says in my ear: "I know that you'll look after her. I trust you."

Antonia leaves and we stay with Aunt Mathilda and Uncle Andreas. We're clean and well fed, but we can't go out of the house because of the foreign soldiers and the general disorder. Aunt Mathilda is afraid something will happen to us.

We each have our own room now. Sarah sleeps in the room that had been her mother's; I sleep in the guest room.

At night I draw a chair up to the window and watch the square. It's almost empty. Only a few drunks and soldiers wander through it. Sometimes a limping child, younger than me, it seems, crosses it. He plays a tune on his harmonica; he goes into one bar, leaves, and goes into another. Around midnight, when all the bars close, the child heads westward through the town, still playing his harmonica.

One night I point out the child with the harmonica to Uncle Andreas.

"Why isn't he forbidden from going out late at night?"

"I've been watching him for the past year. He lives with his grandmother on the other end of town. She's a very poor woman. The child is probably an orphan. He plays in bars to earn a bit of money. People are used to seeing him around. No one will harm him. He's under the protection of the whole town, and under the protection of God."

I say, "He must be happy."

Uncle says, "Definitely."

Three months later Antonia comes for us. Aunt Mathilda and Uncle Andreas don't want us to go.

Aunt Mathilda says, "Let the little girl stay. She's happy here and has everything she needs."

Uncle Andreas says, "At least leave the boy. Now that things are settling down we could start making inquiries about his brother."

Antonia says, "You can start making inquiries without him, Father. I'm taking them both. Their place is with me."

In the capital we now have a big four-bedroom apartment. In addition to these rooms there is a living room and a bathroom.

On the evening of our arrival I tell Sarah a story and stroke her hair until she falls asleep. I hear Antonia and her friend talking in the living room.

I put on my gym shoes, go down the stairs, and run through the familiar streets. The streets, side streets, and alleys are lit now; there is no more war, no more blackout, no more curfew.

I stop in front of my house; the light is on in the kitchen. At first I think that strangers have moved in. The light in the living room also goes on. It's summer and the windows are open. I go nearer. Someone is speaking, a man's voice. Stealthily I look in through the window. My mother, sitting in an armchair, is listening to the radio.

For a week I come to observe my mother, sometimes several times a day. She goes about her business, wandering from room to room, spending most of her time in the kitchen. She also tends the

455

garden, planting and watering the flowers. At night she spends a long time reading in the parents' bedroom, whose window looks out onto the courtyard. Every other day a nurse arrives on a bicycle; she stays for around twenty minutes, chatting with Mother, taking her blood pressure, sometimes giving her an injection.

Once a day, in the morning, a young woman comes with a full basket and leaves with it empty. I continue to do the shopping for Antonia even though she can do it herself and even has a friend to help her.

Mother has grown thinner. She no longer looks like an unkempt old woman the way she did at the hospital. Her face has reassumed its former softness while her hair has its color and brightness again. It is done up in a thick russet bun.

One morning Sarah asks me, "Where do you go, Klaus? Where do you go so often? Even at night. I came into your room last night because I'd had a nightmare. You weren't there and I was scared."

"Why don't you go to Antonia's room when you're scared?"

"I can't. Because of her friend. He sleeps here almost every night. Where do you go so often, Klaus?"

"I just go for walks. Around town."

Sarah says, "You go to the empty house, you go cry in front of your empty house, don't you? Why don't you take me with you?"

I say to her, "The house isn't empty anymore, Sarah. My mother has come back. She's living in our house again, and I have to go back too."

Sarah begins to cry. "You're going to live with your mother? You're not going to live with us anymore? What will I do without you, Klaus?"

I kiss her on the eyes. "And me? What will I do without you, Sarah?"

We're both crying; we're lying tangled together on the living room sofa. We hold each other more and more tightly, laced to each other with our arms, with our legs. Tears are flowing down our faces, in our hair, on our necks, in our ears. We're shaking with sobs, with trembling, with cold.

I feel wetness in my pants between my legs.

"What are you doing? What's going on?"

Antonia separates us, pushes us far apart, and sits down between us. She shakes my shoulder.

"What have you done?"

I cry out, "I didn't do anything bad to Sarah."

Antonia takes Sarah in her arms.

"Good God. I should have expected something like this."

Sarah says, "I think I peed in my pants."

She throws her arms around her mother's neck.

"Mama, Mama! Klaus is going to live with his mother."

Antonia stammers, "What? What?"

I say, "Yes, Antonia, it's my duty to go live with her."

Antonia cries out, "No!"

Then she says, "Yes, you should go back to your mother."

The next morning Antonia and Sarah go with me. We stop on the corner of the street, my street. Antonia kisses me and hands me a key.

"Here's the key to the apartment. You can keep coming whenever you want. I'll keep your room for you."

I say, "Thank you, Antonia. I'll come see you as often as possible."

Sarah says nothing. She's pale and her eyes are red. She looks at the sky, the blue cloudless sky of a summer morning. I look at Sarah, this little girl of seven, my first love. I will have no other.

I stop on the other side of the street in front of the house. I put down my suitcase and sit on it. I see the young girl arrive with her basket and then leave. I remain seated; I don't have the strength to stand up. Around noon I begin to get hungry; I'm dizzy and my stomach hurts.

In the afternoon the nurse arrives on her bicycle. I cross the street at a run with my suitcase and grab the nurse by the arm before she has entered the garden.

"Ma'am, excuse me, ma'am. I was waiting for you."

She asks, "What's the matter? Are you sick?"

I say, "No, I'm afraid. I'm afraid of going into the house."

"Why do you want to go into the house?"

"It's my house, my mother's. I'm afraid of my mother. I haven't seen her for seven years."

I stutter and tremble. The nurse says, "Take it easy. You must be Klaus. Or are you Lucas?"

"I'm Klaus. Lucas isn't here. I don't know where he is. No one does. That's why I'm afraid of seeing my mother. Alone, without Lucas."

She says, "Yes, I understand. You did well to wait for me. Your mother is convinced she killed Lucas. We'll go in together. Follow me."

The nurse rings and my mother shouts from the kitchen, "Come in, it's open!"

We cross the veranda and stop in the living room. The nurse says, "I've got a big surprise for you."

My mother appears at the kitchen door. She wipes her hands on her apron, looks at me wide-eyed, and whispers, "Lucas?"

The nurse says, "No, it's Klaus. But Lucas will probably come back too."

Mother says, "No, Lucas won't come back. I killed him. I killed my little boy and he's never coming back."

Mother sits down in one of the living room armchairs and trembles. The nurse rolls up the sleeve of Mother's bathrobe and gives her an injection. My mother lets her do it. The nurse says, "Lucas isn't dead. He was transferred to a rehabilitation center, I told you already."

I say, "Yes, to a center in the town of S. I went to look for him. The center was destroyed in a bombing, but Lucas isn't on the list of the dead."

Mother asks very softly, "You're not lying, Klaus?"

"No, Mother, I'm not lying."

The nurse says, "What's certain is that you didn't kill him."

Mother is calm now. She says, "We have to go there. Who did you go with, Klaus?"

"A woman from the orphanage. She went with me. She had relatives near the town of S."

"Orphanage? I was told that you'd been placed in a family. A family that took very good care of you. You have to give me their address. I'm going to thank them."

I begin to stammer: "I don't know their address. I wasn't there very long. Because, because they were deported. Then I went into an orphanage. I had everything I needed and everyone was very kind to me."

The nurse says, "I'm off. I still have a lot to do. Would you see me out, Klaus?"

I walk out to the front of the house with her. She asks me, "Where were you these seven years, Klaus?"

I say to her, "You heard what I told my mother."

She says, "Yes, I heard. Only it wasn't the truth. You lie very badly, my little one. We checked the orphanages and you were at none of them. And how did you find the house again? How did you know your mother had moved back in?"

I am silent. She says, "You can keep your secret. You undoubtedly have a reason for it. But don't forget that I've been taking care of your mother for years. The more I know, the more I can help her. When you show up out of the blue with your suitcase, I have a right to ask where you've been."

I say, "No, you don't have the right. I'm here, that's all. Tell me what to do about my mother."

"Do what you think is best. If possible, be patient. If she has an attack, telephone me."

"What happens when she has an attack?"

"Don't worry. It'll be no worse than it was today. She cries out, she trembles, that's all. Here, here's my telephone number. If something goes wrong, call."

Mother is sleeping in one of the living room armchairs. I pick up my suitcase and go unpack in the children's bedroom at the end of the hallway. There are still two beds, two adult-sized beds that our parents bought just before the "thing." I still haven't found a word to describe what happened to us. I could say drama, tragedy, catastrophe, but in my head I simply call it the "thing" for which there is no name.

The children's bedroom is clean, as are the beds. Mother was obviously expecting us. But the one she is waiting for most eagerly is my brother Lucas.

We are eating silently in the kitchen when suddenly Mother says, "I don't in the least regret having killed your father. If I knew who the woman he wanted to leave us for was, I'd kill her too. If I hurt Lucas it was her fault, her fault entirely, not mine."

I say, "Mother, don't torture yourself. Lucas didn't die of his wound. He'll come back."

Mother asks, "How could he find this house again?"

I say, "The way I did. I found it and he'll find it too."

Mother says, "You're right. At all costs we must stay here. It's here that he'll look for us."

Mother takes medications in order to sleep and she goes to bed very early. During the night I go look at her in her room. She sleeps on her back in the big bed, her face turned to the window, leaving the place that had been her husband's empty.

I sleep very little. I look at the stars, and as at Antonia's I thought about our family and this house every night, so here I

461

think about Sarah and her family, about her grandparents in the town of K.

When I awake I find the walnut-tree branches outside my window. I go into the kitchen and kiss Mother. She smiles at me. There's coffee and tea. The young girl brings fresh bread. I tell her that she doesn't need to come anymore, that I'll do the shopping myself.

Mother says, "No, Veronica. Keep coming. Klaus is still too small to do the shopping."

Veronica laughs. "He's not that small. But he won't find what you need in the shops. I work at the hospital kitchen and that's where I get the things I bring here, you see, Klaus? At the orphanage you were spoiled when it came to food. You couldn't imagine what you have to do to find something to eat in the city. You'll spend your whole time lining up outside shops."

Mother and Veronica have quite a bit of fun together. They laugh and kiss. Veronica tells stories about her love life. Stupid stories: "So he said to me, so I said to him, so he tried to kiss me."

Veronica helps Mother dye her hair. They use a product called henna that restores its old color to Mother's hair. Veronica also tends to Mother's face. She makes "masks" for her, she does her makeup with little brushes, tubes, and pencils.

Mother says, "I want to look nice when Lucas comes back. I don't want him to find me ratty, old, and ugly. Do you understand, Klaus?"

I say, "Yes, I understand. But you'd look as nice with your hair gray and no makeup on."

Mother slaps me. "Go to your room, Klaus, or go for a walk. You're getting on my nerves."

She adds to Veronica, "Why didn't I have a daughter like you?"

I go. I circle around the house where Antonia and Sarah live, or I wander through the cemetery looking for my father's grave. I only came here once and the cemetery is big.

I go home and try to help Mother out in the garden, but she says to me, "Go play. Get out your scooter or your tricycle."

I look at Mother.

"Don't you realize that those are toys for four-year-olds?"

She says, "There are always the swings."

"I don't feel like swinging either."

I go into the kitchen, get a knife, and I cut the cords, the four cords of the swing.

Mother says, "You could at least have left one of them. Lucas would have liked it. You're a difficult child, Klaus. Nasty, even."

I go up to the children's room. Lying on my bed, I write poems.

Sometimes in the evening Mother calls us: "Lucas, Klaus, dinnertime!"

I go to the kitchen. Mother looks at me and puts back the third plate meant for Lucas, or she throws the plate into the sink, where of course it breaks, or again she serves Lucas as though he were there.

Sometimes too Mother comes into the children's room in the middle of the night. She fluffs Lucas's pillow and talks to him: "Sleep well. Sweet dreams. Till tomorrow."

After that she goes away, although she sometimes also stays longer, kneeling next to his bed, and she falls asleep with her head on Lucas's pillow.

I remain motionless in my bed, breathing as softly as possible, and when I wake up the next morning Mother is no longer there.

I touch the pillow on the other bed; it is still damp with Mother's tears.

Whatever I do is never good enough for Mother. When a pea falls from my plate, she says, "You'll never learn to eat properly. Look at Lucas, he never soils the tablecloth."

If I spend the day pulling weeds from the garden and come back inside all muddy, she says to me, "You're filthy as a pig. Lucas wouldn't have gotten dirty."

When Mother gets her money, her little bit of money from the state, she goes to town and comes back with expensive toys that she hides under Lucas's bed. She warns me, "Don't touch. These toys have to stay new for when Lucas comes back."

I am now familiar with the medications Mother must take.

The nurse explained everything to me.

So when she doesn't want to take her medications or forgets them, I administer them in her coffee, her tea, her soup.

In September I begin school, the same school where I went before the war. I should have found Sarah there. She isn't there.

After class I ring Antonia's doorbell. No one answers. I open the door with my key. No one's there. I go into Sarah's room. I open the drawers, the cupboards. No notebook, no piece of clothing.

I leave, throw the apartment key in front of a passing streetcar, and go home to my mother's.

At the end of September I run across Antonia at the cemetery. I've finally found the grave. I bring a bouquet of white carnations, my father's favorite flower. Another bouquet is already resting on the tomb. I put mine down next to the other one.

From out of who knows where, Antonia asks me, "Did you come to our place?"

"Yes. Sarah's room is empty. Where did she go?"

Antonia says, "To my parents'. She has to forget you. She thought of nothing but you, she was always wanting to go see you. At your mother's, anywhere."

I say, "Me too. I think about her all the time. I can't live without her. I want to be with her, no matter where and no matter how."

Antonia takes me in her arms.

"You're brother and sister. Don't forget that, Klaus. You can't love each other the way you do. I should never have taken you in with us."

I say, "Brother and sister. What does it matter? No one will know. We have different names."

"Don't insist, Klaus, don't insist. Forget Sarah."

I don't answer. Antonia adds, "I'm expecting a child. I'm married."

I say, "You love another man and have another life. So why do you still come here?"

"I don't know. Maybe because of you. You were my son for seven years."

I say, "No, never. I have one mother only, the one I'm living with now, the one you drove insane. Because of you I lost my father, my brother, and now you're also taking away my little sister."

Antonia says, "Believe me, Klaus, I regret all that. I didn't want it. I couldn't imagine the consequences. I truly loved your father."

I say, "So then you should understand my love for Sarah."

"That's an impossible love."

"Yours was too. All you had to do was leave and forget my father and the 'thing' would never have happened. I don't want to see you here anymore, Antonia. I don't want to see you at my father's grave."

Antonia says, "All right, I won't come again. But I'll never forget you, Klaus."

Mother has very little money. She gets a small amount from the state for being an invalid. I'm a burden on her. I must find work as soon as possible. It's Veronica who suggests that I deliver newspapers.

I get up at four o'clock in the morning, go to the printing press, and pick up my packet of newspapers. I cover my assigned streets and leave newspapers in front of doors, inside mailboxes, under the closed steel fronts of shops.

When I get home Mother isn't awake yet. She doesn't get up until around nine o'clock. I make coffee and tea and go to school, where I have lunch. I don't get home until five in the evening.

The nurse gradually extends the time between her visits. She tells me that Mother is better, that all she has to do now is take sedatives and sleeping pills.

Veronica too comes less and less often. Just to tell Mother about the disappointment of her marriage.

At fourteen I quit school. I take a typesetting apprenticeship offered to me by the newspaper I have been delivering for three years. I work from ten at night until six in the morning.

Gaspar, my boss, shares his nightly meal with me. Mother doesn't think of making me a meal for the night; she doesn't even think of ordering coal for the winter. She thinks about nothing but Lucas.

At the age of seventeen I become a typesetter. I'm not earning bad money compared to other jobs. Once a month I am able to take Mother to a beauty salon, where she is given a recoloring, a perm, and a "makeover" for her face and hands. She doesn't want Lucas to come back to find her old and ugly.

My mother criticizes me constantly for having left school: "Lucas would have continued his studies. He would have become a doctor. A great doctor."

When our tumbledown house leaks water from the roof, Mother says, "Lucas would have become an architect. A great architect."

When I show her my first poems, Mother reads them and says, "Lucas would have become a writer. A great writer."

I don't show my poems anymore, but hide them.

The noise of the machines helps me write. It gives a rhythm to my phrasings and sows images in my head. When I've finished composing the newspaper I compose my own texts, which I sign with the pseudonym "Klaus Lucas" in memory of my brother dead or disappeared.

What we print in the newspaper completely contradicts reality. A hundred times a day we print the phrase "We are free," but everywhere in the streets we see the soldiers of a foreign army, everyone knows that there are many political prisoners, trips abroad are forbidden, and even within the country we can't go wherever we want. I know because I once tried to rejoin Sarah in the small town of K. I made it to the neighboring village, where I was arrested and sent back to the capital after a night of interrogation.

A hundred times a day we print "We live amidst abundance and happiness," and at first I think this is true for other people, that Mother and I are miserable and unhappy only because of the "thing," but Gaspar tells me we're hardly an exception, that he himself as well as his wife and three children are living more miserably than ever before.

And when I go home from work early in the morning, when I cross paths with people who themselves are on their way to work, I see happiness nowhere, and even less abundance. When I ask why we print so many lies, Gaspar answers, "Whatever you do, don't ask questions. Do your job and don't think about anything else."

One morning Sarah is waiting for me in front of the printing press. I walk by without recognizing her. I turn only when I hear my name: "Klaus!"

We look at each other. I am tired, dirty, unshaven. Sarah is beautiful, fresh, and elegant. She's eighteen years old now. She speaks first.

"Won't you kiss me, Klaus?"

"I'm sorry. I don't feel very clean."

She gives me a kiss on the cheek. I ask, "How did you know I worked here?"

"I asked your mother."

"My mother? You went to our house?"

"Yes, last night. As soon as I arrived. You were already gone."

I take out my handkerchief and wipe my sweaty face.

"You told her who you were?"

"I told her I was a childhood friend. She asked me, 'From the orphanage?' I said, 'No, from school.' "

"And Antonia? She knows you came?"

"No. I told her I had to go enroll at the university."

"At six in the morning?"

Sarah laughs. "She's still asleep. And it's true that I'm on my way to the university. In a bit. There's time for us to have a cup of coffee somewhere."

I say, "I'm sleepy. I'm tired. And I have to make breakfast for Mother."

She says, "You don't seem so happy to see me, Klaus."

"What a thing to say, Sarah! How are your grandparents?"

"Well. But they've grown old. My mother wanted them to come here too, but Grandfather doesn't want to leave his little town. We could see each other a lot, if you want."

"What are you going to study?"

"I'd like to do medicine. Now that I'm back, we can see each other every day, Klaus."

"You must have a brother or sister. Antonia was pregnant the last time I saw her."

"Yes, I have two sisters and a little brother. But I'd like to talk about us, Klaus."

I ask, "What does your stepfather do to keep such a crowd?"

"He's high up in the Party. Are you trying to avoid the subject on purpose?"

"Yes. There's no point in talking about us. There's nothing to say."

Sarah says softly, "Have you forgotten how much we loved each other? I never forgot you, Klaus."

"Nor I you. But there's no point in seeing each other again. Can't you see that?"

"Yes. I've just come to see it."

She waves down a passing taxi and leaves.

I walk to the stop, wait for ten minutes, and take the bus the way I do every morning, a smelly and overcrowded bus.

When I get home Mother is already up, which is unusual for her. She has her coffee in the kitchen. She smiles at me. "She's quite pretty, your little friend Sarah. What's her last name? Sarah what? What's her family name?"

I say, "I don't know, Mother. She's not my little friend. I haven't seen her for years. She's looking for old classmates, that's all."

Mother says, "That's all? What a pity. It's time for you to have a little friend. But you're probably too awkward for girls to like you. Especially girls like that, the well-bred sort. And with your menial job and all. It would be completely different with Lucas. Yes, that Sarah is exactly the kind of girl that would suit Lucas."

I say, "No doubt, Mother. Excuse me, I'm terribly tired."

I go to bed and before falling asleep I talk to Lucas in my head the way I have for many years. What I tell him is just about what I usually do. I tell him that if he's dead he's lucky and I'd very much like to be in his place. I tell him that he got the better deal, that it is I who is pulling the greater weight. I tell him that life is totally useless, that it's nonsense, an aberration, infinite suffering, the invention of a non-God whose evil surpasses understanding.

I do not see Sarah again. Sometimes I think I see her on the street, but it's never her.

One day I go to the house where Antonia used to live, but none of the names on the mailboxes is familiar and in any case I don't know her new name.

Years later I receive a wedding notice. Sarah is getting married to a surgeon, and the addresses of both families are on Rose Hill, the richest and most elegant part of town.

I was to have a great many "little friends," girls I meet in bars around the printing press, where it is now my habit to go to before and after work. These girls are factory workers or servants; I rarely see them more than once or twice, and I bring none of them back home to introduce them to Mother.

I spend my Sunday afternoons with my boss, Gaspar, and his family. We play cards and drink beer. Gaspar has three children. The eldest daughter, Esther, plays with us; she's nearly my age and works in a textile mill where she has been a weaver since the age of thirteen. The two boys, who are slightly younger and typesetters too, go out on Sunday afternoons. They go to soccer matches or the movies or walk around town. Gaspar's wife, Anna, a weaver like her daughter, does the dishes, the laundry, and cooks the evening meal. Esther has blond hair, blue eyes, and a face that recalls Sarah's. But she isn't Sarah, she isn't my sister, she isn't my life.

Gaspar says to me, "My daughter is in love with you. Marry her. I give her to you. You're the only one who deserves her."

I say, "I don't want to get married, Gaspar. I have to look after my mother and wait for Lucas."

Gaspar says, "Wait for Lucas? Poor madman."

He adds: "If you don't want to marry Esther, it would be better if you didn't come see us again."

I do not go back to Gaspar's. From then on I spend all my free time alone at home with Mother except for the hours when I walk aimlessly around the cemetery or the town.

At the age of forty-five I become the head of another printing press, this one belonging to a publishing house. I no longer work at night but from eight in the morning to six in the evening with two hours off at lunch. My health is already very bad at this point. My lungs are filled with lead and my badly oxygenated blood is poisoned. This is called saturnism, a disease of printers and typesetters. I have stomachaches and spells of nausea. The doctor tells me to drink a lot of milk and get a lot of fresh air. I don't like milk. I also suffer from insomnia and great physical and nervous exhaustion. After thirty years of night work it is impossible for me to get used to sleeping at night.

At the new printing press we produce all kinds of texts— poems, prose, novels. The director of the publishing house often comes in to oversee our work. One day he examines my own poems, which he has found on a shelf.

"What's this? Whose poems are these? Who is this Klaus Lucas?"

I stammer because usually I have no right to print personal texts.

"They're mine. They're my poems. I print them up after work."

"You mean to say that you're Klaus Lucas, the author of these poems?"

"Yes."

He asks, "When did you write them?"

I say, "Over the past couple of years. I wrote many others, before, when I was young."

He says, "Bring me everything you have. Come to my office tomorrow morning with everything you've written."

The next morning I go to the director's office with my poems. They add up to several hundred pages, maybe a thousand.

The director hefts the package.

"All this? You've never tried to publish them?"

I say, "I never gave it a thought. I wrote for myself, to pass the time, to amuse myself."

The director laughs. "To amuse yourself? Your poems aren't what you might call amusing, exactly. Not the ones I've read, anyway. But maybe you were more lighthearted when you were young."

I say, "When I was young, certainly not."

He says, "True. There wasn't much to be lighthearted about in those days. But a lot of things have changed since the revolution."

I say, "Not for me. Nothing has changed for me."

He says, "At least now we can publish your poems."

I say, "If you think it's a good idea, publish them. But I beg you not to give my address or tell my real name to anyone."

Lucas came back and left again. I sent him away. He left me his unfinished manuscript. I am trying to complete it.

The man from the embassy didn't announce he was coming. Two days after my brother's visit he rings my doorbell at nine in the evening. Luckily Mother has already gone to bed. The man has curly hair and he is thin and pale. I usher him into my study.

He says, "I don't speak your language very well, so forgive me for being blunt. Your brother, that is to say your alleged brother, Claus T., committed suicide today. He threw himself under a train at East Station at two-fifteen this afternoon, just as he was being repatriated. He left a letter for you at our embassy."

The man hands me an envelope on which is written, "To the attention of Klaus T."

I open the envelope. On a postcard I read: "I would like to be buried beside our parents."

I hand the card to the man from the embassy.

"He wants to be buried here."

The man reads the card and asks, "Why did he sign it Lucas? Was he really your brother?"

I say, "No. But he believed it so much that I can't refuse him this."

The man says, "How strange. Two days ago, after his visit with you, we asked him if he had found anyone from his family. He said no."

I say, "It's the truth. We weren't related at all."

The man says, "But you'll still permit him to be buried beside your parents?"

I say, "Yes. Beside my father. He's the only one in my family who's dead."

We follow the hearse, the man from the embassy and I. It's snowing. I'm carrying a bouquet of white carnations and another of red. I bought them at a florist. There are no more carnations in our garden, even in summer. Mother plants all sorts of flowers, but not carnations.

A new grave is dug next to my father's. My brother's coffin is lowered into it, and a cross with a different spelling of my name is erected over it.

I come to the cemetery every day. I look at the cross inscribed with Claus's name and I wonder if I shouldn't replace it with another bearing the name of Lucas.

I also think that the four of us will soon be reunited. Once Mother is dead there will be no reason for me to go on.

Not a bad idea, the train.

Born in Hungary, Agota Kristof left her homeland during the revolution of 1956 to settle in Switzerland. She still resides there, where she also writes for the theater.